UPLAKE

AN APOCALYPTIC WILDERNESS ADVENTURE

BY

GEORGE THIELMAN

Copyright © 2013 by George Thielman.

All rights reserved. Published in the United States by George Thielman.

All rights reserved. No part of this publication may be reproduced or transmitted in any form or by any means, electronic or mechanical, including photocopy, recording, or any information storage and retrieval system now known or to be invented, without permission in writing of the author, except by reviewer who wishes to quote brief passages in connection with a review written for publication in print and electronic form.

This book is a work of fiction. Names, characters, places and incidents either are products of the author's imagination or are used ficticiously. Any resemblance to actual events or locales or persons, living or dead, is entirely coincidental.

Cover photograph © 2013 George Thielman

Book and Cover design: Vladimir Verano, Third Place Press

ISBN: 978-1-60944-069-5

Printed at Third Place Press, Lake Forest Park, on the Espresso Book Machine v.2.2.
thirdplacepress.com

ACKNOWLEDGMENTS

To Mike and Kim for allowing me to tap into their power supply, thus powering up my computer and cabin lights.

To Tammy Gunderson for editing the first draft.

To Doug Dykstra for vetting the book for the final time.

To Vladimir Verano for his great design skills.

To Cathy A. and Kathy S. for your great advice and support.

To Mike Scrudsveg for the critical drinking and thinking sessions.

To O-dog for patiently watching out for my me while I wrote.

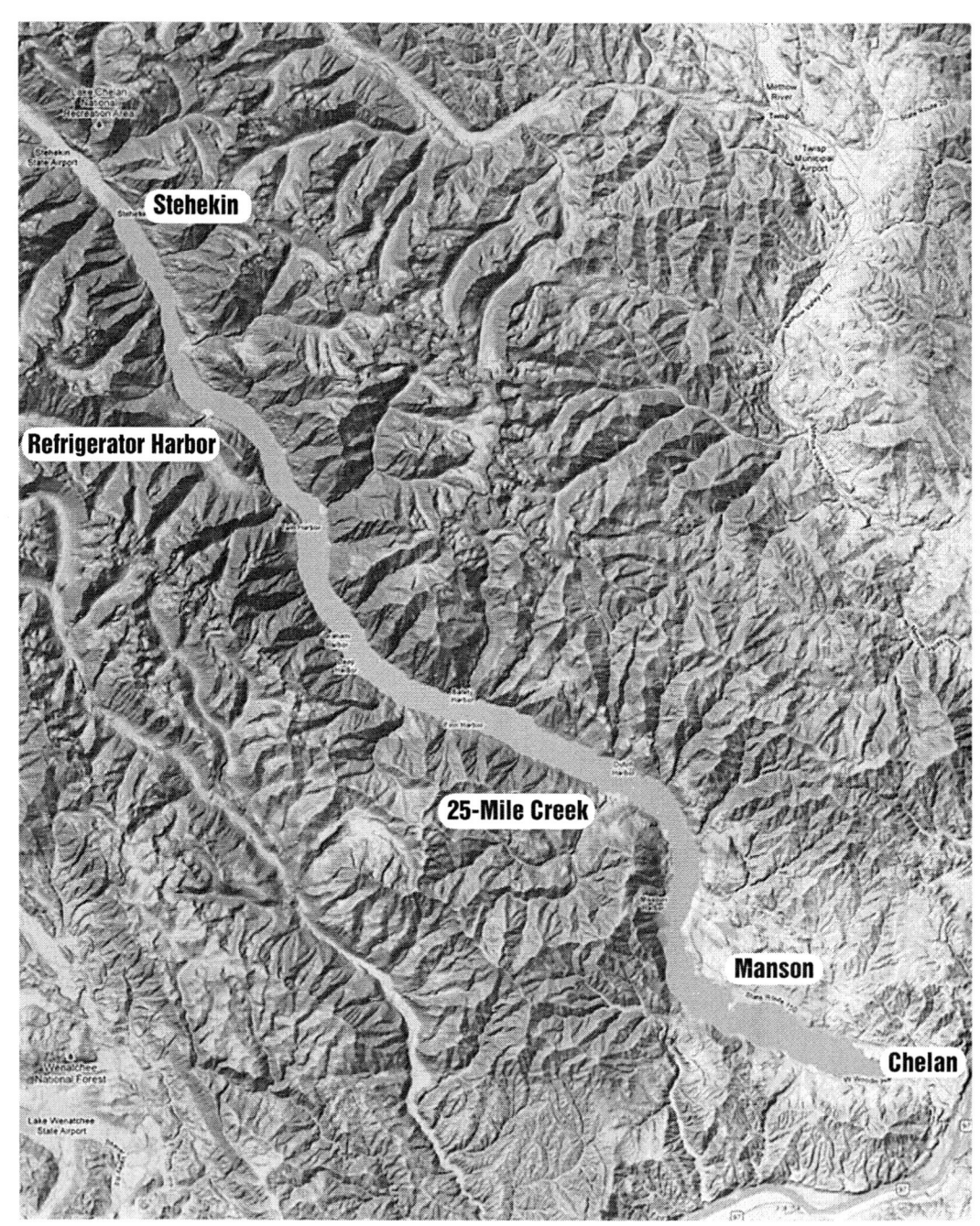

Lake Chelan, Washington

UPTAKE

THE CABIN ON THE ROCK "UP THE LAKE"

CHAPTER 1

She stopped, nose slightly up in the air, nostrils twitching as she took in the scent. Again she looked up over the sagebrush, and heard no sound but the wind. Her coat blended with the grey sagebrush, a cloud of dust clung to her. She was smooth and soft, unlike her matted friends. The pack jogged on, cautious but playful. Their hunger was overpowering; ears straight up listening for any and all threats and anything that could be eaten, eyes moving, heads darting from side to side, looking always looking, smelling, sniffing, then jogging easily. The pack had traveled over thirty miles that day. Now tired and hungry, they were looking for supper and a good sleep.

This morning they'd left Hanford Reach as a pack. The big scraggly male had stood up, circled the pack then started walking. The rest stood up and followed him. They had soon moved easily, seeming to bounce effortlessly across the soft dirt, stopping for water and to rest a few times, sometimes chasing a rabbit or two. The pretty female loved this land, the smell of sage abundant food to eat: stink bugs, lizards, and snakes. Her favorite food was chicken, tasty and easy to catch. Sometimes the pack stayed near the Columbia River. Hunting was good along the river. Fish were caught and ate, and ducks and other waterfowl could be hunted. This land was theirs to rule. This winter they had stayed in a craggy area overlooking Hanford. They loved the great scenery, could keep track of all creatures great and small, and had cover from the cold winter.

Today was a sunny day, though clouds from the Puget Sound were starting to spill over the Cascade Mountains, threatening future rain. She looked to the west at Mt. Adams without knowing what she was looking at. It had been there her whole life, a giant stagnant thing that blocked the sun, snowcapped, looming larger than all the other mountains. She put her head down then took off in a gentile trot. In a spit second she had caught a rabbit in her mouth. She looked to her right. Her friends were in a gulley going after a group of field mice, and she would have the rabbit to herself. She held the rabbit's body down on the ground with her front paws, and reached down with her mouth crushing the twitching rabbit's neck; warm blood flowed into her mouth. Familiar taste. It was good. She raised her butt in the air playing with the rabbit as she chewed. She then turned to her favorite part; the stomach was chewy, just what she needed. She looked around, tail wagging, muzzle red from the delicious blood. She licked her lips. The rabbit, though void of its brain, kicked a couple times. The canine reached back and bit what was remaining of the head. Life was grand. She felt a violent tug on her hindquarters. A loud bang. She tried to move. A bullet had severed her spine. A tug on her head from another 7.62-millimeter bullet dropped her to the ground, dead, mouth full of rabbit liver.

Two hundred yards away, Private Peter Nubbinskiy looked up, smiling. He snapped the plastic cover over the scope.

"What the fuck. P. Nubb, we're gonna get flunked 'cause you wanna shoot a stupid coyote," ranted Nick Mose. Vibrating and beeping from their packs interrupted his rant. A laser, triggering the signals, had shot them. Private Mose spit out the words. "Fuck man, you killed us."

P. Nubb laughed, "Don't worry man, we're cool." Their bodies vibrated again, and P. Nubb laughed.

The radio buzzed and a hoarse voice commanded, "Nubb, Mose, get back to the shack. You're dead. Chop, chop, boys!" Mose and Nubb jumped upright, no longer hidden by the camo suits, brush-covered helmets, faces colored with tan, green, and black paint.

Mose groused," You jackass, we're fuckin' dead, man."

P. Nubb kept smiling. "Come on Mosie, We're all good." They started to run the two miles back to the rally area. With their rifles in their arms they ran quickly, sweating, but barely breathing hard.

Captain Tom Trainer watched from his hiding place, as the two Lieutenants ran down the dirt road. His staff sergeant laughed, "You gonna flunk 'um sir?" Tom slipped out of his gillie camo suit, then rolled it up and stuffed it in his pack. He looked at the two bodies running down the road.

"Naw, they already passed. Let's fuck with 'um a bit' let 'um run back. They're good men, work hard. This is just a course in escape and evade, a refresher course so to speak. Besides, the exercise has been over for two hours." He looked at his sergeant and winked. "Let's get a beer. I'm thirsty." They gathered up their gear, binoculars, canteens, chew, range scope, and two bolt action sniper rifles set with the laser tag game on the end of the barrel.

Captain Tom pulled a silver flask from his combat vest, took a swig, and then passed it to his sergeant, who took a good long drink then gagged. "I can't stand tequila, thought it was going to be whiskey."

Tom laughed, "You pussy." They ran down the hill opposite the privates to a hidden Humvee, jumped in, peeling out in the gravel. Tom took another big swig from his flask, draining the bottle. It'd been filled with Patron Anejo, one of his most favorite tequilas. They passed Nubb and Mose, purposely making more dust with the Humvee. Nubbs and Mose kept running through the dusk seeming to not notice the dirt flowing into their lungs.

Tom pulled around a thirty foot high, and thousand yards long, pile of dirt, set up to contain stray bullets in the middle of the shooting area. At the southern end of the range was a concrete building with a thick metal roof. It was an old army bunker built for the nearby Hanford Nuclear Reservation. Now used by the military for weapons training and logistics exercises, it housed a schoolroom, a kitchen, and two small offices. The south side of the building housed a fifteen by fifteen foot vault set with shelves and gun cases. Over a thousand rifles of all kinds were stored there along with pistols and other small arms. Outside to the north, were target ranges set for different weapons and exercises. Several Humvees, pickup trucks, and rental cars were parked neatly in perfect military order. Not far away barbecues were smoking away. Coleman coolers of every color and size were filled with ice and bottles. Men and women gathered around tables. Most wore the military camo, or BDU, short for battle dress uniform. Some were wearing civilian garb, and a few sported business suits.

This was the Yakima Proving Grounds, a massive expanse of high desert in south central Washington State. Nearby was the mighty Columbia River. The grounds, owned by the military and used for training soldiers in tank and mock battles, were a great place to train and explore. The dirt was fine with sagebrush, snakes, lizards, bugs, deer, antelope, and of course rabbits and coyotes. The highway split through the area with underpasses so military vehicles could pass under. The civilians could get off the highway, but they couldn't go anywhere. Basically the proving grounds were on their own mountain range. The best part was that from most any hill was a great view of the Hanford Reach to the east, and the majestic Cascade mountain range to the west. South were the towns of Yakima, Richland, and Pasco known for agriculture of all sorts, lately for award winning wines.

Captain Tom Trainer was in the Air force, a member of the Air Force Special Operations team, a highly trained specialist in communications, combat and rescue. Tom had joined the Air Commandos after serving with the Army Rangers for five years. Initially he became a Para-rescue Jumper (PJ), trained as a medic, a combat specialist, search and rescue, and he could call in missiles and bombs to their exact point of impact. He taught all the above disciplines, and was decorated several times in his twenty years as a warrior. He was deployed to Persian Gulf War I from '90 to '91 then Somalia in '93. From there he spent time in Bosnia, Kuwait, Turkey, United Arab Emirates, and finally, Pakistan to help train their military people. After a year in Pakistan as a (PJ) trainer, he was sent back to the states to train U.S. military. Mountain Home, Idaho, became his next home. Then Alaska, Colorado, and Arizona where he taught desert survival to pilots and flight crews. When the Twin Towers fell to the ground on 9-11 he, along with his highly trained operators, were called to service. His training and experience in faraway high and dangerous places placed him at the front of the list to be sent to Afghanistan. Less than two weeks after 9-11, a handful of highly trained and secretive warriors were sent. Joining with the Northern Alliance they killed and chased the Taliban out of Afghanistan. With experience in high-altitude climbing, he fought for two years in Afghanistan, loving every moment in the dry country, slinking about the rocks and brush searching for targets. Gulf War II; Iraq, was his next area of combat. After a year of fighting there, he was sent back to Afghanistan for several more tours, fighting in most of the conflicts throughout the region. He loved Afghanistan, the high mountain passes and long thin valleys. If it weren't for the war he would have been one of the first to climb and backpack throughout the region.

After ten years serving in Afghanistan and Iraq, he'd been shot five times, blown up, and stabbed, all in less than two days. Trainer used eighteen years of training and experience to make it out of his last battle alive. Severely wounded and fighting to the end, he finally ended up being sent back to the U.S. to recover from his wounds. While recovering in the hospital he thought of all the great adventures, climbing, hiking throughout the world's pretty places; the Alps, Himalayas, trekking through the Baltoro region of Pakistan with its twenty thousand foot rock towers, then the beauty of the American Wilderness. He thought of all these grandiose places and decided then and there that he would finish out his twenty years and move on to civilian life while he was still somewhat young and able to climb, raft, kayak, hike or just do nothing.

◆◆

After four months of surgeries and hospitals, Tom took a two-week leave in Washington State. He chose Stehekin, Washington, a small resort town deep in the North Cascade Mountains, and at the end of the super deep and glacier-fed Lake Chelan. With a mountain bike, a bike trailer, and eighty pounds of gear and food, Tom stepped off the Lake Chelan Ferry, after riding northwest from the town of Chelan toward the Sky campsite. Tom rented a small private campsite, bought firewood, set up his tent and campsite then went about limping through the campsites, still feeling the effects of his wounds.

Mountain bike riding was easy on his wounded body, so he rode all the easy roads and trails. Tom fished for trout every day, swam in the freezing lake, kayaked and canoed up the lake and Stehekin River, sharing the freezing water with mountain trout, beavers, muskrat, and deer. Every night he had a campfire at his own campsite.

Tom spent the evenings eating and drinking at the nearby Sky Café and Bar. Late one night he was introduced to Sally Sky who owned the campsites and café. Sally invited Tom to visit her family's ranch a mile away. Tom accepted Sally's invitation, and the next morning, in great military fashion, he was at the gates of Sky Ranch at seven am. Sally Sky, an older woman of sixty-two, was born and raised on the small ranch. Four generations had been raised at the twenty acre Sky Ranch, one mile away from the family owned café, bar and campsites. Small cabins were built for rentals, with wood stoves, bunk beds and private bedrooms. Sky Café and Bar could be seen from Lake Chelan. It was a two-story building with a full basement for storage of food and supplies. The cabins at the ranch were made of fir and cedar trees, all harvested from the Stehekin Valley. The barn was L-shaped, full of hay for the two cows and one bull. Eight horses were kept in another barn, and a large chicken coop opened to a two-acre garden. Semi-truck sized bread-shaped rocks dominated the northeast corner of the small ranch.

Tom kept his wounded body under wraps, not wanting to frighten people. He had high hopes that he would be able to run again in the near future, but for the time he limped and rode his bicycle. Sally and her family were both impressed and horrified by Tom's wounds. They were polite and tried not to look. The most notable was a y-shaped scar that started on his left cheek, about even with his nostrils. At the eyelid the scar went left and right forming a capital 'Y' that finished at his hairline. Tom had earned his scar in a hard-fought knife fight with a talented young Taliban fighter.

Tom had been shot on his left side, through the back, bullet having entered the skin but exiting, after tearing its way around a couple ribs. One bullet entered his left thigh, one grazed the back of his left leg behind the knee, tearing up tendons and muscle, another bullet entered his left lower forearm entering and exiting with little damage. The fifth bullet did the most damage, entering his left shoulder from the back. That one shattered his upper arm above the shoulder. His arm was covered with cuts from bomb fragments. Considering all the damage to his body, the worst was the left shoulder and the left leg that took two bullets, one of which broke his femur. Other than that, none of the bullets or bomb fragments did much damage other than tearing flesh and muscle. His scars were still pink and showed like a neon sign. People were polite and curious with many questions about America's longest running war. Tom's explanations were short and to the point. He tried not to sensationalize or expand his stories beyond what was asked.

After a dinner of buffalo burgers, Tom sat with Sally outside her own house on Sky ranch. Near the garden, four anti-bug torches burned, attracting bugs then burning their little bodies. After two hours of whiskey drinking Sally was tipsy. She looked at Tom.

"What," Tom asked.

She smiled at him. "You know, even with all those wounds, you're pretty damned cute."

Tom laughed. Two days later Sally and her grandson took Tom the sixty miles back to the town of Chelan by boat. Tom vowed to come back the next summer. Sally said she would save her favorite cabin for him when he returned then gave Tom one of their ten week old puppies, reddish color with brown ears, big paws, and an oversized head. Bigger than the rest of the litter, he was a little athlete right out of the whelping box. Tom accepted the fuzzy little critter, said goodbye then left for McCord

Air Force Base, south of Tacoma. He would have to endure another nine months of service. Rather than taking work as a paper-pusher, he spent two months working as a gunsmith. When he was healed enough, he transferred to the Yakima Proving Grounds where he finished the remainder of his twenty years.

◆◆

Today he celebrated twenty years of military service, his last day as an American warrior. The celebration and get-together at the concrete building were for him, his retirement party so to speak. Tom walked into the vault carrying his sniper rifle and Colt M4 and he set them in the gun racks. The staff sergeant was taking inventory of the many weapons in the vault. Rifle racks filled to capacity with old-school M16s still in use, new school M4s, state-of-the-art with small combat scopes, short barrels, long barrels manufacturers such as Colt, Fabrique National (FN), Armalite, Heckler and Kock (H&K,) Remington and Bushmaster. Plastic and metal cases held new weapons glistening with gun oil, camo colors to break up the image of the weapon. Tom helped put away four Remington 700s bolt-action sniper rifles with huge scopes. Next to those were other sniper rifles: Winchester model 70s, chambered in .308, and the newer and bigger .300 win mag, a bigger charge to send the .30 caliber further and providing a bigger punch to the target. They checked out the new H&K 416 and 417. The 416 chambered in the standard .223 caliber a much smaller round but very dangerous. The 417 was chambered in the .308 or its metric equivalent 7.62 millimeter. The 417 was heavier and a bit bigger. Tom preferred the 417 in country. Colts M16 had quite a history in the world, released in the 1960s to replace the M1 Garand, and M14. It was thought to be too small and flimsy with plastic parts. It looked like a toy and was made fun of for decades. It had however worked well for the last five decades; many different styles and makes had created demand for it as the world's foremost weapon of choice.

In a corner were two massive rifles, five feet long and over twenty-five pounds each; they had the look of a M4 on steroids. With a large scope, it fired a bullet over four inches, made to disable trucks, armored vehicles, and even tanks. It shot a fifty-caliber bullet, sending it over a mile, and was used for sniping throughout the world. Copied by several gun manufacturers, it offered the shooter incredible accuracy with serious punch power. It was a semi-auto that offered the sniper second and third shot capability without working a bolt to chamber the next round and eject the spent casing.

Tom took in his final look at the vault. He was a bit sad. A self–confessed gun nut, these weapons had been the tools of his trade for twenty years. After tonight he was finished with his trade, the defense of his country.

He set his Colt 45 with the rest of the pistols. Colt, Kimber, Beretta, Sig Sauer, and Springfield lined the racks. Next to the pistols were gun racks for fully automatic machine guns, for shooting rapid fire, a fixture in military weapons. Most military rifles had a select fire switch that could change the weapon from single fire to two and or three burst shots then to fully automatic fire, which fired all the ammunition in the weapon until it ran out; they laid down deadly fire rarely accurate. Captain Trainer was an expert in the use of all these weapons. He left his four clips on table in front of a young, bespectacled private quietly writing away in a ledger. He was recording which weapons were returned, and tagging each with a corresponding number that was entered in a Dell laptop.

Major Mohamed, the men referred to him as Major Mo, was black and known as a fair man. He had never seen the kind of action Tom had experienced. He was Tom's landlord as well as his boss. Major Mo walked to Tom, swigging from a Budweiser. "So Tom, you still leaving? Sure you can leave all this fun?"

Tom smiled, "Yah, I can and, well, they won't let me back in combat. Seems my only choices are recruiting, training, and go to Washington to push paper. I'm doing none of that shit … I'm going away for a while."

Billy Wilson, the Heckler and Koch rep., came up to Tom and Mo, "So this is it, huh, Captain? I'm glad I could come and see you off. If you need a job we could get you lined up with H&K."

Tom laughed, "So I can wear khakis and a polo shirt? I don't think so."

Major Mo spoke up, "He's going to Stehekin to live in a cabin without power, like Gilligan's Island, as primitive as can be."

Billy said, "You should get married, have kids, settle down … It's not so bad you know."

Tom replied, "Marriage is for other people. Most of them go tits up and rest are screwing around on each other. Naw, I'll do what I want this time." Tom rolled his eyes. "No wonder so many vets kill themselves after returning from combat, pure boredom … I think I'll continue to the wild and crazy wiles."

Major Mo said, "Sounds like a rough way to live, bugs, wild animals, dirty toilets, and no football. A hard way to live."

Tom looked off into the darkness, "No, I don't think so … it's going to be fun."

Billy said, "What about money? The retirement check after twenty years is not that big."

Tom laughed, "Twenty five hundred a month. Don't have a house payment, my pickup is six years old, and my Beemer is ten years old. Hell, I don't even twitter, wouldn't know how to twitter. Couldn't imagine Face booking with my face." They all looked at Tom. "Exactly! That's what I'm talking about!" He laughed and added, "I'm canceling my cell phone. Think I'll keep my e-mail though."

Billy said, "What about your family?"

"My mom and dad are gone, brother and sister are religious nuts and think wars are good for business … they think I'm crazy. All I have in this world are my friends and my big puppy dog." Tom raised his flask, "To friends, to puppies, here."

Major Mo said, "You should see his pickup! Full to top of the camper with food, chainsaw, tents, sleeping bags, and fishing gear. Man, so much stuff. Even has that motorcycle trailer full to the top."

Tom said, "Everything I own is in that pickup and trailer."

"So you're going to move into a tent in the Cascades?" Billy asked.

Tom smiled, and then looked off in the distance, "No, I'm going to a ranch; it's been there for eighty years, run by a family, with cows, horses, and chickens. The cabin is old, near the Stehekin River. The Sky family owns campsites, cabins, and a café, and bar. Spent some good time at that bar. I think there's only ten miles of road once you get there. Only way there is by boat, floatplane, or foot. It's a wild place that's for sure. Stayed there for two weeks last summer, camping every night, sleeping on the ground. Some people offered me a place to stay and I'm going. Tomorrow night I'll be there and I can't wait."

For three hours the men and women drank shots of tequila and whiskey. Beer bottles littered the area. Chicken and rib bones had been pitched in the bushes. With a war on, few of Tom's friends were present at the party. Billy Wilson, being the head guy for H&K, presented Tom with the latest version of the USP combat pistol. The lower part of the pistol was made of super strong plastic, and the mechanical parts were all metal and encased in the plastic lower. It had extended clips that added four more rounds. The barrel stuck out with threads to receive a suppressor or silencer. The plastic handle was done up in olive drab green. The caliber was .40, a good round bigger than a nine millimeter, yet smaller than the hefty forty-five. Tom was to be well armed in his retirement. His men gave him a hot-rodded Colt M4, completely done up with all the bells and whistles, stainless barrel, custom muzzle flash, and carbon fiber clips. The weapon was made up like a Formula One racecar. He ordered a few parts from the reps, to further customize his new M4 then said goodbye. Major Mo drove Tom home to Yakima, dropping Tom on his bed in Major Mo's basement.

Finishing up the patrol of a small village he smelled the air. Must be near the shitter, Tom thought. The air was dry and freezing. He looked at the mud, dirt and steel of the corrugated shacks. The dirty citizens were not present; no looks, no peeking around corners at the well-armed Americans. There was a filthy stink in the air. Captain Trainer thought they must have been burning plastic trash again. Smoke was rising from a nearby mud shack; Tom took the lead, his M4 butt stock sitting on his shoulder making the weapon shorter and easier to manage in tight situations. A tattered, dirty blanket hung as a door. It moved with a slight breeze. The stink was overpowering. Tom made a quick move inside. With two of his best specialist behind him, they surrounded the hut. Tom looked around, eyes straining to adjust to the darkness inside the shack. The roof had a big hole with the corrugated, rusted metal bent down like a giant had torn the ceiling down to get fresh air. In the middle of the hut was a smoldering pile of stink, plastic, an old burned up corner of a blue blanket, crap that could not be identified, and the toxic smell of death. Small log ends, un-burnt, poked from the ash heap. Tom pulled a stick from the pile. Pushing the burned pieces around the ash, he exposed the layers below. The soldiers held their hands over their mouths to shield from the stench. Straining to look at the burn pile, he pushed a layer of paper aside, uncovering a half-burned hand. Moving the ash around him exposed more of the heap: body parts, and feet, black and grey. It was not clear how they had been separated from the bodies. They were robbed of all body fluids, skin black and grey, dried like a cooked pig. The soldiers gasped at the sight.

"Goddamn, what the fuck is wrong with them? Fucking bastards," a soldier spit out. Tom pulled a small digital camera from his pocket and photographed the scene for the paper-pushers at base. He took in the scene. It was as disgusting and foul as a scene from the Saw movies, but real, incredibly cruel; a heap of chopped and burned bodies mixed with bits of plastic, trash, and wood,

Leaving quickly, and once outside the soldiers leaned against the outside wall, gasping, trying to fill their lungs with unstinkable air.

UPLAKE

They walked to the center of the village, Tom was about to call base when a bomb blast from ten feet away went off Sergeant Danny Holt was picked up by the blast, slamming him into Tom. Both flew backwards. Tom landed in a big hole. Firewood and dirt from a nearby stack fell on him. Even with the ringing in his head he could hear his troop being shot up. Bullets snapped everywhere. He regained himself, and reached for his M4. The bomb blast had torn it free of him. He reached for his sidearm, a Heckler and Koch .45, rolled to his side, his hands bloody from what he didn't know. Clicking the safety up he was about to sit up when a RPG flew past directly over him, slamming into the wall of the hut they had just exited. The force of the blast covered him in dirt, rocks and other crud. The ringing eventually stopped and two more bomb blasts came from - he didn't know where. His left hand was searing in pain, he looked down at it covered in dirt and blood. He couldn't see the source of the blood. Two people ran past him, almost snagging on him. They wore the funky hats of locals, with long grey man-shirts and camo jackets with combat vests. Tom realized he was so covered in dirt and sticks he was invisible to the Taliban punks.

One of the Taliban turned around looking at Tom with ratty-assed teeth set in an ugly snarl. Tom fired one round at the ratty teeth. The bullet entered just above his upper lip, and his head slammed backward with brains and bone splattering onto the comrade behind him. A body dropped to the ground. The dead man's friend turned around, AK 47 ready to fire. A double tap to the chest from Tom's H&K, spun him like a top before he fell to the ground. Tom rose from the hole, dirt and sticks falling from him like an Ork from Lord of the Rings being born from the filth of the earth. RPGs landed, and body parts from the hut were blown and came down on Tom. He turned away from the dead guys, the Mark 23 up, ready to fire.

Two Taliban fighters, five feet from Tom, were startled by the sight of a American soldier, not only so close, but emerging from the ground with hands and feet falling like some type of monster, Both men panicked, moved their AKs, but were too slow. Tom fired one shot, point blank, at the shitheads. The fat 45-caliber bullet tore the top off the arm of one. He screamed in pain turning into his friend. Tom shot them both dead then rolled to the left, taking cover behind an ancient mud wall. He looked around for a weapon. Another Taliban ran past, just twenty feet away, and then another. Tom watched the men, in a zone, a state of grace, his only thoughts dealt with threats. He fired four shots, killing both.

He noticed Danny Holt's M-249 in the dirt nearby. He picked it up. The huge see-through box of ammo was full to the gills. He racked a round in the chamber then looped the strap over his right shoulder and neck crouching behind a mud hut. Danny was moaning near him. Tom whacked him on the head with his hand "Danny, how ya doin' yo." Danny rolled close to Tom then leaned against the same wall. He was bleeding from his left eye socket.

"Can't see a thing, Cap."

"Open your other eye," Tom advised. Tom wiped the blood from Danny's face. The left eye was missing. A bullet had gone at an angle into Danny's head, entering then taking Danny's left eye on the way out. Tom bandaged the area with a thick compress then pulled Danny's Beretta 9 and put it in Danny's hand "Now you watch my back."

Danny yelled, "Where's the rest of our troop, Cap?"

Tom snapped back, Not sure, but I'm going to find them. Look for my M4. I think those assholes are regrouping behind the first mud huts." Fire came from the other mud houses not far away, four fire signatures, four assholes. Tom called and thought of them as assholes, uneducated, stupid, and bigoted. jerk-offs. Taliban had been taught to hate fiercely anyone or thing that came from the west, and Tom had learned to hate the Taliban. Fire came from one of the huts. A young Taliban fighter ran out, trying to move the fight closer to Tom. As the kid ran shooting his AK from the hip Tom calmly fired a twenty round burst at the kid and his buddies. Racked by 5.56 bullets, he was doing the rag doll. Another fighter moved from a mud hut, again in open view. Tom ducked, pulled a grenade, and threw then slipped over a small wall and fired a long burst of fire. Through the space between the mud houses three Taliban fighters ran for the cover of a nearby rock. Tom saw them get up and run for cover. He fired through the five feet between the huts, a continuous blast that sent over forty rounds into the area. Around them dirt kicked up, obscuring them from sight. The gun stopped as the 100 round clip went empty. Tom turned to Danny. He held up another clip, reloaded, and ran to a nearby hut. He found his remaining soldiers dead. Tom found a working radio then called base with his position. He picked up two M4s and twenty thirty round clips from his dead men and stuffed them in a ratty blanket before he ran back to Danny. RPGs and bullet fire were raking the area; Tom threw a smoke bomb to signify a hot LZ then switched to a M4. Taliban rose up from behind rock with RPG. Tom fired a quick burst from the smaller rifle at the fighter. The first round grazed the top of his head. The second round hit him square in the nose. He went backward as four more rounds tore his head apart then he fell flat on his back with the RPG straight up in the air. Fingers clenched down on the trigger, he died shooting his weapon straight up into the air.

A grenade flew through the air, as if in slow motion. Landing on the roof of the hut, the explosion rocked Tom and Danny. The contents of the hut, rained on the two soldiers.

Tom woke, out of a deep sleep. It was not always the same dream, reliving a stressful day in Afghanistan. It wasn't the first time he relived that day and would not be the last.

With a splitting headache Tom rolled out of bed at five thirty sharp. When he woke he looked over at his dog, Woody, who was lying on his back, legs straight up, snoring. He had pushed Tom against the wall, which left most of the bed for the now seventy pound dog. Tom put on a pair of swimming trunks and a sweater. He heard a noise behind him, turned and saw Mo's five-year old daughter, Mina, standing in her one-piece swimsuit.

"Tom, can I go to the hot tub with you?" He scooped her up, carrying her upstairs to the kitchen, holding her while he made coffee. The other kids were watching TV.

Tom asked, "Where's your mom and dad?"

Mina said sweetly, "They're kissing in the bedroom." Tom grabbed his coffee, and went outside to the Jacuzzi with Mina in his arms. Woody followed with a rubber dog toy in his mouth then sat down trying hard to chew the tail off the blue toy. Major Mo finally emerged from the house. It was Saturday - no work.

"Hey, Jeremiah Johnson, ready for the wild mountains?" Mo said sarcastically. He slowly dunked himself in the hot water "Oh man. That feels good."

Tom asked, "How long are you going to stay in the Army?" Major Mo and Tom passed Mina from one to the other since the little girl not capable of sitting still.

"You know Tom; you could have been a coronel by now. Made more money, easier life you know."

"Yeah, I know. Guess I never wanted to be a politician, push paper and the like. Besides I like the action."

Major Mo remarked, "Mr. Action Captain can't live with paperwork. Well you can always come back."

Tom took a big drink from his coffee cup. "If I can come back. I well as long as I can be in the field. I am taking a year off though."

"Taking your box of medals and heading for the wild. Well, good luck my friend." Mina shifted from her dad's lap to Tom's, unaware of the placement of her little feet in Tom's crotch.

She asked Tom, "Are you coming back here to see us?" and crinkled her face in concern.

"Yeah I'll come back, not for a while though."

Mina asked, "Can we come to your house and stay, but only if there's no bugs. My mom hates 'um." Tom and Major Mo laughed. She then ran her tiny fingers over the scars on Tom's face. "Do these hurt? They look like they do."

Tom said, "They don't hurt anymore, but they itch." They dried off then went to the kitchen for pancakes and eggs. Tom said goodbye to his friends. Woody jumped in the passenger seat of the Tundra. Tom waved goodbye, with Woody leaning his young body between Tom and the steering wheel. They drove north on Interstate 82 past Ellensburg, then north on 97 past Wenatchee and north along the great Columbia River to the town of Chelan.

◆◆

Tom stopped at a natural food store for rice, granola, wheat, flour, sugar, ten pounds of organic shade grown coffee, tea, yogurt, vitamins, emergency energy packets, spiralina for plant protein, and a box of Power Bars. At the liquor store he bought five bottles of Cazadores tequila, four bottles of Jameson Whiskey, a dozen bottles of vodka, and rum. Dannoe's Feed Store was next; two fifty-pound bags of dog food, two cases of canned dog food. And they were done. On to the outdoor shop, Ray's Northwest Sporting Goods. The old solid block walls were whitewashed long ago, had since been painted with murals of duck hunters, people in the woods, speed boats pulling skiers, hikers, mountain climbers, campers with canvas tents, the proud father watching his family with his pipe in his mouth. The outside was lined with stacked trashcans, three Old Town canoes, and a couple lake kayaks. Inside the main store was open to the second floor, and the outside perimeter was lined with loft-like clothing displays. He walked through the lower floor picking out small green propane bottles, fishing gear; Patagonia fleece, shirts, and a lightweight down coat then three pairs of trail running shoes. The owner, a tall chunky man, helped Tom with his purchases. He was over six feet tall, over sixty, and didn't look like fat guy.

"Nice jacket. You in the Air Force?" Ray asked.

Tom looked up to the roof pretending to be thinking." Well not anymore, finished up last night."

"How long were you in?" Ray asked.

Tom replied," Twenty years, moving to Stehekin for a while. Air out and cool off. Oh, do you carry bullets by the way?"

Ray pointed upstairs. "Follow me, my man." In a corner upstairs the walls were lined with large gun safes, four feet of walking space between the safes, and glass display cases filled with pistols, bullets, knives, and other technical gear for the milspec cops and gun nuts. Gun cases were off to the side, but complete with hunting rifles, some used some new.

"Well this is my kind of place. I spent some time as a gunsmith in the service. Did weapons and tactical training for the last year," Tom said.

Ray cracked a big smile. "So can you fix guns, and reload bullets?"

Tom said, "Can do most of anything related to weapons."

Ray stuck out his hand. "Weehlheel, let's do business together. I could use a gunsmith and someone to reload custom loads that come in here… by the way, where are you staying in Stehekin?"

Tom thought in his secret military brain that maybe he should shut up. Then he thought that he should network and chill out and allow the local gentry into his life. "I'm staying at the Sky Ranch … By the way, I have to be in 25 Mile in an hour. How far is it?"

Ray pointed. "It's twenty-five miles along the east shore. Can't miss it. Big log entrance with elk antlers at the top. Do you have reloading equipment with you?"

Tom said, "Yes, I do have a small rcbs press and other stuff kinda-sort-of customized to suit the work I've done."

"Great, I'll send you some casings with instruction of things needed!" Tom paid a hefty bill, just over twelve hundred dollars. He drove out of town toward Twenty-Five Mile Creek.

He thought of expenses and how he would pay them. He had two thousand, six hundred dollars a month coming in from retirement every month for the rest of his life. Living the way he planned, he could do fine. Eventually he would have to get a job like all the other schmucks in the world. He wanted a year of traveling in America. Already he had spent most of his life in foreign countries; this time he would discover the U.S., maybe Stehekin, Washington would be his new home forever. In his head he thought of his investments. His IRA account had been split in half by the recession. Now it was worth around one hundred twenty five thousand dollars. He had twelve thousand dollars in the Chelan County Bank and five thousand dollars in cash stashed in his gear. As a young man he had started to buy gold from shops in faraway countries. He had learned the trade of buying and identifying gold, and had bought small coins and little one ounce rectangular bars, rings, bracelets, necklaces, and even rough pieces of gold still full of impurities straight from the ground. All told, he had quite a bit of money and gold. Still not enough to buy property and build a home to the standards of the State of Washington, but enough to buy property and build a small cabin, one without electricity or running water. This is what he wanted. The problem was building codes. Those demanded the building of cookie cutter style homes that looked more like the track homes of Seattle.

Tom pulled over along the shore of Lake Chelan looking across the half mile at all the condos on the north side of the lake. They seemed to continue along the shoreline for ten miles before petering out past the town of Manson. After that foothills gave way to steep mountains, giving way to even steeper mountains. Occasionally there would be a big gulley between two mountains; there for eons, avalanche debris would flow down the gullies creating suitable and stable places to build a cabin, house, or even communities with several cabins and houses. The sixty-mile long lake and its interesting little areas fascinated Tom.

He walked to the shoreline with Woody, who looked immediately for stick, found a six foot branch, picked it up in his mouth then proceeded to try to break it by moving it quickly back and forth like a teeter totter. Finally it broke in three pieces. Woody picked up a two-foot piece, turned to look at his master, then wound up his neck shaking the big stick back and forth. He let go of it and it flew five feet, landing near Tom's feet. Tom picked it up, and threw it into the water. Woody jumped in with a big splash. They played like this for fifteen minutes.

Tom found a patch of bushes then reached into his Camelback Pack. He pulled out a small pipe, and a baggie with wallet sized peace of Afgan hashish. He snipped off a piece about the size of a raisin then smashed it into his pipe. He looked around; trying not to be obvious then took a big drag on the pipe holding in the sweet smoke in his lungs. Weed was not tolerated in the military, but many did it. When piss testing started, marijuana use dropped off dramatically. Tom had never stopped or started using weed on a regular basis. He was tested enough that he couldn't allow himself to become regular user. The last couple of months he had been smoking more and more. He told none of his friends except his rock-climbing buddies from Yakima. From Afghanistan Tom had brought ten ounces of pure hashish, formed in the shape of plates. He found a potter that had covered them with a fake ceramic coating, painted them terracotta color and then painted stripes on them. When finished they looked like six Afgan plates. They made it through the military post office. When he made it back to the states he unpacked the plates, broke one in half, then peeled the fake ceramic coating off the hashish, and had a smoke. Hash was similar to smoking weed because it's made from marijuana; it gives a person the same euphoria that weed does. Tom found the smell of his hashish to be less aromatic, and harder to identify by smell. He found that weed decreased his anxiety about his past military life, his dreams were more easygoing; they became more about pretty places, and not so much about war and battles, Hashish was lightweight and he never got a hangover.

Tom loaded his sopping-wet dog into the back of the camper. Not long after, he found the entrance to the Sky's property. He drove his truck under the log entrance and down a long, naturally manicured, driveway to a big brown metal barn. Near to the shore of Lake Chelan was the house, made of brown painted logs, windowpanes painted white, with a brown metal roof. The house was two stories, and two dormers on each side of the ridgeline expanded bedrooms above. On the east side was a burly rock fireplace. From the house a round-graveled front driveway led down to a sturdy dock.

Garrett Sky walked out of the house to greet him. A short, skinny bookworm-ish type of guy, Garrett ran the business side of things from thirty-five miles away. He was the accountant and bookkeeper, and preferred to live somewhat close to regular civilization with its movie theaters, coffee houses, gas stations, and big box stores. Campers fixed on spending time at one of the Sky family's campsites or cabins would start their tour at Garrett's house. The family boat picked up campers at the boat dock on the property. Tom was waiting for that boat to take him to his new home.

Tom unloaded everything from the back of the Tundra, leaving a big pile of stuff. He heard a low rumble and looked out at the lake. A silver and red boat came into view. Made of aluminum, it was similar in shape to police and border patrol boats. Almost thirty feet, it was powered by two big Mercury outboard motors. Two men were in the boat's cabin. The driver skillfully cut the engines then slid easily backward into the dock. They tied up next to Tom's pile of gear. The back of the boat read "Skyboat." That name was everywhere around here.

A tall young man with a green hoodie jumped off the boat "Are you Tom? I'm Philip. This is my dad, Darren Sky." Darren stuck out his hand and shook with Tom.

"Glad to meet you again," said Tom. "I met you last August. You all gave me my dog." Woody ran up to both of them and stood up, placing his big paws on Philips shoulders

"Wow. That's a big dog. Need to train you." Philip pushed the big puppy to the ground. Woody ran to a soccer ball in the yard, pushing it around, trying to get his mouth around it. It rolled into the water. Woody

GEORGE THIELMAN

followed it in, proceeding to get wet again. They all laughed which emboldened Woody to continue entertaining the humans. He jumped at the ball, splashing the water. Finally his young teeth penetrated the ball. It deflated in his mouth. He swung it side to side then let go of it, launching it ten feet back on shore. He ran back to shore proudly displaying the deflated soccer ball.

Tom laughed "That dog was given to me by your mom last August. He's quite a dog. Full of energy. Loves sticks and squeaky toys." Darren and Phillip loaded the boat as Tom kept moving more of his stuff to the dock. "You sure that boat can carry all this?"

Darren said, "No problem. This boat can carry over a thousand pounds. That's why we bought it."

The boat's cabin was big enough for eight people to sit or stand. There were two captains' chairs and bench seats along the back wall. The heavier stuff was stored low to keep the boat from becoming top heavy. The packs and duffel bags went forward of the cabin. Eleven milk crate size plastic totes were stacked up in the back. Four big old green duffel bags were set on top the totes. Darren picked up mail and packages for the Sky Ranch and some their neighbors. Tom went back to his pickup pretending to look about the camper while he smoked another hit from his pipe then hopped on Skyboat. They left 25 Mile Sky with a powerful wake. The big boat lifted the front easily, and the front end bobbed just a bit, riding the waves smoother than Tom thought possible for boat its size.

Lake Chelan is one mile wide in most places, and sixty miles long. The lake's elevation is 1,100 feet above sea level and it's one of the deepest lakes in the country. At one place the lake is over four hundred feet below sea level making the deepest part of the lake near to fifteen hundred feet deep. In its past Lake Chelan was covered with a five thousand foot deep glacier that carved the deep lake from the Columbia River past the town of Stehekin. The lake was the roadway and path to uplake outdoor activities. In the late eighteen hundreds white men searched for a trail over the Cascade Mountain Range. Northwest of Stehekin white men followed Indian trails over Cascade Pass, hiking for thirty miles to the lake, then rode canoes to the town of Chelan. Due to the steepness of the cliffs that surround Lake Chelan a road was never found. Some mining was done with little success. With the North Cascade National Park at the northern end of the lake the area became a quiet mountain getaway. Campers, climbers, horse packers, boaters, and adventurers of every kind rolled through the area some looking for nothing more than a quiet place off the grid to survive.

It was cold on the boat. The two big Mercury outboards were four stroke and brand-new. They were fully loaded with enough oomph to get the boat riding fast and high on the water. The deep water became deeper. Tom watched the depth meter, over five hundred feet deep, hard to believe. The temperature went down to 46 degrees. Tom put on his camo field jacket with his rank and all the other patches. Darren offered Tom a beer, a new one called Blue Moon. Tom took it, drinking half right away.

Darren said, "So you are Air Force, huh … Captain? How many years were you in?"

Tom finished his beer. Phillip handed him another just as Tom pulled out his now refilled flask of Patron Anejo Tequila. He took a big drag off the flask then handed it to Darren. He drank it back, "Man, that is smooth and good …whew." He handed it to Phillip who took a big swig without so much as changed look. "So how old are you, Philip?"

"I'm eighteen. Thinking about joining the military in another year. Made a deal with my dad that I would help him around the ranch doing guiding for the ranch. The best part is I won't have to go to school and I'll be getting paid to horseback in the mountains."

Tom asked, "What do you want to do and with which service?"

Phillip thought for a minute, "Maybe Army Rangers, not sure yet. What do you know of the Rangers?"

Tom replied," I was Army Ranger for the first five years of my career. They are awesome. Well-trained and take care of their people. Went to the Air Force because I was shot up, and tired of living at Fort Bragg, so I resigned my commission and joined the Air Force. Promised a job flying if I made PJ school, so I did all that. Spent a lot of time training at Nellis Air Force Base in Las Vegas, then Colorado Springs. Then I became a member of the Air Force Special Forces finishing my time at McCord, and Mountain Home, Idaho. Then 9-11 happened and I spent the last ten years outside the country serving mostly the Middle East and places like that."

Phillip asked, "Why did you quit?"

Tom said, "'Cause they thought I spent enough time in country. I was wounded several times and I didn't see myself becoming a general… too stuffy! I saved my money and now I'm taking time off, on vacation as it were. I'm not retired. Who knows, maybe someday I'll join up again. It's not for everyone you know but I did have fun, more so than the guys stuck in traffic on the freeway sucking dirty air every day going to work. But there are boring jobs in the military too, that's for sure. I was lucky to stay clear of the boring part."

Darren asked, "Where was your favorite place to serve?"

GEORGE THIELMAN

Tom thought. "Hmmm. I loved Mountain Home. It was small, in great country, as was McChord and Colorado Springs. I think my fave was Mountain Home. Outside of America my favorite was Afghanistan, high mountains, tough edgy environment, and close to the Himalayas. What a cool place."

Darren asked," What about weapons? What do you like and what have you used?"

Tom smiled. "Weapons, well that's the cool part of being a shooter. Few people on this earth get to play with weapons. Favorite rifle is the M4 or the AR10, sniper rifle H&K model 91, or a bolt action Remington or Winchester works just fine. For pistols I prefer a bigger .40 or .45 caliber to the smaller nine mil. All are capable of killing people, but the .40 caliber offers the best balance for me.

Woody was laying on top the packs in the back of the boat; sun and wind blew through his strawberry blonde coat. He was still somewhat wet from swimming at 25 Mile Sky. He shined in the sun, his big semi-floppy ears bobbed as the boat moved with the waves. The guys in the cabin drank tequila and beer. Tom watched the mountains go by, campsites and private property had docks for boat camping, state campsites had nice aluminum docks, private property could be seen with wood docks. Halfway there they pulled into a campsite called Prince Camp, a big expanse, once again in place only because avalanche, stream debris, dirt and rocks had rolled downhill for thousands of years. It was probably 100 acres of huge pine trees. Forest fires had ravaged the outer edges of the campsite. They walked up the trail for a short hike. A chair had been cut intro a large stump with a chain saw. There were metal fire rings with grills that hinged up, picnic tables, and small cleared areas for setting up tents. Snow was on the ground on the shaded north side, but the trails were clear. The sun was going down. Getting colder, they hiked to Prince Creek. Its creek bed full of river rock, maybe 100 yards wide, and spanned by two single log bridges, flat topped by a chain saw joined a rough cut hand rail cut made from thinner logs attached with steel bolts. They continued on with Woody in the lead, tail straight up and wagging back and forth. Strutting with an easy bounce, he spotted two deer not far away, and looked back at his master.

Tom said, "What's that Woody? Get him." Woody ran for fifty yards, growling then turned running back to Tom proudly showing off his speed and bravery. The guys smiled at his antics. He backed himself under Tom's legs seeking guidance from him. They continued on until the snow became too deep. The pass to the north would require snowshoes or skis.

They turned back toward the boat noticing a family camping with a big campfire. A blonde-haired seven-year old girl with pink pants and a black north face down jacket waved at them. She walked to Woody carrying a two foot rubber snake, "Are you going to camp with us?" She put her hand out to pet Woody's big head. He had grown up around Major Mo's kids and didn't mind little kids. He stuck his head toward the little girl, letting her hug him. "He's nice. I like him." The guys talked with the family then went back to the boat and to Stehekin.

They passed the town of Lucerne, an old miners' town, now full of small cottages. Up the road was a large Lutheran camp. Continuing up the lake, the boaters finally moved into Stehekin Harbor. Big docks with boats buildings, stores, a hotel, post office, park service museum and gift shop, and smaller gift shops, most closed for winter, lined the harbor. Big red busses were parked nearby waiting for the summer touristas. They continued on to the outlet of the Stehekin River. To the right was a huge flat area of land. Small cabins could be seen. A few were puffing wood smoke. Fifty yards away from the cabins was a two-story cedar building a sign said "Sky Café." To the right of the café was a large dock and on shore were canoes and different types of kayaks.

Spotty snow covered the ground from a late snowfall, and was piled up on the north side of the Café. The final gasps of winter, it was colder here, stuck in the nook of the North Cascades the mountain peaks and lower hills were covered in snow. The bigger peaks were capped with deep snow; many held powder all year. Lake Chelan was down low as was the Stehekin River. The water level in the rivers and creeks was still low as frozen snow and ice waited to melt; still too cold to send melted snow downstream; waiting. Clouds were spilling over the Cascades from the Puget Sound like a tsunami, with tails of clouds flowing both before and behind the bigger condensed clouds. Tom watched the crazy clouds move like a living being, sending its cloudy tails first, to explore a path for the large mass that is to come. Lights were turned on in the café. A fire was burning inside and easy smoke was pouring from the massive rock chimney. The café was larger than he remembered. Like Garrett's house, it was made of logs with a green metal roof and had with three dormers on each side of the ridgeline. Each upper bedroom had access to the second floor deck. Where the café had expanded the outside walls were clad in cedar siding. On the east side of the building was a big porch with wood handrails to keep the customers from spilling onto the sandy beach. Darren turned to Tom with a big smile "It's pretty, isn't it? I've lived here my whole life and the wonder and beauty of it all never ceases to catch my attention."

Tom continued looking at the great sight, "It's a great sight alright. The beauty is really something, wild and rife with nature." He bent down to pick up his gear. Philip stood looking at the upper mountains.

"Let's take all your equipment to the pickup." A brown and white Ford pickup sat near the docks, a carpenter's rack on the back bed. They unloaded the boat, piling all the stuff carefully in the bed. It fit easily since it originally fit in the back of a small Toyota Tundra. When the truck was loaded Darren turned to Tom, "Well, buy your dinner and have some more drinks. Have to give my mom a ride to the ranch. She hurt her ankle a few days ago hiking, limping around a bit. It usually closes in an hour and a half, but we'll keep it open for a while. My mom is waiting for you." Philip added, "Yah, and we have a great bar with a big screen TV. My Uncle Garret at 25 Mile Sky records drag racing, NASCAR, and football, along with other forms of sports so my grandma can play it on the TV in the bar. We don't have cable of any type so all we have is the DVD and VCR tapes, have lots of them." They walked to the café. Tom turned back to the loaded truck. His weapons were sitting for all to see in their plastic and aluminum padded cases.

"What about my stuff. Is it ok? Don't want anyone to make off with the guns,"

Darren and Philip looked at each other and laughed, "Don't worry, Tom. There's nobody here to steal anything."

Tom shrugged his shoulders went to the truck and pulled off two nylon black gear bags and followed them to the café. He looked at Philip and Darren; "I'll feel better with these near me!" The café had a storm entrance with old thick glass wavy from many years. Sagging as old glass did, like a slow liquid, which it was. Inside the café fifteen six person rectangular tables took up most of the room, with a lunch counter made of the same shiny knotty pine as the tables. The ambiance of the café/bar was clearly mountain-like. Several thick coats of clear finish had been added over the years on the tables and bar tops, and the walls were clad in knotty pine with painted pictures of mountain scenes. A black and charcoal drawing of Sky Café and Bar hung from the water hung on the wall. It must have been old; a fifty-seven Chevy pickup sat in the same spot that the 1990 pickup now sat. Another photo had waterfalls cascading down, creating a gorgeous stream that continued down to Stehekin Valley then to Lake Chelan itself. All the pictures had water flowing from one place to another, feeding the lakes then flowing to the mighty Columbia River. Eventually the water would reach the Pacific Ocean. They walked through the empty café to the bar on the east side of the building. The bar held ten small knotty pine tables with another knotty pine bar. The back wall was full of bottles: Jack Daniels, Seagram's, Old Crow, Crown Royal, Captain Morgan, Jameson, tequila, rum, Bacardi, brandy, gin, Popov Vodka, Smirnov, and all the liqueurs. A fairly complete bar, Tom thought.

Darren disappeared into the kitchen. He came back to the bar and filled two glasses with Blue Moon Belgian beer, "Straight from the tap… Sally's in the kitchen. She'll be out in a few minutes. Tom picked up his beer mug and walked about the bar looking at old black and white photos of Sky Ranch and the surrounding areas. Each old photo had a caption typed with typewriter. In one photo an old Indian man stood with a Sharps buffalo rifle. The front of a building read, "Traders Post." The caption read, "1907 the original Samuel Sky, then 42, in front of the first building he made at this very location, a fur trading store catering to trappers and adventurers." Another was of the opening of the Sky café in 1969 with Sally and her husband standing with a pitchfork, as in American Gothic. Sally's husband was wearing stripped bell-bottoms and a vest with a marijuana leaf hanging out his pocket. Sally was wearing a thin dress that clearly shows her young shape. Tom thought about how attractive she was. The caption read, "Sally and James, opening of Sky Café 1969, big party."

A loud, old voice broke up Tom's thoughts. An old man moved into the bar, wearing an old, dirty red Patagonia jacket. The sleeve were in tatters, his hair, long and butchered by some terrible barber, was uncombed and was mostly grey with streaks of black. His bushy eyebrows swooped forward, and his forehead was furrowed and tan. He wore a grey wool sweater under the Patagonia with pleated dirty, black slacks and his fly was open. The cuffs of his pants were stuffed into old leather hiking boots, which were laced up perfectly. An old worn brown leather belt held his pants on his body. Darren jumped behind the bar, "What'll it be, Joe?" Joe seemed to think for a minute, scrunched up and scratched at his unshaven face, and took a big breath like he was going to blow out hundreds of birthday candles. He held the breath then seemed to yell out, "Well, goddamn-son-of-a-bitch, shit ill have whut I always have ill-tell-ya-whut!"

Darren said, "The house scotch on the rocks, huh."

Old Joe yelled back, "Shit- fire-to-fuckin-hell-boy- ill-tell-ya-whut- shit, looks like a cold one tonight better stoke that fire boy-ill-tell-ya-whut." With that he sat down on a stool and took a swig of his drink. "Hmm, neckter of the gods ill tell-ya-whut right there like fuckin hell boy. Philip how ya doin god damn haven't seen ya in a coons age, spitten image of ya dad there kid you join the marines yet? Get ya out of here lickety split, that's for sure ill-tell-ya-whut-shit!"

Tom was amazed at the decibels and the way the old fart could cuss. Sally came into the room. She was prettier than he remembered, straight up with a strong body. She was wearing a fleece vest with "Sky Ranch" and a jagged mountain, a river, and a stick figure catching a fish.

"Hello Joe." She poked Joe in the back. He raised his glass to her and took a big drink, saying nothing. She came to Tom and her grandson grabbing Philip by the cheek. He scrunched up his face as she kissed him on his forehead. Sally walked behind the bar to Darren. She grabbed him with either hand around his head, pulling it to her. He did the same as his son, as his mother kissed him on the lips. She let him go and gave him a slap across the cheek. "My boys, how ya' doin' today," with a fake New York accent. She looked at Tom and hurried back around the bar to him. She put her hands on his left arm drawing him closer to her, "Captain Tom Trainer, how are you? You look better than the last time, that's for sure." She hugged him. Tom smelled the definite aroma of weed on her.

He said, "I'm doin' good Sally. Glad to be here, thought of little else since last summer,"

She hugged him again and said," Joe, have you met Captain Tom Trainer of the U.S. Air Force?"

Joe looked at Tom "How ya doin' there son. Always glad to see a man that wears the uniform. Looks like you've seen some combat god dam if that ain't a sumbitch ill- tell- ya- whut- shit." Then Joe took a big breath and yelled out, "Well ill-tell-ya-whut, was too young for World War II, but I did fight in Korea, fighten off those yeella Chinese, livin in muddy foxholes for weeks, god dam if that wasn't sumthin, why they would always attack in force, not much for sneaken up on ya with bomb under their clothes like those goddamn ragheaded sand nigger camel fuckin boo rabb cowards in the middle east, while ill -tell –yaw-whut what we should do is give the Jews all the money and weapons and let them kick the shit out of all of um, do a lot better than were doin'. I'll tell yaw whut, right there to fuckin hell boy, shit." Old Joe then reached down to his crotch grabbing the whole mess with full open hand, cleared his throat with a loud sound, and swallowed the mucus. He sat back down with a thump, picked up his glass, draining it. He set it down then looked at Sally. With a swirling motion with his finger he communicated to Sally his desire for a refill. Sally smiled a huge, pretty, toothy smile then looked at Tom.

Tom said simply," Very well put. Glad to meet you Joe!" Joe lifted back his third highball in a toast.

Sally stood smiling behind the bar, "Ok, you guys hungry? I have buffalo stew and buffalo stew. So what'll it be? Ok buffalo stew it is!" She left the room. A few minutes later a big chunky man in a cook's jacket and hat came out carrying six bowls of stew and two hot loaves of bread.

He set them down, "Dig in boys. It's on the house."

Sally came back with a glass of wine in her hand. "Tom, is that the little mutt we gave you last summer?" Tom nodded yes. "Well bring him in, must be starving. She went out and came back into the bar with Woody, a bowl of water, and bowl of stew for the dog. "Now you go ahead and eat up, big boy." She stroked his head. He looked at Tom.

"Go ahead eat up," Tom told him. Woody bent down and started lapping up the delicious stew.

Philip said," There's not an animal on this planet that doesn't like my grandma. She's like the Dr. Doolittle of Stehekin."

They sat outside for an hour talking. When they closed up, the dark clouds were still forming. Old Joe walked by them, stopped twenty feet from them. He stood spread his legs like he was bracing himself for a stiff wind. He stuck his right hand up to the sky made a fist then pulled it down, like he was pulling a train whistle. As his arm came down a loud squeaky fart followed as his arm lowered. When the arm made it passed his waist the noise stopped for a second then continued in short burst that were highlighted by a short punch from the same right arm. He then yelled out as he walked into the darkness, starting for home. "Gonna be a cold one ill tell-ya-whut-godamn-sumbitch nice to meet ya Tom, ya, bad ass fuck."

Philip and tom looked at each other smiling. Philip then laughed kicked at the ground then looked at Tom. "Old Joe is a bit colorfull and enjoys a good drink. Most of his joy seems to come from a good fart." He laughed again. Tom and the Sky's drove the mile down the gravel road to Sky Ranch in darkness.

MOVING IN –
THE CABIN ON THE ROCK

CHAPTER 2

SKY RANCH WAS ONE MILE NORTH of the café along an unnamed gravel road. They crossed a log bridge over Miners' Creek, which bordered the ranch along the east side. A log gate similar to 25 Mile Sky's, with log posts supporting a log crosspiece marked the entrance. A wood, shaped shield with elk antlers decorated the entrance. Dried moss hung from the antlers. Two houses made of rock and cedar, with brown and green metal roofs, hid behind large huckleberry bushes. Grey boulders and small cedars decorated the front yards. Garbage can-sized rocks lined the inside of a four-foot wire fence. They passed an L-shaped brown metal barn and parked next to two bus-sized grey and white bread loaf-shaped rocks, which mushroomed at the top.

Sally stepped out of the truck, reached for the closest duffel bag and headed off down a dark path. They lost sight of her through a stand of fruit trees. They took off after her, carrying bags and boxes along the dark path. Big flat stones had been set, making a walkway. Gravel had been set to the height of the stones making the path higher than the damp ground. They passed through two smaller bread loaf-shaped rocks. Scattered stunted cottonwoods grew along the trail. Tom walked between two of the biggest bread loaf rocks. A clearing opened up with the dark outline of cabin and the river in the background. To the left was a small bay with a huge logjam in the middle. He walked up four rock steps onto the covered porch. Tom stomped his foot on the solid rock porch. A light flickered on inside the cabin as Sally found the oil lamps and lit them. Sally had lit three oil lamps along with six fat candles upstairs.

The floors were rock, not stone tiles. The house was, in fact, built on a large flat rock. The inside was twenty feet by seventeen feet. The first three feet of the walls of the cabin were made with mortar-set rocks more than a foot thick. Most of the square-shaped rocks were drilled and pinned into the much larger rock to keep them from creeping and cracking, Sally's grandfather and father had been miners as well as traders and farmers. They had drilled the rocks carefully and framed the house with solid four by eights made of sturdy cedar and Douglas fir wood, all cut and fabricated in a nearby lumber mill.

Inside was an L-shaped loft that looked down on the small living room below. The balusters were made from squiggly driftwood from the river nearby. The walls and ceiling were insulated and covered in cedar planking, giving the cabin a cedar smell and keeping the bugs away. The cabin had a bit of a musty smell, but cedar dominated the smell of the cabin. The stairwell was in the center of the cabin, held up by eight-inch thick beams that continued to the ceiling. Along the east side of the stairwell were two wood stoves separated by a rock wall, one black wood stove faced the northeast back of the cabin for heating, and an old chipped up blue enamel cook stove faced the kitchen in the front.

Sally bent down and lit the black wood stove. "With both of these stoves going in the winter, the heat will build up so good that you'll need to open the windows. This is the coziest of the cabins we have, real nice!" She crumpled a sheet of newspaper and lit it. The newspaper caught fire and the cedar kindling began snapping and popping. Rocks had been carefully collected from the property; again most of them were square-shaped, not thicker than six inches, the floor was not completely flat so the mortared walls took up the space created by the irregular rock floor. There was one big four-inch drop in the floor in the northwest corner; you had to be careful not to trip in a few areas. The kitchen was left of the front door with old brown painted cabinets and lime green Formica, an old chipped white enamel sink with a pump type hydrant faucet, and the upper cabinets had glass windows so you could see the contents.

Sally stoked the fire then spoke to Tom as Darren and Philip quietly hauled in all the equipment and supplies. An old Lazy Boy chair was the only furniture in the house except for a small three-foot by three-foot table with three chairs that did not match.

GEORGE THIELMAN

Sally informed Tom, "Now the faucet is under pressure, but still requires a couple of pumps. Because the river is the water table the water is cold and clean. We left you four oil lamps and some candles. The wood stove heats up the cabin in about fifteen minutes. In an hour the temperature well be over sixty. Because of the insulation, the house stays very comfortable." She walked to the kitchen area and opened the lower cabinets. "We left you a bunch of canned goods and dry goods like rice, noodles, and granola. Now out the side door," she waved Tom over to a side door on the west side of the house. Outside they stood on the rock, looking down at a sort of carport, the roof was made of rusting tin bent down in some areas, fifteen feet across and held up by sturdy wood beams. Like the house, the walls were three feet high with full windows on the west and north ends. The south end was open with old lawn mowers and farming tools left to rust in a heap. "Okay Tom, I'm out of here. Make a list of things you need and we can get them whenever you want. We usually go to Chelan a couple of times a week for one thing or another, so stay in touch with Philip. I'm sure he'll be around you quite a bit. Good night. Maybe we'll see you in the morning!" With that she was out the door with Darren following behind her. Tom turned his attention to making trips to the truck with Philip. After fifteen minutes they had all the supplies scattered everywhere on the bottom floor.

Philip sat in one of the kitchen chairs obviously interested in some of the equipment. "What kind of guns do you have in the cases and are you a hunter? I'm pretty good myself. Most of the guns we have here are old, but we take care of them."

Tom opened two rifle cases. One held a black Winchester bolt action with a big scope; the other held the Colt M4 given to him at his retirement party. He pulled each out of the case and handed them to Philip, whose eyes lit up.

"Man, these are nice, I like the camo colors on the M16." Tom corrected him. "It's an M4, but semi-auto only."

Philip said, "You have a screw-on silencer. That's cool, man, and all kinds of green carbon fiber make it super light. Did you use Colts in the Army?"

Tom replied, "Not always. Sometimes I used Armelite and others. The latest are from FN and H&K, I saw dozens of assault rifles from all different makers. They each make great weapons in two calibers, but I think when I get done with this Colt it well be as good as anything I've used. Now the Winchester model 70 is chambered with a 300 win mag, a good round that will fly flat for several hundred feet. It's not new and I've shot with it many times. To answer your question, I do hunt. Hope to go with you this fall."

Philip stood up and stretched, "Well, got to go Tom. Maybe see ya in the morning. Do you fish?"

Tom replied, "Yes I fish, but I'll bet not as good as you. Maybe you can show me?" With that Philip waved with a big smile and was gone down the steps.

Tom looked through the plastic totes. He walked upstairs to the loft with Woody following. He looked around; the ceiling was high enough that he could walk without bending over. He was only five foot ten, a perfect size for this cabin. He noticed two cedar cabinets. One was a chest of drawers; another was a small closet type with a few cobwebs. Specks of mice poop here and there dotted the floor. A window faced south about knee high. Individual windowpanes held swirly old glass, with the putty dried and flaking away. Tom looked out at his front yard, a pile of firewood, brown grass, snow patches, and the bread loaves. He hauled up two duffel bags and two totes full of bedding and clothes. He unrolled two fat Thermarest mattresses, snapped them together to make a double sized bed then laid out a double Coleman sleeping bag. Near the bed he laid two folded wool blankets, one pillow, and set up a digital clock next to the bed. Tom hauled up his weapons and some clothes. Downstairs he unloaded his kitchen stuff; coffee, stainless coffee press, two ceramic cups, tea, bowls, and a few paper plates. In the upper cabinets he found ceramic plates, bowls, cups, and glasses. Nothing matched, but Tom didn't care. This was his first home. He could pick and choose where and when he sat and ate.

He sat down at the table pulling out the bag that held his hashish, filled a bowl, and walked around the house christening the place with smoke. It was not lost on him that most people would not choose to live this way. He opened a bottle of Cazadores Tequila and poured two shots into one of the Boy Scout cups he had found in the cabinet. "Here's to Sky Ranch and freedom." He raised his glass to Woody, who was sitting up looking at him curiously. His tail wagged. He continued unpacking one plastic tote full of reloading equipment. He unloaded a couple hundred pounds of food: soup, ravioli, peaches, pineapple, pears, chicken, turkey, dog food, beans, chili, rice, flour, wheat, bags of dried beans and all the other stuff he would need.

His first night in the cabin he was excited just to go to bed. He thought of the times his parents would take him on vacation at the national parks on the west coast: Yosemite, the Grand Canyon, Glacier, Yellowstone, the

GEORGE THIELMAN

Grand Tetons, and the parks of Arizona. As a boy his excitement could be seen in every action he took as they traveled on holiday. His dad would set up the nylon dome tent as Tom would pull the gear out of their little Nissan pickup that his mom and dad seemed to make last forever. He would crawl into his own sleeping bag next to his mom and dad and dream of the day's adventure to come. Tom felt that way tonight. With his big puppy following him they ascended the stairs to the loft. The Thermarest mattress had inflated itself. He set the new H&K next to his pillow, stripped off his clothes, and crawled in bed. He then reached over for his pipe for a smoke, taking two hits from his pipe then drank a pint of cool water. He wondered how it was possible that water could be so delicious. The wood in the woodstove snapped and popped quietly. Tom opened the loft window. The sound of the river and wind was all he could hear; no hum of electricity or car sounds, no human voices or fireworks going off. He laid down on his thin bed, smiling, and groaned in complete pleasure. Woody walked over to him, put his head down and jammed his forehead against Tom's leg then collapsed at the foot of the bed. They fell asleep with no dreams of death this night.

At two am he woke and threw on his jacket and walked downstairs to piss. There was no bathroom in the cabin, so he had to pee outside. Two owls were hooting in the distant darkness trying to find each other. One of the cows mooed; the wind was kicking up pine needles. It was in the thirties. Woody walked quietly, sniffing as he stood peeing on the long grass. Clouds were moving in fast through the valley, the smell of snow was in the air, the mountains looked small. The wind picked up. Tom stood looking up at the clouds. They were moving and changing fast like mutating cotton balls. He yawned, a deep hard yawn that rolled throughout his body. The clouds had holes with incredible light behind them. Massive lighting, like that of pulsating runway lights, lit up the sky through the holes in the clouds. There was an incredible flash of light then a big bang. Thunder then dry snow started to fall. He looked up to the clouds watching the natural show, and couldn't take his eyes off the sky.

Through a hole in the clouds a flash of light then furry face looked at him. Then cute black eyes and nose black lips formed a smile. It had white fur like the clouds, and was moving behind the clouds, the light emitting from his body like a searchlight behind the clouds. It was like Bono at a U2 concert moving the light as the Edge played his electric guitar to the tune of "Bullet the Blue Sky." Tom stood mesmerized by the crazy sight above him. The clouds sped up, the light breaking through to the valley below then it would shut the light down, and the valley would become dark. It hit the mountains west of the ranch then traveled down across the ranch like a helicopter light looking for criminals. It stopped at Tom and Woody. He stood looking up. He wasn't sure, but thought he saw a monster look around the search light at him. The light took off traveling across the river then disappeared in the trees.

Snow started to fall. He looked at his watch. It was 2:39. He took two steps then said, "What the fuck." Tom stood watching the sky for more of the show. He looked at Woody. Woody looked up at his master, his coat covered in snow, as was Tom. "We were out there for a half hour?" Tom was baffled and rubbed the sleep from his face. He scratched his head. Inside he dried Woody with a towel. He smiled, then went back to sleep, dreaming of cartoonish snow monsters.

Snow fell all night covering the ground; a good dusting. He woke at 5:30 as usual, feeling rested. The fire was out and the cabin was cold. One of the cows mooed in the early morning. Mist was rising from the warmer river. As the snow fell it was quite a sight, like a Hallmark card; the banks covered in snow, the river flowing, moving branches and trees to new locations.

Tom started a fire in the old wood stove. He stacked small kindling; the size of a big kitchen knife, on the bottom then stacked another layer, laying it horizontally across the first layer. He crumpled newspaper, laid it across the kindling then stacked more kindling like a tepee on the top of the paper then lit the paper. He blew on the fire lightly then gave it some time to take.

It lit right away. The small douglas fir kindling snapped quietly as he added bigger pieces and let them burn. He lit an oil lamp then set his Coleman stove on the lime green kitchen counter. He found the coffee pot, starting the boiling process then went back to the wood stove to add the bigger pieces of wood. He chose Starbuck's Pike Place for his first morning brew, added a little milk the Skys had left him, and poured it in a ceramic cup he had bought in Chelan. He dressed in sweat pants with a sweater and his new down parka and walked out the front door across the ranch out to the horse pasture. Walking along the riverbank his footprints sunk down in three-inch deep snow. Cold and dry, it moved like dust when his boots hit the ground. He spotted fresh deer tracks, and a family of raccoons crossed in front of him.

He walked past Darren's house. Only thirty feet west of Sally's, it was a carbon copy of hers. A light was on in the kitchen, and someone was preparing coffee or tea. He continued on north past the vacant bunkhouse to the barn. Sally was outside carrying firewood into her house. She saw Tom and waved. He walked over to her taking the wood from her.

"Nice morning," she said. "How was your first night of retirement?"

Tom laughed, "Don't say that, makes feel old and sickly."

Sally replied with a long stare. She moved her head upward and nodded," Well, you're not sickly, that's for sure! Why don't you come in? I have coffee on." They went inside the warm and cozy house. A fire burned in a wood stove. Tom threw some logs on her fire, and then sat down at a large rectangular kitchen table.

"Sally, you can fit over a dozen people at this table." They sat talking.

"My great, great grandpa wandered through Stehekin Valley in the late 1890's, after the army. He moved to the café location, opened a trading post, and bought the Sky Ranch to grow food for the travelers. The old place burned to the ground in '39. My grandfather built this house in 1941 then went to war, leaving my grandma alone until '45 when he came back. That's when he built the cabin you're staying in, right after the war. He was a bit messed, up bad dreams and the such." Sally was fishing for signs of Tom's trauma, but she saw none. "Ya, that cabin saved my grandpa. He spent days and days collecting the rocks and wood he would need to make the cabin. They made their own cement and mortar right here. When the materials were in place he started building that very night. Sometimes he would sneak back to the cabin. My dad and his brothers could see his pain in everything he did. Fought in Europe, starting on D-Day, chased behind the 1st Rangers, spending most of his time as a medic. Everyone gave him space as he worked on the cabin, meticulously setting just the right rocks in just the right way as he wanted. He mortar set the rocks, drilling and pinning them so the four foot footings would not creep off the big rock. He framed the cabin with six-inch thick cedar beams in the modern style of stick framing that's done now. He was a visionary.

Sally continued, "After four months he completed the cabin and tried to move in alone, but he was in love with my grandmother. As time went on he spent more and more time with Grandma. My father went to Vietnam in '62 came back in '64, messed up much like my grandfather was. He left. Me and my husband to take care of the farm. I ended up owning the farm 'cause no one else wanted it. My dad moved to Spokane to run a quarry and I stayed here with my hippie husband. Ran the place ever since with my kids. My dad moved back in the late seventies and drank himself to death in that cabin. He told me once that the cabin on the rock kept him alive. He loved that place."

Tom asked, "Why don't you stay there?" Sally looked at the ceiling and rolled her eyes.

"I actually lived in it from '71 to '75 then I became a young mother. Our family got too big so we kicked the renters out of my place and Darren built his place. Garrett and his sister moved east. It's been a great life; the café took off and we made the campsites and cabins. Over time it all grew into what it is. I wouldn't trade it for anything."

The back door burst open. It was Philip. "Grandma, I'm ready to go! Hey Tom, we always ride our bikes to the café for Sunday breakfast. Want to come?" With the road full of snow, they road mountain bikes, the knobby tires gripping the snow easily. Woody and two redheilers ran alongside, sniffing and sprinting ahead, only to put the brakes on when they got the smell of a critter. They'd sniff wildly then jump up, sprinting to catch up. At the café the cook, big Kenny Delanny, cooked up French toast with elk sausage, and potatoes chopped and cooked with onions, garlic, basil and hot peppers; a perfect meal for a cold snowy day. The dogs all got a bowl of stew mixed in with dry dog food.

The café porch floor was made of cedar with bench seating. There was always a couple of ceramic bowls full of fresh water for whatever animal needed it. A screened-in porch on the lakeside was used in the summer when the campsites were full; many locals ate and drank there. It served as a place for parties, weddings, birthday parties, and community get-togethers. Locals and cabin owners were the only people in the café this morning, Two local couples, and four at the bar enjoying the Seattle Seahawks and Raiders game from a week earlier enjoyed the cozy atmosphere. A warm fire snapped nearby.

Outside the windows a light snow fell, the dogs walked in circles bugging each other, poking at Woody. Woody was the new and youngest one, but he was also the bigger dog. Woody snapped at Philip's dog, Bandit, who stepped back looking from the side at Woody's snarling mouth. Another dog, a blue heiler, stepped between them, breaking the tension. Suddenly all three took off running around the café, two laps, happily racing each other. They ran, tails wagging, straight onto the nearby boat ramp and into the frigid lake. Bandit and Hunter swam out then came back trying to lure Woody into the water with them. Woody stood in the water up to his belly watching his new friends with his mouth open. Just as quickly as before, they ran back to the café porch. There they lapped up water from the old Crockpot, sat down, and stared out at the empty campsites. They watched Sally's little poodle mutt, Zippy, slowly walk to the café, looking for her master. She walked straight to the Crockpot bowl, took a big swig then sat down, her curly brown poodle fur now coated with snow. She was usually left at home because she was old and small, but she was as stubborn as could be. If she could, she would always try to keep up with Sally. One eye was glazed over from cataracts, her tail was hairless and scrawny, and her scrunched up ears neither stood up nor flopped down. She looked old and was, but she was loyal to the Sky family. She walked by Woody, her tail proudly standing straight up. She seemed to dance in front of him then let out a loud bark. He sat bored, simply glancing at the little old mutt.

Sally, Tom and Philip left the café with the dogs both behind and running in front trying to bother each other and to herd the humans. All but the old mutt were at least partially of heiler blood; a herding breed that worked sheep, cows, even people on bicycles. At the ranch they would herd the chickens and horses. They pestered the horses and the two mules. Both had been kicked several times, yet still continued pestering of any and all people and animals in their company. They were happy as dogs could be. Like the humans who lived in this isolated country, they were healthy and happy; healthy food, clean water, and nothing manmade polluting upstream to bother them. Tom thought of the monster in the clouds looking at him with his big dark humorous eyes. All here seemed harmonious, clean, isolated, and healthy. Tom thought this was going to be a good place to heal both his body and mind.

Tom went back to his cabin to organize his things. He started by putting away clothes in the two chests of drawers in his bedroom loft. On the dressers he laid out his meager nick-knacks: a six-inch metal die cast of the robot from the movie "The Day The Earth Stood Still," a headlamp, two Gerber daggers, and several small framed pictures of him and climbers and soldiers. One picture was of Tom, on a shot-up Russian Ural motorcycle pockmarked by big bullets through the tank. He had a big beard, dyed black to fit in better with the local gentry in Afghanistan, and a new style Springfield M14 slung over his shoulder, set up for sniping with large scope painted in a desert camo. With canned paint he had painted the brand new match grade rifle himself, sitting on the steps of a big Sikorskey helicopter. Another picture was of three of his rock-climbing friends in the early '90's mid-way up the famous El Capitan, a Yosemite big wall rock climb. All tied together, looking down 500 feet to the valley floor, their hair was messed up, and faces and hands tanned from days exposed to the hot sun. The expressions on their faces were of mock fright. They were brave people risking their lives for nothing but fun, and to stave off life's boredom. Another picture was of Tom as a young boy, ten years old, camping in a snow cave in Canada, a huge toothy smile on his face.

In the corner of the cabin he set his locked rifle and pistol cases. In front of that he'd fashioned a pole to hang his clothes on. He'd set his iPhone on top of his Dell laptop. Neither had any use in the valley. His keys sat nearby, useless.

The front door burst open, Philip, standing with two fishing poles and a tackle box, yelled, "Tom, let's go fishing right now. Grandma wants to have a fish fry tonight!" They'd walked less than 200 yards to the shoreline of the Stehekin River. Snow had stopped falling an hour before but it stayed cold. Philip led Tom to rock sticking out into the Sky's small bay, created by a huge beaver dam. "This is called the finger." Philip traced the rock with his hand, clearly pointing out a hand with its middle finger sticking out.

It was so perfect that Tom started laughing, "What a great place to be," he belted out in a coughing laugh. "Okay kid, show me how to do this!" Philip opened the tackle box, and pulled out two very well used lures. "I make these out of old spoons; have since grade school. Caught some great fish with these babies." He was excited to have such a friend. He tied the lures on the end of the two lines, showing Tom the right knot to use, and how to tie the spinner to the lure itself. He stood back and launched the pole, sending the lure forward into the icy waters then dragged it back slowly, teasing the fish below. Tom did the same. Cast after cast they worked the lures trying to get the attention of the fish. By the end of the hour they had five good-sized trout. They stayed another hour and caught five more. Philip dressed out the fish on the rock leaving the entrails on the rock for the black birds to eat, "We'll take half of them to the café and they'll sell them tonight.

They packed the fish in ice at Sally's house. She packed half of them in a plastic bag and into a small igloo cooler for the café's use. She made the fishers a lunch of potato salad and sourdough bread. Philip took off to do chores while Tom went back to his cabin to continue straightening up his stuff. Darren came by with the pickup truck full of log rounds.

"Just split these and they'll burn real well. Should be enough for the rest of the spring. We have the job of keeping the tree branches out of electric wires. That's where the wood comes from."

Tom asked him, "Darren, I need a gun safe or something lockable in the cabin. Do you have anything I could use?"

Darren thought for a minute. "Yes, I think I do. Come with me." They drove to Darren's house. In his garage was an old cabinet standing over six feet. It was beat-up, gouged, and scratched. "This should work," he said. "I think they call these Armoires. Not sure about that though. What I'll do is beef up the hinges and add solid oak to the inside. We can make slots for the rifles to sit in, and add a shelf or two for your handguns and ammo." They loaded it into the pickup and drove it the three hundred feet to Sally's L-shaped barn. They carried the big chest past hay bales stacked fifteen feet high, through a door, and into an old woodshop. The tools were newer. A stack of old tools took up the east wall.

Tom said, "Man, it's warm in here. Maybe I should move in here rather than the cabin." Darren made an irritated face that Tom did not see.

"Sally keeps the shop heated to keep me in here making furniture and knickknacks to be sold at the store!" Tom thought no more about it. They left the piece of furniture, and walked outside, along the empty one-acre garden. The chickens pecked at the meager grass and weeds poking through the snow.

Tom drove away with Darren, northwest, following power lines. The power poles were much smaller than what he had seen in the big cities. Trees had been long ago cut to minimize falling tree branches messing up the electric grid.

Darren said, "Whenever we see a tree leaning or a branch ready to fall, we cut it away. This way we have fewer electric interruptions." They drove to the small power station, a solid block building with a large old-style water wheel, the driveshaft of which disappeared into a small shack; the powerhouse. A day of work, and to see every bit of the valley and how it operated, was Tom's goal for the next couple weeks. This would bring all he didn't know about the valley closer to him and make it seem smaller to him. He was in a hurry to establish his new life and to make new friends.

The driveshaft entered the shack and turned a generator that powered the valley. They cleared away logs that had the possibility of clogging the water to the water wheel. Long poles that had bent down, with blades for moving the logs pushed out into the flow of the river.

Darren pulled out an ancient banged-up Coleman cooler. Out of it he pulled out a couple roast beef sandwiches. He handed Tom a jar." It's apple cider from last fall. My wife makes it in five gallon buckets. I think she made over twenty gallons from the bad apples that you don't see in the grocery store. The roast beef is actually buffalo from one of the small ranches near us. We even make our own mayonnaise and mustard. We do buy cheese from the big stores down lake, and sometimes we make our own. We try to make all we can here."

Tom had never thought about where grocery products came from and what was in them. He moved in his seat. Darren asked, "You in pain, Tom?"

Tom said, "My shoulder and left side took a few bullets. It gives me trouble, need a hot tub. One of the bullets entered from my left side behind the ribs. It wound through my ribs and traveled around the big ball joint in my left shoulder. Did a lot of small damage that mostly just bugs me."

Darren replied, "When I was in the army never saw any action. Did my time in Korea and Japan, standing around keeping machinery running. Always looked up to the Special Forces guys."

Tom looked back at him. "Thanks Darren. I'm glad to hear that, and I want you to know that those of us Special Forces guys that did a lot of the shooting looked forward to coming back to the machines that kept our lives moving forward and comfortable."

After lunch they drove back to Sky Ranch. Tom went back to his cabin, and looked through his supplies, wondering what he could use to make life better in this remote place. His food supplies were massive, Skippy Peanut butter, strawberry jam, Nutela spread, and a case of canned chicken, turkey, tuna, and salmon. In the cupboard he had boxes and bags of Bisquick, baking powder, cane sugar, raisins, flour, wheat, and chocolate chips, along with thirty MREs that he stole from the Army in Yakima. In a big plastic tote he had dried food for backpacking, beef stroganoff, spaghetti, stew, dried eggs, pancake mix, granola, and two cases of Power Bars. From Cabela's he had two big cans of pheasant and two seven-pound cans of smoked ham. As retirement gifts his friends had given him boxes of cheese, crackers, and sausage; the kind sold at the mall kiosks for when you don't know what to buy for someone.

He walked a few steps to the wood stove to poke the wood in the fire. From his pocket he pulled his antler pipe, filled a bowl, and smoked up, watching the smoke rise past the loft. He laughed thinking about where he was and how fortunate he was to be in the valley. It was exactly where he wanted to be. He had enough food and supplies to last a couple months. With what he could hunt and fish he thought he could live a long time in the valley; with his current expenses he could live for years. If he moved to the big city he probably couldn't get a credit card without a job, and his retirement money was considered just above the poverty rate. He didn't feel poor or rich in this place; life would be different. Because of past purchases and acquisitions by the Sky family, twelve decades of collecting and building cabins and houses, digging fire pits, nailing together picnic tables for the campsites, not to mention the early purchase of key properties, the family had never in a century sold any of their pieces of land. They had stayed together, helping each other get high school and college degrees. Some had gone in the service to take advantage of the GI bill and go to school on the government's dime, and to receive medical care from V.A.

Enough of them had come back to this place to keep it relevant to the world of Lake Chelan. With Sally's leadership, the holdings of the family had grown and become more stable than at any time in the last century; there were no loans, and no stock portfolio. Every financial deal was tied to the valley, and all the property was paid for, including 25 mile Sky. There were accounts for the supplies needed for the café, bar, and store, but nothing else. The cabins and the campsites paid the taxes and for the six people it took to hire to maintain them. The Sky family took good care of the people that worked for them, giving them rooms above the café or a cabin to stay in, along with healthy food and a positive place to live while they took care of the Sky family holdings.

Since it was the second week of April, few people visited the campsites. A few rented the small cabins for honeymoons. One couple spent an entire week, barely moving from their cabin. The café would deliver meals to campers or cabin renters. One old man had been renting a cabin all winter using the time walking and boozing with old Joe Spadafore. The rumor was he had terminal cancer, and that he was living out his last days and using the last of his social security living in the valley enjoying the café and bar. He was scrawny and not very tall. He wore old Hager slacks, no denim or cargo pants. He received mail and a few packages. Sometimes he would take the three-hour ferry ride back to Chelan, come back a few days later, happy to be back where things were simple and clear. His name was Bill Battling from Tacoma. He'd worked at the old pulp mill 'till it closed then worked for a lumber mill as a sales manager. He had sold everything when he was diagnosed with cancer. He'd thrown everything he'd wanted in his bulbous '92 Chevy station wagon and headed for 25 mile Sky. The wood-paneled wagon sat next to Tom's Tundra in the parking lot of 25 mile Sky. The back of it was covered in two decades of political bumper stickers. "Rush is right. Mega dittos Rush. Remember Ronald Regan. Ross is boss, I'm the NRA. When guns are illegal only criminals well have them. Ted Kennedy's car has killed more people than my gun. W in '04. Abortion is a crime." Then he had a sticker Dole-Kemp in '92 that had another sticker of the same font and size that said Role-Hemp with a marijuana leaf between the two names. Bill wasn't quite as colorful as old Joe, but he did have the same old-man fire that kept them pissed off at the world. He claimed the reasons for the pissed-off old man attitude was simple. One reason was because sex wasn't going to happen again, because with every movement he felt pain. The most relevant reason was that at Bill's age, you could look back on your life and know that things were never going to be that good again.

Tom's third evening was spent at the bar drinking, watching a NASCAR race from the day before. He'd been cutting and splitting fire wood for six hours that day, and the big Ford pickup was packed with wood for several households in the valley, at least. They walked inside the café and didn't have to wonder who was telling tall stories in the bar. They walked around, through the café, to the bar. Tom Darren and Philip looked at each other and laughed. Old Joe Spadafore was standing in front of a table of young men. Most wore Harley-Davidson jackets or shirts. Joe was in mid-story, yelling each word to the men. He was gesturing with his hands, again his fly was open, and he had he nose hairs hanging from his nose.

"So I'm in there, in my pickup, when this kid on a rice burner runs a red light. Shit, he hit one of them construction trucks with all the tools and lumber on it. Well you know, what the fuck. Gotdam truck bed tore his head right off his body, helmet and all, so I jumped out of my pickup." He then pretended to pickup and hold a severed human head. "Picked up that helmet with the head inside, turned it over, flipped up the glass part, and I'll be a gotdam, sumbitch motherfucker if he didn't look at me and say, 'Help me please?' Well I took one look at him and I cradled that head in that helmet and I swear to gotdam shit fucker that I said then, in a very soothing voice, 'aint one gotdam thing I can do for ya, son. Your head is defucking detached from your fucking body.' Gotdam, I swear to fucking Jesus H. Christ I'll tell you whut shit." With that Joe turned to Kenny Delanny behind the bar, "Give me another one of them, gotdamit." Kenny smiled a big toothy grin at Tom and Bill and poured another shot for Joe. Joe slugged it back and left for the restroom, yelling about how he had to piss like a gotdam racehorse, ending with, "I'll tell ya whut." Everyone in the bar shook their heads in humor, and went back to their conversations.

Two days later, Tom's fourth evening, Darren asked Tom to come to Bill's cabin, and to bring a first aid kit. Bill was on the floor, his mouth foamy with white liquid. He had finally died, and was found by Joe just minutes before they tried to get his old heart going. He was too old and sick, and had died peacefully in the place of his choosing, living out his last days with people that gave a shit about him. Darren called the Sherriff in Chelan on the short wave radio in the café office. He was told to wrap

Bill up and bring him to Chelan, which they did. Tom rode with Darren, Sally and Philip to Chelan. They arrived in darkness. An ambulance took Bill to the coroner's office, and Bill's friends left for 25 Mile Sky to spend the night.

It was a sad night. The end of a life of a lonely man. They wondered about his family and friends. Who would care about his death? As it turned out, family members from the Puget Sound area claimed the body. In the morning they rode the boat back to Chelan. Sally and Darren went for supplies while Tom and Philip walked to Ray's Sporting Goods where they picked up a thousand empty shell casings for reloading. Upstairs they did business with Ray.

"So what can I do for you two boys?" Ray asked. Tom ordered a silencer for his Colt .45 and the H&K, along with bullets and reloading supplies. Tom went to a nearby coffee bar, and plugged in his Dell laptop for two hours. He replied to e-mails, and checked websites. He ordered a cedar hot tub with a wood fired woodstove, two portable solar power kits that would give him enough bright light at night so he could read by, and two car-like batteries to contain the energy from the solar panels. At a home furnishings store he bought five six-foot by four-foot Persian style rugs made of hemp. Two were decorated with Indian designs, and the others had different designs of mountains and streams. He also bought insulating mats to go under his new rugs. Because of the rock floor Tom felt the cabin needed something to insulate him from the cold.

Again the hard-working aluminum boat was fully loaded with supplies near to the point of being overloaded. They made it back to the café dock after a long and rough trip. The white caps on the lake were crashing hard on the bow of the boat. All were happy to make to the Sky's boat docks, and again they went in the café for a drink. Sally unloaded supplies from the boat, stocking the bar shelves with four different types of tequila: Patron Gold, Cazadores Gold, Cabo Wabo, and Don Julio.

The rugs and mats worked well, warming the cabin and really held the room together. The next day, Tom bought two floor lamps from a shop in Stehekin that carried products made by Darren. It was made from an old cedar branch, painted with a sealer, and the shade was made from deer hide. When Tom rode up on his mountain bike with two lamps made by Darren, Darren laughed and said, "You do know that there is no electricity in your cabin!" Tom laughed, "There's going to be soon enough. I have a plan."

For the next four weeks Tom remodeled the cabin, adding insulation and paneling over the insulating paper showing through. He cleaned out the carport area then took a rototiller to the dirt floor chewing it up. He tore the old rusted metal roofing off and replaced it with strong corrugated clear panels made from recycled plastic. They were a quarter inch thick and could easily hold snow load with a little more support. From an old house he scavenged insulated windows and installed them on the three-foot high rock walls that bordered the carport. He added a big glass door and he reframed the spaces between the windows with cedar two by sixes, matched with the cedar siding the cabin. The result was a south-facing greenhouse.

May started with sunshine and a big delivery for Tom. His solar unit showed up, along with his wood stove, and cedar tub. He set the wood stove up on the rock porch in the greenhouse. The cedar tub was round, five feet across and forty inches deep. It came as a kit and required one to put the floor together first. The cedar was tongue and groove, so fit together only one way. The cedar pieces for the walls were identical and fit together as the floor did. On the outside of the tub, two long bolt straps were provided. One attached on the bottom and the other on the top half to hold the cedar together. When the tub started to leak you simply tightened the two bolts. On the inside of the tub Tom anchored the wood snorkel stove to the floor and to the walls, and set up a fence to keep people away from the hot wood stove. The wood stove sat inside the tub with the bathers. It was a top loader and simply heated up the water as the wood burned. The metal was thin stainless steel powder coated for cleanliness. Darren made benches inside then tied up four layers of thin insulation to the outside to help insulate and keep the heat inside the tub. Tom cut a hole in the roof of the greenhouse and ran the stovepipe through it to vent the woodstove. It took just under an hour to fill the tub and an hour to heat the water.

Sally, Darren, Darren's wife Chris, and Philip came over to christen the tub. When full of people the tub overflowed onto the big rock porch and to the greenhouse floor below. It gave Tom an idea.

The next day Tom set up four flat rocks on the greenhouse floor to serve as a shower floor below the spigot that emptied the tub. Now one could shower before entering the tub keeping it clean. Also, a hose could be attached to the spigot to direct the emptied water to the plants growing in the greenhouse. From Chelan Tom brought ten six-foot bamboo plants that he planted in circle around the new shower floor to be used as a shower curtain.

Sally showed up with a wheelbarrow full of vegetable starts; lettuce, onions, potatoes, squash, zucchini, and tomatoes were planted along with herbs and two small Japanese apple trees. In less than a week the old carport was now transformed from a caved-in junk heap to a closed-in bath and greenhouse. The addition of the bamboo and other plants gave the room a comfortable feeling. With time the plants would give off the scent of a thriving garden.

Morning coffee was started before anything. First Tom had to pick the coffee he wanted. With thirty pounds of ground Starbucks coffee he had quite a choice, Starbuck's Pike Place roast was his favorite; not too dark, not too light, with a good taste. There were no electric coffee makers in the cabin. He had two choices, to heat up water with the wood cook stove or the small two-burner Coleman stove, which was the easiest. It had an automatic sparker. All that was needed was to turn on the propane and flick the red sparker. His favorite coffee-making method was the French press that forced the water and beans together, making a thick and tasty brew. Using a metal Malita with brown cone filters was the cleanest and didn't leave coffee grounds in the teeth. Both methods made great tasting coffee.

Tom poured milk into his coffee and went to the greenhouse, watering the veggie starts while sipping strong coffee. All the plants were set in rich horse and cow dung. The smell hung in the air of the greenhouse.

Earlier in the week he had set up his four solar panels on the southern side of the cabin and had run cords down to a converter that sent the new power to two big truck size batteries to store the power until needed. At night he had bright lights, used a small Bose stereo, and a short wave radio with an AM-FM radio. Tom enjoyed National Public Radio from Spokane, Rush from somewhere in Idaho, and an Indian from Buffalo Run, North Dakota who seemed to be singing in some sort of Indian dialect. With a newfound power source he could now charge his cell phone or his laptop computer. There was however, no service for either. He tried to run a toaster but it drained the batteries in a short time. Tools could not run with such low power, but he was thrilled to have lights when he needed them, Music was never something he listened to; radio was good. NPR in the morning with coffee cured loneliness.

Several days after moving in he realized smoking pot and unpacking had become his most frequent pastimes. Feeling lazy, he began a workout regimen. He would run, walk, hike, mountain bike, or kayak every day to stay fit and sharp. He road his mountain bike on a hot day in May. Sweat poured from his pores, his muscles felt strong and tight, and he wanted to sprint the remaining mile to the café, but bears were popping up everywhere he went. It seemed that someone had opened the cave door and shooed them out onto the valley roads. Woody and Tom caught up to one walking the same way they were. The big female just turned around, and looked at them. She turned her attention ahead of her, lumbering on while Tom walked his bike and tried to keep Woody from chasing after her. Woody eventually did, growling and barking like a mature male dog that he wasn't. The big female black bear left the road running uphill so fast and easily that she left Woody wondering what to do. He turned back at Tom, looking in puzzlement at the swinging branches where before a four hundred pound critter was. Tom called his dog several times. Finally, Woody came back to Tom's side. Between the café and Sky Ranch they spotted another; this time a much bigger male; who jumped from the bushes just to cross the road and disappear into the bush on the opposite side of the road. He startled Tom, who pulled his small Glock forty- caliber pistol from his pack, holding the sights on the bear until it disappeared. Near the creek that bordered the ranch Tom stood on the log bridge, looking at the stream bank. In the mud was a line of bear tracks walking to the ranch. Woody stuck his nose in the air, taking in an irritating smell of something. He moved his head back and forth like he wanted to sneeze, and was clearly bugged about something. Tom thought it was the frequency of the appearance of the black bears. Woody stuck his nose to the dirt, taking in a big smell, carefully trying to translate the smell for his brain.

Tom laughed at his young dog, "Come on dude." He ran, pushing his bike to the gate of the ranch. Woody stopped. Tom ran into him. Stooping down Woody was watching something ahead, listening. They heard a loud yelp, a small dog yelp of pain and fear. Tom heard a scream from a woman, one of pain and frustration, then another scream. He dropped his bike, pulling the mini Glock from the waistband of his shorts. He pulled back the slide chambering round As he ran through the gate he spotted Sally's mutt laying on its back, its fur now stained red with blood, its little ribs poking from a tear on its right side. He heard Sally scream, "NO! Out of here!" then a grunt. He rounded the corner of Sally's cabin and there was a big beautiful Cougar holding onto Sally by her right forearm. The big paw dwarfed her small arms. Its claws dug deep, holding her with its own right paw. Sally and the cat, face to face. He smacked at her shoulder with his left paw, but she hit him hard on the nose with a stick the size of an axe handle. It recoiled, pulling her to him. She hit again and again, each time on the nose. Woody, already agitated, ran at the big cougar, barking and biting. The cougar would not let loose of Sally. Tom ran to within six feet of the big cat. Woody moved to Sally's left side. The big cat swiped at Woody, but missed. The overmatched cat moved away from Tom, dragging Sally like a rag doll. She screamed in pain. There was a snapping sound like a stick breaking. Woody snapped at the cat. It swiped at him again, this time hitting him along the left thigh. He jumped back then surged forward, sinking his teeth into the big cat's ribcage and drawing blood. The cat let go of Sally. It was now backed up against Sally's house. Tom aimed and fired his small Glock, point blank. As the cat raised his paw, the bullet smashed through the outstretched paw, the cougar growled in pain then raised his big head showing his teeth. He desperately lunged forward at Tom his head back. Tom fired two shots, one- two. The cat's head jerked back violently. Both bullets entered his head from under the jaw. Forty caliber solid balls rolled through his brain matter, squashing all electric impulses killing him immediately. He dropped like a stone to ground; his head flung back, eyes open, but rolled back like he was on a pleasurable trip on heroin. Woody ran forward, biting at the cat's neck. Woody shook the head then dropped it and proudly turned to Tom, and strutted back to him, teeth red with the cat's blood.

Tom ran to Sally, picked her up, and carried her to a wicker couch on her porch. Tom checked her arm; it was broke below the elbow. Four deep puncture wounds from the cat's claws were seeping blood. He made her sit up, trying to keep the wounds above her heart.

Darren's wife, Cheryl, ran from her house with a shotgun, she set it down next to the couch. Tom said to Cheryl, "Go into the house find some clean white sheets or towels to use as bandages, then find me some tape, any kind well do." She had lacerations on her back from the left paw, and one on her forehead, Philip showed up then ran into the house where he called the North Cascade Rangers station and a mobile EMT helicopter from Chelan, Philip ran to Tom's cabin to get the big first aid kit. They cleaned and covered the wounds with bandages, and put ice in a big plastic baggie holding it on the broken forearm. Darren's daughter, Jackie, held ice on her forehead. "Don't worry Grandma, you'll be alright. We're going to take you to the hospital."

Sally patted her on the head. "Thanks little girl; thanks to Tom and Woody. Tom, I'm feeling woozy." She rolled her head to the left and passed out.

Tom said, "She'll be alright, just passed out, loss of blood and a little shock. It's all normal. She leaned her head back and became conscious. "I'm all right, thank you very much," she slurred and passed out again.

Philip quietly said, "Chopper's coming from Chelan, be here in fifteen minutes and my Dad's on his way with the pickup. Said we'll drive her to the pasture, and the chopper crew wants a signal flare."

Tom went to his cabin and brought out three can-sized smoke bombs. He put them in his shoulder bag and walked to the end of the driveway. When Darren showed up with the pickup, Tom put Sally inside the truck. He held her up, as Darren drove. Again she came to. She looked around, and vomited in Tom's lap. She spoke weakly, "Sorry Tom, I didn't know that was going to happen." She passed out again. Darren stopped in the middle of the pasture. Tom gave little Jackie one of the smoke cans. He pulled a tab. Lighting purple smoke.

She threw it in the truck bed laughing," That's hella cool, huh mom?" and giggled some more. Darren asked Tom, "How is she?"

Tom was holding Sally's hand, checking her pulse. "She's ok I think. Broken forearm, deep cuts,"

"Well, what about the vomiting?"

Tom looked back at him, "Normal sometimes. Got a head wound, probably dizzy. She'll be all right. Seems strong." Cheryl looked at Tom," I don't see how you can say that after what happened to her," It was the first time he got a close look at her. She was almost strikingly beautiful. "I say that Cheryl, because she will be just fine, … you'll see." He stepped out of the truck and winked at little Jackie, who was still dazzled by the purple smoke. He reached into his bag and pulled another can out, and pulled its tab orange. Smoke poured from the can, which started Jackie giggling even more. Philip walked to her. He put his hand on her shoulder; holding onto his little sister, he pretended to laugh with her, Tom smiled at them both, and in the distance he could hear the chopper as it came into the valley. It screamed past them, and banked hard to the left. With landing gear out, it landed with an easy thud. Two EMTs hopped out, ducking their heads. Tom raised his hand They went to Tom and he yelled to them," Deep lacerations on the forearm, back of the right shoulder, cuts to her back and forehead, broken right forearm and slight head injury… not sure about that."

They loaded her in the chopper, with Cheryl riding with her. Tom looked at Sally, strapped into a gurney.

"Tom, make sure you water the plants for me." She looked up at him and winked. He agreed, even though he didn't know which plants she was referring to, he thought she meant them all. The orange and white chopper lifted easily in the cloudy haze, its back end higher than the front. It stopped, the wheels retracted and it made a twist to the right and it took off heading southeast. When it was out of sight Tom walked back to his cabin.

Darren came after him, "Where you goin'? The rangers will be here any minute,"

Tom asked, "What are they going to do? Little late, don't you think?"

Darren looked toward the dead cat, "They want the cat. Most are tagged with a computer chip like a dog. Probably'll cut him up, measure his balls, you know."

Tom laughed, "measure his balls, ya right. Ok I'll help load the thing in their car, but I'm not touching the balls. I'll put it in the tractor scoop for them. Tom drove the Sky Family to the boat docks. A half hour later they were up on the waves, heading to 25 Mile Sky then on to Wenatchee to check on Sally at the hospital. Tom walked to the bar for a drink and a burger, still in his shorts. Only a few people were eating. They looked up at Tom then back to their meals. He decided to eat in the bar so he could watch a two-week old NASCAR race. Joe was in mid-sentence; his favorite story complete with gestures. His legs were spread, pants hanging on his hips. He wasn't skinny; it was just that his pants were too big for him. Fly was zipped, old dirty ranch coat with a denim shirt and messy hair, unshaven for days his gray whiskers made him look older. Ear and nose hairs stuck out like overstuffed grass in a soda bottle. His hands were big and spread apart, "So there aw was. His eyes looked at me and said, 'Help me ... then his eyes rolled back and he died ... boom! Deader than a doornail, on the ground god-dam-ill-tell-ya- whut-shit! Gotdam motor-cycles shits." Tom ate his meal then drove back to the ranch.

Two park rangers were unloading the cat from the tractor scoop into a faded Chevy S-10. They looked at Tom as he pulled in the garage. Woody ran to them as Tom approached them. Woody strutted to the rangers, his nose in the air taking deep smells. His nostrils moved as he took in the smell of the dead cat. They set the cat in the back of the green pick-up; National park stickers on either door were faded and peeled. One of the rangers, a big man wore a huge belt of gadgets: gun, mace, two extra clips for his full size Glock, handcuffs, and flashlight. He smiled at Tom. The ranger was bothered, having received word earlier in the day that their budget would be cut again, and again, as usual, the only way they could make up the deficit was to raise park fees and ticket more drivers. This was a big concern, and required two cops to patrol Highway 20, focusing on stopping the crazy crotch rocketiers blasting between Rockport and Ross Lake. It was the only place he could set up a speed trap. They would undoubtedly make up their deficit, but it would take his precious officers off much need duties. Not only did he need to find more money, but also he had his boss from headquarters with him. He didn't care one single bit about the cougar, he was happy that Sally was ok, but the park would surely be blamed for the cougar's malfeasance, and he hated his boss's method of talking down to everybody. He wished she would stop wearing her pants above her belly and get a larger size. Her long sleeve green ranger shirt was tight and she surely needed the next size bigger. Her big gut stuck out and provided a good resting place for her mammoth missile-shaped breasts. He giggled at the thought; through her uniform he could see an indentation where her belly was. She looked back at him, annoyed. Squinting through her thick glasses, she flipped up her attachable flip up sunglasses, looked up at Tom walking up then back at him with a pissed off, disapproving look. He felt she had just tried to communicate with him, but had no idea what the hell she was saying. Her deep throaty voice stabbed into his brain without speaking, like the bulbous-headed shiny mu-mu wearing aliens in the early Star Trek series. They talked to each other through telepathy. He felt the thought stab at his grey matter.

Tom saluted the rangers. "Hello, my name is Captain Tom Trainer, U.S. Air Force, at your service." It was direct and to the point, the way the military taught. He didn't like the woman right away, and the big ranger dude seemed distant, inattentive. Tom looked at the woman. Her badge said Pat Skully. The big ranger's said Dan Lennings.

The male ranger said, "My name's Dan Lennings. This…"

She butted in without shaking Tom's hand. "I'm Captain Pat Skully. What exactly happened here?" Tom did not like the tone of her voice. She spoke too loud, like a politician. Woody sat beside him looking up at the two rangers. He was curious about them. Tom ignored her and looked back at Officer Dan, "So where are you taking the cat?"

Pat jumped in, "We'll take it down to Chelan and examine the bullets and determine the cause of death."

Tom stood back and blinked hard, smiled then shook his head. "What do you mean cause of death? Two bullets entered from the bottom of her jaw and rolled around in its skull, tearing the brain apart … I'm sure they're still in there." She stood back, widened her stance on her stubby legs, and pulled up on her utility belt, tightening up her camel pants.

"How would you know that, Sir?" Tom smiled. He had dealt with people like this in the military and marveled at their sense of self-purpose.

"I'm the one that put the bullets in the cat." From his back pocket he pulled the pistol, handed it to her with the small clip in the other hand. She recoiled at the sight of the pistol. Clearly, she was threatened and stepped back.

"Sir, I don't need it right now. She put her hands up.

Ranger Dan stepped forward taking the pistol in his hands. "Thanks Captain." He inspected the gun, pulled the slide back, checking for a bullet in the chamber. He snapped the slide back then pulling the trigger, he looked at the silver-tipped ball ammo. He handed it back to Tom who slammed the clip back in the gun and put it back in the pocket of his Patagonia shorts. This unnerved Ranger Pat. She stepped back, again blinking, looking back at Ranger Dan. Tom felt her brain waves jab his brain again. He winced in pain, having no idea what she trying to say.

Dan said to Tom, "So tell us what happened here as best you can, please?"

Tom gave them the story in full military detail giving no hyperbole or nuances. When he was done Ranger Pat said," Why didn't you let it run away? Instead of shooting it to death." Ranger Dan rolled his eyes not trying to hide his disgust of her.

Tom put his hands on his hips. "Lady, are you sure about that? I don't think you would do any different if you were in my shoes." He kept his voice low, feeling no threat from Ranger Pat, but clearly bugged by her. He continued teasing her, wanting her brain to explode with a gooey grey and red pop, but it didn't. "Me and my dog Woody saved a Stehekin icon from death today and you want to vilify me? Now, I'm drawing a line in the sand." He stepped back and scratched a line in the pine needles. He was smiling inside, and "there," he stood back.

Ranger Pat said, "Well, we need your I.D. to make a report!" Tom stood rock still, "No, you cannot look at my I.D."

Finally Ranger Dan said, "I think we have all we need. Thank you, Captain." He turned to the faded pickup, and opened the door for Ranger Pat. She stood her ground, staring at Tom. He looked back. Finally, he winked at her. She recoiled, wincing as though he had just shoved her. Finally she turned and walked to the jeep, sitting down first, facing the outside of the cab then pivoting to the left like a ballerina, she sat looking straight ahead as Ranger Dan closed the door. He waved to Tom, and Tom waved back, amused. They drove off, leaving Tom and Woody looking at each other. Tom patted Woody on the head then bent down wrapping his arms around Woody's barrel chest. "What a good boy you are."

Tom raked the blood into the ground, picked up bandages, and walked back to the chicken coop. He opened up the adjoining storage shed and sprinkled chicken food inside the chicken run. He tried to corral them into the run, but they wouldn't go. Finally Woody ran over, pulling from his little brain the red heiler genes that showed him how to herd. He jogged easily, rounding the chickens into the run. Tom closed the door, amazed at his dog. Next he went to feed the horses, breaking off chunks of hay for each of them. The two cows and bull all mooed as Tom poured food from a big sack. He had no idea what it was, he just poured, and then filled the troughs for the animals. He watched as the cows ate, big teeth, tongue licking the food back inside their mouths. The big-horned bull walked over, bumping the cows gently.

Tom and Woody walked back between the big muffin top rocks to his greenhouse. Earlier he had filled the cedar tub with water. He started a fire in the snorkel stove. The water would take at least an hour to heat. He stoked the fire from the top loading hole then hiked back along the East fence through the small orchard behind the big L-shaped garage next to Sally's house. He inspected the fence posts. They were old as were the square four feet high wire fence. At several places the fence was bent over, the post rotted through at the bottom, only the wire held the fence up. Along the roadside of the fence were two gates, one at Sally's house, and the other at Darren's. Tom continued along the inside fence line behind Darren's garage/barn. He walked along the west fence then hiked off course to check on the two houses. The back porches were both screened in to keep bugs out of the house and to serve as homes for the more tame cats that lived on the farm. He rummaged through the kitchen looking for cat food. Finding a big plastic tub full, the cats happily scooped up the cat food. Two small kittens both with long tails sticking straight up in the air; one a grey, the other an orange tabby; followed Tom and Woody as they continued along the fence perimeter. Behind the bunkhouse he found a break in the wire fence, clearly stomped over by something big. Tom bent it back up then checked out the bunkhouse. It was more of a cabin than any of the buildings. Made from real logs, it had a kitchen and two rooms with bunk beds that could sleep eight and had a good size bathroom with a shower. It was built close to the barns and chicken coop. Like Tom's cabin, it picked up the smell of the cows and horses. It was cozy, with floorboard heaters running on low.

In the storage room of the horse barn he found a glass jar full of sugar cubes. He pulled out seven and fed them to each of the horses. Back to the chickens, only the two roosters stood in the run strutting, guarding, as the two baby cats hunted in the late evening. They lay in the brown grass, looking straight ahead at the two roosters who were ten times their sizes. Stalking the chickens and roosters, tails moved, slowly curling upward as they watched their prey. One kitten jumped at the wire fence. The roosters moved forward to fight the little cat, but the fence held them back. Tom laughed at the kitten's bravery.

Sally had plants everywhere. Succulents, ferns, even cactus. The west side of her house was a greenhouse, built into the side of the building. Planters full of veggie starts, and small trees he didn't recognize. In one corner he found fifteen marijuana starts about eight inches high. Popsicle sticks next to the plants, all had, "Juicy Fruit" written on them. He said to himself, "I thought juicy fruit was a gum."

He left, walking back to his cabin through the big one-acre garden. The ranch was really quite small, only twenty acres. The family leased pasture from two neighbors and the forest service, most of it along the river, and a fence kept the critters from the bank. Three small creeks dissected the pasture. A windmill kept pumping water into a big trough that watered not only the horse and cows but also deer and elk.

Tom walked below the cedar tub in his greenhouse, stripped off his clothes, and showered with water from the tub. Salty sweat ran threw his mouth. He walked up the steps to the tub. The water was perfect, around one hundred degrees. He eased his sore body into the water. It was a great feeling. He sat back on the bench, warm and cozy. The snorkel stove heated the greenhouse. Already moisture collected on the clear plastic ceiling. He watched it run down the panels, sticking to the plastic until it hit the south wall and collected in a rain gutter, before it drained outside. He dried off and went into the house naked. From a stainless steel cooler he had found floating in Lake Chelan he pulled out two micro beers and his antler pipe. He filled the pipe with his hashish and went back to the tub. He stepped back inside with a beer in his hand. In the tub he sat, relaxing. The warmth enveloping him, soothing his many wounds, and the tightness along his scares loosened. He smoked from the pipe, drawing the sweet smoke into his lungs and delivering its relaxing effects to his body and mind. His mind went through the events of the day. *Was it possible to let the cat escape? The answer was a "for sure, NO!" He was a soldier, a master of inflicting pain and punishment to anyone or thing. He was an instrument for his country, no matter what he felt about an issue, his job was to inflict the will of his nation. How much of his past job was in vain? How many innocent people had he killed? Was the big cougar innocent? How many unnecessary homes and buildings were needlessly destroyed by bomb strikes called in by him? How many times had he painted a target, a group of enemy in a hole or cave? Sometimes he would get a view of the bomb or missile as it came down from the sky obliterating the bad guys in a orgy of beautiful colors of flame and building materials flying through the sky, bouncing off other buildings, bending trees over, ripping leaves from the branches.* He shook his head making the thoughts disappear.

The two tabby kittens jumped up on the benches above the edge of the tub. They walked along, swiping at each other, not sure of the hot steaming water. Tom splashed them. They jumped back sideways, and pawed at the water. A muddy stick flopped into the water. Woody stood up on the top step hoping to have a throwing session before bed. Tom threw it to him, and he snapped it in midair. The tabbies attacked Tom's fingers and swiped at Woody's big head as he walked by. Woody jumped backward having been attacked by cats at Major Mo's house while a puppy, something few dogs forgot. After an hour of soaking Tom added cool water to cool down. He got dressed in sweat pants, and made dinner of potatoes and trout. He fed the trout skin to the tabbies. Later he walked with Woody through the ranch in the darkness of evening, enjoying the quiet; the cows and horses shuffled around in their stalls, the chickens were quiet, and he checked the houses. In the distance, he saw a headlamp go through the front gate and disappear in Sally's house. Tom quietly walked to the side window and looked inside. He saw Kenny Delany, from the café, disappear into the pantry. He was gone a long time. Finally Kenny reappeared, turned off the light, and went outside by way of the back porch. Next Kenny went to Sally's L-shaped barn and again pulled a disappearing act. For forty minutes Tom sat on top of the hay bales, watching and waiting. When Kenny came out Tom held onto Woody so he wouldn't go after Kenny, who was carrying a big paper sack. Tom smelled weed. Kenny put the sack in his backpack, put the pack on, and rode off in the darkness. Tom walked into the woodshop in the barn. He looked around, trying to find the source of Kenny's time. Nothing was moved. Everything was in place. The shop was a bit warm, but nothing stood out. His armoire was lying on its back on the floor. Strong one-inch hardwood had been added to the inside, and new hinges had been added. On a table were two pieces of wood, undoubtedly to be used to hold the rifles in place. Tom was impressed. He shrugged his shoulders and went back to his cabin.

Even though the fire was dying in the cabin, it was a bit too warm, so Tom opened the windows in the loft. He sat down on the bed. In the darkness he could see the two tabbies curled up together on Woody's Cabala dog bed. Woody came up the stairs, sleepy from the exciting day. He looked at the two sleeping cats, looked at Tom, and went to the rug nearest the window. He looked out the window then seemed to collapse on the rug, curl up, and sleep.

Tom lay there thinking about the simple things that made this place so special; fighting off a wild animal, the great food, the chickens, cows and horses, and the river with all it brought: Fresh fish, a huge beaver dam, big rat-like critters, and the garter snakes that hung out at the water's edge eating bugs. A deep sleep overcame him. He dreamt once again of Afghanistan, a great dusty place where the water wells were poisoned with massive infusions of poisons on purpose by first the Russians then the Taliban, none having any regard for the locals who would occupy the land in the future. It was in some ways like Vietnam, mined with small cluster bombs on top of or below the surface, waiting for the day when they could wreak havoc on an unsuspecting person or animal. Even the rivers were full of waste, barbed wire, sharp metal thrown in heaps in the river bottoms, piles of trash, no thought or reason to the placement of refuse.

For every attempt at normal civilization there were ten attempts at pulling it back from any normalcy. Even the few rich living Afghanistan, living the so-called "good life" stepped carefully, the tension always at critical mass. Unsure looks wherever one traveled, never really knowing who is friend or foe, who might blow up your home and family simply because they have made a small amount of money, or purchased a wheelbarrow. Sneaky people that were alive because of their ease at changing sides, holding allegiances to whoever held the weapon in front of them. A country mined and poisoned in every term of the word. Anyone could hold sway over another - just hold an AK47 and spout ill-formed religious verses. Broken people not sure which way to turn or look, wondering what to admit to, never really sure which answer was the best. A nation that could only be sure of one thing that," God is great."

His thoughts cleared. He fell asleep again, dreaming. He was walking with his men, patrolling, trying to find Taliban fighters who had mixed in with the locals. They were next to a shop selling kabobs and glazed walnuts; chickens hung from a stall. A bomb went off triggered by a person nearby. The blast lifted the men, throwing them against a thick mud wall. His men were dazed; shopkeepers' goods were destroyed, as were the shopkeepers, laying in poses of death, guilty of nothing more than being a shopkeeper at the wrong place. Tom rolled to his side weapon ready, ears ringing, waiting for another bushwhack. It didn't come. He never found out what that bomb was for, who triggered it or why. None of his men were seriously hurt. Two shopkeepers lay on the ground with massive holes in their bodies where before there had been none. The dream made no more sense than the bombing, reliving itself as though it was an entity itself, trying desperately to survive like the people in the dreams, long since dead and gone. He snapped awake, feeling dazed, the second time he had dreamed in such a way.

Outside it was dark. The sound of the river drowned everything else out. He sat up, and looked at his watch illuminated in the dark night. 11:08PM. A cool mist hung over the river. He heard the sounds of the enemy outside. Woody jumped up, growling, "Wrrrraaaaat," over and over. Tom grabbed his Colt M4, screwed on the new silencer, put on a Black Diamond headlamp and fleece jacket, and walked outside. With Woody's help he found the enemy. Two fat raccoons were trying to make their way into the chicken coop for an easy meal. They stood on the ground, trying to find a way in. Woody chased them to the roof of the coop where Tom shot them both. Two easy thumps no louder than a refrigerator door opening. He carried them to the river, throwing them in for the fish to eat and went back to bed.

Raccoons were a big problem in the mountains. They open windows and doors, unzip tents and packs, and ate any thing man ate. If they were allowed to prosper they could destroy the chickens in a few days. They were like the Taliban; their very existence depended on the destruction of something dear to the modern world; at least that's how ranchers saw it.

Back in the cabin he drank a big glass of water and went upstairs to the loft. The kittens were now asleep in Tom's bed. Woody was already sacked out on his own bed. Tom pushed the kittens over, smiled, and went back to sleep, this time dreaming of cloud creatures coming down and walking amongst the earth creatures.

In the morning he made coffee and eggs and the remaining trout then went to the chicken coop. He spread out feed for them, and fed and watered the horses and cows. Kenny showed up at 7:15 to gather eggs and milk the cows. He showed Tom the ins and outs of both, gave him six eggs, and a quart of milk and headed back to the café to make breakfast for the customers. Tom wanted to ask about Kenny's late night foray into the woodshop and Sally's house, but didn't figure it to be his business.

Tom walked the property, fixing the bent fence where needed, digging new fence posts and placing them, nailing the wire fence to the post. He inspected the chicken coop looking for breaks but found no weak points. It was framed with cedar then overlaid with six foot high one inch by one inch electrically welded galvanized wire nailed to the wood. Even the floor of the chicken run was laid with the same wire four inches under the dirt. He couldn't think of one more thing to do to make it sturdy. Its walls were cedar overlaid with rusty corrugated tin, as was the roof. The barns all matched; the same uncoated metal rusting away in the day.

Mid day found him weeding in the outside garden. He watered outside and in Sally's greenhouse. While inside, he checked the kitchen. She

GEORGE THIELMAN

had a very new industrial refrigerator freezer, and all the appliances were new, energy efficient, and smaller than usual. She had a thick wood table big enough for as many as twelve. A big eating bar divided the dining area with room for another five. The stove was propane. Countertops were combination two-inch cascade granite and two inch thick wood that matched the table. He opened the pantry door again wondering where Kenny had gone the night before. Continuing the tour, the dining area opened to the living room that was a library and TV room. The top floor was three bedrooms and a bathroom. Sally used a bedroom that adjoined the west greenhouse on the ground floor. A big wood stove sat next to the couch in the kitchen. It was a green enamel wood cook stove that kept the house warm in the winter. Opposite the kitchen was an office with a desk and bookshelves and the short wave radio, and a large laundry room that always seemed to be in action. The drain field for the two houses came together in Sally's backyard then proceeded under the large vegetable garden. The waste leached through, helping to keep the garden rich and moist. Behind the houses was a shared backyard with a kickball field and a volleyball area.

For four decades people had been arriving at the café in late May. Most were college students looking for a summer job or to spend the summer working for the family, working at the café, guiding the river for fishing or working for the campgrounds. It was uncommon for there not to be people hanging out in the Sky kitchen playing cards, Monopoly, or other games. Sally's 42-inch TV was on most nights. She had a couple hundred CDs and DVDs from Kelly's Heroes to Joe Dirt, most pirated from Garret in 25 Mile Sky.

Gardening was taken seriously, compost bins of every type were next to the garden, all labeled: one for horse and cow manure, another for household scraps such as banana peels apple cores, old lettuce coffee and filters with newspaper, brown paper towels, and all other fruits and veggies. There were metal and plastic containers cooking up compost tea from all the available mixes. The chickens were allowed to graze in the garden, pecking up the bugs and slugs as well as fertilizing the soil further. A hundred yards away was the biggest heap of compost on the property. It was mix of every kind of fecal matter, a living-heaving heap creating warmth, gurgling, and digesting every moment. It was mixed with the tractor, and used for the gardens when it was ready.

Tom's cabin was in the northeast corner of the lot closest to the river. The huge bread -shaped boulders surrounded it. From the air they looked to be ameba-shaped. Of course from the ground they were muffin-topped bread loaves, some as high as ten feet. Because of the boulders the view from the cabin was the boulders, except north where he could get a good view of the river. Long ago a glacier had dropped the boulders there, all right side up, none on the side or upside down.

Darren's barn was set up with a portable lumber mill that could make up to a twelve inch cut. Most of the wood milled in the shop was from Sky Ranch. Some of the trees were scavenged from the river. Sawdust was used for the compost pile. Neighbors brought their logs to be milled then used for projects in the valley. Compost was applied to plants in different methods. On the ranch, buckets were used to pee in. Combined with sawdust, it made a good addition to the soil. Along with chicken scat, horse and cow poop, and the fact that the garden was situated on top of the leaching field made for incredible growth in the huge garden. Still April, portable greenhouses were set up in the garden to give the crops a longer life. Greenhouses were made of PVC pipe snapped together making a hooped support. Over the top the workers dragged thick construction plastic and wire tied it down to the ground. Already lettuce had gone through several cycles and had been cut to the dirt. Within a few days they were big enough for a meal. Tom composted his crap in a series of buckets then sprinkled sawdust on top and mixed it in with the rest of the compost for use on the soil. The compost pile seemed to never change, always steaming on a warm day. Worms were added to digest and filter the compost. The mound did everything but pull unsuspecting animals and small people into its giant blob.

Tom and Woody sat on finger rock quietly watching the beavers work on tearing apart a log jam on their dam. The beavers munched the branches from the logs then disappeared under the water to tuck the leaves inside their den somewhere in the jumble of logs and branches. They'd pop up, patiently swimming back to chew and save the leaves for a meal later on. They seemed unfazed by the presence of humans. Unafraid, they had never been shot at or trapped. Living in a small bay on the river they posed no threat to downstream properties or creeks. If they'd felt threatened they'd have disappeared with a loud slap of their tails. From special places in the logjam they'd look out, safe within the confines of the massive structure. The big beaver dam kept the big eddy swimmable. Without it the water would flow fast and hard. Kids would row out in one of the small rowboats curious to anxious to see the beavers. Logs were not the only materials to get stuck up in the jam, Tom had found his silver Coleman cooler, paddles, a life vest, full cans of beer, even a bent up canoe washed up one night. From Finger Rock the beavers could be seen playing and hauling any and every type of branch and tree. The river was a delivery device for food and building materials. Logs that were too big or were rejected would flow back to shore getting caught by Finger Rock then dragged on shore to dry, eventually to end up in Darren's small lumber mill. If the logs were too big for the mill, they would be cut to size. If it were too big in girth to fit on the mill table, the center would be cut by a chain saw until it was small enough.

THE MMM

CHAPTER 3

FIVE DAYS AFTER THE COUGAR ATTACK, the Sky Family landed at the docks. Despite Sally's arm in a sling, her bandaged forehead and back, she was smiling, happy to be back. She was tough. She walked straight and true, greeting the few people that were milling about the café. Inside she began work, serving food and drinks with her one good arm. Philip drove back to the ranch to bring Tom back to the café. Tom and Philip walked in the door then to the bar. Joe Spadafore was once again in his stance; wearing baggy chinos, a dirty ranch coat with filthy pockets, and shredded sleeves; talking loudly having thrown back three whiskies. "Why that girl had blue hair, dark eyes, and so many piercings in her face that I asked, 'Hey, why don't you come with me fishing, I'll use your goddam face, wouldn't even need fish hooks." Then he started in a loud laugh that seemed to go on forever. When it ended he continued, "boy il'll-tell-you-whut-god-dam-sumbitch-shit." Then he laughed some more and walked to the restroom.

Sally was in good spirits, behind the bar mixing drinks. The last of the sun shown through the windows. She insisted on pouring Tom his Patron tequila guzzlers on the house. She fed the dogs outside on the porch. Beef stew mixed with dry natural dog food. They lapped it up quickly so the others could not get at theirs. Special of the Night was trout caught that morning by Tom and big Kenny, potatoes, carrots, salad and fresh sour dough bread. Tom, Woody, Philip and the two dogs jogged back to the ranch. Tom let Philip beat him to the gate and acted like he was exhausted, coughing and limping back to his cabin. Philip didn't believe him and told him so. Tom walked back to his cabin a happy man. Fourteen months before he'd been shot and blown up, and for the first time in a long time he'd ran almost full out, keeping up with a teenager.

Back at the cabin Tom stripped, stood on the big flat rock shower and drenched himself with hot water from the snorkel tub. He walked up the steps and into the hot water. The warmth surrounded him. Sitting back on the cedar bench the tightness of his wounds relaxed. The top of the snorkel stove snapped. It was burning down; the water temperature was 105 degrees, just about too hot.

The greenhouse door opened with a bang, he meant to put a stop on it, but had put it off. Sally walked through the greenhouse door, along the rock path and up the eight steps. She knocked on the wood tub. He stayed quiet, but Woody gave him away. She looked his way only his head was sticking up. She laughed at him then said, "There you are. Hiding out, huh?"

Tom said, "You should come in, the water's perfect." She put her hand in the water then looked around. "People will talk, Tom."

"You sure about that?" Tom replied. "It's my cabin … Well, it's your cabin and it's a free country."

She looked around. He couldn't see her face in the darkness. "Well, ok. I'm coming in, but I can't get my arm wet." He watched her undress. Her shiny white bra stood out in the darkness. Nipples standing up, she took off her pants and unsnapped the bra, set everything on the upper benches, and carefully climbed in the hot tub. Tom stared at her, not talking. She splashed him in the face, "What are you looking at, dude?" With her left arm out of the water she waded to him, putting her arms around his neck. He felt her naked body rub on his. Her knee rested in his crotch. In the dark she was gorgeous. She seemed younger, and more playful than he thought possible. She said to him, "How do you like that big boy?" She pressed down on his crotch with hers then reached up with her right arm taking Tom's face in her hand. She kissed him on the cheek. "You and Woody saved my life. I owe you big, my badass dude. She slapped him lightly the way he had seen her slap her son and grandson. She rolled to the bench next to him. Woody's head came into view, showing off for her, and the two kittens jumped up on the upper benches looking for fun. They swiped at the water then at big Woody. He backed up, annoyed. Tom could tell he was still playful. He patted Woody on the head, pulling him closer in the range of the kittens. He took a drink from a canteen then handed it to Sally. "That's some good water," she said. "Missed it. Wenatchee water is not so good…. glad to be home, that's for sure." She reached into her small pack, pulling out a pipe and lighter. "Now I know you smoke! Can smell it on you! It's ok 'cause I do too." She filled a big pipe made of wood then handed to Tom. She lit it for him, holding it to his mouth. He inhaled the sweetest, tangiest pot he had ever smoked. It was good tasting, like her buffalo stew, close to perfection. They sat in the water watching each other, neither was sure of what to do next. Tom had never been with a woman as old as her and she hadn't been with a man a young as Tom in a few decades, so, they passed the pipe back to each other until they were sufficiently baked. She stood straight up, water glistening off her body. Her breasts stood up more than Tom thought they would. He thought, "Jane Fonda workout."

"Tom, I'm not going to beat around the bush, but here I am naked in the water with you, a man twenty six years younger than me, and I'm stoned. Anyway, I feel I owe you a life, can't pay you in money, but I want to offer you a job with us running the ranch and its satellite businesses. 'Specifically, I want you to be the driver of the boat picking up the customers, making deliveries, and I bought a new coffee roaster. We have five hundred pounds of coffee beans to practice with, and we have packaging. We'll set it up in the back room of the café. We have product already out there. Your job will be to roast it and deliver to Chelan and Wenatchee areas. Also there's one more thing I want you to do for me and I'll only tell you about it in the morning after we have breakfast together. So, think on it and I'll see ya at seven thirty in my kitchen. She climbed out of the tub, took Tom's towel, dried off, and put on her clothes as Tom dried off. He stood naked in front of her clothed body. She looked back at him.

"You're coming right?"

He replied, "I'll be there. Don't worry."

He slept in, with the kittens and big Woody all snuggled together. Later, he rolled out of bed to Sally's house. She made a light breakfast of eggs and toast with some of the best coffee he had ever tasted. She poured in some fresh milk. The mugs were big, homemade, and muddy brown.

She stood up. "Ok, let's go."

Tom was surprised, "Where are we going?"

She waved him out of his chair. "Bring your coffee." She walked to the pantry, and opened the door. She looked at Tom then turned back, and stuck her hand under the third shelf. She seemed to push a lever then pushed with her body on the shelves. They pivoted and moved inward.

GEORGE THIELMAN

Sally walked down a flight of steps with Tom behind her. Stopping at a solid-looking door, she looked back at Tom and turned the doorknob. The door opened with a gentle thump. The air was warm. Big light bulbs hung from the ceiling. Humming. Over twenty marijuana plants, five feet high, all heavy with ten-inch buds, green with the telltale five-leaf symbol. Half the plants were sitting in soil, bedded plastic five gallon buckets. The other half were in smaller buckets full of small pea gravel. Small plastic drip hoses ran to each plant.

Sally said, "We've been growing weed for four decades in this basement. For the first time we're experimenting with hydroponics. With hydroponics we grow in small rocks rather than soil. So far the plants in soil seems to be growing better than the hydro, but we'll see!"

Tom said, "Man this is the greatest grow operation I've seen. Not far from budding and completion. Great smell!"

Sally looked at him and smiled, she put her good hand in the air making a gentle sweep. "Thence into beauty, you like it? Now come with me!"

They retraced their steps, out the back door to the L-shaped barn. Four big scraggy cats poked their heads up from the hay bales, watching them. Sally opened the big door that led into the wood shop. She opened a closet, again pulled a lever under the second shelf and pushed. Down another flight of stairs they went, to another solid metal door. She pulled the door open. The aroma was overpowering, a fruity fragrance deep and intense. Sally said, "This is called the dungeon, the house is called the basement. We grow most of the plants in here. Over there, two hundred starts." She pointed to a corner. One hundred plants were budding six feet high with heavy branches thick with ten to twelve inch buds.

The huge seventy five by thirty foot room was divided into three parts. Simple fluorescents, growing little eight inch clones on a table. Small branches cut off a bigger plant then dipped in a chemical to help the little branch grow roots created clones, perfect copies. Dark green plastic divided the clone area from the other two parts of the dungeon, so the clones received constant light. When the clones were tall enough, they were moved to another area where bulbs were brighter. There they stayed for a month or longer. They then moved to the flowering area which held much more powerful bulbs to mimic the longer days of summer. The last two stages were on timers, faking the light of the day then shutting them out to mimic night. All the plants were in five gallon buckets; holes drilled so water could escape out the bottom. When plants were ready to move on to the next stage Sally changed the bulbs rather than move the plants themselves. She continued, "We have another growing area where the baby clones will be going. It's outside. The plants grow to eight feet and make near to five ounces each. Everything here in the dungeon is watered and given light with a timer." The walls and floor were solid concrete painted white. A couple work tables held razors, scissors, and pots. A laundry type slop sink occupied a corner.

In another corner was a small area, ten feet by ten feet, bordered with 4x4s holding sand and pea gravel. A grow light attached with a timer mimicked the day and night; a small five-foot waterfall had been built with a little pond. Bamboo was grown around the area they called the beach. Two beach chairs were set up, and an old beach ball, partially deflated sat at the water's edge. The walls were painted with a full size mural copied from a Hawaiian picture: sandy beach, palm trees, blue ocean, and a motorboat in the distance, with surfers riding waves. Sally said, "We love the small beach, helps us get through the long cold winter." Tom sat down on one of the beach chairs. He noticed Two small green tree frogs hopped about on the waterfall.

Tom could tell that a great deal of thought had been put into making the grow successful. "So, what do you want me to do?" he asked.

Sally said, "I want you to handle the grow outside. I need you to be the security of the ranch, make deliveries in Wenatchee, ride the boat, make contact with my nephew from the west side, and deliver to him. He'll make the deliveries to the dispensaries we want to supply."

Tom replied, "Sally, I'm not sure I want to go to jail. I like smoking up, but I really don't know any of you that well. To risk going to jail for so little. Im now free to live my life how I want. Being a pusher of weed and going to prison is not what I envisioned when I retired from the military." He shrugged his shoulders. "I enjoy getting a buzz, but I'm not hard up for money, or that much into it to get busted. No matter what we might think, if the law finds this place we are going to get busted big time. If and when that happens, and, I don't want to kill people over weed."

Sally looked back at him smiling, "Tom you're the most capable man I've known. We have never been busted in over forty-five years, never. This is a good life. I'm not sure we would have this ranch if it wasn't for the grow operation. The café kind of pays for itself, the campgrounds are the same, our coffee, or guiding, all of it, combined along with the grow keeps us chugging along." She sat down in a lawn chair on the beach then motioned Tom to sit down. "We can pay you fifty thousand a year and a good bonus if all goes well. Plus you can live in the cabin for free. I'll reimburse you for your deposit and first month's rent paid and sign the cabin over to you. It will be yours forever, to do as you see fit."

He blinked heavily, not sure what to think. "Are you sure, Sally? That's a big price to pay for so little,"

She interrupted him, "Let's not forget that you saved my life and that is a big deal to me and our family. This grow operation helps so many people by keeping all of our little offshoot businesses going, it puts money in the pocket of more people than you might think, and contrary to what you may or may not know, we are a legal grow operation; have licenses for most of it. I admit we are pushing the limits of the laws that leave an aura of tension that makes living here a bit dangerous, a little risky. We like it that way."

Tom stood up and stretched. "Alright Sally, I'll do it. But I'm not selling to scumbag dealers. I moved here for a reason. I want to live a simple life, shovel snow and chop wood. That's my idea of heaven."

Sally smiled, "Don't worry about selling to small dealers, most of the contacts are people I've known for decades and they are quite safe. We'll need you to make delivery to my son Garrett and my nephew from the west side. Coffee deliveries will be made along with pickups of customers and campers."

Sally stood with her hands on her hips and turned to look at the plants. "Ok Tom, we usually grow at least 250 plants at a time. They make almost three ounces per plant. With the profit we provide health insurance for all that work for us on a full time basis. The part-timers that come for the summer to work in the garden, café, campsites, or guide for us all get half their health insurance paid by us. Soon we'll start the outdoor grow operation, not far away. It's a great hike and cool place to grow. All you have to do is hike one and a half miles to the grow area, water, hang out, keep the deer and other critters away, and feed good nutrients to them. What do you think?"

Tom thought and scratched at his scarred face. "I want your word that you will do everything to get me out of jail in the case I get busted."

She laughed, "We'll get you out and give you the best lawyers in the state. That I promise." They shook hands. "It's a deal."

Tom went back to his cabin. He dressed in his running gear, the latest running shoes, light running pants, thin long sleeve shirt, and then the lightest camelback pack with first aid kit, knife, and the Glock compact. While running he thought of his new job. He was most excited about being the new delivery guy. Riding the Sky Boat would be the most fun, with sixty miles of lake shore, most of it wilderness, he was more than happy. He had found a home, and he was quite sure that he would enjoy his job.

Woody happily ran at his side. His first run in over a year and a half. He ran for ten miles, stopping several times to enjoy a stream or watch an animal. Deer, squirrels, and a bear were seen, water was everywhere; creeks, streams and waterfalls created a backdrop of noise, water falling from the cliffs, down the side of the mountains to the valley below. Snow was just about gone except above on the mountains. He jogged easily, muscles remembering their old movements. His left leg was a bit sore but the actions of his leg fell in line with the other.

He stopped at the café said hello to big Kenney, talked for a bit and ran further to the ranch. He walked to the bunkhouse for a shower. At his cabin he went to work, using a table he'd set up for the job of reloading. It took two hours to reload one hundred rounds of .308 caliber for the Chelan County Sheriff's Department. Twenty rounds each of .270, .223, .300 win mag, .30-06, and a new round making headlines with Snipers of NATO .338, a new powerful round known for accuracy and long range. Every shooter had a preference for long-range calibers. Most wanted a powerful round that would put the hunted, whether it is man or beast, to the ground quickly. For long range Tom preferred .300-win magnum, a monster round that fit well for long range shoots. The big round flew flat for almost a mile and had reasonable recoil. He liked the 30-06 a monster round, but it didn't fly as long as Tom would like. During the Persian Gulf War Tom used a Remington 700, a classic bolt-action rifle with a big scope chambered in the smaller .270 caliber. The bullet flew far and fast, it was easy to handle, and it was smaller and a bit lighter. He had wreaked havoc on Iraq's forward bases in 1990. The Iraqis invaded Kuwait; the America could not stand by while their friends were taken over, along with a considerable portion of the U.S. oil. Tom was sent in with his Rangers. He had made corporal and was one of the squad snipers. While the conventional forces gathered in Saudi Arabia for the upcoming invasion to knock the Iraqis out of Kuwait, Tom and his crew of Army Rangers were tasked with acquisition of enemy information. They would hang-glide behind enemy lines, stash hang gliding gear then hike and run to one of the forward observation posts of the Iraq military. Guards would be shot or stabbed quietly. The small group of Special Forces would then wipe out the remaining enemy, steal information, code, radios, and sometimes prisoners. Sometimes they left the Iraqi post intact; other times the complete post was blown up. They would then run to a waiting chopper, extract back behind the lines to Saudi Arabia. The next night they might do the same.

GEORGE THIELMAN

Tom boxed rounds as samples for Ray's store; four fifty round boxes of each size bullet. He would do pistol rounds another day.

Darren and Sally came to guide Tom to the big grow on the hill. They carried fifty starts in backpacks; eight-inch baby plants made by cutting small branches then planting them separately; clone. With seeds you never knew whether you had a male or female plant. With the clone coming from a female you knew you had a female, very simple.

It was an out-of-the-way trail that crossed the road, followed a creek then zigzagged. They went up over and through layered rock for a half a mile then hiked over four fat fallen cedar trees. Without knowing the way, one would be lost in a jumble of dense forest, sticker bushes, and loose rock. It was essential to zigzag up the layered rock. The fallen cedar trees were used as trail as well. Branches sticking up were used as hand holds and had to be moved around carefully. The trees still had their bark so the footing was solid. After passing cedar trees they stepped onto a rock ledge near a mossy waterfall. Darren and Sally stepped under the waterfall and continued through to a deep, damp cave. Darren stopped after twenty feet at a locked gate. He turned the dial on a fat combination lock and swung the gate aside. Tom looked at the fence, carefully made from cedar logs the thickness of a thermos, nailed and bolted together. They continued under three house-sized boulders that were leaning against the side of a cliff and crossed a stream. Under another huge boulder, and the party walked out from under the boulder into sunshine. Blinking in the sunlight, they arrived at a flat ledge, about two hundred feet long. Pine trees twenty feet apart dotted the ledge. In a far corner a waterfall dropped to a series of car-sized pools of clear clean water.

Sally stood, her arm splinted, forehead scarred from the cougar attack. She spoke, smiling happily, "My great grandfather found this site in early 1909, He, along with my grandfather and father, mined this area finding small amounts of gold, silver and copper from the cliff here. She pointed at an eighty-foot high cliff, and one hundred feet long. Tom could clearly see a scooped area thirty feet deep with a small cave entrance that stopped forty feet from the opening. She continued," Three generations mined here. Just enough was found to keep them interested. My father quit in the late fifties. It had become a bit of a hobby for him. The trek to carry the minerals out of here was never worth it, but they continued year after year. I hiked up here with my grandfather in the fifties. After college I started to hike up here with my husband and friends, looking for a place to grow marijuana. We flattened the area, covered the tailing and rock deposits with soil from around the ledge then started to grow good weed. For four decades we have hauled soil and compost up here in five gallon buckets. We have carried up thousands of pounds of soil over the years and continue to this day. Now the soil is so fertile that we only have to carry compost up here along with the starts themselves. The grow area is southwest, facing the big cedar trees that kept the old mine invisible to airplanes and helicopters. Keeps the grow area camouflaged, but allows the hot sun onto the crops. The south-facing cliff held the summer heat on the ledge. Two hundred ground holes had been dug over the years. Each year they were dug, up marijuana starts were planted in the same spot. To make compost tea, last year's plants had been left in the hole. The waterfall dripped into a pond dug many decades before," Sally said.

Sally explained more. The key, the incredible height and weight of the mine operation, was the mineral rich water, cool and clean, void of sodium or fluoride. It flowed downhill from the glaciers then through the rocks and into the trees and soil picking up everything it needed to sustain man and plants then dropped to the ledge below to help the plants flourish. City water, filtered and contaminated with fluoride, flowed through old dirty pipes and holding tanks then passed through old galvanized water pipes. In the newer homes the water carried through copper pipes and the even newer homes now used plastic hose to pass water into the human body. City and Rural counties where humans lived had used pesticides without care for centuries, applied to weeds and bushes they didn't like. Sky Ranch and the Valley had none of the uphill contaminants of the cities. The water was clean and cool, flowing everywhere. Downhill in Seattle the cute little creeks that once flowed through the Puget Sound area were now, for the most part, nonexistent. City workers manicured the remaining creeks throughout the Puget Sound area in hopes that salmon would return. Thinking was, all you had to was make it look like a native stream and the salmon would come back to spawn. They weren't coming back. The cool, pretty water was now toxic with unseen chemicals that ruined the livers and kidneys of unsuspecting and beloved cats and dogs. Salmon used to make it to Lake Chelan. Now very few, if any, made the trek up the heavily dammed Columbia River. Now the worst polluters of Lake Chelan were the many boats that ran up and down the long lake. Their exhaust pointed straight into the water that now was used as a muffler.

Sometimes Sally would get into arguments about pollution with her friends. The conversation was always the same. Her antagonist would state that the newer boat and car motors put out few pollutants. Her reply was always the same, "If you believe that car and boat exhaust are safe then hook a hose to your bedroom. Hook the other to your car or truck motor and hang out in the bedroom. See how long you live." She would laugh and move on.

The MMM area was a great place to grow, warm during the day and cool at night. During the summer solstice the plants grew tall, good growing weather. Sally sat down on a rock, "This grow area has been responsible for the expansion of the ranch, campsites, and café, Tom. The money from the sale of the crops has helped everyone in our family in one way or another, to go to college, buy houses, make it through hard times, it's done all that and continues to this day. My husband named it the Magical Marijuana Mine. We call it the Triple M. You, Tom, are the addition we didn't see coming. Now this area will sustain you. Darren and Philip will help you haul everything you need."

Tom, not knowing intricate nuances of growing weed, said, "What else do we need to carry up?"

Darren said, "What you need to carry up here is composting materials from the ranch."He stopped and looked at Tom. "Remember when you asked me, 'what do you do with all the compost materials?'"

Sally stood up, with her broken arm in its cast she made a gentle movement like a conductor, "This is where the compost goes. Hundreds and hundreds of pounds of it. We carry it up in backpacks, stuff a bucket in a internal frame pack, and hike it up here."

Tom scratched his head, "So, what do I have to do? I have to hump a thousand pounds of compost material, starts, water it every day, and kill rodents. I get all that."

Sally stood up, grabbed Tom's cheek like he was a little kid then gave him a gentile slap, "That's it, my man. By the end of the summer you will be in the best shape of your life from the hiking. Now let's get back to the ranch. I'm hungry for lunch."

For two weeks Tom hauled full buckets of compost material five gallons at a time, four trips per day. Finally he was up to five trips a day. He spent several nights at the MMM in a small tent, hunting curious and hungry rodents that would munch the starts to a small stump. Sally gave him a big jar of ladybugs to sprinkle on the plants to kill pests.

As the plants grew in size he had covered them with camouflage netting, set up eight feet high on rope, strung back and forth from the big trees that dotted the grow area. Camouflage of illegal plants was the challenge of the day for all growers of weed. Buckets were painted green and brown, as were shovels and garden tools. Nothing was left laid out that could look to be man made. Plants were set up with no order to them. No straight lines. The forest service choppered in, looking for fires. Other people flying around could spot the grow area. The farmers hoped the camo netting would hide the plants, and so far through the years they had. Sally wasn't sure if the authorities looked for grow operations. She had never heard of others in the area. She had flown over the grow area once, looking to see if she could spot the MMM from the air. She couldn't; it was tucked away in a small valley. Nondescript, it looked as normal as the forest that surrounded it.

Sky Ranch was void of neighbors and leased all the forest service land next to the ranch. Popular hiking trails were far away so hikers didn't come by. Also the hiking trails in the area were so plentiful and scenic that no one thought to explore the MMM area.

Tom had fallen into a routine. Up at six, he made coffee, made breakfast, hiked to the MMM, watered all the plants, mixed in compost tea, hung out, drank his coffee, and ate breakfast before hiking back to the ranch. By June he had hauled all that was needed for the grow area. The loads were light. Every morning he found dead mice in traps at the MMM. Skunks, and porcupines were enemies of the area. Deer would have decimated the area if allowed to. With a cliff on the north side and south side and the locked gate in the cave deer could not enter the site Tom and Philip had found signs that a bear had slept in the cave next to the gate from time to time, but he had moved on.

As Sally said, Tom had become fit like never before. His leg was healing, he was faster and stronger, and clothes seemed baggy. Running and hiking had made him lean and mean, and natural, low-fat food helped as well. Tom discovered the bread loaf boulders that surrounded his cabin were dotted with hand and footholds, some small, some big. Every night Tom and Philip, along with Philip's cousin Karen Sky, could be seen climbing laps around and over the boulders. Gymnastic chalk used by climbers to keep fingers dry and sticky dotted the grey and white rock showing the good hand holds. Small stains of blood from torn fingers marked the chalky holds. Grass at the base of the rock was smashed down from falling and being repeatedly stomped. Two games were played. One was to boulder left to right, trying to stay on the rock as long as possible to gain strength and endurance. The other was to first pick out a line or route. Climbers could go up or side-to-side. Some would start sitting down. Bouldering had become an art in itself, training for the big mountain climbs without the danger of long and deadly falls. Tom was the best climber, Karen was close behind, fit and strong, a college student from Boulder, Colorado, she had spent the last three years climbing in the crag rich area around Boulder when she wasn't attending class. They worked hard trying complicated moves that were every bit as difficult as some of the most demanding gymnastic moves. Bouldering stretched the muscles and tendons, loosened up the shoulders and neck and took pressure off the spine. It was just what Tom needed to finish the healing of his shoulder wounds. When the evening was over and the three felt strong, loose, and spent, a quick bike ride or run to the café for a drink finished off the evening.

    Karen Sky had arrived at the docks after hitching a ride on a friend's boat. Her third year of college complete, she unloaded her mountain bike with side bags hanging over the front and back wheels. A small cargo trailer full of possessions followed behind her to the café. She ate lunch at the café then left to run up the valley. She caught up to Tom after six miles then ran together back to the café. At twenty-two her maturity was that of a thirty year old. Blue shorts, thin tank top, short black hair, strong tanned legs; they talked as they ran. She was one of Sally's six nieces attending college. She stayed in Sally's cabin with her, and had been coming to the ranch since she was a little girl. All year she looked forward to spending summer at the ranch. This year she was surprised to see Tom living in the cabin on the rock. She wondered what spell he had placed on her aunt to make her allow him to live there. After a few days of running together she got together with Tom and Philip for an evening bouldering session. Beers where downed and hashish was smoked. Tom was clearly the better climber and made them both look bad, but his kindness and helpful nature overrode his ego. That night she took a hot tub with the entire family squeezed into Tom's cedar tub. Late that night, after the family went to bed, she left Sally's house, walked right into Tom's cabin, up the loft to Tom's bed, moved the kittens aside' and climbed in. From that night on they were together, enjoying each others company as men and women do. Tom changed his morning routine so he could get in six miles of running with Karen then ride bikes to the café where she would start work at the café. From there Tom would hike to the MMM and back down to continue another hour on the trails or roads. He enjoyed moving quickly over the paths that had for centuries carried Indians, white explorers, miners, trappers, and wayward lovers of the far-reaching lonely glacier formed lands. He was happy his body could obey his demands.

    Sally knocked on his door, a new practice after finding her niece Karen in Tom's lap on a kitchen chair in his cabin sans pants. Sally carried on like she hadn't seen anything, knowing full well what was going on. She swore long ago not to be an uptight mom or grandma that went from child to child expressing sexual tension by way of blithering on about moral traditions and values. Sally let them be adults and knew what they were doing. Tom's work at the MMM was showing rewards already. The plants had grown two feet. The weather had been perfect, around seventy degrees during the day. Many days it would reach eighty-five. The ledge would become hot. Without a place for the wind to go the plants seemed to grow just fast enough to see them moving, though of cause this was not possible. Sally's strain was called Eastern Promise, bred from seeds from Hindu Kush and a weird strain someone called Mazier; one from Afghanistan and one from a gorgeous region in India, and both known to be hearty enough to grow in the North Cascades. She had bred them five years earlier and now had enough seeds to continue on for decades. She had cleaned up a section of the dungeon and planted twenty seeds of Mazir and twenty of the Kush. The Kush sprouted only females and the Mazir luckily sprouted one male. She then grew them to a foot tall. When the male sprouted small sacs on top the branches, she carefully squeezed the sacs on the male plant then shook the male sperm, as she called it, and, voila. The females flowered and created a combined seed that worked well in the varied conditions of the valley. She was proud of Eastern Promise, a big hit in California's Hemp-A-Luza, a weeklong event in Humboldt County, California. One of Sally's nephews had made the trip, and entered the pot in a contest. It was well received. Now, four years later, it was in demand. Only a few people knew where it came from or what it took to breed it, so the Sky Family had huge orders, most of which were going to Seattle's ever-growing medical marijuana dispensaries. The Sky Family was hoping for a bumper crop of Eastern Promise. To make the great harvest happen, the grow would need constant water and nutrients. Most of all it would need near to perfect weather straight into September.

 Tom read three books on growing weed. Much was learned. Marijuana was first grown in Afghanistan. It could grow most anywhere under any circumstance, but it will only mature and make great THC-rich buds under near perfect situations. Hot weather was essential, along with good water. It liked the tropics. It could grow without soil; hydroponics. It depended on timers to send water at the same time every minute or hour. Growing in soil seemed to be the more natural way to grow, seemed more organic.

 Tom was now hauling fish oil and molasses to the MMM. That, and five gallons of Sally's special concentrated compost tea. At the MMM there was a hole two feet deep scooped out of the rock ledge that was used as a spot to make compost for the grow. Last year's plants were composted in the bottom along with Sally's new formula making for a great mix. Sally's super steroids, as her sons called it. Stalks seemed to thicken and climb with aggressive results, complete expansion. Tom had no doubt that the Sky Family knew how to grow weed. He was a part of every phase now from picking and trimming, to cultivation and delivery. Once a week he would hike twenty six miles to highway 20 along the Pacific Crest Trail to make a five or ten pound delivery to Sally's youngest brother, Karl. Karl would drive to the trailhead along the P.C.T. and Highway 20, sit back, and wait for Tom to arrive from the ranch, 26 miles hiked in eight hours. Tom found the hike to be less dangerous and it filtered out any riff-raff. They could see cops from a distance and could easily disappear into the brush to hide. Five pounds of weed made the ranch ten thousand dollars easy money. With Sally's house, the dungeon under the barn and the MMM all growing good weed, Tom hiking and making good deliveries, all the grow areas producing good-tasting, strong pot, it was clear to Tom how people got into trouble with grow operations. Easy to see how only dollars were seen.

Mid-June the 100 Juicy Fruit plants in the dungeon were harvested. They were five feet high, big and fat, with twelve-inch buds. The dungeon had once again created a bumper crop of its own. It was what they called middle-of-the-road, walk around bud, always good, but wouldn't win a contest. It did however make the ranch twenty thousand dollars after all expenses, a tidy sum, all cash no taxes.

MID JUNE

Sally threw a big party. Relatives from the west side came, every room in the cabins and bunk house were full, tents were set up, salmon, chicken, and buffalo were barbecued every night. They played volleyball, kickball, horseshoes, and the kids were all over the ranch. The cool people frequently used Tom's hot tub; that is the ones that drank or smoked pot. Karen's father showed up. A huge hunk of a dad, six foot five, owner of a nursery in Woodinville, over on the west side, he was the main go-between for the grow operations and the one that Tom hooked up with on Highway 20. He hooked up the dispensaries and good pot dealers with product from the ranch, got along well with Tom, and treated his kids with complete respect. Karl Sky was fifty-nine. He had a good gut hanging over his cowboy rodeo belt, wore tight Wrangler pants with a denim-buttoned shirt. He talked softly and had the habit of smacking people he liked hard on the back when he got excited. He had long since discarded cowboy boots for hiking boots; only the best for his worn out knees. Loud and jovial, he ran his big hands over his belly then hooked his thumbs in his belt on either side of his oval belt buckle, laughing as he watched four kids playing badminton. He stopped laughing when he saw Tom and his daughter together. He knew they were shacking up together. Sally had calmed him down, calling him an old fuddy-duddy. Karen elected to say nothing until her large dad spoke up. She let him have it with both barrels, ordering him to keep his nose out of her love life, and it was all going to be over in September when she went back to college in Colorado. Karl was more worried that Tom would somehow subvert his daughter's innocence. As usual he forgot the power that women had over men. He feared Tom's past would change his daughter. He realized she was more grown up than he was, as she pointed out he made most of the family income by selling weed.

By mid-July the plants were over three feet tall and the leaves were big and green. Small pistols, the size of a snail's antenna, were growing at the crotch of each leaf. These would become the bud that would be smoked. The stalks of each plant were thicker than a big pencil. The MMM had taken on a smell, tangy, like fruit. It permeated the area with its strong aroma. Darren hiked up with Tom one morning; from his pack he pulled what looked like a sort of animal liver. He cut them open with his knife letting stinky juice drop into a paper plate. He looked at Tom sticking his finger up in the air. He was wearing blue surgical gloves, and the smell was overpowering, "This, Captain Tom, is the smell sack from a skunk. I have four of them ... been saving them for months." Darren walked around dropping skunk smell here and there, covering the perimeter then dropping the smell sack on the ground to help disguise the marijuana smell and keep predators away fearing the stink of a skunk.

Sally's monstrous vegetable and herb garden was now flourishing, bearing heads of lettuce of every kind, grown together making a pretty lettuce medley. Corn stalks grew high. Cucumbers, tomatoes, onions, squash, and other veggies were growing. Green was the color, and bushy potatoes were pushing out. As the plant grew to ten inches they would add six inches of soil to force the potatoes to grow another tier of spuds.

Six summer employees were now working at the store, cleaning cabins, hauling firewood for campers, raking campsites, picking up trash, and working in the café, store or bar. Canoes, kayaks, rowboats, and small sailboats were rented to campers paddling up the Stehekin River then paddling back downstream. Campsites were near to full capacity, as were the cabin rentals. Four more workers were brought on to cover the increased work needed. Two were hired to guide rafting and hiking trips. They worked with Ray's Northwest Outdoor Outfitters in Chelan. He would send people to the ranch after buying the necessary tents, sleeping bags, hiking stoves, fleece clothing, sleeping pads and pocketknives from him. Business was great for all involved.

Tom reflected on his life three months into his retirement. He was making money selling reloaded ammo to Ray, who would sell to his diehard hunters that appreciated the consistently high quality of his reloads. He spent most of his time driving the boat to pick up campers, and at the MMM or the dungeon working, watering, and clipping leaves, "from killing to gardening; what a difference." He stayed away from the campsites and store except for evening drink. The noise of kids and families going about camping was nothing Tom understood. He hiked with his dog and girlfriend, running the trails, and to the MMM twice a day, still hauling compost material. He was in the best shape since coming back wounded from Afghanistan. The only wound he felt was behind his left knee, which took a bullet scraping along the muscle. Sometimes it would ache so badly it would make him limp. It would just appear for no apparent reason. His left side was still sore from the two bullets that went exploring through his rib cage, exiting below the left shoulder. An evening in the snorkel tub was all he needed to sooth the pain out of him. With Karen, a couple of beers, good sex, and to bed, bodies, strong, sore and tired. In the morning they would wake up and start the day the same as before. It was a simple life, without having to pay bills, commute an hour each way to work, easy and clean, the ranch was self-sustaining. Little was bought from down river except booze and bulk goods. The café and bar was full most every morning and night with drinkers and eaters, all enjoying the quite life without the sound of modern cities.

BECKY

CHAPTER 4

EAST OF CHELAN THREE MEN HIKED along Naysay Creek in sight of the Columbia River. They were laughing, carrying new guns, and looking to blow things apart. They had two hundred bullets each. Mini-Mike took a swig from his seventh Icehouse beer. Finishing it, he threw it into the stream then set his shotgun upright against a small rock. He took off his pack, snapping another beer from its cardboard cube box. He held the beer at his mouth, downed it using his whole body then threw the beer can into the stream, yelling, "Ya bitch, that was shot-gunned, you fuck!" He moved his body spastically like a football fan celebrating a touchdown, his foot knocking the shotgun over. It slid down the length of the rock, the trigger hitting a stick poking out of the ground. The shotgun went off, making his two companions jump.

Dorn ran to the gun, picking it up. He shook it at Mini-Mike. "What the fuck man! Are you stupid or what, god dammit. Be careful!" Mini-Mike grabbed the shotgun from Dorn who towered over the smaller man. Dorn gritted his brown multi-stained teeth, his scowl turned to a sneaky smile, which made Mini-Mike smile.

"Ok man. Fuck man, sorry."

Dorn's younger brother, Ted, much bigger than Dorn, towered over both of them. He looked down at Mini-Mike, "Hey, asshole?" Mini-Mike didn't look up. "Hey, Asshole?" Ted repeated. Mimi-Mike didn't look up again. Ted grabbed the shotgun barrel, Finally, Mini-Mike looked up. Ted was huge, an ex-football player and wrestler from Washington State University He shook the shotgun barrel, which shook Mini-Mike like a rag doll. "These guns cost us lots of money. If ya can't control yours, I'll take it away. Got me?" He let go of the gun barrel, and Mini-Mike almost fell over.

"Ok, man. Fuck off." Mini-Mike walked off ahead, upstream, mumbling to himself.

Ted said to his brother, "That punk is going to get us killed. You have to keep an eye on him, and I don't want you to give him one of the Glocks!"

Dorn replied, "Ok, I'll watch him and I won't give him a Glock!" Money had come from the sale of crappy weed and meth from one of their Mexican suppliers. They had sold everything to the beeners, and white trash meth heads in the area were making big profits. Recently they bought three Glock pistols, two shotguns, and two Yugoslavian AK47s to protect their drug operations.

They were happy living on Mini-Mike's mom's property outside of Chelan. The compound, as they called it, held several rundown buildings. Two plywood cabins housed the punks and Mom. One house was for Mom and her champagne bottles. Mom paid the bills with her Social Security money and her husband's railroad pension. She washed the punks' black clothes and cooked most of the food. Large pots of mac-and-cheese with hot dogs cut up for meat, cheap white bread, and Wal-Mart milk kept the bellies full. The punks claimed to be the worst gang in the area, and most of their time spent hiding in the surrounding hills from the local law enforcement. They hid in concealed campsites they had made with green plastic sheeting held up with cut branches. They slept on foam pads with goose down sleeping bags. Trash dotted their campsites. At the compound there was an old pickup truck, its bed overflowing with empty beer cans, and its oil spots dotted the pine needles. Mixed paper and plastic trash littered the ground. Mini-Mike drove a dented black primered Nissan SUV; stickers covered the back, Metel Mulisha, The Insane Clown Posse, and other screaming metal music stickers dotted the back window.

Cabin living was easy. Ted lived in a small travel trailer a hundred yards away, so he wasn't woken up every night by the constant partying by Dorn and Mini-Mike. Ted didn't like Mini-Mike, but had lived for two years on his family's property, ate his mom's food, and shit in the dirty outhouse they were forced to use because the county had closed down their outdated septic system. He hated the cold morning shits, sitting reading gun magazines. At one point in his life he wanted to be a cop, but that would have put him at odds with his younger brother, Dorn. His thoughts were interrupted by the sound of shooting coming from up the creek. He ran forward, hopping over logs and around a rock. He saw Dorn, his baggy cargo shorts hanging near the ground. Dorn pulled up his pants then fired into a dead, bloated cow lying in the stream. It was hot, and the cow was puffed up twice its normal size. Most of Dorn's bullets missed the target. He yelled, "Ya man! Finally, got something to shoot at. Yow!"

Mini-Mike stood with his shotgun at his hip, legs apart, facing the cow. He put his hand in the air then yelled, "Are you lookin' at me? Are you lookin' at me, bitch? Ya that's right, fuck ya!" He pumped six rounds of twelve-gauge double buckshot into the cow. He turned around, reloaded his gun, and fired another six rounds into the dead cow. He laughed, "Ya bitch, fuck ya, man!" He walked, laughing with Dorn and Ted. The gases the cow held inside its stomach and intestines escaped with loud, gooey fart sound. The punks looked back at the cow, laughing, when suddenly the disgusting gasses hit the punks with a stink they had never encountered. The stench hit Mini-Mike first. He dropped, made a face of pain then dropped his shotgun, running away sideways into Dorn and Mini-Mike. All fell over in painful laughter.

Ted grabbed them both pulling them backward out the smell range. "Godam, that's fuckin bad yo! Whew!" They backed up, reloaded and downed a couple more cheap beers. They fired off another couple hundred rounds into the cow leaving it a torn up mess of disgusting guts and bone. They walked back to the compound, satisfied with the day's activities. It was time for sandwiches and more beer.

By nightfall Dorn and Mini-Mike were smashed from large amounts of Crown Royal Whiskey and Keystone beer. From his trailer Ted yelled at them to take it easy. His request went unheeded; the music remained as loud as could be. Ted walked out of his travel trailer to the door of the cabin. He opened it. Dorn and Mini-Mike had their backs to him. He yelled at them, "Hey assholes!" He reached down, pulling the plug from the stereo. It went off quickly. Dorn turned around, a glass pipe in his mouth. Ted stepped forward, took the pipe from his mouth, threw it on the ground, and crushed it with his big foot.

Mini-Mike already drunk, stepped forward, "Fuck you man! What's your problem?" Ted stepped forward.

Dorn stood up between the two. "No problem, Teddy. We'll go to bed and knock off the bullshit. Ok man?" He slapped Ted on the back and smiled, showing dirty yellow and brown teeth.

Ted cocked his head,"Just stop with the shit. I thought you sold it all anyway."

Dorn's voice was calm, "No problem, Ted. That was the last of it" Ted took a long look at the two shitfaced punks, shook his head, turned around and went to his trailer, leaving Mini-Mike and Dorn smiling at each other.

Mini-Mike said, "Fuck man, that's shit man! A bunch of shit! I'm gonna' kick his ass!" Dorn slowly pulled a baggy out of his shirt. He swung it back and forth in front of Mini-Mike's face. Small crystals shined in the bag. They smiled at each other then went out the back door to Mini-Mikes old fort in the back yard. They continued their assault on their bodies and minds, drinking and smoking until they passed out, which was an hour before Ted woke up.

Mini-Mike and Dorn wandered out of the little plywood fort around noon. They smelled bad. Both were wearing their baggy black cargo pants with chains hanging from belts to wallets, and new Vans skateboard shoes. Dirt and grass clung to their black hoodies. Ted was chopping wood when they emerged from the fort, eyes sunk in their heads, dark circles under their eyes. They were stressed, and out of their beloved meth. Ted said, "We have to go water the plants. You guys coming?"

Dorn was tired and pissed off now, "Fuck off man. I'm lying down." He was thinking about how to get more crystal; tonight would be bad if they were out. He needed to sleep but the burning need for more drugs ruled his thoughts.

Ted shot back at his younger brother, "Naw, man. Don't worry I'll take care of it by myself. You guys stay here and get things ready for tonight," Ted replied, "get ready for what?"

Ted turned, grabbed his small pack and shotgun, and left. Hiking up the creek bed for two miles, he passed the rotting, blown apart cow then turned left at a small creek. He hiked for a hundred yards to a bushy area. Two-foot tall marijuana plants poked up above a small fence. He picked up two five-gallon buckets, filled them from the creek then watered each of the thirty plants. When he was finished he sat down on a rock, proudly looking over the grow area. He pulled out the remains of a small joint, took two puffs then put it away for future use. He was proud that he could make a joint last for three days. He liked the grow area, especially when the punks weren't around. He didn't like the guns and meth, but he was going to back his brother to the end.

When Ted came back two hours later, Mini-Mike, Dorn, and the Nissan were gone. Two days later Mini-Mike and Dorn showed up, stocked with a new supply crystal meth. They arrived late and went right to bed. When Dorn finally passed out Ted went in Mini-Mike's bedroom. He flipped him on the bed face down then quietly said, "Where'd you get the rock?"

Mini-Mike said, "Fuck you man. I'm not telling you nuthin'!" Ted increased his grip around the back of the punk's neck. He picked him up just enough to slip his other arm under Mini-Mikes neck, something he had done many times while wrestling for the Washington State Cougars. He knew just how much pressure to put on Mini-Mike's neck so he would not be able to breath. Mini-Mike tried to fight, but went limp. Ted pulled him up, slapping his face softly waiting for the blood to start flowing again. When Mini-Mike came to Ted asked again, "Where did the meth come from, Mike?" Again Ted flipped him over and started the same process,

"Ok, Ok, man. We robbed the beeners that we sold to man. That's all. Fuck man!" He was struggling to breathe.

Ted poked his big finger at Mini-Mike's face. "You better stop your crap with my brother or one day I'll break your neck!" He jabbed his finger at him for effect again then walked out of the room.

Mini-Mike yelled back, "Hey man. It was Dorn's idea. Man, this is bullshit." Ted walked away knowing full well that Mini-Mike was right. When Dorn woke, his bag of rock was empty. He thought they smoked it all, not recalling the night before or the hand of his brother taking the rock out of the bag. He showered then went about with the posse chores, cleaning up the grounds for Mini-Mikes mom's monthly inspection, when she finally left her own filthy cabin and had bitched the punks out for their filthy living. Then she'd go back to her own cabin to watch TV. Dorn promised he wouldn't do any more crazy stuff, not defining what crazy stuff he was talking about. That night at the old plywood fort he explained to Mini-Mike his next move, raiding the Mexicans cabins while they worked in the orchards. Robbing the Mexicans was just too easy. They would need to move on to make money and they would be out in a few weeks.

The next day they took off early, breaking into two for the cabins on the outskirts of an orchard. These were the cabins of the guys that supplied meth to the punks. Even though reinforced, they made it inside. They found two ounces of cheap Mexican weed, enough meth for a week, two Taurus .45 pistols, and two thousand dollars of hard-earned money. It was too easy. The following night, while Ted sat in his trailer watching the History Channel, they snuck out again, this time robbing two vacation homes of flat screen TVs, stereos, DVDs, and anything else they wanted. Two days later they pawned everything at a pawnshop in Chelan. They had become thieves.

From her Chevy Blazer, Ranger Becky Smith watched two men load beach ball sized rocks into the back of their red Dodge power wagon pickup. The radio chirped. The dispatcher's voice was slow and bored, "Becky, Boss said to wait for backup. These guys have been picked up before, have some history of violence" Becky keyed her mike, "ten four base." Out loud she said, "pussies." She set her microphone on the seat, and pulled out her new Smith and Wesson M&P, a good copy of a Glock. She pulled the slide back checking to make sure a round was chambered, set the pistol back in her holster, and hopped out of the small SUV. She hiked uphill before she crossed the road, quietly walking through brush until she was thirty feet from the two men. The older bigger man said to the other, "I think we have enough for the outside wall." Becky walked forward with her pistol drawn. The men sensed movement and turned to face her. Their expressions were of surprise and dread. "Oh shit!" one said.

Becky spoke clearly and loudly, "Whatch ya doin', boys?" The bigger man walked away from her around the truck. She did not want them on either side of her. She yelled, "Stay where you are, both of you! Put your hands on the truck and spread your legs." She handcuffed the bigger man. He tied to squirm, but she held him easily, twisting his big hand sideways while applying pressure on his middle finger. He yelled in pain.

From the north end of the dirt road another beat up Blazer appeared, lights on, siren off. Two officers jumped out, guns drawn, but already the robbers were cuffed. The men would be booked and spend some time in jail. Maybe the truck would be taken from them. The park service used trucks like that all the time.

At base Becky filled out her reports for the day, a report on the computer and a hard copy. She set the copies, along with her day report and time card, into her bosses' organizer on his desk and left for the locker room. She dressed in worn black running tights, jog bra nylon vest and a camelback pack. She packed her Smith and Wesson semi auto pistol in her locker and set her backup lightweight Smith and Wesson snub nose thirty-eight in a pocket of her small pack. She rubbed on bug juice, took a big drink of water from the fountain, and stepped out into the evening for her big run of the day. A mile into her run she came to a row of cabins, under a sign, "Yellowstone Bedrock Acres." Her friend and running partner, another park ranger, shouted, "Hey Beck, how was the day? Shoot anybody today?"

Becky laughed, "Nobody today. Lots of tickets, for trash violations, a woman washing her hair with Suave shampoo in a stream, busted two guys for stealing rocks, were gonna' make a rock wall, too cheap to buy them."

So what happens to them?"

Becky took a big breath as they jogged along the road," They'll get their hands slapped, maybe a big ticket, might take their truck from them, but I doubt that." They picked up the pace with six miles to go. An eggshell Dodge Charger with matching powder coated custom wheels slowed down, and drove alongside the two women.

The women smelled cologne as one of the men in the car stuck his head out." Nice butts. You girls need a ride to our cabin?" Becky looked at them then laughed. The guy hanging out of the car had a shaved head with a heavily cultivated beard, and of course, he wore a gold chain. She yelled at them, "No thanks, got to meet our lesbian group for a talk on venereal disease." The bald guy's face changed. Both girls cracked up laughing.

"Man that's good, Beck. Leave it to you."

"I could have told them I was a cop" They ran on finishing with a good kick.

Becky scooped up the stuff in her locker and walked, sweating, to her Toyota Prius. She hurried to her small cabin, stripped, took a shower then filled her old bathtub. She poured a big glass of red wine and then slowly lowered her strong body in the water. "Damn, that feels good. Nothing better." She lay in the water wondering, "Is this how I'm going to live my life? What an idiot." She thought of her training as an Air Force MP in Alaska and Kuwait. That led to a job as a Park Ranger specializing in law enforcement at one of the greatest parks ever; Yellowstone. Her territory was the north end near Mammoth. It was her nineteenth year in the park service. She taken two years of college, served five years in the Air Force then spent three years working as a part time ranger on the north end of the Grand Canyon. She studied animal husbandry, was working on her bachelors, and looking forward to winter when she would study the hibernation habits Yellowstone's bear population. She wanted out of law enforcement, and wanted into the world of animal studies. With the long recession, jobs with animals just weren't available. Now, at age thirty-nine, she felt stuck, but happy to have a job. It was her choice, so she had little to complain about.

People came to the National Parks for an experience in nature, but some showed up with three hundred thousand dollar RVs, spending their entire time sitting inside watching TV and breathing the fumes from their generators. The days surrounding July Fourth were crazy days in the National Parks. There were campers that wanted to get away from fireworks, and those who had to carry them every place they went and didn't understand why or how they were prohibited in the park. Becky was looking forward to the evening shift.

Microwave, bread makers, George Foreman Grill, coffee maker, meat grinders, waffle makers, and all other Teflon lined, plastic coated devices were all off limits in her kitchen. One modern convenience in her home was a toaster oven. She toasted up two big pieces of sourdough bread and coated it with butter and organic grape jelly. She walked out of her cabin, sipping her coffee, and munching on her over-toasted bread. The small cabins the workers rented were built in the fifties for park workers. Many decades later they still were used for the workers. Row after row stood identical cabins, twenty feet by twenty feet, with a small bathroom, and a studio type kitchen that opened to the only other room. It served as a bedroom and living room. There was a small porch on the front and back, room for a car outside, and a small yard surrounded by six foot high bamboo fencing. Inside the small yard were six metal horse troughs filled with soil and used as raised gardens. Squirrels had once again decimated the tomato plants, and at night the raccoons that thrived in all National Parks rolled through her garden looking for food, munching on her lettuce, carrots, and anything else they liked. She kept a co2 bb pistol on hand to keep them out of the garden.

For two hours she surfed the Internet, continuing her education. She read several journal articles by animal biologists from Alaska talking about grizzly bear hibernation. The reading gave her some ideas of why factors influencing the start time of hibernation. She was looking forward to having the fall and winter off to study "her bears," as she called them. Most interesting to her was that part of the bear's brain kept them from urinating in their den. How was this possible? How was it possible that bears knew when and where to hibernate for a full winter? Three years into her studies she had learned much about the Yellowstone bears, but had a passion to discover more.

Her phone rang. The dispatcher was calling her to an early patrol of the northeast campsites. The dispatcher sounded bored, but to the point.

"Yes, Beck, we have three forest fires going so everybody is working overtime. Need you to patrol the campsites."

She made the rounds easily, later in the day. Sure enough, campers fired off fireworks, scaring a retarded boy into a restroom. To seek relief from the earsplitting bangs, he had locked the door and would not come out. From outside the outhouse Becky stood, knocking on the door. The kid's mom and dad stood with the ranger. The mother was frightened for the safety her son, and the dad was mildly amused. They called his name, "Josh, honey, come on, unlock the door. The loud noises are gone. No more tonight. Honey, come on now." From inside the restroom was a guttural frightened yell from the traumatized kid. It sounded far-off, like he was in a tunnel. Becky wondered how he could sound that way. She wiped away the sweat from her forehead. The outhouse was only five feet by five feet. He could not be any further than five feet from his mother's crying face. Finally, a young park maintenance worker showed up with the key. When she unlocked the door, and they swung the door open, no kid was to be seen. Josh was gone, the outhouse was empty. The mother looked at Becky; Becky threw a quizzical look at Josh's parents. The mom looked past Becky, pointing at the pit toilet. The lid and seat were in the upright position. Becky turned around, and looked at the toilet. A light was moving from the inside the pit, shining on the ceiling. The dad simply said, "What the fuck?" The mom turned around and punched the dad in the arm. He faked pain then started laughing. Becky took a small flashlight from her gun belt, and looked into the six-foot deep pit. She shined the light down the hole. Josh stood on a pile of toilet paper and fecal matter smeared from head to toe in brown shit. Becky looked down and spoke, "Josh, we need you to come out of there. People need to use the toilet." She turned to the parents and started to laugh uncontrollably. Josh's dad looked at Josh's mom, and they started laughing, all feeling guilty at the same time.

The poor boy looked up, "Hi Mom and Dad!" The boy, only twelve years old, was still small and young. "I dropped my whistle!" He showed it to Becky and his parents then went to put it in his mouth. He stopped before it got to his mouth, and he held it up again," It's dirty, Mom!" The laughing started again, this time constrained.

The dad yelled down, "Josh, boy, put your hands up and we'll pull you out. The dad looked at Becky with a smile," I hate to ask you this, but?" The dad held up his right hand to show his cast. Becky rolled her eyes and handed her hat to Josh's mom.

GEORGE THIELMAN

Becky turned to the custodian, "Could you go to the nearest showers and clear a room for young Josh here?" The young woman took off in a sprint for the shower rooms, two hundred yards away. She was happy to get as far as possible from the feces-smeared boy. Becky and Josh's dad each grabbed a hold of each of the boy's wrists, pulling upward. It was awkward because the hole was just big enough for their hands. She pulled with her right arm, the stronger of her two. They had just got Josh's head sticking out of the toilet hole when Becky started laughing again. This made the dad crack up. The boy's hands smeared in gooey, shit slime started to slip. Not wanting to start the process over again, Becky slipped her strong left arm under the boy's arms and pulled him out of the toilet, bear hugging him.

The boy was smiling the whole time. He said, "Hi, my name's Josh. What's yours?"

She set him down, now covered in the same shit. The dad high-fived the boy then hurried the stinking boy away through the campsites to the showers. Josh's mom apologized and thanked Becky before following her two men. Becky had no extra clothes in her Blazer. She called in to report that she would be coming back to the station. The dispatcher demanded that she check out an accident involving a truck and a moose.

Becky drove to the accident site. A new Toyota pickup was on its side, the front end crunched in. The driver and his wife were ok; the moose had two broken front legs. The bones were sticking through the flesh on both legs, and the animal was in great pain. Onlookers watched as Becky approached the moose. She wanted to fix the moose, but knew there was no way that was going to happen. She pulled her pistol racked a round and fired two shots in the head, "Two in the hat." There were screams from a bright blue Suburban full of kids.

Three hours later she strolled into base, heading for the locker room showers. As she walked past, her boss looked at her, then laughed. "Shitty day, huh?"

"What a bunch of crap, huh?"

One of her fellow rangers walked in. "Becky, what an incredible smell you discovered."

Another ranger walked in and stood in front of Becky. He smiled and said, "What kind of crap is this?" He smiled then broke up in laughter. Becky smiled, gave everyone, including her boss, the finger then went inside the locker room. She emptied her pockets, took off her belt, and stepped in the shower with her clothes on. First she cried for the moose, not the first animal she had to exterminate. She laughed at the boy, and marveled at his parents' incredible love and patience. She whispered, "Unconditional love, fuck off."

In Washington State several years earlier Sally Sky ran an ad in the Washington State University paper for summer jobs on the Sky Ranch. Many students had been hired over the years. Students of agriculture and farming were her first hires; she would pry them for knowledge of modern farming. Sky Ranch was small. Because of the students the garden became smaller and put out more food than ever before. Sally applied her new found gardening knowhow to her grows of weed. Many of the part timers worked at the café/bar/store. With inquiries about handicapped facilities, Sally and Darren refurbished four cabins for handicapped needs: wheelchair access, lower faucets, handrails, and propane stoves. They were finished in time for their first campers of the season.

One young man, paralyzed since birth, showed up in an electric chair and had met a girl of the same age, who had suffered a brain injury in a motorcycle wreck. They developed a friendship that kept them together every moment of every day. They spent the day either enjoying the day in the screened in porch of the cabin or being pushed up and down the dirt road to the ranch and back. They enjoyed raccoons playing in the evening, deer grazing with horses, wild turkeys walking amongst chickens and picking over the same ground, eagles swooping down into the river, catching fish with their talons, then lifting into the sky with their catch twitching. Best of all they caught sight of a couple black bears raiding the garbage of the campsites. Their experience and friendships would last a lifetime.

Rules of the campsite were simple: quiet time at ten, no generators, no fireworks, no shooting of guns, no wood gathering, and food was to be stored in metal bear boxes provided at each campsite. The bear boxes were big enough for a big cooler and food. They had locking mechanisms that could confound any animal with thumbs. In the middle of the campgrounds was a building used for restrooms and showers, and along the back of the building was a series of metal boxes that looked like big mail boxes. One was for food scraps, one for paper products, another box was for cans, bottles, and plastic, and another for plastic scraps. Raccoons were the cutest and peskiest of all critters. They would come out at dusk, snooping through the trash and around campsites. They were capable of unzipping packs and tents. They were well-fed, thus good-sized animals. They rolled through the campsites like a Tsunami, and by morning they were gone.

GEORGE THIELMAN

August was a hot month that not only helped the crops grow well, but also pushed animals ever further uplake to seek out the cooler weather. Twice the campsites were turned upside down by the visitation of two small rattlesnakes slithering through the campsites. Big, tough, macho men jumped on top of picnic tables in fear, leaving their women folk to fend for themselves. Big Kenney Delanny would come with his five-gallon bucket and stick, and would pin the snake's head. He'd just pick it up by the back of the head and drop it in a bucket. He would set them in an empty aquarium at the back of the bar until someone had time to take them for a boat ride. They'd be dropped into the lake a few feet from shore.

Tom's final days of August were busy. Most of his time was spent in the final cultivation process at the MMM. Cutting and trimming required tedious clipping with small scissors. First the plants would be cut at the bottom and then the leaves would be cut of at the base of the branches. The stem and branches would then be void of all leaves, leaving just stems, branches, and the bud. thirteen inch buds that were thick as a beer bottle. Tom would flip the plants upside down for three days to make all nutrients and THC flow into the buds. Finally, the plants would be cut loose and hauled to the ranch where they would be hung in the dungeon to finish. They dried slowly, for seven days, with fans blowing and fresh air was circulated to keep the plants from molding. Hiking the remains of two hundred fifty plants took Tom and Karen over six days. They did four trips per day doing over nine miles a day. When they were finished they did other jobs; Tom hauled campers in the boat for a late evening pickup, and Karen would spend the evening working in the bar or café.

Tom came home one day to find that Karen had framed all of his coolest photos from climbing and soldiering. One photo was of him in boot camp, dirty and young, with a youthful smile. Another was after Ranger School, proudly wearing his badges and sitting with others on a smoldering Iraq tank. Another showed Tom parachuting with full battle gear, and another was four of his Ranger buddies, walking away from a mud building in Somalia. The mud wall had four piss stains on it, a satire of "The Who's" album from the early seventies. There were pictures of ice climbing, high altitude climbing in Pakistan and Nepal, and rock climbing from all over the world. One of the pictures was of one of Tom and his buddies giving Tootsie Roll Pops to young Fagan girls, who could show only their eyes behind colorful veils and headscarves. Tom's favorite photo was one of several of his Special Forces buddies in a junkyard outside of Kandahar. Tom was on a shot-up Russian Ural motorcycle, and his buddies in or on various former Russian planes or drop tanks. All were fully armed and smiling; seasoned veterans, they had seen more than most soldiers.

The modern U.S. military, fully volunteer, fought battles as much as they wanted, pulled off special ops, and constantly kept the Taliban on the run. Tom's face was very different compared to the smiling eighteen year old in boot camp. Karen had nailed the pictures up on most every space of the walls. Tom was proud of the pictures and what they represented. He gave Karen a gold necklace from Morocco that he'd kept for many years. They made a great night of it: chicken with gravy, good wine, a dip in the snorkel tub followed by an hour of good sex.

In Tom's greenhouse, plants had taken off. Every form of veggie thrived. Bamboo had grown many spikes and now made a great cover at the base of the shower below the tub. Flat rocks were hauled in for more stepping-stones. The spices and herbs gave the green house a healthy strong smell. The two kittens had moved in, spending time chasing mice and small snakes, they would also dart out from the cover of the plants to attack any passerby, mostly Woody, who would never remember to look for them. He would jump back from them and snarl. They would retreat to the safety of a plant looking back at him. The two long-tailed tomcats hunted small birds, moles, shrews and rats. As the kittens got older and bigger they would be seen stalking the chickens, their small bodies low to the ground, tails swirling like a fly fisherman's casting.

THE SHITTY DEAL
END OF AUGUST

CHAPTER 5

Tom was walking in Afghanistan, heavily armed, his men on every side of him, making a formidable group. All of his men were wounded, or torn to pieces. They were the walking dead. He was running, the bullets snapping at the ground behind and around him. He was running away but they caught up to him and started tearing him apart. He was being picked apart one chunk at a time. The pain was unbearable. He withstood it with only a wince, moving his gun from side to side, reloading. Finally, the pain was too much. He looked down at his hands. They were shot off, and blood spurted from mortal wounds.

He woke up sweating. He looked around, the stars shining through the window. The kittens were curled up in Karen's legs, fast asleep with her. Woody was awake looking at him. He stood up, dressed, walked downstairs then outside to the front yard. He looked up at the cloudy sky. The mountains acted as a frame for the blue and grey clouds. The river was flowing high, making more noise than ever. He looked back up again. "What? What do you want from me?" From behind him he heard," Who are you talking to?" She was wrapped in a fleece blanket, her short black hair messed up, and blue eyes were squinted. Not a strand of gray hair. For the first time he realized how much older he was than she. She was leaving in two weeks. He walked to her, pulled the blanket apart, wrapping his arms around her. Picking her up he carried her upstairs. She smiled as he carried her; they moved the kittens to make love on the bed.

Karen's final weekend they had a horse ride all planned out. It would serve two purposes. One was to have a good time; another was to carry fifty pounds of great weed to Karl Sky. He was riding his six horses from Highway 20 south to Stehekin to meet up with Tom, Karen, and Philip. They would load up and ride back north to the highway. The ranch would see $100,000.00 of the crop. The great part was that there was more weed almost ready to go, drying in the dungeon. Tom sat on Finger Rock drinking coffee and looking out on the river. His fishing line tugged.

They left at two p.m. Karl was in the lead on his big American stud. Tom was in the rear, with Philip and Karen in the middle. Each person had a packhorse, but no coolers or chairs, just the basics and fifty pounds of great weed. They were well armed with Karl packing a Colt 45 and a Winchester 30-30. Philip carried an old style Ruger .357 and a Winchester like his uncle. Tom carried a Colt Python four inch barreled .357 revolver, a gun tuned at Colt's custom shop. Under his vest he carried his back-up Glock .40 caliber. Under his pack was his match grade Colt M4. He kept it covered with a tarp. The weapons were not only for security, but also for fun. They found it to be cool and made them feel like cowboys. They sipped good tequila and smoked weed the whole time, with big Karl quoting lines from Clint Eastwood movies. "Hey Blondie, you know what you are?" On and on, he made his companions laugh. Riding within small valleys, they were always in earshot of water flowing over and through rocks and branches and logs. They heard rocks shifting and moving, and branches moving with the flow of water, in the small creeks. Camp was made on the top of a fifty-foot rock. A fire was made against another rock, blackened from decades of campfires. The horses tied up, munching on green grass and oats enjoyed the cool, soft earth under their shod hooves. Water noisily flowed under the big campsite rock. Tom's fish, caught earlier in the day, was cooked over a small grill taken from a Weber barbecue. They heated up baked beans from the café, and drank Heineken from cans. Sleeping in the open, with no tents was fine since the rock was high enough that the bugs would stay away. A cool wind blew from the north at about ten miles an hour. It was the magic number that made it impossible for mosquitoes to maneuver. It was a great evening. They slept soundly, the fire smoldering all night. Again Tom woke in sweat, breathing hard, the same dream bullets snapping at him, raking the ground, until finally catching him then tearing him apart. He felt the pain again. He crawled to the fire, set wood on the fire, and sat watching the flames.

GEORGE THIELMAN

He wondered if what he was going through was PTSD, Post Traumatic Stress Disorder. "Is that it?" He wasn't sure. After an hour of poking at the fire, he went back to bed, sleeping soundly until morning. He was the first person up and started the fire, again heating water for coffee, Sky Valley Coffee. They now had stickers that matched the ranch label; big mountains in the background with a fisherman in a river boat. House Blend was his favorite. He sat and drank. He wrapped the French press in a down jacket to keep it warm for the others. By the end of the day they were at Karl's truck. Karl drove two of his horses back to the west side. Philip, Karen and Tom rode back to the ranch.

Four days later, Tom drove Karen back to 25 Mile Sky. When they docked Karen said, "You know Tom, I don't want to come back here to live. I want to travel and start a career. I love this lake, but it's not what I'm going to do. I want to travel the way you have, and maybe have kids sometime. I know you don't want them, but I do." Tom shrugged his shoulders, "I agree with you. I've enjoyed our time and won't forget you. I think you should go and have fun." He smiled at her. "And I hope you have a great life and everything you want."She left in her small Subaru with a wave. Tom walked to Garrets house, stashed a ten-pound brick of weed in the garage, and picked up a wad of cash from the same place.

He drove back to the town of Chelan then to Ray's Sporting Goods where he dropped off five hundred reloaded bullets for hunting. He was given another thousand empty casings to reload. He handed Ray four ounces of fresh weed, picked out a few things in the store then went upstairs to talk weapons with Ray. Ray had two shiny AWT AR-10s, similar in every way to Tom's M4 but chambered for the larger .308 caliber bullet. AWT was a private company from Spokane that jumped into custom weapon manufacturing after 9-11. It's owners were former military and avid hunters that, along with others, banked on weapon contracts from the military. AWT stood for Applied Weapon Technologies, and they fabricated a customized Mil-Spec M4, and a bigger brother, the AR-10. Changing the barrel and other minor parts could easily change both weapons from one caliber of bullet to another. All the parts were custom made on CNC machines that the owners said were more accurate than any used by weapon makers. These weapons had a big emphasis on lightweight and strength. Tom inspected one with a light OD green and tan camo- finish and a twenty-inch barrel. Without the handle of a M-16 and a rail system in its place on the top of the barrel and below it, one was free to mount any number of small combat scopes, lasers, flashlights and magnifiers of various makes, making the weapons not only expensive but a cluster fuck of deadly technology. Tom picked out a lightweight scope that worked as a combat scope with a green or red crosshairs. A battery and small chip let you decide which color reticule to use. The colored crosshairs allowed the shooter faster target acquisition along with better aiming, Tom's scope was small enough to use for combat and big enough to use for long range shooting. The problem with these scopes was that one needed batteries to power the scope. Modern day battles could go on all day, easily using up the battery life. With Tom's new scope when the battery went dead' the scope switched to an etched black crosshair.

He made the purchase of the rifle, scope, eight super light Kevlar 30 round clips, plastic case and a bigger scope for hunting. The weapon was built to Military Specifications or MIL-SPEC, which means that parts were made the same as all Military parts from other manufacturers. Tom called the H&K rep and ordered other parts for his weapons. His bill was almost four thousand dollars. He paid Ray and left for Stehekin.

On the ride back to Stehekin Tom felt alone but relieved. It had been a long time since he lived with a woman. Karen was fun. From the first day he knew they would not be together long, so he never really allowed himself to fall in love. As he bounced on the waves, he smiled, channeling young Karen all the best luck in the world. The Sky Boat was loaded with supplies again, most of them for his cabin. For the café he had picked up two hundred pounds of coffee for the coffee roaster. Also on board were liquor for the bar, and other supplies for the store. At the Sky boat docks he loaded the pickup then brought the supplies into the café, bar, and store. He went to the bar for a drink. It was two days before Labor Day weekend and the bar was slow. Campers were trickling in from downlake.

Sally was tending bar, "So, you are going to miss Karen?"

Tom looked at her and said," Yes, I'll miss her! She's a good person. I have no doubt that she will find whatever she is looking for."

Sally looked back at him while she poured a double Tequila Guzzler; tequila, lime and ice. She said, "You think she's looking for something?"

Tom nodded, "We're all looking for something, Sally!"

She laughed, "Not all people are lookin', some are happy with the way things are."

Joe Spadafore burst through the door. "Ok, Sal, give me the usual, hair of the dog and don't stop 'till the fat lady is singing." He slapped Tom on the back with his big hands, moving past Tom to two of his fishing buddies. The fishing buddies sat at the far corner of the bar and immediately started cracking jokes. Tom heard the punch line of Joe's joke, "So the owner of the porno store comes in and asked his worker, 'How's business?"

His worker said, 'Pretty good, sold out all the dildos. The best part is that I sold your thermos for 150 bucks." They erupted in laughter. The spirits were such in the café that even people that hadn't heard the whole joke or were offended by it still laughed. Tom and Sally both laughed along with them. Sally pushed a note to Tom and whispered, "Need you to pick up a family tomorrow around noon, at 25 Mile. Darren and Philip are taking them on a horse trip, and we have coffee and weed ready for deliveries." Sally looked around the bar then waved Tom to follow her to the office. Once inside she pulled out her small pipe, preloaded. They smoked a few puffs then she pulled out an envelope, a half-inch thick,

"What's this? "Tom asked.

She smiled at him. "It's twenty thousand dollars in cash. There'll be more." Tom slipped the envelope in his pocket next to the shoulder holstered Glock .40. He smiled as he sipped on his double shot Patron,

"So the MMM did well did it?"

She laughed, "It did better than ever. We sell weed for two thousand a pound to the dispensaries in Seattle. Karl handles. All of it his sources are loyal. Bunch of his high school and Army buddies started four dispensaries with our money. We own the business. Those guys run it, provide security, and best of all legal customers. From the dispensaries we have made up a distribution center for the world of weed." Sally's cast had been removed a few days earlier. She scratched at the skin. She put her pipe back in her fanny pack.

"You still packing heat, Tom?" Tom nodded yes. She reached into a fanny pack revealing a shiny snub nose thirty-eight. "This baby should do, don't you think? Got it from Ray a couple months back. It's light as a feather and holds five bullets. Ray said they're called Plus P ammo, supposed to be more powerful. I wouldn't know about that!"

They strolled back to the bar. Sally said, "Philip wants to join the military next spring. He wants to be an Army Ranger, like you. His mom is sick with worry, afraid he's gonna end up," she stopped. Tom finished for her, "end up like me, is what she means. Yah, I know what she means. I think Philip will do well. He's strong, great kid, endurance, and self-discipline. Everything the military wants."

Joe was drunk and loud already. He was standing, legs spread, his hands in front of him, "Well god-dam if that bastard of a rattlesnake wasn't under the table. Why I jumped up, and it's goddam head was four feet off the ground. Most of its body was coiled up, it's tail rattling' so hard I couldn't hear myself think. Why, it struck at me over and over, missing' my body then we tussled." He sat down picked up his scotch and downed the contents then looked at Sally pointing to the empty glass. She walked over and started to fix another. One of Joe's friends asked, "What happened next, Joe?"

Joe looked hard at him, took a drink, leaned back then leaned forward and with a big growl he yelled," What happened? We'll I'll tell yaw whut happened. What happened, he killed me!" They all broke out in raucous laughter. Tom and Sally laughed hard at that one. Old Joe walked out of the bar laughing, "Huh, huh, god-dam, he kilt me, sure as shit fire it fuckin-hell boy ill-tell-ya-whut-shit-fire."

Tom rode the boat back to Chelan the next day. He made the coffee deliveries before ten using his mountain bike with Woody running alongside. They hurried back to the boat then to 25 Mile. He wanted to make the drop off of weed, before the customers started to board. Garrett was in a good mood for once. The transaction was made. Tom was given over ten thousand dollars in cash from past sales. The new customers were waiting and packed, all their bags in the boat. Onboard were two teenage boys with pants hanging down past their butts flaunting their red-checkered boxers. They wore colorful hoodies, and their faces never seemed to leave their Game Boy devices, thumbs moving fast. The little girl was cute as could be and no more than seven years old. She couldn't keep her eyes off big Woody. She sat in front of him staring into his eyes, occasionally she would stick her hand out and pet Woody's soft fur. Her Mom looked like the usual Bellevue, Washington housewife; bored to hell, she was trying to keep her family together, and have a good time. Her husband looked like the father on Dennis the Menace: dark hair with little bit of grey, white polo shirt with slacks, and loafers. The Mom was trying to make conversation about the lake for the benefit of the kids who had no interest in the goings-on around them. They disembarked at the docks then walked to the café to rent a cabin. An hour later the family was seen in the café, the little girl squiggling in her seat with excitement. The two boys stuffed burgers and fries in their mouths and continued with their game boys.

Tom drove the pickup back to the ranch with Philip. They unloaded supplies then went into Tom's cabin. He pulled the AWT rifle out of its case, and laid it on the table. Philip picked it up, checked the gun for a live round then turned a knob on the scope and selected green for the color of crosshairs. He calmly scrutinized the gun, with a slight smile he looked back at Tom. "So what made you buy this brand? Why not a Colt or H&K or Bushmaster?

Tom shrugged his shoulders, "I knew the owners of Applied Weapons Technology some years ago, and I knew the quality they demanded in their machine shop. The weapon is one of the best I've seen. Plus, Ray only has so many Assault Rifles at his shop that are Mil-Spec and hardy enough to take into battle right out of the case. Most of the assault rifles you find at the gun stores are not made for battle. Round after round this gun will do everything a guy would want it to"

Philip smiled at Tom," I want one!" Philip looked out the window, "I want out of here for a while. I need something more, to see the world, travel in the U.S."

Tom butted in, "You should go on a road trip, check out the west camp out in National Parks and see the sights. If you want adventure, ride a motorcycle across the U.S."

Philip scrunched up his face" I promised my Dad I would help them with the guiding this summer and that I would wait until spring to join the military." Philip laughed, "Well Tom, I gotta' go prepare to take that family on a horse packing trip. Boy that's gonna' be fun!" He left to saddle up the horses.

Tom smiled, remembering his first days as a Ranger. Only two weeks out of Ranger training he was in Iraq, inexperienced as a soldier. At a young age he had traveled to rock climb, spent time as a hang glider and parachutist, and he'd traveled across the States on his dad's old 79 BMW 1000 by himself at sixteen.

When he decided to become a soldier he already was a proficient hunter and marksman. He was promoted to squad leader, excelled at everything, and became sought-after for covert missions behind the lines. He was put in charge of a six-man squad guarding a town that bordered Kuwait and Saudi Arabia. Authorities had evacuated the Saudi town of one hundred and fifty. His troop was given specific orders to only watch the desert for Iraq's finest soldiers. After four days of looking out over the vast deserts of Kuwait, a Captain straight from West Point showed up and took charge of his troop. His name was Captain Graulich from Phoenix, Arizona. He was hard on all of the men. With no practical experience in soldiering, he was trying too hard, yelling about sandy weapons and dirty boots in a place that had nothing but sand and dirt. Tom and his buddies had found a stash of hashish and secretly smoked up at guard duty, getting high was a great way to ease the boredom and the abuse of the Captain.

One day he was on guard station with his buddy, Private Mommar Mohamed, when they spotted a column of six Iraqi tanks heading at them from the east, white flags flying from their turrets. Captain Graulich and his corporal drove to the gravel road. Tom heard him over the radio, calling his superiors. "Yes sir. They are coming straight at us with white flags flying, our first surrender."

Tom called from his position a hundred yards away, on the only hill in the area, "Captain, this might not be what you think!"

Captain Graulich yelled back, "Shut the fuck up, corporal. Keep this line clear!"

Tom, already stoned at seven in the morning, replied," Captain, we should," He was cut off again by his Captain.

"Trainer, shut up and keep this line clear!" Tom and Mo looked at each other and laughed. They were in a sandbagged bunker camouflaged with netting and old cement blocks. Tom aimed his Winchester sniper rifle at the first Iraqi tank commander who was standing up in the turret. The tank pulled up to the roadblock, and they watched Captain Graulich and his corporal approach the tank. They could not hear the conversation; the tank commander was clearly talking to the Captain when he dropped down into the tank. Captain Graulich stepped back. His corporal aimed his M16 at the tank then back at the tank behind them. Tom and Mo watched as the second tank opened fire with its machine guns onto the Captain and Corporal. The bullets tore them to pieces. The tank calmly drove through the roadblock.

Mo looked at Tom, "Well, I guess you're in charge again. What are your orders?" They watched as the two lead tanks turned their turrets toward them.

"Get out of this bunker!" Tom ordered. With weapons and packs, they rolled down the opposite side of the hill just as two shells hit the bunker, blowing it to pieces. Tom and Mo, safely behind the small hill, hurriedly put on their gear. Tom slung on his M16 and took off after Mo as they ran to the cover of the old mud brick town. They looked back at the bunker on the hill as two more shells blew the blocks into the air. The American flag stood up in the midst of the carnage then fell over into the dust.

Tom said to Mo, "Well, I guess we gotta fight now!"

Mo looked at him and laughed," Where's the rest of the squad?" He keyed his radio. No sound came out. Together they pulled the radio out of Mo's vest. A small chunk of steaming metal had embedded itself into the body of the radio, severing the connection.

Mo yelled," Where's your's?"

Tom looked back at the bunker and pointed, "It's back there. I was working on it this morning, piece of shit." They took off jogging through old alleys, from one road to another. Each home was connected to the other. Each home had a seven-foot high courtyard with old thick gates.

Tom thought it looked like a scene from Indiana Jones where they ran through the town looking for the bad guys who'd kidnapped Indy's girlfriend.

Mo said as they jogged, "Where we goin', man?"

Tom turned toward him, jogging sideways." We are going to get in this fight, right now." They ran out of alley to the main road that dissected the small dessert town. Tom glanced toward the old roadblock. The tanks were out of sight. but a dust cloud and noise gave up their positions. They heard gunfire and three explosions. They turned and ran faster to the sound of fighting, gunfire and dust showed the way. Down an alley they ran then down a dirty street. Tom stopped dead in his tracks when he saw three tanks emerge from around a corner. The tanks turned toward him and Mo. Tom broke down a gate, pulling Mo into a courtyard as the tanks' machine guns opened up on their previous position. Locked in a courtyard, Tom looked through the open gate. The tank sat, puffing diesel fumes. The front door was locked. They pushed and banged \ on the door, but it would not give. The tank's turret was rotating toward them. Tom and Mo scrambled up an outside oven the to the top of the thick, seven foot high wall. Tom made the roof first then looked back at Mo who was still on the top of the wall struggling to find balance with all his gear and weapons. "Come on Mo, let's go." The tanks turret was almost aiming at them.

An old telephone pole stopped its motion, the hatch opened; the commander jumped out and manned the machine gun unit's tripod. Mo ran over the last little bit of wall then jumped behind the mud parapet wall on top the roof. Tom exposed a kneeled-up M16 aiming at the tank. He fired a burst from the weapon hitting the tank commander with eight rounds, splitting his guts on the top of turret. He fell backward. Tom pulled a grenade and threw it toward the tank, trying to drop it into the open hatch. It landed on the dead commander's chest detonating and blowing him even further apart. Mo turned to Tom, "Fuckin' awesome, Dude!"

Tom and Mo jumped from one roof to another. They looked back as the first roof was blown to pieces by tank fire. They climbed down to a second floor window, smashing their way into the abandoned home. They ran through cozy bedrooms, nice rugs, and a poster of Michael Jackson's Thriller album. Tom looked out to the front where the tanks were. He saw the back of one disappear around the corner. He ran back to the window they had come from and looked down the narrow alley. Two tanks were slowly driving down the long alley. The lead tank had its turret pointed forward, the second was pointing backward. Both had their hatches open.

Tank commanders were outside manning the machine guns. Mo ran toward Tom, M16 ready. They laid low until the first tank passed. They carefully and quickly fired almost point blank at the commanders, killing them both. Setting M16's down, they pulled grenades. Tom threw his into the following tank. It entered the open hatch and blew up. Mo's grenade hit the hatch as it was being closed. It exploded outside the tank, Mo dropped another grenade down the hatch of the same tank Tom had dropped his down inside. A blast emitted from the open hatch. The tank driver was hit in the head with grenade fragments, and he pulled the throttle back all the way, making the tank surge and rear-end the lead tank. The lead sped up and hauled out of the alley.

Mo and Tom climbed back up to the roof. The lead tank was now out of the alley and the tank, which had lost the commander, could be seen at the opposite end of the alley. Cannons fired at Mo and Tom's location. Tom and Mo climbed down into the courtyard and ran out the gate, straight in front of a tank and through a space between buildings. They emerged, red and panting, out of harm's way as the tanks started complete destruction of the homes nearby. Mo asked, "What should we do now man?" Tom said," Not much we can do if they're buttoned up. Without radios we're helpless. From the west two A-10 Warthog Jets screamed overhead. Two massive explosions destroyed two tanks. The Warthogs circled around to bomb the others. From their rooftop position, Tom and Mo saw the rest of their guys signaling.

Tom and Mo's performance that day brought them out into daylight as some of the first heroes of the Person Gulf War. Mo was promoted and sent to officer's training school. Tom joined up with a group of Delta and Navy Seals that were being used for Special Ops behind the lines for the rest of the war.

Tom stood looking out over the farm from the porch of his cabin. He was smiling. Woody was crouching in the grass with a rubber fish toy in his mouth, the sun was going down, and it was light out, 7:39 pm. He had to prepare for a long run to Highway 20 for another delivery to big Karl. He was going to be gone for three days. On the floor he laid out his lightest pack, a three pound sleeping bag, small down jacket that folded up the size of a big softball, three packets of freeze-dried spaghetti, four veggie burgers, raisins, dog food, Power Bars and a small bag of equipment. His pack weighed forty pounds, light for three days.

Woody and Tom hiked fast making the 26 miles to Highway 20 in eight hours, a little over three miles per hour. Karl was asleep in his pickup when Tom made the trailhead. He snuck up on Karl, surprising him when he woke, as he saw Tom stand by his open window.

Karl hopped out of his truck, "Godamn boy, can't believe you! Coulda got shot man. I'll tell ya." He calmed down when Tom started telling him jokes, and finally Karl cracked up. On the pickup truck bed Tom dropped the big bale of weed. Karl's eyes lit up … until a light green pickup pulled up into the trailhead parking lot. A tall park ranger stepped out and set about checking parked cars for parking passes. Tom covered the pot with his fleece jacket. Karl didn't care about the ranger; he found them to be nosey and bothersome. Karl loaded his big pipe and set it in his pocket, waiting for the ranger to leave. He snapped open two beers then poured two shots of tequila. They threw the tequila back and started on the beer. Woody trotted over to the ranger who was checking cars for parking passes. After issuing two tickets he sauntered over to Tom and Karl.

"Hello! How you guys doing today?"

Karl said smugly, "Juss fine officer. How 'bout you?" Tom just looked at the ranger while sipping on his beer.

"Whose dog is this?" the ranger asked. Karl pointed to Woody who was holding a stick in his mouth, wagging his tail.

"Zsat is not my dog."

Tom spoke up, "It's my dog. Why?" he asked, annoyed.

The ranger walked closer. He was bigger then Tom." Well, he's a good dog, but he has to be on a leash."

Tom laughed, "Sorry, but I don't have one on me at the moment, and I'm not going to put one on him when I do find one."

The big ranger didn't know what to do. He stuttered, starting to sweat, "Well, if I see you on the trails I'll have to give you a ticket or make you leave the area."

Karl was becoming angry, annoyed at this man's insistence in interrupting his day. He stepped forward smiling. He downed another beer in front of the ranger then crushed the can, laughing as he did. The ranger turned, sweating, face now red. Humiliated, he walked quickly to his pickup and drove off. Tom smiled, "Dude, we have to go. That guy is scared and you're carrying a big bundle of weed! I'm out of here, and so should you!"

Karl said, "Ya you're right. Let's get out of here." He stuffed the weed in a stinky blanket then threw old firewood and his fishing gear on top the blanket. "See ya, Tom." He peeled out, driving the opposite direction of the ranger. Tom double-timed his paces back to the cover of the forest. He walked as fast as he could for two hours, covering six miles. Finally, he stopped along a creek. He emptied the camelback bladder then refilled it with fresh water. Woody stood in a small pool of water the size of a pillow. Tom ate a Power Bar then gave his dog a big chunk of buffalo jerky. He took off, hiking quickly again. The trail traveled across the North Cascade National Park for several miles. He hoped the rangers would be elsewhere. By the end of the day Tom and Woody were near the trailhead to Stehekin. They crossed a creek and hiked up a small rise to his mountain bike, left against a tree. He strapped his pack to the titanium rack. As Tom was about to start riding, Darren and Philip came by with the Greenman Family from Bellevue. Darren was in the lead on his big, black, American stud. Next came the little girl, a smiley little blond who could not sit still in her saddle, she said nothing but her smile said it all. The father looking so much like Dennis the Menaces' dad, wearing a white polo shirt with designer jeans that did not seem to fit or look good on him, was on the next mount. His pretty wife rode by and waved. Their two teenage boys rode past on the two most docile horses the ranch owned; both boys had their little computer games thumbs working hard as they rode by. After six packhorses had passed, Philip rode up to Tom. He put his finger to his head. With a big smile he pretended to shoot himself in the head, but kept riding. Tom rode back to the ranch where he filled the snorkel tub, unpacked his pack, and took a long hot bath.

The next day was spent doing business for the ranch in Chelan. He dropped off coffee to four coffee shops. At Ray's Outdoor Shop he dropped off reloaded bullets, and then picked up several boxes of supplies. He borrowed Ray's Chevy pickup to haul loads of canned goods, rice, flour, sugar and wheat to the boat. Again, the boat was almost overloaded. Tom thought Sally must have been stocking up for the rest of the decade. He drove to Garrett's place at Twenty-five Mile Creek to pick up mail and more supplies sent by way of UPS.

Tom drove back to the café and then went for a drink. Sure enough, being it was dusk, Old Joe showed up. The bar was crowded. Joe was quietly joking with his same group of fishing buddies. Tom left to unload supplies for the café. After he finished working, Tom went fishing on Finger Rock, catching two twelve-inch trout for supper. After supper he sat back, happy to do nothing in his Lazy Boy chair, where he fell asleep. Outside the river moved southeast to fill Lake Chelan. The beavers had another round of babies. They swam, playing. Their mother kept them in line, playing with them, chewing on branches of captured logs and branches safe in the little bay.

GEORGE THIELMAN
FALL

Summer finished, the workers left for their homes and schools. The campsites and cabins emptied except for retired folks. This was the time of year Kenny Delanny loved the most. He was up at six am start coffee. A few of the older residents would wander in sometimes for breakfast, most for coffee only. He read books in the bar or café as customers ate. Sally or Tina would cover for him if he ever left the café, but he seemed never to leave. September stayed warm right up until the last day of the month.

October began with rain and wind. Tom, Philip, and Darren dragged half-logs into the barn, cut them up into twelve inch rounds, and split them with heavy splitting axes. They cut over fifteen cords of wood dragged from the river throughout the year. The additional logs sat in an orderly pile the size of a RV. All the homes were heated with wood. Darren's and Sally's were heated with electricity as well. Toms was exclusively heated with wood. He stacked over five cords of wood under cover on the porch, and under the eaves he'd stacked to the top of the windows, two rows deep.

Two cords of wood were hauled and stacked at Joe Spadafore's cabin while he was at the bar drinking Scotch. Three other nearby friends received firewood from the Sky Family for free. Wood was a lifesaving commodity in the valley, used for heating and cooking. Some was used to dry fish for the winter. Firewood was essential for almost every home and business, as essential as water.

With hunting season around the corner, Tom and Philip prepared. They reloaded bullets and cleaned and oiled rifles. They tested their rifles for accuracy. Tom and Philip spent three days at 25 Mile cleaning and working on rifles for Ray's customers. They reloaded over three thousand bullets. Calibers from .243 to .338 were loaded with Tom's bullets and powder. The bullets were not really much different than the boxed rounds bought in the store, nor were they much more expensive. They were loaded the same way, slowly and carefully, so the shooter got exactly the same powder charge every time. Sometimes the factory bullets could be inconsistent, giving the shooter a gun that shot differently each time it fired, making hunting difficult.

In the dungeon a new crop was finishing. It would be ready for delivery in November. The big garden was again covered in clear plastic, and the greenhouses were held up with bent PVC pipe to protect the crops from early frost. Greenhouses pushed the productive growing season further, another two months. Sally spent the fall canning veggies, making salsa and catsup. She made cases of crunchy pickles. Coffee was roasted and bagged. Over five hundred pounds of coffee was prepared for sale then delivered downlake. The most popular roast was called,"Uplake House Blend." Of medium roasts Tom found Granite Blend was smooth and chocolaty, followed by Espresso Roast, then a Breakfast Blend, the weakest of the blends.

    The first year the roasting machine paid for itself. The company ran out of packaging and had to reorder. A thousand pounds of new beans were delivered for winter roasting; another thousand would be delivered before the end of fall.

THE BADASS VIRUS

CHAPTER 6

IGNACIO DELE CORTE MADE IT to the old warehouse in the slums of Mexico City. Along with fifty other men and women, he'd be making the trip north to the boarder under orders from a drug cartel he didn't know. All he knew was that he was signed up to haul drugs for another season; this time all the way to the source in Washington State. He had done this for five years with great success. His bosses now trusted him completely, allowing him to choose where he wanted to deliver. This was the first time they delivered so far north. They were delivering heavy loads of meth, and weed. Some people would come across the border with the drugs hidden in clothing, stuffed animals, guitars, inside sealed energy cans, many stuffed it up their anus, or if they were women crammed the drugs into a baggie of suitable size then jammed it into their vaginas. Some swallowed sealed Baggies then shit into a strainer the next morning. Some of the people were simply trying to get into the U.S. to work in the fields and restaurants. To pay for their travel, the cartel came up with a deal. If one would haul a certain amount of drugs across the border successfully without being busted by the patrol, their traveling cost from Mexico City north would be paid entirely by the cartel. This particular cartel was showing heart to the people that carried their drugs, hoping their own fairness would be remembered in the following years.

Others like Ignacio, veterans of the importation of drugs, would move it through a tunnel dug by hand using a compass and a GPS. The tunnels were high enough and wide enough to move four wheeled quads. They were known to have lights, gravel floors, and wood beams for support. Beams four to five feet wide were nailed to a half a sheet of plywood or particleboard, premade to prevent soft, grainy dirt and sand from dropping on the travelers.

Just outside the tunnel entrance were the ragged edges of biggest dump in Mexico. Paper flew in the wind. The stink lodged itself into the nasal passages. The open sewer ran along dirt streets. The combination of filth and sewer was a stench that burned eyes. Little kids ran in the dirt road, splashing through the ditch that was used mostly for the transport of human waste.

Ignacio was called a coyote, a deliverer of drugs to the Americans. For the delivery of a pound of weed he got one hundred bucks. For ten pounds of meth he made five hundred bucks. The risk went up with amount of meth and so did the money. Mostly the Americans deported the drug runners back to Mexico. Ignacio looked out over the massive trash heaps.

"Chingow!" he said through clenched teeth. His eyes hurt; this smell would take days to get out of his system. A mother came out of her small shack, yelling at the kids to come in for dinner. She yelled again for them to wash up before dinner. He wondered how they would wash up or live in such a place. A door opened and a woman holding an old plastic bucket dumped filthy contents into the ditch outside her front door.

A dozen tough-looking young men and women from the southern jungle approached the warehouse. The bosses, the guys with the guns, admitted them. These were the scary ones, young and mean. Morality was a word they had little use for. On their hips they carried long wicked-looking knives in sheaths. On the other side of their hips they carried handguns, and semi autos of all kinds. The top boss carried a pistol with a pearl handle. Eight big men carrying Russian-made AK47 assault rifles surrounded him. No person was allowed close to him. They made life into nothing by killing, always killing, sometimes chopping bodies into pieces, and dropping acid into human orifices, making the coyotes watch as a lesson as to what would happen to them and or their families if they screwed up and lost the drugs. They were ugly. Everything about them was caustic. Petulant young people with no fear of consequences. Ignacio hated this place. His time as a coyote was almost up. This time he would travel north to Washington with a big load of weed and meth. This time he would make real money. This time he would stay in Washington with his cousins. He had paid their way north and had several thousand dollars in an American bank. He would pick fruit in the fields along the Columbia River. He had no desire to come back to Mexico; he had pushed his luck too far already.

The coyotes had to buy into the cartel at a good price, leaving a type of bond with them in case they got busted or the drugs were stolen. They'd travel north, usually somewhere in the states where they had connections with workers or family members. In Ignacio's case, he had worked on the apple and cherry orchards of Washington from Wenatchee, north along the Columbia River. The job of drug runner was dangerous; the pitfalls and mine fields, many. He wasn't a violent man, and he had defended himself many times, both from white people and dark skinned. He watched the jungle people gather outside the trashy building. They looked bad, sick maybe. Maybe they were not used to the filth. He wasn't sure. They were sweaty and dirty, and he didn't like the idea of being inside a tunnel with them.

After a two-day bus ride he sat on his backpack in a tunnel, the worst he'd ever seen. People had pissed in there. His leg was in a puddle of something. They were packed in like sardines. He tried not to lose his stomach. He and the jungle people were under a border town. Waiting in the tunnels was never fun' they had been there for hours. It was dark and dirty, and he had to piss. Most of the coyotes were coughing. It was hot and dank, and smelled of mold. A few people had candles in their hands, and three women from the jungle openly prayed. Shadows danced on the dirt roof and walls. He looked back at the short woman behind him. She was cute, but sweating like the rest of them. As she coughed, deep mucus spit from her mouth to the puddle they were sharing. Finally, they moved forward, but the movement was painfully slow. He, along with his fellow illegals, all struggling to keep it together. He was taller than his friends so he had to crouch down almost to a crawl. They moved for almost a eighth of a mile, and crawled up an aluminum ladder into another shitty, smelly warehouse. One by one they were allowed to leave the building.

When his time came to exit he hurried out of the building, ran down an ally, and up a street. When Wal-Mart opened he was the first through the door. He bought Lee dungarees, a blue buttoned shirt, and a light fleece vest with the name Sun Devils printed on it. At the shoe department he bought a pair of the most expensive New Balance running shoes. His straw cowboy hat was left in a garbage can, replaced with a University of Arizona baseball hat. As he walked out of the store, he looked more like a University of Arizona Sun Devil student on his way home from college than an illegal or drug runner. He made a point to speak only English. With a peppy smile he bought a ticket to Wenatchee, Washington. At the local Pizza Hut he filled up on chicken wings and root beer. After a long meal he walked to the Greyhound Bus Station, and stepped onto a loaded bus headed north. He wondered how it was that the border patrol didn't bust everyone in the bus, as it was clear to him that all of the people in the bus were wetbacks. He smiled as the bus pulled out of the station and drove north. The trip to Wenatchee would take three days, with many stops. In Reno, Nevada he smoked his own drugs; one hit from the glass pipe just to keep him awake. On the bus he sneezed. He hated the cold weather. At the next bus stop he bought a thick Carhartt jacket and hoodie. He was cold all the time now.

Two days later his cousins picked him up at the bus station in Wenatchee. They drove his cousin's old Honda Prelude to Brewster, Washington north along the Columbia River. His cold had gotten worse. His head ached just enough to bother him, but not enough to slow down his appetite. He wanted to party with his friends. Instead he went to an Olive Garden Restaurant, ate a big meal of beef stroganoff, and had a Redhook beer, real American food, with sourdough bread and butter. He couldn't eat it all, so they boxed it for him and he went to the shack his cousins had shared with friends for a night's sleep.

The shack was one of ten on a big apple farm in Brewster. Ignacio thought it to be the most beautiful place he had been. The stars shined, and the steep cliffs created a funnel that framed the night sky. Here was the smell of progress; the fruity smell overpowering, from the orchard. He walked to the nearest tree. He didn't know the make of the apple, but it was red with a touch of yellow. Most of the ground was used for apple or cherry orchards. Ripe fruit ready to be picked, and at the end of its growing cycle. Everywhere the orchards were lined with beat-up cars and pickups, ladders, pallets, and boxes for packing fruit. The shacks were clean and cozy, with electricity, a bathroom, and two bedrooms. His cousin stayed all year as a permanent employee, choosing not to go back to Mexico.

Ignacio woke up to a full cabin. There were over twelve people sleeping on the floors, couch, and two to a bed. He wobbled outside to get air, light rain, and snow. He smiled, "Chignow." He wiped the sweat from his forehead, and thought, I love this place in the fall. It was the shit. "Chingow." He felt terrible inside. Back in the shack it was warm and cozy. Other than a snore coming from the two bedrooms, it was peaceful. He went to the toilet, coughing, trying to be quiet but the huge gobs of phlegm only came up with the most extreme effort. The amount of crap that came from him was amazing. It floated on the top of the toilet water, and he felt the need to look at it once more before he'd flushed. He fell asleep on the couch, waking with a severe headache. Someone was making eggs, beans, and coffee. He stood, took a deep breath, and wobbled. Ignacio collapsed face down on the floor. His friends helped him into the bathroom where he stayed on the toilet, shitting and pissing until he couldn't go anymore. He was laid down on the couch. He thought of the jungle people; how sick they were. He could taste the filthy dump outside the city and his throat burned.

"Chingow."

The jungle people had the H1N1 virus. At the dump a form of swine flu had developed, had mixed, and mutated with the H1N1. Both strains were different than any before. Their hosts had carried the new virus out of the tunnel and into the sunlight of restaurants and stores. Two illegal travelers had been picked up by the border patrol and sent to overcrowded jail cells. The rest of the tunnel travelers had taken cars, busses, and vans in every direction but south. Three days later the original importers were dead. The virus attacked the throat leaving the carrier with a filthy toxic taste in his mouth, and then went to work in the head, clogging the brain with fluid thus twisting the messages the brain sent for the body.

When Ignacio's cousin's boss checked to see why his workers were not in the orchard, he found all sick with the flu. Ignacio was already dead and hauled to the hospital. Along the way he infected the ambulance drivers, and the State Patrol officer passed the virus to the entire station. Friends and families passed the virus on to hundreds, then thousands.

THE DROP

CHAPTER 7

WHILE IGNACIO WAS CRAWLING THROUGH the low tunnel into Arizona, Tom was making a drop of ten pounds of the best weed, Hindu Kush. Garrett asked Tom to make the delivery for him. He was worried about the amount and sale to one of his customers. Garrett had a bad feeling about this delivery, and had expressed his concerns to his mom, who'd asked Tom to complete the deal. It was to be made at a trailhead near the town of Chelan, on a good size ridge that had a winding four-mile drive to the end of the road. Rather than worry about the winding road and the possibility of ambush, Tom avoided the road altogether and rode his mountain bike in from the other direction.

Garret's delivery was to be to an old high school buddy. Josh showed up on time in a Chevy pickup truck with a small camper. He stopped his pickup then looked at each car in the parking lot. Most of the cars were from people out for a night run or hike. He turned and watched the winding road. When nobody came, he got out of the truck to piss in the fading daylight. Tom popped up from behind some bushes, dressed like a hunter with face paint and full camo. "I came to sell some weed!" Tom yelled.

Josh whirled around, stammering,"Um uh, uh, ya just a moment." He reached for a bag. Tom came near to Josh and whispered, "So you got twenty thousand?" Josh looked around nervously. Tom handed Josh the big square bundle of weed and Josh handed Tom a pack. As he handed it over, Tom noticed movement in Josh's camper window. Two men jumped out of the back of the camper. Tom grabbed Josh by the left arm, pulling him to the ground. Josh stuttered, "This is not my idea, so take it easy."

Dorn and his brother leveled guns at Tom and Josh. Dorn yelled, "Send the weed over here and you won't get hurt!" Tom turned and ducked behind a Subaru. Shots started raining down on the car. From Tom's side bag he pulled two soda can sized tear gas grenades, pulled the tab, and threw in the direction of Josh's truck. With a grip of steel, Tom held on to Josh. Gunshots blasted from the brothers. Windows of cars and trucks exploded onto them. Tom tried to pull Josh behind the car. Dorn watched the can hit the roof of the truck and fall near him. Tom pulled a Glock 9mm from his jacket and fired under the Subaru at the legs of Dorn and Ted. The bullets hit both men in the boots and they screamed in pain. Ted fired from over the hood of the pickup while his brother fired from under the truck. Tom fired six rounds at Ted, hitting him in the shoulder twice. Ted winced in pain then sat down to reload his gun. Dorn was reloading when Tom appeared from around the pickup. Both Ted and Dorn, hit with pepper spray, yelled as the chemicals blinded them. Tom kicked the shotgun from Ted's hands then delivered a kick to his face. Ted hit the ground bleeding. Dorn tried hard to hit Tom with his fist. Tom grabbed the rifle from him and flung it down a hill. He punched Dorn in the face and snatched the big bag of weed. He left the Hopson Brothers on the ground, hurting. Josh was lying dead, his feet shredded from shotgun blasts; another had hit him in his face.

Tom took off down the trail, running north from where he'd come. He ran, taking deep breaths to calm himself down. He heard Josh's pickup start, and positioned himself for a view of the scene. He saw Ted and Dorn driving away and could see that Josh's body was gone. He was relieved to be away, and hoped they'd dispose of Josh's body. Tom had more running before he could reach his mountain bike. He stopped for a moment, looked around, and listened. He heard footsteps and stepped off the trail and behind a tree just in time, A couple came around the corner, chatting. When they'd passed, Tom continued on; he did not want to be seen by anyone. It would be all that was needed to tie him to the death of Josh. His mountain bike was stashed under a tree. Tom cleaned the camo off his face, and put on bright colors that bikers sometimes wear, a helmet, headlamp, and fancy bike gloves. The camo clothes were stashed in his side bags. He donned the clear Oakley wrap-around glasses and a fake grey mustache that smelled of toxic glue.

The ride was easier once Tom made it back to asphalt. The dirt trail was rough, and he'd crashed a couple of times, without being hurt. He rode past a group of women out for a walk, then to the driveway of 25 Mile Sky and to the little room above the garage. He dressed in clean clothes after showering.

Garret came out of the house, hearing his dogs. "Tom, what happened? There was a call on my radio of a shooting. Cops up there right now going over the trailhead."

Tom stopped and turned to Garret, "Man, if we're going to do this, problems are going to arise. Don't worry about it."

Garrett said, "So there was a problem? I knew it. Man, we're in deep shit."

Tom grabbed Garrett's arm and spoke quietly, "Listen Garrett, nothing happened, everything is ok. I'm going back to my cabin and you're going inside to watch TV. In the morning you'll do whatever you do, but you will not worry because there is nothing wrong." Tom let him go.

Garret shot back, "I'm going to call Josh, right now!" Tom stepped closer to Garrett, not wanting to frighten him. He put his hand on Garrett's shoulder. "Don't call him for a few days." He lightly slapped Garrett on the cheek. "Don't worry about it, nothing happened."

Driving home was treacherous. Waves were slamming the boat from side to side. Logs had been pulled out into the water by the wind and wave action. Tom stopped the boat allowing it to idle. He pulled out the Glock 9mm he had used. The bullets were all rubber. Painful, but not lethal. He dropped the remaining bullets into the water, then let the Glock pistol drop from his hand into the lake. "Good luck finding that." He filled his hiking shoes with rocks and let them sink in the deep lake. Everything that could tie him to the scene of the crime was dumped overboard that night. He put the throttle forward making Stehekin at 3:39 am. He was tired. His feet hurt. For once he felt his age; his body ached and something was in his shoe. He lay down and slept in his cabin for three hours. He woke to Sally, sitting next to him. Woody was next to her with a stick in his mouth, his tail moving back and forth like a fan.

Sally asked, "What happened out there? I got a worried call from Garrett. What happened? I'm the boss here, you know. Don't leave anything out."

Tom sat up. "Things were going well. I handed Josh his big bag of weed, then two guys jumped out of the back of his camper with guns. They looked crazy and started shooting. Of course, I did the same. Shot both of them in the feet with rubber bullets. When the smoke cleared I found Josh dead, with buckshot in his face, chest, and legs. I sprayed the bastards with pepper spray, grabbed the bag of weed, and got out."

Sally wiped her eyes, "So Josh is dead?" Sally broke out crying as Tom said, "I had nothing but rubber bullets. They would not have been that lethal. They shot him. Probably robbed him of his buy money, then looked to rob me." Sally wiped her face, "He's dead because of me. Used to play with Garrett, ride with Darren." Tom got up. It was noon, cold and raining. Sally hugged Tom, "You saved Garrett from certain injury. Once again we owe you,"

Tom held her close, and then turned her to face him. "In this business crime is always right around the corner. Those dumbasses tried and failed. All these years you have been lucky not to be involved in trouble of this kind. You have to let this go, and make sure that everyone knows that I spent the night at Garrett's. There is nothing that could tie me to the trailhead."

"What about the shell casings? Doesn't that gun shoot them out?" Sally asked.

Tom laughed, "The casings they will find are for a Glock 9mm. That's now on the bottom of Lake Chelan. Even if I wanted, there is no way to find that weapon. Footprints are of a shoe that they will never find. I'm quite sure that nobody saw me. With that big storm that came in last night I doubt there is any physical evidence that could be tied to us. We have to hope that the body will be buried. Even if they find it, I never touched him. The two that attacked me couldn't recognize me, and I'm not sure I could recognize them." He looked out the side window at his tub. "We'll have to see what happens with those guys."

Dorn and Ted drove to Mini-Mike's dad's hunting cabin, southwest of Chelan. After a hit of crystal they looked for a spot to bury Josh. They picked an area under wood in the rotting woodshed. After burying they moved the firewood over the top of the grave. They gathered up Mini-Mike and supplies, and then moved to the hunting cabin to hide out. Josh's pickup was driven to a field and set on fire. A Chelan County deputy saw the pickup burning and called the fire department. The fire was out in less than a minute. The deputy noticed bullet holes in the camper. Dorn had been seen with Josh the morning Josh disappeared. With that knowledge, the deputies made a visit to Mini-Mike's mom's house in Chelan. She gave up nothing, but the deputies put an APB on Ted and Dorn. Mini-Mike had no idea that Josh had been killed, or that he was buried under Mike's woodpile. But Mike's fear of cops turned out to be a good thing. He spent the last of their money on food for the hunting cabin and they spent Thanksgiving at the cabin deep in the woods, drinking, popping pills, smoking crystal, and had no thoughts of what they would do after they ran out of food. The big storm that rocked Stehekin washed out the dirt road to the cabin. They felt safe and secure after they'd shot two deer, enough food for a couple more weeks.

Tom waved goodbye to the Sky Family. After dropping them off at 25 Mile Sky, he picked up more food and supplies, once again wondering why Sally needed to stock up with so much food. He rode back to Stehekin once again in the overloaded Sky Boat. Tom and Woody would be on their own for two weeks. Even Kenny Delanny would leave for Seattle. Thanksgiving was clearing the folks out of Stehekin. The café and bar would be closed while they were away. Tom was relieved to be alone. Finally all he had to do was to take care of the animals and the plants; no hiking or deliveries. There was ample reason to be worried about the botched delivery to Josh. Garrett had heard nothing. Josh's body had not been found, but his burned pickup was found. The deputies were quite sure of foul play, but with no body they had little to go on. A missing persons report was filed by Josh's mom. That's how far it got.

WILLIAM COLTER

CHAPTER 8

WILLY COLTER CLEANED HIS CABIN, hoping his sister from Brewster was coming. She had sent a letter a few days before saying she would visit. Two days later she hadn't come. The big rock fireplace he had built was full of small cobwebs. With a broom he swept them away, onto the floor, smashing the spiders as they fell. He scratched at his nuts, which were not used to boxer briefs. After the rock fireplace was clean, he went to work cleaning the logs from the inside. The pesky spiders had burrowed into the spaces between logs. He swept them all out, onto the floor, and then cleaned the windows with his cloth towels. The only paper in his house was toilet paper. He would not buy paper towels right away and vowed to start all his fires with dried pine needles, something he had plenty of.

Willy was a survivalist. He believed the financial collapse was just the start of the collapse of the United States of America, It didn't help that a black man had become the president either. His kitchen and panty were full of the raw materials needed to survive for a year. Five gallon buckets of wheat, flour, rice, oats and other materials. The cabinet was loaded with chili, his favorite food. He had cans from Dennison's and Dinky Moore, just to name a few. In two boxes he had freeze-dried food; the kind backpackers used. They sat on six cases of military style MRE's (meals ready to eat.)

On the closed in porch he had three tin garbage cans full of dog food for his black lab. Eight cases of Alpo canned dog food sat next to the garbage cans. Ten cases of Miller Beer were stacked in a nearby location, along with four monster packs of toilet paper from Costco.

From inside a cabinet he pulled his last pack of smokes. He couldn't wait until he went into town for more, Camel straights was his brand, no filters. He loved that camel on the pack. For Forty-nine years of his sixty-five years he had smoked the brand that John Wayne had pushed onto him.

Today was the day to go to town. He prepared by pushing his dresser to the side. He reached down and pulled up three floorboards, exposing a secret locker he'd built under the floor. Inside were a hunting rifle, and a Colt AR15 assault rifle. Other items inside the box were boxes of ammo and full clips for the AR, along with four handguns. He unlocked a metal safe. He turned the dial on the combination lock then grasped the dial and pulled it up. Inside were neat stacks of cash and other valuables.

Inside the big pocket of his Big Jim overalls he slipped a small Colt .380 pistol. He racked a round then put the safety on. He'd pulled out two hundred dollars then went to the kitchen drawer where he pulled out a Colt .45 and a genuine Marine K-Bar dagger. He stuffed both in his inside jacket pocket.

He drove down the road in his old Ford pickup, his black dog Blackie sat next to him moving as Willy fishtailed around the corner. Willy spoke to Blackie through clenched teeth; he slapped the metal where his Colt lay, "You'll never catch me with one of those German or South American guns, ugh buddy?" He rubbed Blackie on the head so hard he fell onto the floor.

"Hold onto something, my old boy!" He drove up to the Post Office first, picked up his mail, two checks from social security, and two from the Masons Union. He cashed them at the local bank, bitching the whole time about how long it took to cash them.

At the local grocer he stocked up on fresh meat and six cartons of smokes, in front of him a scraggly Mexican was buying Sudafed and other cold remedies.

On his way back to his cabin he talked to Blackie, "Godam wetback Mex's everywhere you turn. Never speak a word of English, goddam what is the world comin' to?"

Later that evening he made a loaf of bread in the old wood cook stove, and set it on the table to cool. Willy felt lightheaded and went outside for fresh air. He walked along the riverbank smoking a cigarette. From the

GEORGE THIELMAN

woodpile he carried four armloads of wood inside then set about chopping for a half an hour. In midstroke he felt a pain in his chest so bad that he dropped the axe in the grass, he put his hands to his chest and fell next to the woodpile dead.

SIMON JORDAN
NOVEMBER

CHAPTER 9

SIMON JORDAN WAITED FOUR DAYS for his father to return from the store. His dad had left notes reminding him to stay at the cabin and not to wander off. He was a big kid, nineteen, and carried a serious expression. Most people thought him to be angry. In reality, he really was serious; seriously thinking about one thing or another. He looked down the road one more time, looked at his dad's note, then back down the road. He continued, sights landing on the riverbed. He slipped a Bear Grylls belt through the belt loops of his Bear Grylls survival trousers then slipped the brand new Bear Grylls survival knife his dad had given him before this trip. He slipped his genuine Bear Grylls jacket on, and stuffed a down jacket into his medium-sized REI pack. Small binoculars, a camera, a plastic tarp, a roll of 4-millimeter nylon rope, a water bottle, three apples and six granola bars were layered into the pack. A Bear Grylls down jacket, extra socks, and a pair of fingerless gloves followed. In his Bear Grylls cargo pants and shirt he stuffed a compass. Bear Gryll's pocket knife, 16 foot tape measure, magnifying glass, small head lamp with extra batteries, one cup water bottle, survival radio, notepad with a pen, and mechanical pencil with extra lead and a arrow tip just like the one that Bear Grylls had found on one of his TV survival adventures and secured to a long stick to make a spear. On his head he put a Bear Grylls grey beanie with the name in big bold letters Bear Grylls. Unlike Bear Grylls, he brought along a box of waterproof survival matches and a Bic Lighter.

He put the pack on and across the street, trudging down the embankment to the riverbed. He walked to within six feet of the water line, and then sat down on a huge log. His dad would not let him come down here. Here he was though, sitting on an old log stripped clean of branches and bark. He imagined the log floating on the river spinning, scraping along rocks, and bridge riprap entangling with other logs making log jams. He wanted to stand on a logjam. He loved the idea of a logjam, now he had a chance to do what he wanted. He pulled out from his shirt a note pad and pen, both encased in a Ziploc baggie, then the tape measure. He measured the circumference of the log; he measured the length of the log, and then wrote all the measurements down neatly in his pad of paper.

Several rocks stuck his fancy so he measured them then sketched them as best he could. With the important work done he sat in heaven with river rocks all around him, big ones bigger than beach balls some smaller some a little bigger, he noted the size differences of the rocks. Sitting on the logs he pulled out his compass took a bead on North then took a look behind him that was south; he took his glasses off and studied everything without them on. Without the transitional tint he found he was squinting, and he noted that.

The sun was warm bearing down on the dark skin of his hands. He was suddenly worried about heat exposure. He looked at the small thermometer: 50 degrees. He didn't have to worry. He looked at the hairs on his hands concerned by what he saw. He took off his jacket, survivor shirt, and technical sweater, now he could get a good look at the whole of his arm hair. He focused on the arm, holding it up in front of his face as one would hold a bug for a closer look. The sun felt good on his arm. Looking at the black hair on his arm, he saw a shape of an old bicycle, the kind with the huge wheel in the front and the tiny one in the back.

With his other hand he lightly ran his hand over the hairs moving them. The effect was immediate. A shape in that of old German submarine appeared. He moved the hairs again. This time he saw a pirate ship papered with black sails and skull and crossbones. He put his sweater and jacket back on, then pulled out the notebook and made notations and sketches of what he saw on his arm. He underlined the pirate ship and German U-boat, noting that he wasn't happy about seeing them. He had an idea. He ran up the riverbank to a large log that was hanging over the river. Carefully he made his way to the end of the log. Here he could get a good look at the river rock below him. Holding onto a branch he strained to look at the rocks. Sure enough, an image appeared. His eyes linked rocks to make the image of the Titanic, and he noted that in his notes.

From his pocket he pulled a lime green shape the size of a big egg. On the back was a small piece of rubber attached to a string on either side. He pulled the rubber, and the string came out He attached it over his beanie, and shook his head to see if he could make smallest headlamp in the world fall off. It didn't fall off. He pulled it off and clicked the button on. The light came on, he clicked it again and the light flickered like a survival beacon. He put it away, and then looked out over the river rock before him. He looked hard. Finally a shape appeared, an old British castle with a tower off to one side. Out came the pad and pen. He liked the castle but not the tower.

Finally he had the chance to do something he never did before. He pulled out his Bear Grylls survivor knife and measured the blade length, four and three quarter's inches the overall length was ten inches. At the end of the handle was a hammer with serrations like a framing hammer. At the end of a small lanyard was a whistle. He blew it, then, embarrassed he put it away. He looked around to make sure nobody saw him blow the whistle. In the sheath, folded up behind the knife, was a metal sharpening stone. On the front of the sheath was a small t-shaped object. It was a fire-starting rod. He put everything back in its place and took more notes. He wasn't sure if, when taking notes, he should spell out the numbers with letters and words or if he should just write down the numbers. As he read them with a tape measure, he was frustrated about that and groaned, a child's groan. He wondered if other people saw and heard him groan. He looked around, nothing but trees and bushes, and he could still see the cabin. He tried the groan again. The way he talked and sounded had changed several years in the past but he still missed that little kid groan he was so used to. He couldn't do it and wrote that down," not happy at the sound of my groaning." Again he was frustrated. He put his hand to his forehead hitting it four times, bap, bap, bap, bap. Now he could think.

He emptied everything in his pockets, laying them in a straight line; had to be straight! He smeared special bug juice that was combined with sun block onto his arms. He looked at his library card then bus pass, then put them where they would be ready when he needed them. He had several playing card size survival cards. One showed how to signal air planes. Another showed the different knots one would need in the wilderness. Another was about bugs. One was about trees and bushes, another about fish, and another about wilderness animals. He stacked them all in his front chest pocket. He pulled everything out, when he realized he had not measured them. When he was finished stowing his stuff back in his pockets he turned to the cabin and looked at the compass. The Entiat River was flowing north. He looked back at the cabin one more time then turned his attention north, happily hopping from one rock to the other. When he got to an area without river rocks he balanced across logs and sticks. After a mile he ran out of rocks and sticks and logs. He pondered what he would do, but first he would write it down. "Out of sticks, rocks and logs - ready to walk on gravel and sand." The sand created new difficulties and he noted that. He remembered that to get out of the wilderness Bear always put a leaf in the water to see which way the lightweight leaf would flow. That was the way to go. He decided he wanted to stay in the wilderness, so he went upstream. He noted, "Didn't have to put leaf in water, and could see which way it was going because of the speed of the water."

Simon had a form of Autism called Asperger Syndrome, a high functioning form; he could read and write at high level. When it came to social interaction he was inept. Some people thought he was retarded. He could do great things with math and science, and read books at fast clip, but he had never spoken a word in his life. He had some other maladies, but his dad had never told him what they were. For the last year he had been seeing shapes in books, letters, magazines, rocks on a beach, and sand. He always sketched what he saw in one of his notebooks.

Also a year ago he had discovered the survivor shows on the Discovery Channel. One show stared a Canadian that went into the wilds by himself, with cameras that he could attach to a pole, and filmed himself as he traveled through the remote places. He carried a water bottle and a multi tool, a tool that resembles pliers. The handles held a file, screwdriver, big blade, small blade, can opener, bottle opener, and a wire cutter. The Canadian was careful, deliberate, and rarely took chances. He tried hard to survive, and rarely killed animals, eating mostly edible plants.

Of the survive show stars Simon's favorite was Bear Grylls from England. A former member of Britain's elite Special Forces group, the SAS, he had stood on the summit of Mount Everest. He was loud and somewhat of a showoff, serious, and highly capable in any situation. He would start the show by jumping backward off the skids of a helicopter into his adventure. To keep things interesting he would land his parachute into an iced-up lake, swim to shore, strip down to nothing, wring his clothes out, and then go about surviving. Viewers were grossed out by the things he ate. Snakes were gobbled up after he bit the head off and swallowed like a piece of licorice. He ate disgusting grubs and bugs, and was not afraid to vomit up his meals. Raw frogs, fish, and lizards were his meals. One show he found a five-foot boa constrictor. Not ready to make camp for the day, he slipped the big snake around his shoulders. When he had covered a few more miles and was ready to camp for the night, he snapped the snake against a rock like a wet towel, then started a fire and cooked the snake for dinner. He climbed trees, train trestles, mountains, canyon walls, and traveled the oceans with his self-made rafts. In one episode Bear needed to swim across a cold bay in Scotland. He was cold and tired, and the Northern Atlantic Ocean water was extremely cold. On a rock Bear found a dead harbor seal. He'd gutted it and skinned it in such a way that he had a custom tailored seal vest. With his new duds on, he jumped in the water and swam to civilization and the end of the episode.

All the survivalists in shows spent a great deal of energy making camp, and wood or bamboo beds high enough to get out of the way of marauding nocturnal animals of the night. They made shelters with roofs of palm leaves, bark, bushy tree limbs, and sometimes even made an awesome shelter from man made junk that happened to float down a river or was just sitting on the beach. Simon was thinking about what to make for a shelter. He was formulating an idea as he hiked. He stopped, looked around, and noticed a good flat spot above the riverbank. He carefully hiked to the riverbank to investigate the place for his building. He pulled out the notebook then went about his sketch. He would look about at times then go back to sketching. He was smiling, nodding his head, raising his eyebrows, and rolling his eyes. The sketch looked great when he was finished. Along the riverbank he found a nine-foot branch. He placed it about four feet up, between two trees on two branches of equal height. This was the main support pole. At the riverbank he found more branches around eight feet long. He leaned the branches against the support pole then added flat pieces of bark. Inside he layered boughs from a cedar tree. He stood back and admired his work; his first lean-too.

At the opening he made fire pit with a two-foot fire ring. The back was higher so the fire and heat would reflect back on him. He gathered firewood, big and small, and dry pine needles. From the woodpile he picked out an eight-inch high bough with a stem about one inch thick. It looked like a Christmas tree. He held it in front of his face, smiled, and pulled out his Bic lighter. He flicked the lighter and held the small flame under the wood Christmas tree. It caught fire easily. He set it on pine needles and added more sticks and small pieces of wood until he had a great fire going.

He stood back smiling,"Ya!" He had just spoken the first word of his life. The pine needle bed felt good to him. He munched on an apple as he lay, looking up at his first creation.

GEORGE THIELMAN

Without a fire or sleeping bag, he got cold when the fire died out. He woke up refreshed but cold. He was happy and content. Breakfast was a canteen of water and a granola bar. He took a picture of his lean–to then took off, hiking north. His solar-powered Casio watch said it was 9:36 AM. He clicked a button; the altimeter said he had gained 222 feet since he had left camp two hours earlier. He made notes of the time, a description of the place he was standing, and noted how long it took to write and sketch the description of the description. Along the riverbank he hiked. The air was colder. He looked at his breath, and then made a note and a sketch of him blowing his breath in the morning air. For three hours he hiked along the river bank, snooping, and looking under rocks and logs for snakes and lizards to eat. A squirrel would do nicely so he went about making a snare. He spent three hours making and trying to lure a squirrel into the snare. He went to bed hungry, sleeping next to another fire on pine needles. Three times in the night he had to add wood to his campfire.

Again he woke up groggy, sore and hungry. He hiked away from the river, and up a mountain where he found an old patch of huckleberries. For two hours he collected, filling a baggy. At camp he ate the blueberries then walked to the creek to wash up. On a large flat river rock he laid on his stomach, arms in the water. When he finished, he opened his eyes, looking into the stream at hundreds of salmon. Back at camp he pulled out the old arrowhead, attached it to a ten-foot branch then crept to the river, staying low so as not to disturb the salmon. He rose up slowly with the new spear ready. Slowly he moved closer to the water. From three feet away he stabbed at a lazy unsuspecting fish. The arrow pierced the fish dead center. Simon's fish was slung to the shore, gutted, and cooked over the campfire; the pink fillet fell away from the light bones. Two days later he was in the same camp spot with another lean-to. This one was smaller with enclosed sides. He ate salmon each day. On the third night the snow came. With it came twenty-degree temperatures and rain. The wet snow made it through the bark roof.

Cold and wet, he went to the creek, this time to a deeper and fast-moving water. He raised the spear then, moving to a wet rock for more room. When he stabbed at the fish he slipped on the rock, sending him headfirst into the river. He hit his head on a rock, and the water carried him to deeper water, then into light foamy rapids. He pumped his arms and legs, but the water was too shallow to swim effectively. As hard as he tried he could barley breathe Finally, he figured it out, as the water moved him forward he would get on both hands and feet and hop from one spot to another until he grabbed a hold of a branch, he pulled himself out of the water. He still had his pack on and had lost only the spear.

Ten minutes later he was naked in front of a small fire, his clothes hanging in front of the fire. He had no intention of hiking back to his camp a quarter mile upstream. Fire ripped through the dry pinewood growing and spreading warmth. Simon looked out at the river that had almost drowned him; no thoughts of regret or fright. Wet snow fell all night. Luckily he found a pile of cut firewood. All night he stood and leaned against a tree shivering and holding his clothes over the fire so they would dry. He had no idea or thoughts of why there was a big pile of stacked and cut firewood, or why the ground and grass growing out of it was flat and cut. A terrible stink came and went with a slight breeze. He didn't care.

He fell asleep against a tree, sitting up, the firelight dancing on his face. Two inches of snow had fallen. It was cold. His down jacket was still sopping with the river water and his shoes were wet. Early in the morning he had put his clothes back on, damp and uncomfortable. The cold had gotten bad in the night. He couldn't handle the freezing cold anymore, the clothes helped, but shivering was all he could do. The firewood saved him.

The sun came up, or in his case down, over the mountains. It was cold, but still life-giving. His attitude changed; he smiled, shivering against the tree with his wet clothes on. Never had he watched with such joy as the sun came up. He remembered the movie 127 hours where the young man, Aaron Ralston, his hand stuck in between the rock and the canyon wall, waited in pleasure as the sun came up just enough to lift his spirits for a few minutes every day.

Following the sun he walked away from his campfire, and past the woodpile. He looked down in the grass. On the opposite side of the woodpile lay a dirty body He looked at it. A bloated man lay in the dirt, skin almost grey, and eyes and mouth wide open. His body looked unusually fat. Red flannel jacket, and an old pipe in his hand, he was wearing Big Jim denim overalls. His boots were old and untied. On the body laid twelve to sixteen inches sticks. All around the body were tennis balls, old, and nearly worn out. Near the old man's feet were four salmon carcasses. The terrible stink drove him backward, his hands in front of his face, trying to shoe the vial, disgusting smell from his face. He stepped backward several steps, stopping against something hard and flat. He turned and looked backward at the object. It was a log cabin. He was eye level with the window. Inside it looked warm, a messy kitchen table with a loaf of breads a butter dish nearby.

GEORGE THIELMAN

The old rusty doorknob turned and the door opened. It was still cold inside; not as bad as outside. No thoughts of whose cabin it was. He went to the moldy bread, cutting off a big slice and slathering it with butter. The bread was stale. The inside was soft and chewy. He found a carton of milk in the refrigerator, took a swig then another. It was cold and delicious. Several scoops from an applesauce container and he was no longer hungry. He rubbed his belly, and walked to the river rock fireplace. It had a two-foot hearth that was eight feet long and two feet wide. The rocks continued curving up to the ceiling, from a rock cubby he pulled small kindling then cut it small like a Popsicle stick. Outside he found dry pine needles under a tree. They laid them out on old ashes. The unburned outer rim of fireplace box was littered with cigarette butts.

Simon started the needles then started the fire, stacking wood slowly on the growing fire. He stepped back looking at the inside of the cabin. It was one floor, rough, like it was made by hand, a little bit of a pitch, the rafters were wide open, stuffed with the owners favorite pieces of wood; all of them about an inch in circumference. Against a wall were hiking sticks: three foot four and five foot high each with a hole drilled in them and a red flannel handkerchief tied and stuck in the hole, some had been sanded and finished with shellac. Four old matching kitchen chairs surrounded a worn out table, the finish worn off, and numerous stab wounds in the top from a knife.

Several paintings of pastures with cottonwoods, one with an Indian with full headdress, another three Indians riding hard after buffalo decorated the walls of the cabin. He pulled out his camera and took pictures of the paintings then sat down on an old couch. The fabric was ripped up twill. He sat deep in the cushions then got up and tested out a recliner near the fireplace. It was perfect. He leaned back, relaxing for the first time in days. Looking up he noticed a rifle over the fireplace. A western type rifle like the western movies. He didn't want to touch it, so he left the Winchester 30-30 hanging on the two nails.

There was one bedroom with two twin beds, two dressers and a closet with a few flannel shirts neatly hung up. Two pairs of dress shoes and a pair of red wing boots lived in the corner. The windows were old, with thick pains of glass. They were stuck shut and just a bit wavy. He lay down on the bed, pulled a blanket over him, and dropped into a deep sleep that lead him to dreams of his mother and father. He spoke to them in full conversations He told them of his adventure hiking along the river catching salmon with his custom made spear, and the great fires he had made, they were so proud of him his mother kissed him on the forehead then walked away.

He woke. Lying on his back he looked up at the ceiling, old sheet rock that needed to be cleaned and painted, rolling over on his side he came face to face with a dog. He was startled and moved against the wall as far from the dog as possible. The dog's tail wagged and he smiled at the man." Hello dog," he spoke for the second time in his life. The dog had a black and pink mottled nose. He pulled out his mechanical pencil, looked at the eraser, then at the dog's nose. He touched the pink part of the nose then smiled. It was the first time he had touched a dog, the first time he had not been afraid of a dog, and the first time he spoke to or smiled at one.

In the kitchen he poured milk into a dog dish on the floor. The big black lab lapped up the milk and looked back up at Simon. Simon looked through the cabinets finding a case of canned Alpo dog food. In the pantry were two fifty-pound bags of dry dog food. He mixed the wet and dry food in the dish. The dog ate, taking huge scoop shovel bites then sat down, tail wagging, looking straight at Simon. Whenever Simon looked at the dog its tail would wag. The kitchen stove was an old cast iron oval with a small oven. He started a fire then cooked up a can of Dennison's chili. Eating from the can he looked out the window at the river. The sun was down but it was still light, and a deer walked across the opposite side of the river, munching on leaves. The night was cold. Simon kept the fire going all night. He slept on the old man's bed, waking up with the lab curled up beside him.

In the morning Simon opened the door for the dog and went back to the table to make notes. When he finished, he went outside to retrieve his pack at his fire pit. He walked around the outside of the house, and saw the dog lying against the dead man. The dog looked up at him, wagging his tail. From the pack Simon pulled out his tape measure. He measured the old man from head to toe, and measured his width. He picked up the fish carcasses and threw them into the river. Under a tree Simon wiped two inches of snow from the ground. Carefully he marked out the appropriate size rectangle with small stones, all carefully chosen from the streambed. They were as round as he could find and all were near to the same size, about the size of a Ping-Pong ball. Two hours later he finished the three-foot by six-foot hole. The measurements were written down in his notebook. He then sealed the notebook in the baggy, put it in his pocket and walked out to the old man. From the old man's house he brought out a blanket. While rolling the old man onto the blanket a pocketknife fell out onto the grass. He kicked it out of the way, wrapped the old man in the blanket, and pulled him into the hole. Before he started to fill the hole back up he pulled out the tape measure. Satisfied, he filled the dirt in the hole.

When the old man was covered, Simon looked at the remaining dirt wondering what to do with it. He sat down thinking about the dirt and why there was so much left over. Then deduced that the old man's skinny body had displaced the dirt. He pulled out the notebook and noted the size of the hole he dug then measured the amount of dirt left over and noted that.

When he came back to the woodpile there were two salmon laying on the ground. The black lab looked up at him wagging his tail. Simon kneeled down next to the dog. He hugged him then looked straight at the dog, "Thanks, buddy." He picked up the fish then noticed the pocketknife. He picked it up holding it to the light. The handle was made of bone with reddish-brown wear markings. It was in great condition. On the blade he read a laser-etched inscription, "John Wayne, True Grit," He pocketed his new knife then went back to the house to cook the salmon.

A week later the salmon were gone, spawning season over. Simon was crushed. He sat by the banks early in the morning sipping hot tea. The snow fell, yet he sat, parka on. The black lab brought him sticks. Simon threw the stick. It flew through the air, hit a branch, and landed four feet into the water. The lab jumped in the river after it. Simon noticed smaller silver fish scatter as the dog swam. He stood and shouted," Trout!" He ran to the house. In the rafters he found two fishing poles, and a fishing tackle box filled with homemade lures, spinners, weights, fishing line and bobbers. He checked out his survival cards for the correct knot to use to tie the spinner to the line. He spent countless hours learning how to cast with the Okuma spinner. Two days later he snagged his first trout; not a big fish, ten inches. He cooked it in a cast iron pan. Curiously it curled in the pan. Good eating. He had found his fresh food. As time went on the trout became much more difficult to catch.

JANUARY 4

Other than dog food, Simon was out of food. He made a hard decision, dressed up in his warmest clothes and took off down the road to the cabins that lined Entiat River. He never thought to check the stacked up five gallon buckets for food or the stacked up boxes of canned food. He had never seen food in buckets or boxes. In the first cabin he found cans of food, enough for another month. He broke into the second and third cabins; all were vacant, being vacation cabins. He helped himself to clothes, toilet paper, plates, cups, knives, soda pop, a hatchet, barbecue briquettes, batteries, blankets, survival books and magazines, and all the other stuff one would find in a home or cabin. With the hardy black lab following him they survived, fishing every day.

One snowy day he was bored and pulled the rifle down from the rock fireplace. He held it then laid it on the kitchen table and looked at it. He had never shot a gun. He was hesitant and worried about what to do with it. He thought hard about where he'd seen that type of rifle. With his father he used to watch western movies; that was the type, "a Winchester rifle." He picked it up and pulled the lever with the loop in it. It clicked hard. Inside he could feel things moving. A bullet popped from the ejection port. He set the rifle down and picked up the bullet. It was long and brass colored. He put the rifle back on its pegs.

He looked through the collection of books he'd picked up from the other cabins and found one called, *A Hunter's Guide, a Handbook for the Hunter.* He sat down and read the book from cover to cover. He went back to the shelf, found hunting magazines and read them. After two days of reading everything he had, he hiked to another cluster of cabins where he found more books and magazines along with food and clothes. At one of the cabins he found a treasure chest of food, beans, sugar, rice, flour, oats, pasta, cases of canned goods and packages of macaroni and cheese, popcorn and candy. In a storage shed he found a blue plastic sled. He loaded the supplies onto the sled and secured them with bungee cords. Four trips from the house to the cabin, and he was supplied again for a couple months. Simon fished every day as he read the books and magazines he had found. As more cabins were raided, the old man's cabin began to fill with stuff: boxes, paintings, pictures, and on the fireplace hearth was a new collection hatchets and fishing poles.

At the start of Simon's adventure he had no thought of why he was hiking away from his family's cabin or why he sat on a rock for six hours just to see how many shapes he could see in a field of river rocks. Four months later he was thinking for himself, looking ahead to the next day and week, soaking beans for a full day so they could be cooked the next day. Now he could be seen thinking through his days, fishing for food, reading then applying what he learned to his own fishing tactics. Success did not come easily. The snow was two feet deep but he carried on. The clothes he had found were perfect for foul weather. He wore snowmobile clothes outside and always stayed on the dirt road track.

GEORGE THIELMAN

February found him hiking along the dirt road. He stopped at a mailbox with the name, Gurdy Clausen painted with black and pink paint. He looked at the cabin; its fireplace chimney was spewing smoke. He could see a garage and a storage shed. Inside the cabin Gertrude sat at her red speckled table with chrome legs, sipping her tea and playing solitaire. She wore a long fleece sweater given to her by her son. Under her sweater was a thick pair of sweat pants. Her feet were cozy with REI extra-warm socks and Sorel slip-on boots.

Two days before, a family of raccoons had decimated her cat's litter of kittens. They'd lived in the screened-in porch, but the raccoons found a tear and entered, eating all but the mother. Gurdy said out loud, "Damned dirty birds, killing such cute little kittens!" She turned over a couple of cards then looked at her wood stove, then at her timer. In fifteen minutes left she would have roasted chicken. Garbage was thrown into the river at a small six-foot cliff at the end of the garden. She had grand ideas for the upcoming spring garden. Seeds were already packed away in small envelopes and she had several paintings of the layout; cute watercolors that could have easily been used as covers for "Mother Earth News," with red lettuce, yellow Kruk nick squash, onion bulbs sprouting and a sandstone path between the rows of award-winning vegetables.

Gurdy nibbled at a slice of sweet squash bread, and picked up an issue of Readers Digest. She had read them all, and now she was snowbound and hadn't seen her son Collin in four months. On top of that, the power went out, the mail stopped coming, and her kittens were eaten by a family of hungry raccoons. She crushed her cigarette into her 1955 pure glass Elvis ashtray. She loved menthols, smoked twenty a day, and had lived to be eighty-three. She coughed hard then spat a gob of gooey spit in the sink. She hobbled back to her chair, checked the timer then flopped her butt in the chair. She had gained so much weight that all she could fit in were her sweatpants and some dresses. Her sweatpants smelled bad. Before supper she would take a whore's bath. She pulled a three-gallon black enamel pot from the table without so much as a grunt. She was strong from twenty years of living in this place. She pulled off the sweater, then sweatpants, off came the panties. She cleaned herself in the kitchen with an old washrag. Gurdy dried off, and then sprinkled powder on her body. She was humming quietly when the front door shook. She looked up. Through the dirty windows she saw a black man checking the windows. She slipped on her sweatpants, t-shirt, and fleece top, then the boots. She grabbed a small baseball bat that her son used to use in peewee baseball.

UPLAKE

Simon walked through the snow to the riverside of the house, checking windows. He stepped up onto a porch then walked to the side door. He pulled a small hatchet from his jacket that he used to smash windows. With his wet gloved hand the hatchet slipped out onto the icy porch. He bent over to pick it up. The door opened and Gurdy appear with the bat. She swung the bat like a golf club, hitting Simon in the forehead. He reeled back, using the last of his conscious mind to take two big leaping steps backward then launched off the porch into the garden area. He landed with a thump, knocking the air out of his lungs. He moaned then passed out. He was suffocating. Gurdy ran out of the house, down the steps, and held the bat in the air, ready to hit him again. She suddenly noticed he wasn't breathing.

She set the bat down and wagged a finger at Simon, "I'm sorry young man, but I can't let anyone rape me, my, my that wouldn't be right, and I can't let you stay in the garden for the rest of winter, now can I?" Simon was lying on his back, his head toward the riverside. She walked to the riverside, pulling him by the arms to the edge of the six-foot embankment. A minute later she couldn't pull anymore, so she tried to push him, but she couldn't get any traction in the snow. She stood over him then turned her back to the river. She reached down and grabbed through his Bear Gryll's belt. She lifted him up by the belt then took one good step backward.

The slick snow allowed Simon's body to slide more easily than she'd anticipated. Simon slid into Gurdy, and her fingers caught in his belt as she struggled to stay on her feet. Simon's body continued with the momentum started by Gurdy, and he slid over the embankment, with Gurdy sitting on his face, and her face in his crotch. Her hand had slid under his belt to her elbow. He was waking up and jerking as his lungs took in water, pinning his hard belly against her hands. The black lab watched the two of them be carried away in the river; it looked like two people giving each other oral sex as they floated down the river. The dog ran after them, but was forced to give up as they floated past him and down a small waterfall. He ran around a logjam, and to a beach down river, but they had disappeared.

THE FALL

CHAPTER 10

IGNACIO DIED IN HIS COUSIN'S SHACK. The coroner came out to the orchard to pick up his body. The two assistants were curious about the sickness of the Mexican workers. All were sick: runny noses, coughing, headaches, extreme spitting of gross phlegm. That evening one of the attendants drove with his family to Spokane to hop a plane to Florida for a winter vacation. Along with them came the virus bug. Orchard workers headed south, along the way spreading the virus. Every restaurant, bus, taxi, or plane ride or boat ride they met thousands of people, who met thousands of people, on and on, spreading. It was picking up steam, and becoming stronger. For some people death came in 24 hours. Others took over a week to die. God did not intervene, no messiah showed up in robes to heal and feed the sick. Religious people did not survive any often than anyone else. Survivors did not become zombies, or mutated humanoid underground cannibals walking the cities looking for brains to eat. Dead people didn't come to life then become biters of human flesh. Monkeys and gorillas didn't learn to speak and take over the world. Aliens didn't land in saucer-shaped spaceships and proceed to turn cows inside out. Most people died in their beds, dreaming of suffocation and hell.

Tom Trainer knew nothing of a virus, flu, or pandemic. November snow was falling. Already the temperature was cold and wet, in the 20s with rain and snow. All the animals lived in insulated buildings so they were snug and warm. The kittens Manny and Moe followed Tom from his cabin to the barn then back again. They were growing into big tomcats. Both kittens still bugged Woody, who was a year and a half, still young and funny. He lived for hiking and protecting his master. He would herd the cows away from Tom, jealous of his newfound friendship with the bovines. Philips horses were gone for two months, guiding first in the Olympic National Park then in southern Washington for three weeks. Several cats lived on the ranch, some in the massive haystack. At least three lived in the protection of Sally's back porch, and two lived in Darren's cabin. Manny and Moe lived with Tom and Woody and slept in the cabin loft; safe in the cabin to sleep and attack Woody. Woody would look at Tom, hoping for support after a guerilla attack.

The ranch was void of rodents; any rodents that didn't know the cats were there got themselves chewed up in short order. Like city cats, they ate the heads first, leaving the headless corpse next to the outside doors for the humans to find. For the most part, the cats were self-sustaining, surviving on what they hunted and small amounts of Purina Cat Chow.

Unless the cats were hunting or chasing something, they were always standing about when the cows were milked. Cats' tails straight in the air, they were on their best behavior, and always shared a bowl. After fishing the fish were always dressed out the entrails and skins were left for the cats to munch on. When a deer or elk were shot they would take the hide and lay it upside down for the cats to remove the remaining flesh.

Predators of the cats were raccoons, bigger cats such as the cougar, bears, coyotes, wild dogs, and new to the area, an occasional wolf. Sometimes the cats would get a hold of one of the chickens but the big rooster would intervene aggressively by attacking the cats with his claw, it was a great thing to see. One, because the cats were taught a lesson, and two, because it was just fun to see the cocky cats cower and run away.

Cocky was the definition of the roosters. After the successful battle, they would strut up to the hurt chicken walking around it, herding it back to the safety of the coop.

Many decades of farming with chickens in such remote areas as Stehekin had taught the Sky family that the chicken coops had to be bomb proof. The shelter itself was off the ground two feet. The inside was six by eight feet. Boxes full of hay sat a foot off the painted floor. Outside the chicken coop were trap doors so eggs could be taken without entering the coop. The chicken run was twelve by thirty feet and encapsulated the coup within its walls. The entire run was protected with metal wire. More wire kept burrowing predators out. The chicken run was next to the garden so they could forage for worms and bugs. Rarely did a chicken get eaten or killed. They were healthy, received exercise and ate well. Somewhere fat and happy. None had names, in case they where to be butchered. Not all of them were kept for eating. Some were kept alive because they were leaders, and taught the chicks the right way to grow up until they were put in the pot.

END OF NOVEMBER

Thanksgiving came with Tom cooking up one of the fattest of the chickens, gravy, potatoes, mushrooms, and sweet potatoes. It was a great meal and he went to bed full. Snow fell, the first to stick for any length of time. Without TV or a phone Tom paid little attention to the outside world. He had knowledge of the deadly virus making its way around the states. He had decided to not listen to news but to stay on the ranch taking care of the animals and plants.

One cold night he heard the cows mooing and chickens clucking. He put on his headlamp and ran, shotgun in hand, to the barn. Things were bumping around inside. He knew it had to be something of good size. With the headlamp lighting the path in front of him, he walked around the stack of hay. He laughed when he saw the Elk. His horns were stuck on a rope five feet high, used for drying plants. Tom moved to cut the rope. The frightened Elk turned his backside to Tom and kicked him in the thigh. Tom fell to the ground, and the trapped Elk continued kicking, hitting him twice and sending him flying into a corner of the barn. The elk was getting the best of him. Finally, Tom was able to collect himself enough to save himself. At point blank range he fired with the twelve-gauge. His shotgun was loaded with slugs (a fat bullet encased in plastic shell casing.) It sliced through the elk's body. Three rounds finally put the big elk down. It slammed down on the floor with a thump, its big rack stuck in the rope holding the head up. Tom cut the animal free, greatly pained from the kicks. Tired, he threaded a rope through an old block and tackle used for moving the hay around the room, then tied the rope around the back legs of the Elk and pulled it, four feet off the ground, and set a bucket under it to catch the blood. It was all he felt like doing until morning.

Like the wounded warrior he was, he hobbled back to his cabin. It was midnight. His thigh was bruised in two places, and shoulder and ribcage were all kicked bruised and battered. He laughed, looking down on Woody who was still jacked up." Man that was weird, guess I don't have to go hunting anytime soon." Woody looked up at him with a quizzical look. He reloaded his shotgun then went back to bed, once again having to move the kittens so he could find a spot to sleep. Two hours later he woke to Woody growling. He dressed then walked carefully to the barn once again. This time he heard a growl from inside. Once inside he climbed on top the haystack. He shimmied up the light and down on the other side. The elk was being slapped around by a black momma bear, her two cubs moving with the mom's movements back and forth.

Tom fired two shots into the hay to frighten the mother. Sensing danger she ran straight at Tom. Just as his headlamp flickered the big mother was upon him before he knew it. Tom was hit by a paw and sent backward, the shotgun scattering on the opposite side of the haystack. He rolled down the hay ending up unharmed and sitting up on the concrete. He rolled hard to the left as the bear cubs came running out the door after Tom. Behind them came the mother. She stopped at the door, turned to Tom, and raised her big paw to pound Tom some more. Woody harassed her, barking and biting.

He was too much for her and she ran into the darkness, Woody on her tail barking and growling in the night. By the time Tom had found his shotgun the bears were long gone. He sat down with the gun barrel between his knees, breathing hard. He was bleeding from his forehead and right forearm; his head felt woozy.

Woody sat down next to Tom, panting. Tom looked at his mutt. "Don't worry, Woody. I'm trained for this shit, man what a night." He laughed then wobbled to Sally's house and took a long bath and a shower before walking back to his cabin.

He slept until 7:30, and woke up sore and overtired. After feeding and milking the two cows, he fed the chickens letting them run through the fenced garden. The fences needed mending so he spent the rest of the day wire tying the metal wire fencing together. The six-foot high wire fence had one spot where the bears easily ran through. Tom nailed the fence to the back of the bunkhouse, then added another post, and continued nailing up wire fencing adding post where needed. Wilderness fencing was never perfect. Deer easily jumped over six foot fences. Bears were the worst for destroying fences. With their incredible strength they easily swiped posts and gates off their hinges. Tom needed more dogs to frighten away the four-legged trespassers.

GEORGE THIELMAN

After the elk and bear beating, Tom carried his full- size H&K pistol. If he went for a run or bike ride, he carried the smaller compact Glock .40 caliber in a holster under his left arm. He attached a sheath to carry an eleven-inch bowie knife for backup. He was enjoying the solitude, but did miss his friends. He wondered how things were going with the outside world. In a few days he would hike to the café start up a fire and have a quiet drink.

In the barn he dressed out the big elk, and fired up Sally's big barbecue to cook five pounds of elk steak. He laid the elk hide on the ground for the cats. They munched on the flesh till their belly's bulged. Woody ate an incredible steak, then lay down to sleep. The rest of the elk was quartered and put inside one of Sally's big freezers.

Curious about how long the Sky Family would stay away, Tom went to Sally's office, flipped on the shortwave radio and called Garrett at 25 Mile Sky. There was no reply. He called for two days. Nothing. He jumped in the pickup, and drove to the café. He started a fire in the wood stove of the bar, poured a stiff drink of tequila, and turned on the radio. There were nothing but health, warnings. One DJ only talked of death and sickness. How the virus had taken over in every city and town throughout the U.S. and Mexico. It was spreading quickly throughout the U.S. and world. In the storm entrance of the café was a box where mail could be set. Inside the box was a big stack of catalogs bills and letters. One was address to him from Sally.

Dear Tom,
We are having a good time here. My sister is very sick and I'm staying here until she gets better. Seems we all have the sniffles. Philip just left the morning after Thanksgiving to guide in the Olympic Mountains. He took six of his best horses; left the rest here in Karl's stables. Well, see you soon.

Love and kisses,
Sally

Inside was his paycheck for the month. He wanted to cook up some food in the kitchen, but didn't want to have to clean up the mess, so he poured a double tequila and added lime and ice. He sat listening to the DJ from National Public Radio talking about ways to avoid the flu; he couldn't get the Wenatchee NPR station. Back at the ranch he cooked up more elk meat for a massive pot of stew.

❖❖

Winter had come early. Heavy snow fell at the ranch, and for two weeks it was quiet with two feet of snow. Outside Tom looked around and listened. The only sound was a couple crows squawking in the distance. No plane sounds, no boats, and no cars. A couple of days before he had heard a chainsaw buzzing in the distance. Other than these sounds, he heard nothing. Maybe a cow or a chicken would make a sound or a coyote howled in the night. It felt to Tom that he was in heaven. Deer and elk could be seen walking in the pasture, and occasional bear wandered through, but kept their distance from the ranch. Beavers could be seen swimming in the cold river, pulling around small branches. Tom fished in the morning snow and caught a thirteen-inch trout for dinner. The next morning he put on his x-country skis and skated his way to the café.

He fired the woodstove box up, and tried to get something on the radio. Northwest Public Radio was all he could hear: unrest in most cities, government services were inconsistent, and hospitals were overflowing.

The virus had picked up in strength. The government tried to downplay the danger, yet in the same broadcast they stated the danger, leaving citizens with ambiguous information. Biologist and doctors worked hard every moment to find a cure or anecdote for the virus. Nothing worked. The newsman at CNN glumly reported Mexico was the start of the virus. Few in Mexico City were spared. The Western U.S. was the same. Tom shut the radio off, and turned on the shortwave, calling Garrett. Nothing. He called the Park Service. He found himself talking to a ranger at the headquarters of the North Cascades National Park. The ranger reported that most of his co-workers were sick or dead; same with the cops and people of Marblemount, Washington. Tom sat at the bar for two hours sipping tequila and eating garlic stuffed olives.

CHRISTMAS

CHAPTER 11

Ted, Dorn and Mini-Mike had spent the fall at Mini-Mike's dad's hunting cabin. As usual, Mike's mother helped him out with money and supplies, keeping them warm and fed. The Chelan County Deputies showed up asking about Ted and Dorn; all the usual questions. They were investigating a missing person and possibly a murder. Mike's mom gave the investigators nothing. A few days before, Josh's girlfriend admitted, after three hours of interrogation, that Josh was going to meet a guy to buy ten pounds of weed. Someone in Stehekin, who grew weed. The deputy visited the dispensaries and found that there was an illegal grow operation at Sky Ranch. The deputy, having grown up with Garrett and Darren Sky, was more than happy to travel to Stehekin. As he was preparing to travel to Stehekin, his wife and kids suddenly and violently became sick. The trip was postponed. He became sick two days later, and that was the end of the investigation. The Sky Family had been saved by the virus.

Deputies did however search for Ted and Dorn and came close to finding Mini-Mike. They missed him by one quarter of a block, as they drove through the town of Chelan. Fear of prison had kept Ted and Dorn in the mountains, hiding out. They were well-fed, well-armed, and dumb enough to fight it out to stay free another day.

UPLAKE

Dorn counted the last of their money stolen from Josh; three thousand, five-hundred dollars. He had sent Mini-Mike to Chelan to purchase one thousand dollars of food. Instead, Mike spent five hundred on drugs, and came back with five hundred in food. They had a great meal, and then the drugs were passed out. Most of the next month they spent fucked up, drinking cheap beer and eating Spagetti-os. By Christmas they were out of drugs. They snuck in the town of Chelan on Christmas Day. What they found was something out of a horror film. All were dead. Power was off, and they were now the Kings of the World. Anything they wanted, they took. They traveled to Brewster and took over a mansion on the river they'd always admired. They raided homes and stores. The only problem was, they were still fucked up, and bored.

BILL CRYSTAL

CHAPTER 12

BILL CRYSTAL FIRED UP HIS WEBER BARBECUE. Snow was falling, and his life had become simple. He'd lost his job at Hanford and his lover left him for another, all in one week's time. He moved to his family's small cabin near the town of Manson, a small community ten miles northwest of Chelan. He'd moved out of the Tri Cities; left behind in his apartment was all of his furniture and whatever he could not fit in his Chevy pickup. Near fifty, overweight, and jaded, the cabin was a place where could recharge and heal from his rejection. The bosses at the Hanford Nuclear Reservation considered him a whistle-blower. His education was in radiology, with a degree in biology, and a degree in animal husbandry. The authorities at the Hanford site had hired him to study the outlying areas of the nuke site. For ten years he collected dirt, lizards, snakes, bushes, leaves, and anything else that needed to be studied, to check for radiation. He was loyal, never late for work, and did his job well. The bosses didn't appreciate the safety problems he discovered.

Elevated levels of radiation were found on everything living, be it plant or animal. With the elevated levels, Bill expected to find mutated, weird creatures strolling around huge trees and bushes. Instead what he found was a diversity of creatures and plants growing normally. Bill stressed to study the long-term affects of the radiation on the plants and animals, but could not find or show definitive or lasting effects on the creatures.

As most government workers they were not expected to change anything, his findings led to no change. His bosses, embolden by Bill's findings, had fired him with the idea he was not needed. Bill got the ax, and his lover left him for another all in the same week. He lost weight and drank too much. One day he packed up his pickup and called his apartment manager as he was driving out of town. He emptied his savings and checking account.

Along the Columbia River Highway that led to Chelan he tossed his cell phone into the river. His cabin had been passed down to him from his parents. It was paid off, and was simple and cozy, with a big fireplace and stacks of firewood. Just ninety feet from Lake Chelan, it was perfect for fishing and boating. His goal was to get over his heartache and rejection by rejecting everything from his former life.

At Ray's Sporting Goods he stocked up on supplies. He bought a pump shotgun and a civilian version of the Springfield M-14, called the M1A1. Ray attached a scope for hunting, added two spare twenty round clips and five hundred rounds of .308caliber bullets. The gun was all black and scary looking, very different from anything he had owned. He bought a backup weapon, a stainless steel Smith and Wesson .45 caliber pistol. He had two days of shooting lessons, which taught him the basics.

He felt that his loss, and his own rejection of society's norms, had set him free. Thanksgiving was coming. He bought a turkey, a pickup full of food, beer-making supplies and a big collection of booze. Whiskey on the rocks was his drink. Snow fell on Thanksgiving blocking the roads, the snowplow guy never made it as far as his cabin. For eight weeks he stayed at the cabin, every morning brewing Sky Valley House Blend Coffee with bourbon, and then went to the shore to fish. His neighbors never showed up on the holidays. He spent the fall and most of the winter on Lake Chelan alone, drunk, with his pistol under his new Carhartt range jacket.

Redefining his life was his goal. He did it with booze, fishing, and by making beer in his cabin. Life at the cabin required more work than he thought, but he slogged through despite his depression. His time was spent cutting wood, repairing the cabin, and making his food from scratch. He made great pies and bread from his supplies. He spent most of his spare time fishing from his old dock; casting back and forth, and patiently standing in the wind and snow while he caught his food. Cooking fish became another hobby for him.

His rejection of society included completely avoiding TV and radio. He listened to old cassettes and CDs. On Christmas Eve he drove into Chelan. What he found was horrifying. The few people he saw were dead, lying in the street, the roads were dirty, and trash blew around the yards. He drove to Wal-Mart where he stocked up on a pickup truck of free supplies, and then to Rays where he found it locked up tight. At the coffee house he picked up twenty pounds of Sky Valley Coffee. To the top of his camper he tied up ten five-gallon bottles of propane from a grocery display. Back at his cabin he wondered what happened. He turned on his generator, and turned on the TV and radio, but found the channels all snow and the radio nothing but static. He deduced the obvious. That people had died from sickness, and that the survivors were hiding out so they weren't affected. He had dodged a bullet by spending so much time at the cabin. He spent the rest of the winter alone in his cabin.

The end of February he drove back toward Chelan, to the local alternative energy company. He picked up two solar panels, six batteries, two small windmills and all the hardware needed to set up his energy supply.

◆◆

When a three point Buck he had been watching walked onto his small grass yard, he shot it with his M1A1 from fifty feet. He had never shot an animal before, so he aimed at the buck's head. Two bullets tore apart the right side of the head; his body, out of balance, spun to the left and then ran sideways into the water. His body dropped into the water beside the dock, his head resting on the wood dock.

Bill walked outside, the rifle raised as though the buck might rise up, to shoot back at him. Bill drove his truck as near to the dock as possible, wrapped a rope around the big head, and then pulled the buck out of the water. The rope was thrown over a tree then he pulled the buck up into a hanging position. He cut its throat, and then hung it up for a few hours. He cut it from the anus upward to the chest. Guts fell out onto his pants. At first he was sickened by what he did. Then he became all right and proud of what he did. Self-sufficiency was ever expanding in his life. From then on he watched the open range next to his yard for deer and other big game. New Year's Day he shot a smaller deer.

Bill's broken heart didn't mend, but as time went on his priorities changed. Less time was spent dwelling on hurt feelings; more time was spent on living, fishing and hunting, and preparing food. This was now essential for life, and not just a reason to go to the mountains. Several cabinets were full of can goods; he used them only when necessary. Nearby vacation homes were used for collecting supplies; those that held the dead were left alone. At first Bill was conflicted about breaking into another's home. He was concerned about breaking laws. Trespassing was a serious crime, as was breaking and entering.

Other than laws of trespass there was the scientific concern of the deaths; how far reaching was this massive extinction of humans?

From one house he took a Honda generator. In another he found a big stereo; another a TV. Both were hooked up to the biggest antenna he could find. When he turned them all on, there was nothing; static on the radio and white fuzz on the TV. He looked in homes for a short-wave radio, but couldn't find one. He tried both landline telephones and a couple cell phones. They were dead as a seashell. On a pad of paper he wrote all the possible scenarios of the apocalypse in his area. Two weeks after New Years Eve, heavy snow fell again he was snowed in.

With no health care, no government services of any kind, he worried. Every moment became precious time to cook or prepare something to survive. Mornings were spent warming the cabin, and then fixing tea and cereal. Sometimes he would fish. His hunting stopped when the deer stopped coming to the area. When he did catch a trout or two, it was a feast, important for the ego and morale. He had to have a confidence in his own abilities. He was trying.

RANGER SMITH YELLOWSTONE NATIONAL PARK

CHAPTER 13

RANGER SMITH WORKED HARD TO FERRY load of supplies to her mountain cabin. She was fighting the weather. Snow was falling hard. These were roads that were not plowed; more than thirty-six miles of gravel road headed north, near the border of the park. Becky Smith hiked in, food and supplies on her back, the last three miles of the thirty-six mile road. Fifty pounds per load, with the last load, her fifth, she had to wear cross-country skis and pull a seventy-pound sled. Snow was falling hard and fast. She made it back to the old wilderness cabin, which was used by rangers and leased out to winter adventurers. It was hers for three months. It was not big, but boasted four bunk beds, two tables, and locking cabinets. Outside was an outhouse with a deep pit toilet. Water had to be carried from a creek a quarter of mile from the cabin, and a woodshed held an unlimited supply of fuel for the wood stove. Four of her friends had hauled, cut, split, and stacked the firewood for her to use over the winter.

Thanksgiving was her first night in the cabin. She ate turkey sandwiches and enjoyed a bottle of wine. Like Tom and Bill, she was stocked with food, fuel and supplies. The shelves in the cabin were stacked with canned goods, bulk rice, noodles, sugar, flour, and a fifty-pound bag of beans. The many parties who had used the cabin had left food behind so they wouldn't have to carry it out. Because of the large amount of food needed, she had to scrimp on other things. She had five pairs of panties and t-shirts, all cotton and easy to wash. Her winter uniform was the warmest, with a fur-lined hat.

Since she would be studying bears, she brought a Smith and Wesson .357 revolver, powerful enough to stop a bear, with reasonable recoil. For grizzly problems she brought along a Winchester model 70 superlight 30-06 bolt-action rifle without a scope. Weight was an issue with all gear. She'd brought twenty bullets for the rifle, one box. Her notes were all printed on paper. She brought twelve pads of paper and two mechanical pencils, a small radio for emergencies, a headlamp, extra batteries, and a sleeping bag.

She settled into the cabin two days after the virus hit the town of Mammoth. All of the bear dens she had studied the winter before were now empty. She was counting on them being occupied. She waited them out, hoping the big critters would show up. They didn't. Now she was crushed. The effort to get to the cabin and stock it was huge, plus the loss of work for nothing. She held on, searching each day. She found bear tracks, but they lead far from her safety range and so she didn't follow them. By Christmas she had seen two bears and lost them in a thick tangle of brush, again losing her valuable subjects. Then the storm of the decade hit the area, dumping several feet of snow, and trapping her in the cabin for two weeks.

In spite of the weather and lack of studying, she enjoyed her time alone. She was ready to leave on New Years Day but the continuing storm made it impossible. Later in the day she pulled her sled to the creek with two five-gallon jugs that needed filling. The snow was falling hard with winds over thirty miles an hour. For an hour she chopped through the ice to get at the water below. She stood up to go back to the cabin. The wind had shifted; her tracks had filled in. Now she was in a total whiteout.

On the way back to the cabin she got lost. The trees all looked the same, with no more than eight feet of vision in front of her, all her memory was worthless. She hiked for over an hour. She was close to panic, but held it in check. For another fifteen minutes she walked in waist deep snow, exhausted and frightened. In desperation she turned hard and fast to the left. Her head hit something hard. It was one of the eaves of the woodshed. Smiling, she carried the jugs of water into the cabin. Now she felt the cabin more as a safehouse. She would never go outside without a compass again. The wood stove was kept burning day and night as the temperature was below freezing, and with wind chill, it was twenty below, depending on the time of day.

GEORGE THIELMAN

By mid-February she was out of firewood and food. Her friends had never come to resupply. Becky made the decision to leave. She loaded the sled with the last of her food, tent, sleeping bag, clothes and weapons, clicked on her snowshoes and pack, and started down the trail back to her car. Two hours later she was at her car, now merely a bump in the snow. She dug out one side so she could get extra clothes. She changed into clean underwear, pants, and fleece, and then put on her winter ranger coat. She clipped her pistol belt over the coat then resumed her travel.

The road made a series of switchbacks before it crested a hill. This was the spot where she could call out. She turned the radio on; nothing but static emptied from the speaker. She tried every frequency, "This is Ranger Smith calling base, come back." Nothing but static. She tried several times. Nothing. She changed batteries. Again, the same results. She looked at the sky, "OK, I guess I hike on out, no big deal."

For six hours Becky Smith hiked along the unseen road, following the clearing and the occasional road sign. She calculated she was making two miles an hour. Two times six was twelve miles. She had over twenty-two miles to go. The weight was beginning to get to her. The waist straps of the sled were digging into her sides. The pack was becoming a burden as well; her shoulders were burning. Stopping next to big rock, she took the pack off and strapped it to the top of the sled. This made the sled heavier, but the pain was relegated to one spot, her hips. She continued into darkness making another six miles by dusk. Eighteen miles wasn't bad for a day's work. She made camp, digging with a plastic avalanche shovel to make a place for the tent. She stacked up the snow, and then set the tent up. It was a small two-man dome tent. The poles crossed over the top and sides, and the rainfly made it complete. Inside she laid two thin insulated mats down, then her sleeping bag. It was a good one, rated to ten-below, and made from the best Polish goose down feathers, with a Gore-Tex outer shell, it repelled water. Inside the tent she had dragged her stove and food, the absolute last of it: two cans of beef stew, a can of sauerkraut, old saltine crackers, and two freeze-dried packets of eggs. She started up the small stove. The gas cartridge puffed, then blew out. Again she turned the dial to on, and heard gas escaping, but it wouldn't light. She let the gas go on. Finally, it lit in a small explosion. She startled. The tent floor and part of the tent were in flames. She quickly smothered the fire, but it had burned a small hole in her sleeping bag. The whole in the floor and in the side of the tent the size of a basketball. She crawled out of the tent, emptied the plastic sled, and slid it under the rainfly covering the hole. Inside the tent she laid down on the sleeping bag. A stream of fine feathers squeezed through the hole in the bag like a geyser.

She laughed, "For fuck's sake." Outside in the darkness, with snow falling again, she found her small roll of duct tape. She taped up the hole and tried the small stove again. It worked flawlessly. Again she laughed, "Fuck me, man!" She cooked up a can of beef stew, and then went outside to pee, a tough thing for a woman in freezing conditions to do. She had to pull her fleece pants down, and then squat.

The sleeping bag was warm and cozy. She fell into a deep sleep, dreaming of sex with her ex-boyfriend. She woke up horny, but ignored the sensation, and cooked up a packet of dried eggs. They needed hot water poured into the plastic, then to be left alone for five minutes to thoroughly saturate the powdered eggs into a goopy mess that resembled scrambled eggs, like the kind you would get at McDonald's. She sprinkled salt and pepper on them and ate every little drop. They were delicious and filling. After packing, she left in darkness. It would be a long day. The waist harness pulled hard on her hips. She sucked it up, letting her mind and body get into a rhythm, and picked up the pace. By noon she was hungry and stopped to heat up the sauerkraut and crackers.

By five thirty she was in total darkness. She reached the main highway that linked the upper northern east and west ends of the park. Snow was knee deep; she was surprised to find the road not plowed. She just looked west and started hiking down the snow-covered road. After an hour in full darkness, she came to a car. She dug away the snow, and discovered the car was full of snow from a broken window. From the south side she looked at the window. It wasn't broken out. It had been torn out from a bear. Long ago bears had learned how to break into cars. First they set their claws on the top of the roof just above the seam for the window. Then they pried their powerful claws into the roof of the car, pulling the window out like opening a soup can. Bears from Alaska to Yosemite had been doing this for decades, adapting to the changing environmental needs no doubt. The car was a Subaru WRX with a trunk. The bears had found whatever food they were after, but had yet to figure out how to open a locked trunk. Becky pulled the latch, then rifled through the many items in the trunk: a cooler with a frozen six pack of Guinness, a bottle of wine, and two frozen turkey sandwiches. The rest of the small trunk was full of camping stuff she didn't need.

She packed up the food and beer continued down the road. The going was easy, and she felt strong. By midnight under a full moon she made camp by digging the snow in blocks, and then stacking them to make a wall. Inside her coat she had put the sandwiches and two beers. She ate the cold food and drank one beer as she set the damaged tent up. Becky fell asleep, later waking to the sound of wolves howling in the night. She smiled, then went back to sleep waking to sunshine. She ate the last bit of dried eggs, and then heated up two beers and drank them in the sun, enjoying for the first time in two months the sun on her skin.

After breakfast she continued her journey. By noon she had reached a small park maintenance building. She walked around the garage trying to find a way in the doors was locked and the barred windows were over seven feet high. She tried the radio again. Nothing.

"Goddamn. What the fuck is going on?" Finally, she pulled her pistol and fired three rounds at the metal dead bolt. She pulled the door open and walked inside. There was a dump truck with a snowplow and a Snow Cat with a small trailer attached. The Snow Cat was for the rangers' use in patrolling the park in the winter. She prayed it had fuel and battery life. She turned the key. It fired easily and she yelled with joy. She opened the garage door and loaded her stuff into the small trailer. Cat in gear, she drove it out, and then tried to call on the radio. Again, there was no reply. She drove west to Mammoth, arriving late that night. The roads were bare; no movement, no lights. All the stores were locked up, there were snow drifts everywhere, and the sidewalks hadn't been shoveled.

The Ranger Station door was unlocked. The inside was freezing cold. Ranger Smith started the big wood stove and then went to the radio room. She sat at the big short wave radio and called, "Hello this is Mammoth Ranger Station. Is anyone out there? Over." Nothing but static. She turned the dial and kept trying. Finally, she picked up a Russian voice. He spoke, but she didn't know Russian so she shut it off. She closed up the station and drove the Cat to her little house. Lights were out everywhere, and cars littered the roadway. She was tired and hungry and had little time or energy to spend worrying about anything but her immediate needs. She realized she'd left the keys for her cabin back at the wilderness cabin among the things she left behind. She kicked in the door.

After starting a fire, Becky changed into clean clothes and went to her bed. It felt was warm and secure. She wondered about so many things. She fell asleep and woke to a massive storm. She restarted the fire, realizing that was the last of the firewood. In the morning she heated water for coffee with her propane stove. Now in clean ranger clothes, she carried her travel mug to the neighbor's cabin.

Without the sled holding her down she walked easily. She knocked and then went inside. The cabin held a wicked stench. Under the covers of the bed she saw two bodies: her friends and neighbors of two years, frozen solid. She ran from the cabin to the next cabin of a man that worked at a nearby bar. He was also dead in his bed. She walked down the line of small cabins stopping at the tenth, just to find another body. Frightened, she packed up her things in the Snow Cat and moved to the ranger station. It had running water, a generator, a working toilet and warm room to use. She would stay in one of the unoccupied rooms in the back.

She sat down in front of the radio, "Mammoth Ranger Station, calling anyone. Come back, over." She repeated for an hour and was about to rest her efforts for a bit when the radio crackled with a voice,

"Mammoth Ranger Station, this Whiskey 24/7. This is Whiskey 24/7. Over. Come back please."

Becky ran to the radio stuttering, the first words she had spoken to another human in months,"Heeehheeellooo, this Mammoth Station. Come on back, Whiskey 24/7. Whaaaat happened? Over."

"Mammoth, we had ourselves a virus that seems to have killed most everyone. Got a guy in Russia, then got you. What's your name?" The radio faded out. Becky sat down, calling for another hour before she gave up. She went to the kitchen and cooked up canned green beans and chicken soup and went to bed.

The ranger station had a generator that was hooked directly to the electrical panel. All she had to do was turn it on and she had power. The next morning she started the generator charging the emergency batteries in the ranger station. She was making pancakes when the radio crackled, "Mammoth Station, this Nick Thom from North Dakota. Come on back. Over." They talked for twenty minutes then the signal faded.

She turned the dial on the old short wave, "This is Mammoth Ranger Station, calling anyone. Over."She sat sipping the last of her Heineken beer. In her bosses' office she found a bottle of Jameson whiskey, and sipped at both calling throughout the day.

Finally another voice came on, "Mammoth Ranger Station, this is Sky Ranch in Stehekin, Washington. Over." She ran back to the radio with a mouth full of food, "Sky Ranch this is Ranger Becky Smith. Come back?"

"Mammoth, this is Captain Tom Trainer of the U.S. Air Force. How are you?" Becky was in tears she was so happy. Her hopes were beginning to brighten. Tom spoke, "I have food and power, hot water, chickens, milk, veggies, you name it, at the end of Lake Chelan in Washington." She pulled out a map; she looked at Lake Chelan, tracing her finger the sixty miles to Stehekin.

GEORGE THIELMAN

"Tom, I know of Stehekin. It's well regarded as a remote wilderness town, sounds great." She spit her food into a coffee cup, "Air Force Captain, can you fly?"

Tom replied, "I can fly, but don't have a plane. Best to stay away from cities!" They made an agreement to call every night at seven P.M. Later Becky tried the Indian guy, but couldn't raise him. That night she showered for the first time in months. The warm water seemed to take her over. She wished there was a tub in the station, but the shower was wonderful.

The ranger station was powered by electricity and propane for the kitchen with two wood stoves. Becky kept the wood stoves going, then dressed in her ranger garb and drove through the town in the Snow Cat. She collected supplies from the store, loading up the small trailer with all it could carry. On the way home, a moose walked about the streets. She stopped the Cat, Winchester in her arms; she jumped out, running quietly through town, using the buildings as cover. From one hundred yards she shot the Moose through the lungs. The bullet ripped through his front shoulder. In a panic, it stumbled, giving her another shot through the lungs. It slowly fell to the ground. It was alive when she put a bullet through into its head.

She drove the snow Cat over and tied a towline to the Moose. She dragged it back to the station and into the maintenance garage, where she hung it from the back legs then slit its throat and pulled it straight up, letting it bleed in the cold air all night. She had other plans for the day.

This time she had to shower the blood from the Moose away. She stripped, and then looked at her naked body in mirror. She was lean, and strong. Her ribs shown through like a marathoner. Her clothes felt baggy on her. She had picked up new clothes at a fancy outdoor supplier; brand new Patagonia hiking pants, shirts, panties, socks, and jackets. She always wore one of her ranger jackets with I.D. in case someone of authority appeared. In the kitchen at the station she cooked a carrot cake with frosting and made peanut butter cookies. She had made them to lift her spirits and cure loneliness. For a time it worked, until seven P.M. when she couldn't raise Tom or Nick from North Dakota. Every three days she would run the big Cummins diesel generator, heating the two water heaters and charging batteries, then she would shut it off until needed.

She quartered the moose with a chainsaw and then cut it up in pieces the way her brothers had shown her. With a big handtruck, she hauled the meat into a freezer. Two big flank steaks she kept for supper. Barbecuing in a small fenced-in area she cooked up the moose steaks well done. She ate by the radio, but again there was nothing but static.

NICK THOM OF NORTH DAKOTA

CHAPTER 14

ON FEBRUARY 14TH RANGER BECKY SMITH got ahold of Nick Thom of North Dakota. "Nick why can't you get out of there? Come here."

"Mammoth, I'm over three hundred and fifty pounds, fifty two, and I have no cartilage in my knees. Over."

"Nick you have to get out of there! Over!"

"Becky can't do it. Out of food and I can't walk far all alone here. Over."

"Nick you must try. Over." She talked Nick into trying, but didn't realize how bad off he was. He had lived indoors for years, north of Bismarck in his mom's house, watching TV, and collecting government checks, "welfare for Indians," he called it. On February 16th, Nick dressed as best he could, in two pairs of sweat pants, and two hoodies with a beanie. He carried an old tomahawk and a bowie knife tied with two small ropes over each shoulder. His intention was to go out Indian style; not dying with a bag of Twinkies in his lap. His calves had become so big that he had to cut his boots down like a low top shoe then taped the boot to his sweat pants. He was game, that's all there was to it. He walked out the front door into the five-degree weather. The snow was only ten inches deep. He made it to his old Chevy Impala. It started. He made it three blocks before it got stuck. He sat in the car thinking, and then with a big breathe, stepped out. His knees hurt with every movement as did his ankles, but he walked a half a mile to his cousin's house. His cousin was dead in his bedroom. Nick sat in the living room, breathing hard. Finally, he found the keys for his cousin's Jeep, crawled in taking along canned goods from his cousin's house. Somehow he would have to make it from his house to the nearby town of Fort Yates. The old Jeep made it five miles until a pocket of water in the engine block popped the freeze plug into the snow. Now he was dead in the water. He looked around. Nothing but rangeland, frozen grassland, for as far as he could see. He stepped out of the Jeep and onto the frozen ground. He decided he was not going to go back. He adjusted the tomahawk and the bowie knife and started hiking. His future was in front of him. He thought of how many times he tried to stop eating like a pig, but he didn't know he would have to pay for it, maybe with his life. He limped along for two hours, feeling energy from his ancestors, before he realized his overweight body was counteracting any power the great heroes from the past could bestow on him.

Down a ravine, he had to piss. While he did, he felt his left arm go numb. He tried to move his legs, but they tingled, and his heart was racing, pounding, and pushing much needed blood to his body parts. He fell over like a cartoon character. He was too big to catch himself or cushion the fall with his hands. He hit the frozen snow with a thud. With his right arm he pulled out the tomahawk, and in his head he said a prayer to the Great Spirit. He started singing an Indian song he had known as a child, learned from his Lakota Sioux grandmother, the Healing Song. Wani wachiyelo Ate omakiyayo (Father help me I want to live). He stopped when he heard the sounds of sniffing. He couldn't move his head very well, but saw a wolf came into sight, twenty feet from him. Another wolf, and another wolf came. He held onto the tomahawk singing, "Wani wachiyelo Ate omakiyayo..." the song continued until he passed out two hours later.

He woke up expecting to be in the Spirit World, but he was freezing cold in a ravine. The wolves had moved on. He thought he must smell bad enough to scare off wolves, like the skunk, he thought. He moved his arms. They were so cold, and his fingers so solid that they clinked against each other. He rolled over onto his side trying to get up, but his legs were still wobbly. He wondered if he had a heart attack. Didn't matter. He was dying of hypothermia. Which would get him first: the cold, his heart, or wild animals? The next morning when the wolves came back through the ravine they saw Nick, frozen solid his two hoodies off, a t-shirt wrapped around his head like headband, sitting upright. The wolves sniffed around, but left, heading for a nearby sheep ranch where the prey smelled and tasted great.

SKY RANCH

CHAPTER 15

Winter was spent tending to the animals on the Sky Ranch; fishing, hunting and caring for the ranch. Its indoor gardens and critters required much care. Tom's days were often started by getting water for coffee, and then caring for the fire in the wood stove and warming the cabin. The top down method was the best and easiest method for starting a fire. Kindling would be set down in the wood stove. On top he would lay another layer of kindling, facing the opposite direction. Crinkled newspaper would be added on top the kindling, and then more kindling. The newspaper was lit with one match. A few minutes later the fire was raging and warming the cabin. This was his most efficient method for fire starting and could be walked away from for over an hour. Tom used the same method in the tub as well. Breakfast would consist of cereal, eggs, and elk or other sausage from the freezers in the basement; sometimes he would have pancakes with apple cider.

Cows required milking and feeding every morning. Milking wasn't always a perfect science for Tom and the cows. Sometimes the cows only gave a quart of milk; other days, almost a gallon. Tom knew that the quantity of milk depended on factors such as exercise, food and rest. Sky Ranch cows got plenty of exercise and rest. Without a final boatload of food for the cows, he was forced to feed the cows hay, which was saved for feeding the horses. The cows didn't complain and happily munched the hay, but the milk was less than the amount they gave during the summer months.

Cats were always milling about during the milking process, hoping for a drink of warm milk. Tom was more than happy to leave a bowl for the felines.

Chickens were fed in the chicken run. If the sun was out, they were let out into the fenced garden. With so many predators near and on the ranch, the chickens were kept near the run. On the ranch they scattered, but never ventured too far from the safety of the chicken run. Chicken and chicks especially did get pinched occasionally, usually by raccoons and small cats.

Mid-morning was the time that animals hunted. Tom would walk the inside perimeter of the fence looking for breaks or tracks in the snow. If he found tracks, he would set a trap for the predator. Sometimes he would catch a critter; other times the critter would find another way in or move on to easier prey outside of the ranch.

Patrols were done with a rifle of some sort. Tom's favorite patrol rifle was the AWT AR-10 or the Colt M4. He had suppressors (silencers) for both rifles, and the quieter rifles were better for the animals on the ranch in that they didn't startle them. Patrolling was a necessary job on the ranch. Tom enjoyed the simplicity and importance of it. If it was not done, bloodthirsty critters could get in and cause great harm. Woody was a happy member of the patrol. With his great nose he could lead Tom to the predator or point out the fact that there was trouble about.

Fishing and hunting was easily the most fun job for Tom. With the Stehekin valley being a tourist area and bordering a massive national park, animals had been strolling through the area for decades with no fear of being hunted. Without hunting laws, Tom was free to hunt what he wanted when he wanted. Still he rarely shot a deer or elk. Meat was stacking up in the freezer, so he stopped hunting and switched to fishing.

Bears were large in number and were more of a nuisance than a danger. They walked the outside of the fence, sometimes grabbing ahold of the thick wire and shaking it. After the attack on Sally by the cougar, a new fence was constructed with higher wire, and poles set every five feet. The new fence was so much stronger that it put most all of the animals off, including bear. Coyotes were the worst. They could dig under a fence and push the rest of the way under. Woody found two inside the wire. Tom shot them both before they could do harm.

Tom took apart his newer AWT AR10. Tom's friend was representative for the gun company and had sent him additional parts to change it from a long-barreled sniper rifle to a full blown battle rifle that could shoot 400 rounds a minute on full automatic. He set it up with an eighteen-inch match grade military spec barrel and lightweight hand guard with a top rail made to attach a scope. The butt stock was made of titanium, and the thirty round clips were made from plastic. Light and strong, it was stronger and lighter than the stock clips, yet as durable as steel. He installed the trigger mechanism that allowed it to fire at full automatic. The AWT rifle looked very much like the Colt and FN M4s that the military used. The difference was that the AWT M4 used a CNC machining. It was also twice the cost, but Tom thought it fired better than most of the best M4s he had used. This weapon was designed to give the soldier a range over 600 yards with good punch power; something the smaller M4 didn't have. In an urban fight, the .223 caliber round of the M4 was plenty good. It gave good sustained firepower without heating the barrel and the recoil problems of the bigger rifle. He tested the bigger gun in the semi-auto mode; one pull of the trigger, one shot. This went well. The muzzle brake on the tip worked better than he had hoped. On full-auto the gun was in good control but seemed to climb as he fired over ten rounds. The muzzle brake on a rifle was set up to be both a brake and a muffler; at the end of a rifle barrel was three holes in the tip of the barrel, that, when fired, the muzzle brake or tip of the gun barrel directed the flash of the explosion of the gun powder downward and to the side and upward as the bullet shot out in a straight line. He turned the brake so two exhaust ports faced up. This would give the gun more braking to keep the rifle barrel from climbing as it fired. It worked like a charm. The gun fired easily. The rate of fire was below 400 rounds a minute, but it wasn't bad.

Satisfied that he had a gun that could handle anything, he celebrated with a smoke. He held the rifle up aiming through the window at one of the cows. He dry-fired the weapon and looked down at Woody," If they catch me with this I could get a year in prison."

Winter was hard and cold. The freezing wind zapped through his winter clothes. He wondered if all of the towns had been affected by the virus. If he had survived, why wouldn't others? He wondered further about his town of Stehekin. He had been keeping close to the ranch. Trying to stay close to the ranch was difficult. While a loner he was not afraid to socialize. His isolated lifestyle was getting to him. A conversation would be nice, maybe a joke or two; tipping back a drink with another human would be nice. Today he would finally venture off the ranch grounds to check on the neighbors.

VENTURING OUT

CHAPTER 16

SNOW WAS FALLING HARD, big flakes like the paper decorations fell, covering Woody's brownish red fur. He jumped up at Tom, biting at his hand in anticipation of a good jaunt up the road. He grabbed Tom's hand again, pulling him to the ground, and then jumping close to him. Tom laughed at Woody as he scolded him.

Tom snapped on his cross-country skis, shouldered a small pack, and finally, slung the AR-10 across his back. He moved slowly through the two feet of snow. The first steps felt out of balance. Soon he got into a rhythm, sliding the left ski, then the right. His fat cross-country skis were best for downhill skiing, but they moved well enough through the snow and down the road toward town. The first several cabins he came to were empty vacation cabins, the owners seldom visiting. Tom and Woody continued on to the next cabin. Skiing was tough, with almost two feet of snow. Woody followed behind in the deep powder, enjoying the cold conditions.

Tom knew the next cabin belonged to family who often enjoyed it. When he arrived he knocked on the door. With no answer, he walked around the house, and peered in the bedroom window. The beds looked occupied. He beat on the windows. There was no response. At the children's bedroom window he could see the face of the ten-year-old boy he had seen playing over the summer. His skin was greyish, eyes closed, probably frozen, and clearly dead. Tom stayed outside. He took a big breath and then looked away. The death of children always bothered him. He decided not to enter the house. What could he do anyway?

They left in a hurry, quietly moving through the snow to town. Two curious crows buzzed overhead. Woody looked up at them and barked then looked back at Tom. They continued buzzing him, playing a game of sorts; one would fly in from up high, then nose dive to Woody while the other would come in three feet off the ground, and buzz upward when Woody jumped up at them. The crows would squawk and seemed to laugh at him.

Tom stopped at every cabin. Most were not occupied. Two had been broken into by pesky bears; front doors were wide open, cabinets torn open, paper and plastic littered the front yard. An empty bag of Alpo Dog Food was stuck in a spruce tree.

When he made it to town he went to the restaurant. The doors were locked. Only the ranger station was unlocked. Tom and Woody ventured stepped inside. It was cold, and the sleeping quarters on the second floor were empty. They walked outside back to the restaurant. The door to store was open, and its shelves were bare. Tom checked the nearby cabins and found them to be occupied by corpses: one old guy was dead in his favorite chair in front of the fireplace a bible in his lap, his wife was in bed, all had been dead for some time, frozen solid. He then checked the hotel finding all the beds unoccupied.

Outside Tom stood looking out at the lake wondering what to do next. He deduced that all the dead must have died from the same virus. He looked at Woody,"They're all dead, my friend," Woody looked up at him not realizing the gravity of the situation, only the mood of his master.

Tom spent the full day checking every building he knew. Seeing no other people, he finally gave up. He clipped the skis back on his feet and headed back toward the ranch. Outside of town two bears barreled from the bushes and stood in front of Tom and Woody. The bears seemed to communicate between themselves by telepathy, and then simply walked past Tom and Woody.

Tom yelled at them, "What do you want?" They stopped, looked at each other, then turned around, and looked at Tom and Woody. Woody growled and his fur on the back of his neck rose up. Tom unslung the AR-10, clicked the fire select to full auto, and pointed the gun at the menacing bears. Tom quietly said, "Get out of here!" One of the bears cocked his head to the side, and then turned around and walked back toward town. They looked back at Tom a few times. Tom smiled, keeping his eyes on them. Woody bugged, as usual, emitting a low, strange growl as they watched the big black bears walk in their tracks.

They continued along the road to the café. Inside the storm porch, Tom unlocked the door with a key that he had left hanging on the doorknob for anyone that needed shelter or a bite to eat. He went to the woodstove in the bar and started a fire and started the big propane stove in the kitchen. Two big elk steaks were cooked up in a cast iron pan. In the refrigerator he found a beer, and cooked up potatoes and carrots to go along with his steak. He ate at the bar like a regular customer.

The power still worked, so he turned on the TV and DVD player and watched the movie, "Tommy Boy." Woody ate a steak from a plate, and then crawled off to a corner to munch on a bone. He made noise while scraping the meat off the bone. He focused his attention on the marrow, completely engrossed in the demise of the bone. Tom watched his dog as he ate his steak.

When he was done he went to the bar for a drink. On the bar was glass that he hadn't used. He picked up the glass smelling the remains of it. It smelled of whiskey. He thought back. He hadn't been to the bar in a month, and when he did visit, he drank tequila, "hmm". He decided to do an experiment. On each bottle of whiskey he marked with a Sharpie pen the line of liquid in the bottle. He washed all the dishes and set them in their place. When he left the café he had left exactly ten pieces of firewood near the wood stove along with twenty pieces of kindling.

They skied back to ranch in darkness. He fed the cats, who all walked around Tom and Woody tails straight up in the air. Tom picked up each one and rubbed the top of their head.

Tom's cabin was warm from the morning fire, outside it was twenty-six degrees. It took a half an hour for the cabin to warm up enough so he could take off his jacket. He sat at his desk making notes, and thinking about what to do about the dead bodies. He sat for two hours thinking. If he left them, they would rot in the spring and summer, making the area stink. Most of the bodies were in their beds now, frozen. They would be easy to move. He could wrap them in their bedding and carry them out. What would he do with the bodies after he had them out? Bury them or burn them? The ground would be frozen and hard to dig.

After gathering supplies, Tom loaded the tractor with duct tape and chain saw. Tractor bucket down, he plowed to the first cabin which held dead. Sixty feet from the cabin was a two-story cedar barn. The old Chevy van was backed out, and tools and supplies that could be used were brought out. With his chain saw he turned his attention to the thirty or so trees that covered the grounds, cutting them down in a one hundred yard circumference around the barn. Firewood was stacked along the inside walls of the barn.

    Snow had stopped, so he plowed a path to the town. It took the rest of the day. With the roads now clear he hooked up an old trailer lined with plywood sides and a wood floor. The next day he started the ugliest work of his life.

    Starting at the southeast end of town, he started to carry the bodies out of any and all buildings, being careful not to miss any. Most of the dead had died in their beds or on a couch. He started by slipping on a white insulation suit he had found at a construction site, He wrapped the bodies in bedding and then duct taped the bedding around them. If they were less than one hundred sixty pounds he hooked a ratchet strap around them and pulled them to the trailer. If they were light enough, he carried them. Some were impossible to get through the front or back doors so he left a sign on the door, and recorded on a notepad the location and the number of dead inside.

    The first day he collected two trailer loads full, near to twenty people. Two weeks he kept at it, carrying the corpses to the barn, laying them on layers of firewood stacked like Lincoln logs at least twelve inches deep.

    Three weeks later he had near to seventy corpses in the barn. Fifteen in various cabins were either to big or were frozen in weird positions that made it impossible to move. They were left in their cabin. When he was sure he had found as many as he could and had cataloged the dead in a notebook, he found a waterproof coffee can, and put the paper with the names inside the can. On the bodies he stacked five cords of wood. The barn was well stocked with old cabinets, boxes, and furniture and hay bales. He poured kerosene throughout the barn, and then lit it. The cedar barn and its contents burned quickly. The one hundred yard no burn ban kept the forest from burning down. Three story flames lit the evening and leapt into the night. The barn reeked of death, burning into the next day when the flames finally burned out.

    Tom erected an eight-foot sign at the base of the fire site, with the can full of names at the base. He had no real flower, so he set a bunch of Sally's old plastic flowers on the can. He said a short prayer and then turned his back on the barn as the snow started to fall.

    That night Tom woke to the same dream as before. Hands and feet blackened from burning, being blown against him as he tried to run out of the area, and the bullets started hitting him; snapping and biting at him taking chunks out of his body. He woke in a cold sweat, feeling the bullet wounds with his hands. He got out of bed, started a fire, and then washed himself. He sat awake the remainder of the night. Within one week the snow had all but covered the old barn, the cross stood, a fitting marker.

Mid-March Tom decided he would stay close to the ranch taking care of the critters and plants. Electricity kept on plugging away, and the old water wheel turning had no shortage of water to move it along. Inside the dungeon he had allowed the current crop of marijuana to grow to maturity, and then he'd picked it and hung it up. He replaced the weed pots with lettuce potatoes, carrots, squash, and all other veggie seeds he had. Food was plentiful. Throughout March he checked cabins for the dead, disposing of the bodies the same method as before; burning small cabins with the dead inside after clearing the grounds of trees and other burnables. While on what he called crematory adventures, he was gathering quite an amount of food and supplies. He stocked the barn and Sally and Darren's homes with all his plunder. The café was stocked as well, with canned goods, bagged and boxed goods; by mid-March he was done collecting from the dead and turned his attention to the farm and his hunting.

MID-MARCH

CHAPTER 17

WHILE TOM WAS SETTLING DOWN to his routine at the farm, winter was ending in Washington State; snowstorms were less frequent. In Chelan, snow could only be seen on the higher hills and mountains. Winter snow kept on falling in Mammoth, Wyoming. Becky Smith stayed at the ranger station, collecting supplies, hunting and fishing and talking on the shortwave radio to Tom. The conversations were always cut short by bad connections, but she got the clear picture of life in Stehekin. She was interested in the remote lake town and intrigued by Tom. For now she was living fine with plenty of food but later without a farm and a big garden she would be in trouble. She could start her own farm at Mammoth, but she came to the conclusion that moving to a location with another live human would be best, especially a place like Sky Ranch that was self-sustaining.

After her decision to move was made, she started to check the roads with the Snow Cat. Record snow had continued to fall, blocking all roads. Avalanches were blocking places on the road, impeding movement. She would have to wait, and until then, she would prepare for the move north. She fired up a Dodge pickup from the maintenance shed, one that was used for road repairs and cleaning of the roads. It had a bucket on the front for pushing rocks and logs and a strong winch to pull logs out of the way. She collected cans of diesel fuel. The truck had a 100-gallon tank.

She would carry ten more five-gallon jugs, along with a chain saw, axes, shovels, her camping supplies and personal items.

"Sky Ranch, this is Mammoth Hot Springs. Come back?"

Tom answered the call, "This is Sky Ranch. Over."

"Tom, I'm coming to Stehekin as soon as the roads clear up a bit. Over,"

"Becky, you're welcome any time." The line went dead as a storm between the two towns blocked the reception.

With Becky's impending arrival, Tom thought he would get things ready for her. He wanted to travel to meet her, but couldn't leave the animals. They were the future for him or anyone else that lived at the ranch. In the barn, he fired up the Sky Boat, charging the batteries and cleaning the sides. The problem was that he could take one-day trips only. A trip to Chelan could take a few hours even if the weather and waves of the finicky lake were at their best. He thought of contracting the deadly virus that killed everyone was frightful. He remembered his Army education about strong viruses and the volatility of them. A virus that was strong enough to kill many people would be considered "hot," "extremely hot," so strong that it would burn out. Without live hosts, the virus could not survive and would die. He was hoping that any surviving people would not have it. His life depended on it. His ideas about the virus were just a guess.

Snow was now giving way to brown grass and bushes. While it was still officially winter, the weather had made a turn. Tom thought hard of making a run down the lake, but he couldn't do it. He was spooked by the unknown, not afraid of fighting but of the virus. He would go when Becky announced her departure. Until then, he grew more plants, kept the animals happy, and biked to the café and bar for a drink.

One day after hiking to the bar while he sipped a drink of tequila, he remembered that he had marked the whiskey two weeks earlier. He got up and checked the bottles he had marked. Two where obviously low. He hadn't drank whiskey since that time; someone else was about. When he left that night he marked more bottles. On the way home he thought whoever it was, was polite and not inclined to take the supplies at the café. He liked that; the guy was so polite that he never made a mess, and always put the key back.

Early one Saturday morning Tom drove the truck with the boat on its trailer to the boat dock at the café. He put the boat in the water and then tied it up as he hurried to take a shit at the café. He walked inside to the back room to pick up a couple pounds of coffee, and then decided to have early morning smoke and a drink in the bar. He slammed back two shots of good tequila.

He studied his map of Lake Chelan. He was dressed in warm ski pants and his Air Force winter coat, with the H&K in a shoulder holster and the small Glock .40 on his belt behind his back.

While he sipped on his third shot the quiet room was shattered, "God dam sumbitch, that was the best shit in years Ill tell ya whut, shit fire!" Joe Spadafore came out of the restroom, sat down next to Tom as if all was well with the world. He slapped Tom on the back, "How ya doin' Tom, shit ill tell ya whut, shit up a storm this morning', been eatin' on a pot roast I made a few days ago. Ha, ha ha shit fire ill tell ya whut, how ya doin, over there at the ranch should come and see ya I should, don't you ever talk anymore?"

Tom moved his head back, "Well Joe, it's nice to see you. How ya doing?"

Joe started in with his usual fast-paced cussing barrage, "Well I juss told ya god damit, been eatin' and shitin', a shitin' storm. Fuck, ill-tell-ya-whut, been huntin', choppin' wood, shot a couple bucks, been eatin good."

Finally, Tom got to tell Joe his side of what he thought was going wrong with the world, "All I know is what a few survivors have told me, and that is that a virus entered America from Mexico, riding with several illegals. Most people went directly to their homes, where they became very cold, like the flu. In a matter of few days they died."

Joe looked out the window squinting, "The Black Plague was spread by Rats, Aids by Monkeys, shit ill tell yaw hut, you should stay here and forget about downlake. Could get yourself dead then bring it back to me, fuck." He looked at Tom dressed in military garb with weapons. "Well shit Tom, if you want to go then ya should."

Tom said, "What killed the people out there was a virus. A virus cannot live in, or on, a dead body. It can be sent through the air, but not far or for very long. It cannot live without live host. I buried and cremated near to seventy people, and I didn't get anything but a backache."

Joe sipped his drink, he set his glass down, and looked at Tom, "So you're tellin' me that you can walk among all the fuckin' dead people in the world and not get that sickness? Come on godamit."

Tom jumped in, "I'm not saying I will stand amongst dead rotting bodies. I'm saying that dead bodies cannot carry the virus, period."

Joe said, "OK, so godam, take me along but don't go all the way to Chelan not yet anyway." There were only two places in the world to old

Joe: Stehekin and downlake. Everywhere in the world except Stehekin was considered "down lake."

Tom talked Joe into coming with him on a ride to Lucerne, a forty-minute boat ride down lake. Lucerne was a portal to the Lutheran village of Holden, ten miles from the lake. They would ride to the docks and then walk to the nearest homes to check for survivors.

Joe walked behind Tom to the boat. They boarded the Sky Boat and then taxied into the lake. Joe said, "This is the first time in eight years that I've left the valley. God damn if that don't make a donkey shit." Tom looked straight ahead smiling, wondering how anything could make a donkey shit. Joe sat in the passenger chair watching the cold lake pass by. He looked at Tom, at one point saying something in Joe Spadafore speak; a mix of slang and cuss words strung together to form a type of sentence.

They slowed the boat down when the first cabins came into sight, before Refrigerator Harbor. Tom honked the horn and then docked. A cluster of cabins could be seen. They could see no signs of life. They tied up the boat and Tom jumped out with his AR-10. Woody ran alongside him down a rickety wood dock. At the front doors Tom knocked then yelled, "Hello! Anybody home? We have some great beer and stew." The cabin all had shuttered windows everything was locked tight, they left it that way.

Refrigerator Harbor was the next stop. From two hundred yards, Tom honked the boat horn three times. They waited for a reply from the cabins. None came. Finally, they docked the boat at the solid docks. Almost a hundred clustered cabins could be seen, small and close together, it had a great community atmosphere. Near the water, at the docks they honked the horn three times. Nothing. Tom stepped off the boat with his rifle in hand.

Joe said calmly, "Maybe you should leave your weapons here, goddam if I wouldn't be afraid of someone armed to the teeth shit fire!"

Tom looked back at Joe and then to his rifle, "I think I'll keep my gun with me." Tom and Woody walked to shore. The road and parking lot was clean, void of trash, leaves, branches, and once again of people. Joe sat on the edge of the boat watching Tom walk back. He pointed back to the cabin community."

"Jus' saw me a person way over there, he took one look at us gave me the finger and ran away, god-damnest thing I seen in a long time boy ill tell ya whut, shit." Then he spit a big luger in the water.

Tom untied the boat. He heard wood splinter, and then heard the report of a rifle. He counted. The shooter was somewhere between three and four hundred yards out. Tom pushed the boat out and fired the engines.

Another splinter of wood from the dock meant the shooter was shooting down on them. Tom pulled Joe to the controls instructing him to troll very slowly.

Joe said, "Ain't this an easy way to get shot?"

Tom laughed, "Guy can't hit shit," Tom pulled out his AWT AR-10, and slung it over the side of the boat. As Joe slowly zigzagged through the small bay, a muzzle flash from one of the cabins.

Through binoculars two older men, one with an Elmer Fudd hat and a red jacket could be seen crouching behind a wood fence. Tom fired six rounds at the house; his scope was not quite strong enough to get a good bead on the shooter. He fired five more shots at the open door to frighten the shooter and the spotter. Both hit the ground, and the gunfire stopped.

He looked at Woody," I'm going to have to get a bigger scope." The boat slowly rode out into the lake. Bullets splashed into the water near Tom. He looked up. A man was aiming at them from a rock perch. Tom yelled to Joe, "Hit the throttle Joe." Tom switched the rifle to full automatic. He aimed and fired a ten round burst straight at the man on the rock. Dirt and rocks were sprayed all around the shooter. One bullet hit him in the leg and he fell to the ground out of sight. They rode back to Stehekin in silence.

Joe yelled, "Boy-ill-tell-ya-whut!"

They drove back to the Sky Café dock. Joe stepped off the dock, farted and then started walking toward the café. Tom yelled, "Hey wait Joe, I'll walk with you."

Old Joe turned around, "Never wanted to walk with me before, shit, "he spat a gob on the deck.

Tom replied, "I never spent four months talking to myself."

Old Joe said, "Well I guess I know whut you mean, has been a bit alone time lately, bring yer dog along and we can do some steppin' together."

Joe lived a half a mile from the café toward town. They turned at a trail and walked for five hundred yards. The old guy walked fast and easy, down the bushy tree lined trail, around two cabins and a barn. Around a large stand of young pine trees, there it was. True to life, Joe's log cabin, a real cabin made with dark colored logs and a green roof. It was the spitting image of the toy Lincoln Log cabin. A woodshed stood on the side yard with a large splitting axe imbedded in a stump.

The cabin was warm from the morning fire. The back wall was nothing but mortar set river rock with a fire place set in the middle, seven feet high the walls were as much as two feet thick. Where the log walls connected with rock wall there were open areas where dry rot had started. The lower logs of the walls were rotting away. From decades of sitting on wet dirt, the cabin was starting to rot from the ground up. The first layer of logs was rotting; almost three quarters of the logs were falling away, leaving a nice pile of wood chip that used to be a log the size of a telephone pole. The logs weren't rotting evenly, so the house was tipping at the front. The cabin had a wood plank floor with plywood nailed over in spots to cover holes in the planking.

"Well ill tell ya whut, aint much but it keeps the god dam rain off my head." He scratched at his grey stubble. "Goddam rats come in at night, crawl through the holes in the floor sumbitches, ill tell-ya-whut-shit," he lifted his left leg waiting to squeeze out a fart which he did, a squeaky sound that went on almost a half a minute. Tom had seen and heard every type of bodily noise and excretion known to man or woman. He shook his head in amazement at Joe's constitution. He laughed and wondered what was next with the old guy.

Tom invited Joe to spend a few days at the ranch, take a shower, and clean his clothes. Joe said he would be there at seven in the morning. They said good-bye and off Tom went to his cabin.

Tom woke up the next morning to the sound of the cows and chickens making noise that only meant they were being moved or were uncomfortable. He dressed and let Woody out the door. Woody ran toward the cows, barking. Tom ran after him, the AR-10 in his hands. He racked a round and clicked the safety off. Around the big bread loaf rock he could see the barn. The bull was standing outside, bugged by something inside the barn. A bucket hit the concrete floor, through the gate and into the barn Tom leveled his weapon at Joe who was sitting down on the milking stool. His right arm and face was spattered in milk and a metal bucket was still rolling on its side.

Joe looked at Tom his mouth open, his hands working furiously on the teets, milk squirted into the bucket in big streams. "Godam sumbitch cow's aint used to me yet, get a bit pesky, old mother almost kicked me in the head. Hit the bucket it did, old mother over there was easy jus put his head in and started eating. I sat down and juss started at those teets, no godam problem. Now this old mother is a pistol. "He shook his head seeming not to notice the weapon pointing at him. He yelled at Tom, "How ya doin Tom? Nice morning, got over a dozen eggs this morning, good godam chickens ya got there."

Tom smiled, clicking the safety on, and slinging his rifle over his shoulder. Once again he was amazed at Joe's candor.

Joe hollered up to him, "Be done in a few minutes, meet ya in yer cabin when im done, take the eggs with ya."He spit a big luger on the ground and loudly cleared his throat. Tom left the room, smiling as usual. He wondered why Joe didn't clear his throat, and then spit.

Outside the barn was a faded orange Camp Trails frame pack that had to be at least thirty years old, from the seventies. It was bulging with items, stretching the old nylon. A faded Coleman sleeping bag was strapped to bottom rails, and a fishing pole was strapped to the side along with a two-foot forest axe. Against the pack leaned a worn Winchester lever action rifle.

Tom picked up the pack it was almost 90 pounds. He walked back to his cabin, and started a fire in the cook stove. He set the kettle on, and then went about dressing. As usual, the cabin was cold. With the house sitting on a flat rock the cabin stayed cool. On very cold days he would start up both the cook stove and wood stove to stomp the cold out of the cabin. It would eventually get extremely hot, so he would have to crack open windows once the cabin was warmed up. Tom would use the cook stove to continue to heat the cabin letting the fire in the wood stove die out.

Old Joe barged through the front door, with two buckets of milk, and set them down. "Them cows is easy, while, in my day them bitches has kicked me from ear to ear godam-ill-tell-ya-whut shit." Tom had never looked hard at Joe he looked like a much bigger Robert Duval. More fit though, baldhead little grey in his beard, his legs was straight as and strong. His back was bent slightly forward from decades of hard work. He wore carpenter pants, a wool sweater and his Carhartt ranch coat stained and frayed at the cuffs.

They ate a big breakfast of eggs and pancakes, and drank a pot of coffee. Tom showed Joe the old bunkhouse. Joe moved right in, placing his rifle on two nails above the woodstove. His clothes were neatly put away in a dresser next to the bunk he picked. He washed his clothes and walked to finger rock where he fished for an hour, catching two good size trout. He dressed them out and walked to his cabin.

Quietly, Joe moved right on in. Tom noticed him making a couple loads from his cabin. On his dresser sat several framed pictures one of a very young Joe in the 50s, leaning against a 57 Chevy, his cuffs rolled up. In his arms was a very cute shorthaired woman. Another picture was Joe in Army uniform in Vietnam standing in front of crate of mortar shells.

Joe took over all the tasks of the farm, saying only that he was better than Tom at ranching. He enjoyed being busy and not having rats crawl over his face at night. Joe stayed close to the ranch. Other than a hike to the café for a drink, he was always fussing with the cows or chickens, messing with the plants in one of the three artificial grow rooms. He was unfazed by the marijuana growing in the dungeon. He watered and weeded. His favorite thing was fishing and watching the cats stalk the chickens. Both the cats and the chickens were his friends. He kept the cow stalls clean, and the chickens were well taken care of. He spent more and more time in Sally's house, preparing food, watching movies, and drinking with a book in his hands.

SPRING

CHAPTER 18

"Stehekin, this is Mammoth Ranger Station. Come on back. Over?" Becky called into the radio.

"Good reception, Becky. Leaving in a few days to clear the path for you. Over."

She keyed the mike to talk. The system went down, all power went dead. She checked the Cummins generator. It would not turn over. She tried to jump it from the Dodge diesel, but it would not fire. Two hours she worked on the big generator, and finally she gave up. Outside she felt a shiver. Wet snow had been falling, creating hazardous driving conditions. Late snow was always a problem. She was packed and ready to go, tired of spending every waking moment alone, she was waiting to leave. Finally, a warm front moved in, rain came with it, loosening and melting the snow. The five days of warm rain falling in torrents washed the roads clean enough to drive.

Becky drove north out of the park. Occasionally she would have to lower the bucket to knock rocks and gravel off the road. April 15,[th] "Tax Day," she laughed at that. Earlier that morning she awoke ready to go, loaded the truck with her food and supplies, extra fuel cans, water, clothes and weapons. On her right hip she carried the Smith Wesson .40 caliber service pistol. Next to her was a Winchester bolt-action rifle. She had left hers behind, choosing instead the more controllable .270 of her boss. A Smith Wesson AR15 semi auto rifle sat next to her, similar to the M-16 she carried in the Air Force. She felt well protected and confident. She smiled, relieved to be leaving the lonely ranger station with the four-wheel drive Dodge and bucket on the front. She felt she could get through anything. Ahead in the road, rocks and dirt had fallen from an embankment. She lowered the bucket, with a shifting lever, the factory-shifting knob was replaced with a silver skull. Sometimes she would play with the bucket while she drove.

    She drove north to the town of Gardiner; a small sleepy town. The roads were not as bad as she thought. Rocks, gravel, branches and occasional cars blocked the road in places. She enjoyed shoving materials with the hefty Dodge.

In the town of Gardiner, she stopped in front of a bar. The roads were empty, it was thirty-nine degrees, and windy. Clouds were backing up against the mountains of Yellowstone. She stood outside of the truck, honking several times. No movement, no sign of life; in the distance cows grazed looking for newly uncovered brown grass. She was in a crappy mood. Her period had started and, of course, she had no tampons or panty shields. She reached down and adjusted the folded up toilet paper she was using for a panty shield. She could deal with the dripping blood but the cramps were like a headache, always nagging and impossible to ignore.

She walked into a ransacked drug store, picked up a shopping basket, and went up and down the isle. She picked up personal items. The pharmacy bottles were strewn about the floor, "Someone was looking for something. Hope they got it."

She walked across the street and into a western-themed bar. The sign read, "Saloon," and had a rope lasso surrounding the word, "open." It was dark and gloomy. The shelves were missing most of their contents. Thieves like herself, no doubt, she thought. She poured two shots of Makers Mark whiskey and bagged two bottles for the road. She spotted a bottle of Patron Gold "Nice." She poured a third shot of whiskey, this time sipping it slowly. "I'm now legally drunk." She put her head in her hands looking at the dusty mirror in front of her. She fluffed out her black short hair. She would have to cut it soon; it was at her shoulders and hadn't been that long in years. Her blue eyes looked, almost like another person, older, more stressed, "That fits!" Sitting at the bar she imagined happier times: swimming with her boyfriend at the hot springs, naked in the middle of nowhere, they had hiked four miles to swim there alone. She wished she could find hot springs; a hot long bath would be great.

A voice erupted from outside. "Fuckin' great, man. Look what I found. A woman was reaching into the Dodge.

Becky opened door of the bar quickly, "Hey! Get out of there!" The woman jumped at the sound of, "Hey!" When she saw Becky, she pulled her arm out of the truck and turned to run away, but rammed into the big side view mirror. She hit the ground hard, first on her butt and then her head hit the concrete.

She was pale and thin. She yelled out at Becky, "Don't touch me, you bitch. I didn't do nuthin,' I swear." She stood up, holding the back of her head. Her stick-like legs seemed to disappear in her dirty down coat. "So what do you want, bitch?"

Becky stood, her hand on her pistol, "I don't want anything from you. You're not in trouble, and don't worry!" The woman crunched up her face in pain, her teeth were yellow, and one in the front was half moon shaped, probably from smoking crystal meth with the pipe in the same place.

"Fuck you, bitch! You're another cop. I hate cops!"

She spat the words at Becky. Her eyes were brown with dark circles under them. She walked away, "Fuckin cops. Fuck you!" she yelled obscenities as she staggered down the street. She turned back to the truck, and then crossed to the opposite side of the street. She kept her eyes on Becky, clearly frightened.

Becky asked, "What's wrong with you, Honey? Are you sick?"

The woman snapped, "No, I'm not, OK? I juss need a hit, that's all."

Becky asked, "A hit of what? Maybe I can help." The woman put her fingers in her mouth biting the tips with her rotting teeth.

Becky said, "Meth head, huh, big tweeker, great."

The woman moved in a circle back toward the Dodge, she slipped again on the icy road. She yelled, "Yah, so I'm a tweaker, fuck you, bitch." The woman slipped and fell again. Becky ran to her lifted her head.

"You're really hurting aren't you?"

The woman spit at her,"Juss let me the fuck go, bitch."

Becky stood quickly, "OK, OK. You can do whatever you want. I'm not holding you!" Her shadow covered the skinny woman lying on the ground. The skinny woman jumped up, just as a shadow moved at the left of Becky. Becky moved like a professional gun fighter, pistol drawn. She ducked down, as she spun around, a gun went off in her face. She felt the heat of the powder explode, and the bullet missing her.

She fired three shots at the image. A big silver revolver bounced to the ground. The black figure was a man wearing full camo. He held onto the right side of his head, blood streamed between his fingers, he stepped to the right and let go of his head. His ear moved forward like a sloppy blood-soaked hinge, skin, and skull fell to the ground. Two bullets had entered under the ear, tearing it from his head. He had put his cupped hand up just in time. Now he fell to the ground with thump. He started to scream in pain, ugly screams like an out-of-control woman.

Becky stood back watching the man in horror. He stuck out his right foot, seeming to try to grab something. His foot hit the wet road. He started to spin himself in a circle, his right hand cupping the head wound. He was moaning, spinning in a circle. Becky was amazed by the amount of blood. She turned away, toward the skinny woman. She lay in a pool of blood, a gapping canoe-like wound to her neck, from the man's big pistol. The woman was alive, blood pumping from her neck wound.

The woman pointed at the man spinning near her, "That's my husband!" The bullet had entered her neck on the left side, piercing her coat. Small down feathers mixed with sticky blood bubbled and ran across her face and then back into her mouth. Her throat sucked a mass of blood and feathers in as she bled out. Her eyes rolled back and she went limp. Becky turned to the man. He lay dead, on his side, in a big pool of blood.

Becky stood between the two. She holstered her weapon and picked up the big revolver lying on the ground. She looked at it. A Ruger Super Blackhawk, it was heavy with a ten-inch barrel. She carried it to the truck and set it on the seat. "He won't need it again, that's for sure."

She pulled the two dead people to a side alley, propped them against a rock wall, and turned her back on the scene. She went back in the bar, picked up her booze, hopped in the Dodge, and drove away, the right wheels of the Dodge leaving a blood trail.

As she drove past the last gas station, four deer jumped in front her truck. She hit one, and the others kept running in front of her, confused. Finally out of patience, she stepped on the gas, and the heavy truck rocketed forward knocking two deer from her path.

She drove for two hours before she pulled over on a dirt road. She was in rangeland. She looked for tracks on the roads wondering if there was something alive out there that wasn't crazy. She drove on slowly, stopping at "The Upper River Lodge." The office door was unlocked, so she picked five keys. She parked the Dodge three feet from a few rooms, and then checked each room. She locked them all and picked the room in the middle to use. Her room was dark and musky. She had noticed a propane tank outside. She hoped it was hooked to the fireplace in her room. It was, and a fire lit easily. She set her candles all over the room, and washed her face in the bathroom with water from a plastic jug. She noticed powder marks on her face from the gun going off in her face, and her ears were still ringing.

She lay on the twin bed. All her guns were there laid out for use. She racked a round in the 12-gauge shotgun, leaned it against the bed and then did the same with the assault rifle. She undid her service belt and reloaded the M&P pistol. The fireplace was warming the room. She laid back, most of her clothes still on. She looked up at the gas flames' reflection dancing on the ceiling. She ran her hands through her thick dark hair, "Man what a crazy fucking day."

She slept fitfully, dreaming of a blue lake that stretched on forever. *She was in a floatplane flying to Stehekin and landed on a snow-capped mountain. Trees hid most of the homes and cabins. She stepped off the plane's float and onto the dock. At the end of the dock was a man too far away to be able to clearly see his face.*

DOWN THE LAKE

CHAPTER 19

TOM STOCKED THE BOAT WITH THE THINGS he would need for the journey down the lake. In the cabin, he bungeed his shotgun next to the Winchester hunting rifle. Next to that were his AR-10 and the Colt M4. Joe was left with his Springfield M-1A1. Joe wanted a better gun to protect the ranch. After two hours of shooting lessons Tom was confident that Joe would be fine protecting the ranch. The M1A1 was a new version of the M-14 a rifle that was designed in the fifties to replace the World War II M1 Garand.

Joe set a cooler in the boat, "This is for you Tom, all from the farm, see ya." He walked to the pickup and drove off. Tom fired the motor. Noon, straight up. It felt good to be moving down the lake. He felt like Columbus journeying to America. Not knowing what the future would bring left him feeling a bit small. He wondered how the world had changed.

When in sight of Refrigerator Harbor, he pushed the throttle forward, keeping the AR-10 in his arms and his eyes on the south shore. The Sky Boat, with its bow high, and moving fast, kept as far to the north side of the lake as possible without hitting rocks. Tom didn't want to get shot at again. Once past Lucerne, Tom relaxed. He stopped at cabin locations along the lake. All cabins were empty but one. A complete family was dead in their beds and the stench was too much to bare.

GEORGE THIELMAN

The Sky Boat road cut easily through the water, another smooth ride. It was getting dark; Tom had spent too much time checking cabins. He wanted darkness so he could look for lighted homes, but he saw none. He docked the boat at 25 Mile. The place was in disarray. Branches lay throughout the yard. Bears had tipped the trashcans looking for food; walkways were dirty, and full of pine needles. The driveway was the same: upswept. There were no tracks that mattered. Dogs, bear, deer and raccoons were the only signs of life.

A hidden key opened Garrett's front door. The house was cold, but secure. Mail and the paper had been delivered until the day before Thanksgiving. In the mail Tom found two retirement checks and a letter from Major Mo, inviting him to Christmas dinner. One letter for Tom was from a cousin in Tacoma. He read them all and then checked out the newspaper. The most recent one told of a deadly virus that started in Brewster, brought to town by seasonal workers. It was reportedly one of the most infectious on record; the communicability rate went through the roof. In less than a week, 70% of Wenatchee residents had acquired the virus, and many had died. The CDC was working hard to find a cure. They were hopeful. Rumors of a link to the Ebola virus was inaccurate. He put the newspapers into a brown paper bag for Joe to read. Tom slept in the apartment above the garage that night.

In the early morning, Tom was happy to find that his Tundra pickup fired easily after sitting so long. Tom drove along the Columbia River sipping coffee. The sun had yet to rise… The roads were messy with dirt, rocks, and branches littering the highway. Cars and trucks sat on the side of the road, their windows so dirty, Tom couldn't see in. He stopped next to a gold Lincoln Town car. Looking in, he saw an old lady wrapped in puffy fur coat, probably her best clothes. Her neck and wrists were heavy with jewelry, a blonde wig sat on her head crooked, and the back seat was full of fancy, colorful clothes. He moved on after letting Woody pee on the side of the road. They continued south, making Wenatchee and turning west on Highway 2 to Blewett Pass, then connecting with Interstate 90 south to Yakima.

They stopped at a rest stop, looking back at Ellensburg. Tom scanned the valley below, looking for chimney smoke. He saw none. Only the wind made noise. To the east, the massive wind generators spun slowly creating electricity for no one. Crows flew overhead hoping for something easy to eat. At the end of the parking lot were two semi trucks. Tom turned and drove away to Major Mo's house.

An hour later he drove into Major Mo's driveway. The doors were locked, and curtains drawn. Toys littered the yard; trashcans were knocked over, their contents strewn about the yard. He knocked, hoping for a response; he kicked the back door in. In the bedroom he found his friends in their beds. He covered their faces. Then he looked throughout the house for a few things he would need. He found Mo's keys. In the wood shed he found a gallon of Coleman fuel. He walked back into the house, spread the fuel around the carpet, and then lit it with a match. The inside of the house quickly burned; black smoke, melting plastic fibers of the carpet, curtains blankets and pillows burned. Tom stood and watched the flames. He didn't want animals to get to his dead friends.

The fire was burned through the attic; flames shot through the roof, burning the roof tiles. He drove away not feeling anything.

He drove back up the ridge to the front gate of the military shooting range, unlocked the gate and drove the dirt road to the shooting shack. He unlocked the massive door. Inside he went to the big metal vault door and unlocked it. The room was as full of weapons as ever. He carried out boxes of his favorite weapons, and stacked them on the tables. He went to the other vault, and hauled out cases of ammo. After a few hours, he walked outside for a break.

In the east, weird clouds had formed over the Hanford Reservation. Owned by the Department of Defense, it was instrumental in the fabrication of nuclear bombs and materials. Warehouses, all for the use with nuclear materials, dotted the massive facility. Storage tanks held toxic materials. Tom drove east, to get a better view of the Hanford area. With his binoculars he scanned the area, but he couldn't see much of the buildings. Steam clouds billowed upward, blocking any sights past Hanford. He had seen enough to know that something big and bad was happening at the reservation.

Fearing for his life, he looked around. Nearby a couple flies buzzed his face, two big beetles walked along together in the dirt, and ants busily worked for their community anthill. Butterflies fluttered by and birds flew. He stood on the hood of his pickup looking back on the shooting range through his powerful Steiner binoculars. He saw movement in the brush. A lone coyote trotted two hundreds yards to the north, ears straight up. It ran to the top of the hill, turned and looked at Tom. Three pups ran about the mother, and then ran down the hill out of sight. He felt relieved. If he saw a radiation cloud from Hanford, it must not have been headed his direction. The sight of the bugs and animals allowed him relief. Three hours later, Tom left the shooting range, his pickup low in the back.

GEORGE THIELMAN

He drove back into the garage at 25 Mile Sky and closed the door. Next, Tom went to Garrett's house where he would be staying. Tom called Joe on the short wave. He told Joe that if he talked to Becky, he should tell her to avoid the southeast corner of Washington, especially the south and east of Hanford. Joe asked why, but the connection went dead before he could hear it. That night Tom ate with Woody in the dark, looking out over lower Lake Chelan. He went over the day's events in his mind. Hanford was his biggest worry. He wondered about the rest of nuclear power plants throughout the world. The nuclear machine required electricity to pump water back into its power source so it wouldn't blow up. He knew enough to worry. Being one man in a world of dead men gave him little power to fix the huge industrial and military machine's problems. He could only keep his mind on his own small world of gardens and hunting. This was his world, his reality. Life was now simple, but the problems were still the same, industrial and military toxins would seep out of containers and into the air and ground. No matter what happened he would have to deal with it.

Still, he wondered how much he should care. How far had the pandemic reached? Had it wipe out everyone in the world? He was curious, but he couldn't find out. He had to stay on the lake, to fend for his own life. The lake was his life.

SIMCOE MOUNTAINS
THE OTHER THOMAS DEER

CHAPTER 20

SOUTH OF YAKIMA, HIGHWAY 97 SPLITS the Yakima Indian Reservation. The ground rises up to create the Simcoe Mountains, the Toppenish and Ahtanum Ridges, steep hills with good timber. Creeks and streams flow through to water the vast farmland that surround the area. The huge Indian reservation extends all the way to the Cascade Mountain Range. Mount Adams, at the west end, and at over twelve thousand feet, is a beacon for most of southern Washington and northern Oregon.

Ten miles east of Highway 97, along a rough Jeep trail, a big white mailbox stood out. It had black splotches on it to copy the hide of a Holstein cow. In blue and red letters were the words, Deer Farm. Tom and Jenny Deer lived a simple life on their five-acre farm. They did not raise deer, and enjoyed the families that braved the rough dirt road to find a deer farm for their children to enjoy. At one thousand, six hundred feet high, a small stream fed the crops. Corn and wheat grew along with apple and cherry trees. A one-acre vegetable garden kept the family table colorful. Three children helped pulling weeds in the big garden. All of the kids were homeschooled in their cement blockhouse. The roof was flat, made of concrete, and held an herb garden. Every square inch of the property was used to grow food for the family and their friends. A small barn was used as a workspace and garage for their twenty-year-old Chevy pickup.

Along the outside walls of the barn were pens for rabbits, and a chicken coop kept the family rich in eggs and fertilizer for the gardens.

Being that they were Indian, Nick hunted, hiking through the pine forest. Sometimes to make extra money he would guide a hunter near his little farm. He knew the area and did everything to sustain his family without having to work a real job. He enjoyed the remote land, gave talks and guided tours to tribal members about self-sustaining mountain living. The couple's enthusiasm for natural living was infectious to other tribal members. Gardens and chicken coupes were popping up throughout the community.

Like much of the country, the economic recession was motivating people to live simpler and to leave less of a carbon footprint. Like Sky Ranch, without having to raise money for electric, gas and water bills, more time was spent gardening, ranching and hunting; a natural tradeoff. The Deer Family was heavily schooled in organic gardening. Along with great soil, the family made compost material from the waste of two milk cows. Chickens and human waste matter was saved to enrich the soil. Instead of the usual ceramic and plastic toilets used in modern society the Deers had a standard toilet seat attached to a wood box that you sat on. Under the wood box were buckets lined with straw or sawdust. The Deer family's fecal matter was dropped into the buckets, which were dumped twice a day into a compost pile. That was dried and mixed with leaves and other organic matter to create a perfectly healthy compost to enrich the soil. This made the plants green and healthy for the family's food. Nick joked that the family food went from, "the toilet to the plate." The cycle of life resided on the Deer Farm.

The family's home was dug out of a hillside. When the house was finished, gravel was placed against the outside of the block walls and dirt was placed six feet deep on the outside, making the house look like it was three feet tall. The building style was like that of the futurist; Paolo Soleri; like Arcosanti, built of concrete and block near the town of Cordes Junction, Arizona. Paolo and his people made a community made of sustainable products and designed and built to use passive solar and take advantage of the wind. Simple four foot by eight-foot solar panels provided the family with the energy needed to heat water for baths and showers. The next thing Nick was saving for was a wind power pole and generating station. The wind blew most of the time from the north, and sometimes from the southeast. The wind generator would work perfectly at the farm, but the money for one wasn't available at the moment.

The virus happened the fall before the Deers hunkered down. They had locked their gate, played board games with the kids, farmed, and tended to the needs of the property. The virus flourished in the Indian Nation and was as murderous to the Native People as it was to the white population. Like the people at Sky Ranch, the Deers were ready; well supplied, prepared in every way for the destruction of the human race. There was no TV at the Deer Farm; they listened to the radio for information. With spring in full bloom and the stream flowing at record levels, the farm was an island of green foliage. Chicken pecked at the ground. Two one hundred-pound Airedale dogs protected the remote little farm with gusto; in their small minds they were the possessors of the Deer Farm, chasing coyotes and mountain lions far from the property.

Fresh food was not a problem at Deer Farm. Rabbit and chicken meat was traded for necessary items such as sugar, coffee, salt, and other items. Little money passed through the pockets of the Deer family. They made t through on very little money. Smart and hardworking, they worked from sunup to sundown. Jenny started the day cooking pancakes or eggs. When the dishes were washed and put away, books were brought out for reading and writing lessons. Math and science was taught, as well as civics and politics. Jenny and her husband were proud college graduates. They'd met in Pullman, Washington when they were attending Washington State University. They had been together for almost twenty years. Now in their late thirties, they were the embodiment of happiness and self-sufficiency.

Along the outer boundary of the farm the Deer family kept a large bee farm. Twelve white boxes; beehives; sat in the sun in front of ten apple trees. With the appearance of flowers came the bees out of their bee boxes; thousands of honeybees buzzed the property keeping the plants pollinated. Pollen is taken from the flowers, brought back to the hive by the worker bees, and used to make honey. Nick and his wife calculated that they had around two hundred thousand bees pollinating and making honey. Along with the bees, hummingbirds buzzed about competing with the bees for the tasty pollen. Bees flew back and forth from the beehive to the flowered plants.

Nick had just come back from a hunt empty handed. He put his gun and gear away. He slipped on a thick wool shirt with leather gloves and put on a homemade mosquito net and a baseball cap. His two girls laughed at him. He gave them both a pat on their butts and they ran outside to help gather honey.

Outside a curious fog was blowing from the south, circling around the Simcoe Mountains. He walked through the garden to the beehives. When he picked the top of the hive off its box, the bees didn't buzz him at all. They seemed listless and clung to the side of the boxes. Thousands of them were walking on the ground as if they ants; something he had never seen. He pulled out the handle that contained the honeycomb. Rather than flying away, the bees dropped to the ground. He pulled out another. This time the bees just dropped to the ground dead. He set the honeycomb down and looked at his two girls. They were watching a hummingbird; it seemed to be having a hard time staying airborne, as a helicopter or airplane would fall from the sky when it ran out of fuel. Nick watched as the little bird fluttered its wings and flew straight into a tree limb and fell to the ground. One of the girls picked it up and watched it die. With his two girls, he buried the bird and went back to inspecting the beehive. All the bees were dead.

One of his girls said, "Daddy, I feel sick … and itchy!" He felt it as well. Not so much a sense of being itchy. He felt sick and weak. He looked around and noticed all the chickens had died and saw three butterflies were laying on the ground dead. He looked at the cloud that was flowing around them. A sense of dread came over him as he realized it could only be some sort of toxic cloud. He ran the girls into the semi-underground house, closing windows and vents. It was too late. The girls were dead within three days. He died a day later. His wife lived three days more, weak and vomiting, and then died.

The big cloud was part of the same mass of cloud Tom had seen from the Yakima Proving Grounds. For months radioactive waste had been escaping into the wind and sky, separating and flowing as several clouds. The morning the Deers began to harvest the bees' honey, a perfect wind blew around Hanford converging and congregating the clouds together. The wind shifted, carrying the toxic and radioactive waste to the Simcoe Mountains and killing the Deer Family. It destroyed organically managed farm and family that did everything to avoid the modern machines.

DOWN THE LAKE

CHAPTER 21

THE NEXT MORNING TOM WALKED to the neighbor's homes to check for survivors. Most were vacation homes and vacant; some were occupied with dead. He left them alone with a sign on the door. At noon he started to load the Sky Boat for a late evening ride to the town of Chelan. He was excited, this was his world. He wanted to find survivors, was sure it would probably not happen in the dense population areas, but hoped anyway.

He unloaded several rifle cases from the Tundra and transferred them to the Sky Boat. The rest he left locked up in the garage. After gassing the boat, he pulled out onto the lake. The fun day would begin. More junk could be seen in the lake as he went further down lake. Floating debris, logs, branches, even boats, bobbed at the lower end of the lake. The lake actually flowed down hill, south to Chelan. Stehekin was a few feet higher than Chelan, making for a big slow moving lake. Because of the movement and the depth of the lake, it was clear and blue; sometimes it was green, but incredibly healthy. Tom drove the boat slowly southeast, dodging logs. He stopped at a few upside-down speedboats, air pockets keeping them afloat. He took out an axe, and smacked the bottom of the fiberglass boat, hoping to chop a big enough hole to allow the boat to sink. He towed a few others to shore, tying the boats, so the debris would not be a maritime nuisance. Tom pulled several other boats to docks nearby. Darkness was coming on so Tom sped ahead down the lake in darkness. A three quarters moon shown in the night, guiding him southeast. Stars lit up the night; it was as though the sky opened for him shining their streetlights. As he rode south he encountered more floating obstacles: boats, wave runners, sailboats, along with all the stuff used in boats: coolers, jugs, life jackets, and dishes. He passed a green inflated floating dinosaur raft. Woody barked at the floating serpent. Tom left it bobbing in the lake.

Manson was the first area he came to. He pulled up to the old wooden docks and secured his mooring. He looked at the bulletin board, half expecting to find a message that would be pertinent to his life. Instead he found fishing and boating rules. He rode the boat out into the lake again, slowly riding off shore to the town of Chelan. He tied to a buoy in the middle of the lake looking for signs of life, an engine noise, maybe a window light or a gunshot. There was nothing but the sound of birds. He sat back on the bench seat looking through the binoculars. No sound.

In the boat's cabin, he pulled the bench seat out turning it into a full-sized bed and climbed into his sleeping bag. Woody jumped up on the bench next to him. They fell asleep rolling with the waves. Tom woke to barking dogs in the distance. Woody looked at Tom, concerned, then looked away into the dark. Outside there were two barks, and then the report of a rifle.

Tom looked at Woody, "Well, we're not alone after all, and they're not dog lovers." He listened for another shot. There were several followed by silence.

He looked at his watch. It was 2:20 AM. He decided to sit tight for another couple hours. He lay back, falling asleep in a few minutes. At 4:30 AM his watch vibrated on his left wrist. He woke up, dressed in cargo pants with a fleece sweater topped by his Air Force camo field coat. His pistol belt was loaded down with extra clips, pouches, and under his right arm was his sidearm H&K .40 caliber. Under the left arm was a twelve-inch Gerber fighting knife. He had started to carry the bigger fighting knife five years back, after he was caught in a hand-to-hand fight with three armed Iraqi Republican Guard soldiers.

At the time he carried a smaller eight-inch dagger. He surprised the three of Iraqis when he walked into a kitchen while the three of prepared a meal. One knocked his M4 from his hands, while another went for his rifle. The third soldier had pulled a big knife from his belt. The guy with the rifle pulled it to within two inches of Tom's face. Tom had kicked the guy in the knee, tripping him, and landed a punch to the side of his head. The fellow with the big knife came at him. Tom feigned to the right, spun around, and took the big knife from the guy. He faced all three with the bigger knife in his right hand and the smaller in the left. He came at them one by one, one knife slashing; the other stabbing. He killed two, and the last gave up, begging for his life after seeing the gory demise of his buddies. Since that time Tom carried a bowie-type fighting knife to keep the odds in his favor.

He pulled the Sky Boat between the two ferryboats. He slipped on his equipment vest that carried the armor, along with all the other paraphernalia needed to stay alive while fighting. The front pouches carried eight thirty-round clips of .308 caliber bullets for the AR-10. Others carried a small five-inch dagger, a Swiss army knife, a small headlamp, a folding knife, three flash bang grenades, and two small tear gas grenades. One pouch carried a small can of pepper spray that shot red paint along with the pepper spray. In a small camelback pack he carried a first aid kit, power bars, and food for Woody. His mountain bike was bungeed to the side of the wheelhouse; he leaned it against a pole and filled the side bags with half of the stuff from his vest so he wouldn't be weighed down. From the boat he pulled a small H&K mp5 submachine gun .9 mm. It fired a sick volley of rounds and was incredibly accurate. When he left the ferry dock he was carrying a hundred pounds of equipment on his person and in the side bags of the mountain bike.

He rode toward town, past the condos and houses. The road was strewn with dirt, leaves, trash, bird crap, and anything else that would fly in the wind. The town was quiet and it was still early. He sniffed the air for wood smoke. Nothing. He rode slowly. Woody jogged along faithfully and happily next to his master, his big tongue hanging out. Cars and trucks sat filthy in the fog, windows dirty.

Empty roads with branches and trash showed the tracks of vehicles that had come through the area; big fat mud tires, from a 4X4, showing thick spaces between tread. At a small doctor's office they stopped. The door was locked tight, and grass and shrubbery had been left uncared for.

If there were survivors, they were still sleeping or had moved away. Through town Tom and Woody continued, straight to the police department. The front door was shot up and glass littered the concrete. Two dead policemen sat at their desks, dead mouths gaping, heads straight back, and eyes closed.

Outside the cop shop Tom took a big breath. He looked left and right. Someone had gone through the police station gathering weapons and who knew what else. Woody stood, his tail wagging, sniffing at nearby bushes.

Tire tracks were up on the sidewalk. It was as if the driver had peeled out on the concrete, fat tires again.

They turned right off the highway. Two blocks to Ray's house, and four blocks up the road. He knocked on the door several times. When he got no response he looked in the windows. He needed supplies from Ray's store. He had to get in. The doors were reinforced metal and the windows were barred over. The back bathroom of the house had a glass block window. In a neighbor's garage Tom found a long framing hammer. The hammer smashed the glass block with a pop. He smashed the mortar out of the way and crawled in. Down the hall Ray was in his bed with his wife, both dead. Tom covered them with a blanket and went looking through the house for keys. He found them in the kitchen. In the soft soil of the back yard he dug two graves. Ray and his wife were buried in the yard.

He backed out Ray's tricked-out Chevy pickup and camper from the garage and drove to the dead end alley behind the store. Fishing through the keys he found the keys for the barred back door and a metal door. Through the two layers of doors and he was inside. Tom unloaded his bike and drove the Chevy to the local organic co-op food store.

From four different stores he carried out bags of beans, rice, flour, coffee, sugar, and just about any other kind of good, including four cases of booze for the bar and six cases of beer from the liquor store.

Next was the feed store for the chickens, dogs and cats at Sky Ranch. Woody laid in the sun, watching Tom as he loaded fifty-pound bags onto the roof rack of the camper. The camper held a Yakima cargo carrier that was perfect for bags of animal feed. Tom loaded over five hundred pounds of animal feed up there. Woody was squeaking a rubber dog toy made in the shape of a cat. The shopping binge had gone well; half the camper was full of food and the pair had plenty of animal food. The sun was out and Woody laid nearby, happy as a dog could be with a full belly and a new squeaky toy. He was working furiously, taking short, fast bites at the toy, trying to kill the squeaker.

He stopped, his head and ears straight up, listening. Tom said with a smile, "What's up buddy?" From the distance came the sound of vehicles, moving fast. By the sound of the whine the vehicles had oversized 4x4 tires. Tom walked to a van near the road. As he looked east, two shiny black pickups appeared, jacked up three feet in air. The first truck, a Chevy, was blocking a Ford, which was trying to pass. Playing chicken with a truck sitting in the road, the Ford would have to pass him or slow down before he hit the derelict pickup in the road. The driver of the Ford slowed down rather than smash into the truck. Horns blew. Two men in the back of the Chevy were shooting at the buildings. As the trucks passed, both passengers shot out the windows of the paint store twenty feet from Tom. Luckily for Tom they ran out of bullets.

As they passed, sets of eyes fixed on Tom and Woody. They looked dumfounded, mouths open, holding shotguns, they pounded on the window of the Chevy, "Turn around Asshole. There's someone over there." Both trucks stopped up the road, the men talking and shouting. The Ford driver slammed the throttle down. The big wheels skidded and hopped as he backed up in reverse. The Chevy did the same, catching up to the Ford easily. The passengers in the back bed of the Chevy held on to a roll bar. Standing up, they jerked as the driver came to a stop, and then did a burnout, driving forward. Dorn was one of the guys in the back of the pickup. He yelled with joy as he almost lost his footing, "Let's get that mother fucker, owwwwowowow!" The Chevy pulled into the feed store parking lot too fast. This time Dorn lost his grip on the roll bar. He grabbed one of the spotlights as the truck bounced again. He fell straight to the truck bed with a heavy thump, and bounced up again by way of Mini-Mike slamming the brakes. Dorn's fellow passenger fell on top of him.

Just as the big pickup skidded to a stop, the Ford rear-ended the Chevy, slamming Dorn's face into the front of the truck bed. Having knocked out one of his rotten front teeth, he howled as if in pain, even though he couldn't feel any. An hour earlier he had taken prednisone and oxycontin for his IBS pain. He picked up his shotgun, and stood in the back of the truck wheeling his gun from one direction to another. He saw Tom's pickup. They were looking for the driver while both pickups idling loudly.

Mini Mike yelled from the Ford, "What the fuck are we looking for? Fuckin' asshole. Let's go." He sat mumbling to himself, "God damn asshole should shut the fuck up, kick his fuckin' ass, man."

Dorn stood looking around, frustrated, He quickly aimed at Ray's Chevy pickup and fired six shotgun blasts at the window. The front lights and grill broke and shattered. The front window cracked, but didn't fall apart. The guy next to Dorn fired his shotgun at the pickup. He broke windows out and then turned the remaining shells on the feed store, breaking up its front windows. He leaned down to reload his shotgun. Dorn was doing the same. As he slipped shells into the shotgun he yelled, "Man this is too easy." Mini Mike sitting behind the wheel of the Chevy, engine running, and took a big swig of his favorite energy drink, Nitro. It was spiked with a healthy dose of alcohol and caffeine, and could only be bought on the Indian reservations. He finished the can, threw it out the window, and he watched as Tom calmly walked around his truck.

Wearing army camo and a gun belt with a huge knife, he mumbled to himself," What the fuck man!" Tom walked straight up to Dorn who didn't see him until Tom grabbed his shotgun. The other guy dropped his shotgun when he saw Tom. With the gun barrel in his hand, Tom pulled it gently from Dorn who held on to it for a few seconds, then released it. With his mouth wide open, Dorn watched helplessly as Tom slammed the rifle butt into his chest propelling Dorn back against his buddy. Both men fell hard on top of empty spent shotgun shells, empty bottles, and empty cans of Nitro.

Tom turned toward Mini Mike's Ford, reeled back with the barrel of the shotgun like a baseball player at bat, and with a mighty swing broke out the Ford's windshield. He turned to Dorn who was trying to get up in the back of the pickup bed and threw the gun with all his might. Dorn ducked as the shotgun hit the back window of the pickup. Its window shattered. The driver, who had seen some of the soldier's actions, knew he was in deep trouble. He slammed the truck in reverse, passing Tom and into the front of the Ford. Mini Mike was doing the same, backing up, cussing in amazement at how brazen Tom was. They peeled out into the road. Dorn looked up in time to see Tom with a pistol in his hands aiming straight at him.

Both pickups were now in the road, pointing west; the Ford followed behind the Chevy. Both drivers stomped on the throttle, shooting forward, as Tom let loose with concentrated, accurate fire at the windshield of the Chevy. He fired into both pickups as they peeled out in front of him. Tom dropped the clip, slammed in another, firing and hitting the pickups as they raced away.

He picked up the empty clip and watched the pickups roar out of sight. He jogged to Ray's pickup, grabbed the AR10 and jogged back to the street to wait for them. They didn't come back. Back at the pickup Tom slipped the combat vest around his neck and filled it with full clips for his rifle. He called for Woody, the big dog came swaggering to him the rubber cat in his mouth. Tom looked at the direction the trucks had gone. "Well Woody, they're either going to hide out at home or they're going to go to war with us," he laughed. He looked at his dog. Woody had blood trickling from his forehead. Tom reached down for his dog, feeling around, found a small piece of buckshot had penetrated the skin between his eyes. Woody stood, tail wagging as Tom pushed the buckshot back out the small hole. He dabbed antiseptic on the small bleeding hole. Woody looked up at him; oblivious to the danger, he wagged his tail and reached down for his squeaky toy.

BATTLE IN TOWN

CHAPTER 22

Tom drove back to Ray's store. The truck windows were shot out, the steering wheel was shot up, and glass was everywhere in the cab. They passed burnt cars and buildings, wanton destruction of property. At a gas station Tom stopped. Two burnt dogs were tied up to post. He poked at them with the big bowie knife and saw entry holes. He stood back up, and muttered in disgust, "God damned. They were used for target practice." Their fur was burnt black, and most of the bullet holes were small with a bigger exit hole .223s. He backed the shot-up pickup into the dead end alley next to the door of Ray's store. He set garbage cans in front of the pickup to hide it, in case the punks came for another joy ride. Over the pickup and camper he laid a camo net from the store to further camouflage the pickup.

Satisfied that he had done all he could, he went back inside the store. He pulled out a list of supplies stacking them by the door, fishing gear, several knives and hatchets, blankets, sleeping bags, outdoor clothes for him. For Joe: pants, shirts, jackets, hats, beanies, two cases of green propane tanks, and cookware, all designed for outdoor use. In the footwear department, he grabbed several pair of New Balance trail running shoes and hiking boots along with a box of socks. He held up a pair of expedition-weight Patagonia socks and shook them at Woody, "Joe's gonna love these babies!" He put everything in the pickup and went back into the store, locking the big metal doors behind him.

Upstairs, in the gun shop, he unlocked the gun vault where the weapons were kept. He pondered what to take. After his shopping spree at the Yakima Gun Range he wondered what on earth he could possibly need from Ray's Gun Shop. Whatever he left may not be available next time he came through here. Maybe the next time, the punks will have ransacked the place, burned it down, or both. He looked around. The walls were made from solid stone. The second floor was all metal beams and tile. Even the roof was supported by metal. He took a ladder to the roof, emerging in a stair room on the roof. The door was made of steel, and the walls were twelve-inch mortar-set stone, the same as the block holding up the building. The stair room was fifteen by eight feet. He unlocked the steel door that led to the roof. The roof tiles were made of slate impossible to burn. The building north of Ray's store was one floor lower than Rays. Looking north he could see a furniture store. In its ground floor windows he could see the reflection of the real estate office next to Ray's and he could see the alley. "Hmm, good thing to know."

Looking east was the big park, with a playground, restrooms, and a big green lawn inhabited by geese and ducks. To south were more buildings, eight feet lower than Ray's old movie theater building. He stood on the roof listening for sounds, but heard none. He thought of the possibility of carrying all the weapons out of the store, but there were too many. Back in the vault he chose the weapons that he would take with him. He thought to himself that he and his friends would use some of the weapons forever, "if I ever find any friends," he muttered out loud with a laugh.

Rifles were laid out on the counter: bolt-action rifles from Winchester and Remington, four pump shotguns and two semi-auto duck guns. Ray had just received six new Colt semi-auto assault rifles for the Chelan County Sherriff's Department. Tom laid them out on the table. From four boxes he pulled four Remington semi-auto rifles designed for hunting. They looked very much like a long barreled M4 with a camo cover and a big scope. Two were chambered in .223 and two in the bigger .308. Remington and other manufacturers had been making assault rifles for hunting and long range shooting for years, by tightening the specs on the rifles. From another metal cabinet he pulled out cases of ammo, and searched through another cabinet for scopes and optics for his new weapons.

Side arms took up less room, so he laid out more of them. Ray was a big believer in the old school Colt .45s called the 1911 models. His favorite maker was an American company Kimber, and Smith & Wesson. He laid 20 side arms in their boxes on the tables. Tom knew that Joe wanted a fancy plastic pistol. Ray was a believer in American made weapons. He carried the Smith & Wesson M&P series. He stacked ten plastic boxes with M & P pistols for Joe to choose from.

Looking through padded metal boxes, he found flash bang, tear gas, and smoke grenades, all tagged for the Sheriffs' Department. He set them on the table. He found a heavy box with a label that read stink/caution. Inside he found a plastic case that held twenty-four stink bomb grenades. Used for crowd control, they were controversial and not yet sold to the military or law enforcement. Contents of the stink bomb were not known. On the floor he set several cases of bullets and reloading supplies.

He went to the corner office to prepare supper. Two cans of Dennison's beef stew were heated over a small Coleman camp stove. He climbed the steps to the roof to look around. On the roof he drank a big mug of tea then smoked a bowl of juicy fruit. He thought again of the events of the day. The supplies he collected for the ranch would help in the near future to put food on the table and protect from predators, both those on two feet, and four. Again he wondered if he could ignore the punks and just go home. He wanted to go back to Sky Ranch, but the responsible person in him kept him from leaving. He was the most qualified person to deal with such a problem. Smoke trailed from his mouth and the pipe. He thought of Mad Max, living in the desert. He looked down at Woody, who looked north, seeing in the dark what Tom couldn't; a dog's sight, with incredible hearing, and an oversized nose. He thought about how Woody experienced feelings in a totally different way than Tom.

Tom walked to the coffee shop nearby; snooping through, he found large amounts of coffee and cookies. Throughout the evening he strolled through shops picking up supplies he could use. From a small medical center he collected medical supplies, drugs, syringes, bandages, antiseptic, and materials to fix and immobilize broken bones, something he would no doubt need in the future.

◆◆

Fog had come in over the lake, making for a dreary night. Ted had just finished applying first aid to his brother Dorn, Andy, Mini Mike, and Doug. Dorn had taken quite a pounding in the back of the truck, knocked out tooth, and had new bumps all over his big head and a bloody nose, on top of being punched in the chest with a shotgun. Ted was pissed-off and was looking to gain vengeance for his brother. Andy and Doug were newer guys that had paired up with a couple, Steve and Karen, and a Russian named Vashilli. Along with Ted's girlfriend, the entire group had happened to meet along the roadside near Brewster.

As a group, they had moved to the Baylands Condos on the north side of town two weeks earlier. The Baylands Condos was four floors high, with four condos on each floor, and a pool in the middle courtyard. All the doors opened to the courtyard, which made for a nice community, had not eighty percent of the inhabitants been hard drug users and thieves.

Steve and Karen had just thrown an old bicycle in the pool. Ted at the railing, looked down at the filthy pool, half full of trash. A barbecue lay in the water, its legs sticking out, along with chairs and a table thrown there by his brother and Mini Mike. Across from him Vaschilli stood, leaning on his railing. looking down at the trash-strewn pool. Both men looked at each other then rolled their eyes in disgust.

Vashilli, the big Russian, watched Mini-Mike tie another stray dog to a tree on the lawn. This was Mini-Mike's fun. Before Vashilli could run downstairs to stop Mini-Mike, he heard a shot. Down the stairs he ran and around the corner. Mini Mike was laughing out loud at his latest kill. Vashilli snatched the assault rifle out of Mini-Mike's hands, set it down, and put his hands around Mini-Mike's neck, shaking him just enough to feel his strength.

With his heavy Russian accent he said, "You stupid sheet, da guy that kicked your ass is out there right now! Stop shooting these dogs! "He shook Mini-Mike one more time, "If you want your gun you can have it tomorrow." When Vaschilli let go of Mini-Mike, the smaller man fell backward to the ground and landed on his butt. Vaschilli pointed his big finger at the punk, and then walked off in disgust.

In his room he slammed the door. There was a knock, and Ted walked in the room. "Sorry man, those guys are wound up and drinking too much. I'll talk to them tomorrow."

Vaschilli stomped his foot at his bigger friend, "That guy dat kick the ass of them is out there, day say he beat them then shot out window and light on trucks. He could have maybe shot dem all dead but he did not, very dangerous. I do not vant to fight this." Ted was bigger than Vashilli and a decade younger. The Russian had been a soldier in his country serving in Afghanistan during the initial invasion and for additional five years. His experience had taught him to respect all adversaries.

Ted was a college football player and wrestler. A bit bigger than Vaschilli, he was stronger and younger. He wondered, as all big strong men did, who was the better fighter. Ted was six foot five; Vaschilli smaller at six three, but still a strong capable man. They talked for a while about camping and hiking. The Russian was trying to get the group to move to a farm so they could grow good crops, ranch, and hunt for their food. He saw the way of their life as unsustainable; scrounging canned food and living off a few fish here and there. He had shot a deer a day earlier, hung it up and gone on fishing trip with Ted. When he came back the punks had torn the deer carcass with machete's and hatchets. The constant drugged and drunken shenanigans were getting old; he needed other people to make the move with him. "Just a matter of time," he thought.

When the punks came back after their ass kicking, Vaschilli was instantly worried. A man that would calmly walk up to armed men without a weapon and inflicted so much pain and let them walk away, was dangerous. The man was military by his dress and actions, "Just another survivor on his own that happens to be a soldier." He thought of leaving that night, but Ted, the only reasonable man, amongst them, talked the Russian into staying. He had to back his older trouble-making brother. Vaschilli would give them a few more days to leave and establish a farm or ranch. Even if it was just Ted and his girlfriend, that would be good enough. He lay down on his bed. Thinking about the day, he got back up to lock his door. He lay on the big bed, looking out over the dark lake wondering if the Road Warrior would come for them tonight.

Ted walked into the room that he shared with his girlfriend, Lisa. "How's your brother?" she asked.

Ted answered, "He's OK. Banged up. Got a tooth knocked out today."

She laughed, "That's all, a tooth? What a big baby. I thought he was shot ten times by the way you guys acted."

Ted looked out the window at the dark town. He smiled,"Yah, he's a bit high- strung, but I promised our mom I would look after him and back his play. "

Lisa stood up and faced him, "A bit high strung? He's strung out on Prednisone, that's a steroid, and he takes oxycontin, smokes crack, or anything else he can smoke. On top of all that, he's a drunk, unhealthy, and the meanest, most uncaring man I have ever seen or heard of."

Ted walked to her slipping his big arms around her small body, "I'm sorry. I'll take care of him, you'll see. Things are going to change." He kissed her on the forehead.

She pushed him back. "Ted, things are not going to change, alright. That army guy is going to come over here and kill all of us. I heard you and Vaschilli talking. He's worried. You're like a guy on a sinking ship, yelling that everything is going to be alright. Those guys down there are evil, immoral, and messed up, I'm afraid when you're gone. I lock myself in the room with my pistol until you come back." They argued for a few hours more. Lisa made sense, Ted knew it. She knew and he knew that whatever happened, he would back his brother's play.

Tom laid out a stack of sleeping pads to crash on. Woody took a look up at Tom, and then curled in a ball, laid his nose between his two back feet and closed his eyes. Tom poked at the fire in Ray's old pot-bellied stove. He sat in the office chair looking at shadows dancing on the office wall while he smoked a bowl. He lay down, staring into the flickering wood stove.

He slept for two hours, waking with a start. The ground seemed to be rumbling and buzzing. He ran upstairs to the roof. Looking north at lights moving, maybe a mile away, the noise was no doubt music from big speakers. He ran down the stairs. He was dressed in dark clothes and his camo jacket with his loaded combat vest. He had changed out the bigger clips used for the AR10 for the smaller clips of the new Colts he had brought from Yakima. The smaller bullets would do fine in an urban fight. Two magazines were clipped together so they would be easier to reload. Outside he locked the door behind him and stashed the keys on top a windowsill so he wouldn't lose them.

With Woody walking beside him, they walked quickly through the park, across the street and turned north along the shore. As they walked nearer to the punks' condo complex, Tom noticed several speedboats half sunken by gunfire. The water smelled of gas and oil. Tom and Woody cut through yards, trying to stay a couple hundred yards from the condo complex. Woody sensed excitement and stayed close to his master, watching him, reading his expressions and actions. They followed the screaming music, and walked around the north side of the complex. The parking lot was lit up by two shot-up black 4x4s. The bass was loud, and it vibrated the ground. He watched from the darkness as a big guy left the condo complex, clearly pissed off. The big guy talked with somebody a few minutes. The music went quiet and the lights were turned down, but the party had just begun.

Steve and Karen stumbled to their condo for the night. Mini-Mike and Andy laid their rifles across one of the trucks and fired a series of bullets at dead dogs. The bodies moved slightly as the bullets penetrated skin and bone. Mini-Mike and Andy ran up to the dog carcasses and fired shotgun blasts into the bodies. They yelled and high fived each other.

Tom jogged to within twenty feet of Mini-Mike and Andy. Both were strapped up with weapons, pistol belts and rifles slung over their shoulders. Tom walked quickly behind them. When they saw Tom, both reached for their empty shotguns. Tom hit them both on the side of their heads. The hand punches from the side were accurate. Both Mini-Mike and Andy went limp and hit the concrete. Tom took their guns and threw those into the bushes. As the two recovered, Tom smacked them each in the face with his fist. They lay on the concrete moaning. Tom zipped-tied their hands behind their backs and pulled them to their feet. M4 pointing at their faces, Tom spoke quietly. Mini-Mike was frightened by his black face paint.

"Listen up punks, I'm running out of patience with you assholes." Mini-Mike started to talk, so Tom hit him in the face with his fist. Mike stopped talking. Tom turned to Andy, noticing a big blocky metal nose ring, he grabbed it. "You want some too?" Andy said almost in a whisper, "No man, not at all."

Tom pulled a small roll of duct tape from his vest. He wrapped two layers around both of their mouths. He slapped Mini-Mike and pulled his big twelve-inch bowie knife from its sheath. He pointed it under Mini-Mike's chin. "Listen to me and do what I say, or I'll kill both of you right now." He drilled the knife's point into Mike's chin to emphasize his point. He did the same to Andy. Both squirmed with pain as the knifepoint hit bone. "Now we're going to go through that entrance to the condos. Let's go." He pushed them forward, past the office and into the courtyard by the pool. Tom reached down, opened a five-gallon can of gas. and kicked it into the pool. He threw a flash bang grenade into the water that ignited the gas leaving a strange flickering light. Tom then whispered into the ears of both of his captives, "Now get on your knees and keep quiet." They did as they were told.

Tom raised the Colt M4 toward the upper floors and fired a twenty round volley at the doors and railings and yelled, "Wake up! Wake up time." He fired the rest of the bullets at the building in a half circle. The bullets broke out windows and penetrated doors. He reloaded as doors opened.

Vaschilli looked down, not sure what to expect, "vhat the hell is wrong with you two?"

Tom cut him off, "Shut up and listen," Everyone was at the railing looking down at Tom and the punks. The gas was floating and burning on the surface of the water. Tom looked up at them, his rifle pointing from one to the other, "if you people don't get out of this town by tomorrow morning, I'm going to kill every one of you." He reached forward, grabbed Mini-Mike, and pushed him into the filthy pool, He did the same to Andy, who hit the barbecue with a painful thud. Tom backed up, threw another flash bang in the pool and two tear gas grenades. He dropped two more tear gas grenades where he was standing, turned and walked into the darkness. The flash bang grenade went off on Andy's back, burning him, and knocking the breath out of him. Then he had to deal with the tear gas. Ted came down and pulled them out of the filthy pool and dragged them both out of the smoke. Ted ran back up to his room, grabbed a hoodie, and his shotgun.

Lisa yelled, "Wait! No Ted! Don't go! He'll kill you!" Ted left.

Vaschilli yelled at him, "Ted, vait! That's not good for you." Ted entered the darkness. The big Russian, grabbed his pistol belt and assault rifle and walked slowly after Ted.

Tom and Woody jogged back slowly the way they'd came. Tom turned the corner of a house, and ran smack into Ted; both men had dropped their weapons on the ground. Tom stood up first, but the bigger man kicked him in the butt from a kneeling position. Tom was propelled forward and fell to the ground. He rolled back to his feet and kicked at Ted. He missed and it made him realize how deadly his opponent was.

They both stood quickly. Ted reached out his longer hands grabbing Tom by the neck. Tom smacked his hands away, and hit Ted in the face with three hard punches. Ted was stunned, but still had the power to hold Tom and punch him several times in the gut. Ted reeled in pain as he hit Tom's extra clips and pistol all nestled in the lower pouches; he pulled back, his hands bleeding. Tom came forward punching and hitting the bigger man. Ted grabbed Tom around the neck, choking him. Tom held Ted's hands, keeping the choke from sinking in further. He was loosing strength. Woody lunged forward, and bit Ted's ass and legs. He let Tom go, and turned his fight to Woody, who jumped out of the way each time he kicked at him. He did this until he felt Tom's bowie knife pierce into his big thigh. He screamed in pain and the light went out when Tom kicked him in the head. Ted hit the asphalt hard. Tom kneeled beside him, and hit him three times in the face breaking his nose.

Tom heard Vaschilli toward him and looked for his weapon. He found it and shot a volley at the big Russian, who ducked behind a van, not wanting to challenge the man. He heard Tom's yell, "Tomorrow morning, or you're all dead."

Vaschilli was surprised to find Ted laying face down on the asphalt. He helped him up and back to the condo. The big knife had penetrated the thigh to the bone; it missed the big artery. Vaschilli cleaned and flushed the wound. He injected Ted with tetanus and antibiotics and gave the big man a shot of Valium to help him settle down.

Lisa stood over him, holding his hand. "How yah doin', big dude?"

He looked up at her, "I'm all right. Got to help the guys." He sat up. Lisa held him on the bed. "Stay still. We just got the bleeding stopped. It's not too bad. It could have been worse. I've got to get going" Lisa calmly said, "That soldier said we have 'till morning to get out of here."

Ted looked at her perplexed, "What the hell are you talking about? We're not going to go anywhere. We're going to get that shithead and put him in a deep hole."

Lisa walked back to him, "Ted, he went through you guys twice with no problem. We have to leave. Now get some sleep. I'm packing to get out of here." Ted laid back, clutching his Glock pistol. He fell asleep with Lisa next to him.

At six thirty the next morning, Doug, one of the new guys, stormed in Dorn's room. Dorn woke with a start.

"What are you talking about man?" He reached for a Nitro, cracked the top, and took a big drink. He looked at Doug.

"I found the guy, the army guy, the one with the shot-up truck, man. I found it, the truck, I know where it is."

Dorn stood up. He grinned, his lower front tooth missing. Head aching, he walked to his dresser and downed a handful of prednisone and two oxycontin. His gut was hurting. He went to the bathroom and sat on the toilet. It hurt deep in his bowels. The fecal matter passing through the tender area of his colon bent him over in pain. He squeezed hard, forcing more pain, but also pushing the fecal matter through and out of him. The relief was immediate. He looked in the toilet expecting to see some sort of gargantuan turd, the size and scale of a great Anaconda, and instead a small turd the size of a small Tootsie Roll floated to the bottom of the dirty toilet. He sighed, and then huffed around the room like child that didn't get his way. He poured two gallons of water into the tank to flush it down. Without power the pumps there was no water to the plumbing system. Every day he had to carry two buckets of water four floors up to his room for flushing and cleaning. There was a knock on the door; Mini-Mike was standing decked out in camo, pistol belt, pack, and AK47.

Tom woke up, his face sore from Ted's punches. He reached down to pet Woody's big head. The big dog rolled over, emitting a low comfortable growl. Tom's watch read 7:04. "Goddam." His hands were sore from punching the big guy. He stood up, undressed and changed into clean underwear. He always found if you couldn't take a shower, it helped to change your underclothes. The office was cold, so he changed into grey pants and light fleece shirt covered by his Air Force jacket. The pistol belt was heavy with gear. He pulled the big Gerber dagger from its sheath. Blood covered the tip and the serrations along the blade. He laughed at the thought of the big guy kicking at Woody, and falling to his demise with Woody standing over him biting at him.

With the Coleman stove, he heated up water for coffee. He put on his combat gear and clips were reloaded. He had fired seventy-two rounds at the punks last night. He'd have to keep an eye on them as they moved out of town. On a big table he laid out twenty full clips, another big set for the AR10, another twenty-five clips of .308, almost a thousand rounds in all. He picked up a Mossberg, a slug gun used for deer hunting. It shot a lethal 12-gauge slug. It didn't fly for a mile like a common hunting necked down bullet, making it perfect for populated areas.

Tom ate two hard-boiled eggs, two Power Bars, and drank down his coffee. He unlocked the back door, walked down the steps to his pickup, unlocked the pickup and walked around the pickup. Woody lifted his leg on a gas meter. He stopped and began to growl. Dorn jumped around the corner in full view with his AK47 leveled at Tom. Tom stared at him, pushed a garbage can down to further distract Dorn, and jumped behind the pickup. He pulled his pistol and yelled to Woody. Dorn fired his weapon at the truck, hoping the bullets would penetrate the truck. Woody attacked Dorn, and bit him in the lower forearm. Woody held onto the bite. Dorn screamed in pain. Moving in a half circle, he kicked at the big red dog, missing each time. Tom yelled for Woody. Woody let go of Dorn. Tom fired four rounds at Dorn, aiming high so he didn't hit his dog. Dorn ran out of sight behind the corner.

Tom slammed the metal door shut, and opened a window and tossed out a soda pop sized tear gas grenade. Toxic smoke spewed from the can. The punks scattered. The window closed. Dorn ran up the road, tears rolling down his face, holding his bleeding arm. Andy moved a pickup to block Tom's truck from leaving. He jumped out and ran into the furniture store. He ran to an upstairs office where he stacked up desks and file cabinets so he could fire at Tom with good cover. He carried an AK47 and a long-barreled shotgun made for bird hunting. He was to cover the west side of Ray's store.

Steve and Karen climbed a ladder up to a church tower. Steve hauled up four loads of ammo and a small cooler of food and beer. His fat wife, Karen, sat down in a lawn chair he'd brought for her. She pulled out a glass pipe, set and lit a small chunk of Chrystal meth, and huffed in the noxious smoke. She passed it to her husband. Steve whipped back his dirty blond hair from his face. He made a yummy smacking noise with his mouth and sucked the smoke into his lungs. They sat back, looking at the top stair room of Ray's store. Karen scratched at her dirty grey hair, "can't believe Dorn ordered us to this church, that fuckhole." She lit a cigarette; menthols were her thing. She put the glass pipe back to her face. Steve took it from her.

"No, more! I have job to do," she spat out. "That fucking Dorn. What a slap in your face this morning." She laughed; it was a deep gurgling sound in her throat that heavy smokers get. She spat out a gob of spit, and picked up her weapon, a Rock River AR15 taken from a cop car. She leveled it at Ray's store and fired two shots at the stair room. They both laughed their guttural smokers laugh.

Doug moved a garbage truck east around the corner waiting for Dorn to give him the signal to move. He saw Mini-Mike drive around the corner with big bulldozer with two big plate steel panels in the bucket.

He heard Mini-Mike on the radio, "Man, this going to be great man. Fuckin' bullshit, man." He laughed and the signal went dead.

Tom locked the back door, and backed away from the back wall. He looked downstairs, wondering about the security of the lower metal storm doors. He ran upstairs to assess the situation. He looked at the furniture store through the barred windows. Andy noticed Tom in the in the upstairs room and fired two rounds at the window. Tom ducked, and then returned fire, ten rounds from the AR10. The big thirty caliber bullets smacked in an arc around the firing area Andy had made for himself. The noise was deafening as the bullets smacked the old metal file cases. Andy looked up from the floor, "Whoa." He doubted what he was doing there. The fire from Tom was accurate and lethal. Andy fired two more shots at the stair room and quickly ducked to the floor.

Tom was happy with his defensive position. He could see a few guys near the alley entrance. He pitched another tear gas can, then a flash bang grenade. Two guys jumped and ran when the grenades hit the sidewalk. Tom threw another tear gas grenade in the alley to keep it clear and two to the front of the building. One rolled down the slate tiles and hit the sidewalk in front of Ted and Dorn before it fired up. Both men hustled their way down the street with the tear gas following behind them. They rounded the corner in front of Doug in the garbage truck. They ran to Dorn's pickup and took off around the park. Tom watched a black Toyota pickup drive up to a house across from the park. He watched through a range scope. The Toyota was at four hundred yards, even terrain, not much wind, and was a good shooting distance. Tom carried four shotguns and a Remington hunting rifle with a big scope. Constant fire continued from above the furniture store and the church bell tower. Tom wasn't worried. It was clear, amateur cover for the other guys setting up across the park. He would have to deal with them soon. A bullet from the south broke out the south window. Tom needed more cover. With rounds coming in from the west, south and north, he could be in trouble. One ricochet and he could be dead. He ran downstairs pulling five big bulletproof vests from boxes. Upstairs he spread them open, and hung them above the windows. They provided good cover for the small windows and could be moved so he could fire at the punks. Fire was now coming from across the park from Dorn and Ted. Both were using bolt-action hunting rifles, firing one after another. Bullets hit the vests, moving them slightly. A flattened bullet fell to the ground. Tom thought at this rate they would be here a long time. He fired at each position with the AR10, just enough to keep their heads down. What he needed to do was to inflict damage. He had been too easy on them. He picked up the slug gun and aimed it carefully at the furniture office window. A rifle barrel appeared. Tom fired three shots; all entered the shooting hole that Andy had made, but missed him. His baseball cap was shot off his head. Again, he fell to the ground thanking God.

Tom turned the shotgun on the church bell tower. He fired several rounds, hitting the bell. The other rounds splintered the cedar siding. He looked through the binoculars at the damage to the building. It was white washed so it was clear what his rounds were doing. He aimed lower and to the left; where he would be if he were right handed. The big slugs blasted a whole the size of a golf ball in the siding. Steve continued to fire at Tom. This time Tom had fired at the right side, where Steve was firing. Two of the slugs slammed through the siding missing him.

Tom heard the faint sound of engines. He looked through the vests and saw a garbage truck backing in front of Ray's store. Across the park a bulldozer, about four hundred yards away, was driving down a side street with metal plates standing upright in the bucket to shield the driver from bullets. "Well, that's something new!" The metal panels were over an inch thick, used for covering holes in the ground when doing road maintenance. None of Tom's bullets would penetrate, and this was their ace in the hole. With the tractor they could bash their way in the store, then what? While the panels were in place, the bucket couldn't do much but smash the front windows. Still, Tom had to keep it from the front of the building. He dropped a couple tear gas grenades down the front of the slate tiles. They hit the ground, spitting out gas. The small cloud drifted to the garbage truck as well as back onto Tom. He wrapped a wet towel around his face, and put a pair of ski goggles over his eyes. The gas was irritating but not nearly as uncomfortable for Tom as for the punks on the street. Bullets continued to hit the outside of the stair room. The hanging vests swayed a little when they were shot; thwack, thwack, thwack; over and over, "Its time to show them the business," Tom said to himself. He pulled out the big AR10, moved a vest aside, and fired at the furniture store office. This time Andy was in place. Two rounds tore through the tip of his ear; the other skimmed along the top of his skull giving him a instant burning headache. The rest of the rounds would keep him on the floor. His head was bleeding and burning. Cold water made his head feel better. Blood streamed down his face. He thought, "I'm in deep shit."

Tom turned his weapon on the church bell tower. With three round bursts, he tore the rest of the cedar siding away from the outside of the tower. He continued with sustained fire to the tower. Karen was hit with big wood splinters in her face. Steve took a bullet in his skinny calf. He screamed and slid down the stairs with his wife yelling for him to wait.

Tom fired rounds on the garbage truck. It was now sitting still, waiting for something. He fired several clips at the tires, mirrors, windows, electric, and hydraulic lines. One of the hydraulic lines squirted fluid as bullets tore the weaker rubber and thin metal parts to shreds. The brakes stopped working. With the truck in reverse, it started to move backwards until Doug turned hard to the right exposing his arms for a second. Thirty caliber bullets ripped his left hand to shreds; another bullet passed through the right hand and harmlessly hit the inside of the door and pinked to the metal floor. He jumped out of the truck with his hands bleeding, flesh and bone mixed together in a painful mass. Tom fired, hitting Doug in the left shoulder, spinning him as though he was dancing. The bullet exited his body and seemed throw him to the floor. With a heavy thump, he rolled a few times, with pained screaming, and passed out.

From across the park Ted, Dorn, and Vaschilli watched the death of Doug. Vaschilli had been shooting one round at a time with his hunting rifle. Through his scope he could see the window Tom was firing from. His goal was to make bullets bounce around inside the room after entering the window, since they were not penetrating. He stopped to reload. When he looked up, the old brick wall he was firing from exploded, sending brick and mortar pieces into his face. One smacked him in the forehead like a rock from a slingshot.

Vashilli, now behind another brick wall, kept his rifle down. He watched Doug get shot to pieces with a unusual smile. A large burst from the window of the store tore up the front of the house that Ted and Dorn were shooting from. They laid their guns down, and watched the bulldozer Mini-Mike was driving, crush a slide and pushed a swing set over. He was taking fire from Tom. As he got closer to the store he had to raise the bucket more and more to keep Tom from shooting him in the face. The bulldozer smashed a small playground and drove across the grass straight at Tom.

Tom waited for the bulldozer to make it to the sidewalk. The dozer drove down hill slightly to the street. Mini-Mike lifted up the bucket so it wouldn't hit the concrete road, which exposed the hydraulic lines. The fire control on the AR10 was on semi-auto. Tom aimed carefully, firing one round after another. The dozer was on the street now. Mini-Mike raised the bucket even higher to cover the tractor cab. Finally, a bullet tore through the rubber of the hydraulic line. Fluid pumped out of the puncture. Without the fluid holding the lifting the bucket, it hit the street with a crash. Mini-Mike ducked in the cab as Tom sprayed the top of the cab. Glass broke as bullets rattled and ricocheted throughout the cab.

Tom ran out of clips for the AR10, so picked up the Colt M4. He went in a circle, shooting the bulldozer and then the furniture store, and then the empty bell tower. The recoil was damn right easy compared to the bigger gun. He dropped down two more tear gas canisters to the road below. Mini-Mike cowered on the floor of the tractor. Tom fired a half dozen rounds into the back metal roof support. The bullets bounced off the metal and bounced to the floor with a wicked sounding stop. Several bullets dropped onto him after hitting the metal back wall. Finally, Mini-Mike couldn't take being in the cab any more. The gas was making him sick, the constant bullets to the top of the cab were frightening, and it was just a matter of time before a bullet ripped into his body. He took a big breathe, grabbed the door handle, and ran from the cab. He fired back at Tom as he ran. Buckshot hit Tom above his ski goggles. He ducked and then took a bead on Mini-Mike's backside. He fired a triple shot. The bullets entered Mini-Mike's ass, tearing apart his hip joint. Another volley tore through his upper spine. He hit the deck in a lively display of spastic movement, the dance of death. Mini-Mike looked up, trying to move, but feeling nothing. His hands and feet would not move. His life fading, no pain, a wasted life spent dealing drugs and in drunken hate, now he lay in a ever-increasing pool of blood. His looked back at Tom on the roof and smiled.

GEORGE THIELMAN

Vaschilli had seen enough. Watching Mini-Mike die left him sick. He hated the little punk, but he was sad for him. He gathered up his weapons and ammo, and ran to the alley behind the house. He jumped in this Chevy Blazer and drove four blocks to the alley behind the house where Ted and Dorn were holed up. Vashilli walk up on them easily, thinking, "God, these guys make terrible soldiers." He shook his head and put his hand on Dorn's shoulder.

Dorn turned around startled, "What the fuck man … shit." Vaschilli crossed the room. A solid wall of 5.56 bullets missed him by a foot. Ted looked up at the ballsy Russian wondering if he was brave or stupid. Vaschilli reached down and pulled Dorn to his feet. He helped Ted and Dorn out the door and into his Blazer.

Tom watched the Blazer peel out from the alley, take a hard left turn and disappear. Briefly he took stock of his opponents: two dead on the road, two or three on the run or dead, and another three just took off across the park from him. He had no idea how many of them there were. The only way to find out was to expose himself. For now he was safe in the store.

After reloading clips for the AR10, he reloaded his vest. He unlocked the steel roll-up storm doors, and carefully slipped out the front door re-locking it. Staying in the cover of the tractor, and then the garbage truck, he rolled around the corner after checking on the two men in the street. Mini-Mike smiled at him, blood trickled through his teeth. Tom fired a bullet through his head then turned away.

He walked as though he was on patrol, crouched with his weapon ready. Woody walked along, all senses working to protect his master, ears straight up, nose occasionally tilting upward to identify a smell. Gunfire had scared the ducks and geese away; whatever was moving before the battle was now in hiding.

Tom opened the back door of the church quietly. He moved to the front of the building where he found a slight blood trail that stopped just out the front door. Tom climbed up the ladder to the bell tower. The floor was littered with shotgun shells and bullet casings, and he was not surprised by the holes in the walls from his gunfire.

Tom and Woody snuck out into the street following a blood trail. He was looking for possibly two people from the church and one from the furniture store. They stopped in an alley and then continued into the furniture store. Blood trailed from the stairs and out the door. He followed the trail north around the block, towards the condos. Three blocks away, two trucks sped by heading south; one was a Blazer and one was a black 4x4.

Tom and Woody circled the condos the same way they had the night before. From behind a car he watched two men and two women load two Toyota pickups. One had a bandaged right ear. His face was covered with dried blood. Another man he had seen in the back of the pickup with Dorn the day before. A fat, dumpy woman with an obvious wound to her hands and face, carried two suitcases. She threw them in the back of one of the trucks, and hurried back into the condo complex for another load.

The guy with the bandaged ear yelled at the other woman, "Come on Lisa, you should come with me." He grabbed her by the hand. She pulled back, yelling at him, "No! I'm staying. I don't want to go anywhere with any of you."

Andy yelled, "Your boyfriend has left you. Come with me."

She yelled at him, "You go. Good luck." She pointed south.

Steve and Karen came around the corner with more bags. They threw them in the truck, and looked at Lisa. Karen said loudly, "Come on, Lisa. We need to get out of here before that fucker gets here." Steve picked up his AK47 and looked around. He was afraid and desperate; he was humbled by the gunfire from Tom and wanted no more of it. He wanted to leave right away, but Karen wanted her clothes and all the stuff she had collected. They were at risk and he knew it.

Steve, Karen, and Lisa stood on the sidewalk waving to Andy. He tugged on his heavy nose ring and put the pickup in gear. He'd driven no more than ten feet when the windshield blew apart from automatic gunfire. Andy's face blew apart with his blood and bone mixed with the exploding windshield. The gunfire stopped. Andy's now near-to-headless body stomped down on the throttle. All eyes watched as the brand new Toyota drove into the side of the condo, smashing a hole in the stucco. The back of the pickup lifted up from the stopping of the truck.

Steve and Karen wasted no time. They ran to their pickup, but stopped when they saw Tom standing with his M4 aiming at them, the eighteen-inch barrel still smoking.

Lisa ran out in between them, hands raised, "No, please! No more shooting. "Steve held his weapon. Tom held his M4 pointed at the group. He was looking about for more threats.

He walked to within ten feet of the group, and yelled at them, "Drop your weapons, now, or I'll kill you where you stand." His voice frightened Lisa further. He sounded ragged, and his face was covered in brown and grey camo paint. Clearly a soldier, he seemed a cruel sadist to her.

She spoke to him, "Please no more killing?"

Tom pointed his M4 at Steve, "I'm not going to tell you again, set the gun on the ground."

Steve set the gun on the concrete sidewalk. "There man, are yah happy?" Steve was trying to be brave in front of his wife, Karen.

What are yah gonna do now, asshole?" Karen snapped at Tom.

Lisa walked to the side of Karen. She said, "Please, I don't know what to say, except that we don't want to fight."

Karen moved quickly from behind her husband, a small pistol in her hand pointed at Tom. She fired two shots at him from ten feet. The bullets pushed him backward a few inches. He pulled his M4, firing at full auto. Twenty rounds tore through Steve and Karen. They dropped like wet blankets to the ground. Tom turned his weapon to Lisa. She was spattered with blood and flesh. She tried hard to not look down at her dead friends.

Lisa said to Tom, "Please don't shoot I had nothing to do with shooting people." She noticed Tom holding his left side. Woody walked to Lisa smelling her. She backed up, having seen what the dog did to her boyfriend the night before. "What are you going to do with me?" she asked.

Tom said, with a wince, "If you want to live, come with me." She walked with him to Ray's store, passing the carnage on the front street. At the entrance to the alley she looked out at the bulldozer. Mini-Mike dead, was now lying in an even bigger pool of blood.

She asked Tom, "Is that Mike?" She started to cry. Inside, she sat down in the office. Tom handcuffed her to a metal post and then fired up water on the stove. Lisa tried to speak several times, but Tom told her to be quiet. She sat watching him as he pulled the combat vest off and then his two shirts. Finally he was down to his t-shirt. He pulled it off, and then set it on a chair. She sat with her mouth open in amazement. She had expected to see a couple holes in his side, but she saw two purple bruises. He noticed her looking at him. He picked up the combat vest and smiled. He reached through the full clips finding what he wanted. He pulled a clip out of the front pouch, and showed it to Lisa. It had two bullet marks from Karen's pistol rounds. He laughed and then went about making supper, his shirt was off. Occasionally he would lay a towel, soaked in cool water, across his chest. She checked out his body. Obvious bullet wounds from the past.

She asked, "Are you in the Army?"

"No, Air Force. But now I'm a regular guy."

He wiped the camo paint from his face, and washed up with soap and water. He turned to her, "Do you want to wash up? Have more water here." He unlocked her cuffs and moved back to watch her. He threw a clean T-shirt at her, and a blue hoodie. He handed her a bowl of Progresso soup. He cuffed her again and went downstairs. When he came back, he announced,"Were leaving right now."

Lisa asked "Where are we going'?" He smiled at her, faced west, and said,"We're going up the lake!"

She helped him load the pickup. Tom moved the black pickup from the front of the alley, and carefully drove across the park following the path of the bulldozer. Lisa noticed her two friends lying in the road.

"Are you going to leave them there?" Tom didn't answer, he was watching for more bad guys. He relaxed after he started backing down the dock to the Sky Boat.

By the time the boat was loaded it was dark. Both he and Lisa wore headlamps. Tom handcuffed her to the passenger seat of the boat and pulled the overloaded boat into the lake. He motored slowly. Twenty minutes later, he pulled up to the dock at Manson.

He looked at Lisa, "Well Honey, now you're on your own."

She looked at him in amazement, "Just like that? You're letting me go? Why?"

Tom said unlocked her cuffs, "Just get off my boat and you're free to go."Lisa stepped off the boat, Woody followed after her, hoping for a hike. Tom called him back to the boat. "So what's your name? "she asked. "My name's Lisa. I'm twenty two and I never picked up a gun with Ted and Dorn."

Tom asked, "Who are Ted and Dorn?"

She replied, "They were the leaders of the group you shot up."

Tom asked, "So, there's a group?"

She said, "Well, not anymore. You killed five of nine, and the rest ran away."

"Tom said, "Where did they go?"

She sighed, "Probably went to Brewster. Don't know for sure. That's where I met them."

Tom set two packs on the dock, big internal frame packs full of new backpacking gear. He looked up at her. "These packs have all you need to make it here. Camp near the dock under the tree there. Good spot, firewood, tent and sleeping bag inside the packs, along with food and equipment, all brand new."

She looked at Tom, tears rolling down her face, "I really don't want to go, and if I could just stay with you, I promise I won't be a problem." Tom reached out, handing her a silver pistol, and then a shotgun.

"Now Lisa, you're not coming with me. You're staying here. I don't want to have to look over my back, waiting for a bullet from you."

She pleaded, "Please, I promise I won't do anything like that."

He shook his head, "No, you're on your own, I'll be back in a few weeks. If you leave a note on the sign over there, I'll check on you. If you follow the road up the hill there are homes and cabins. You can take your pick. Plenty of food. Just be smart and stay out of trouble. It would be best to start a garden, look for crops growing, and there's good fish in this lake."

She looked sad, and using all her charm on him, pleaded, "Please, I don't want to stay here."

Tom pointed to the shore, "You know how to shoot those?"

She unlocked the cylinder of the pistol allowing the gun to open. "This is empty!"

Tom said, "You go to shore and I'll set the bullets and shells on the dock. After I'm gone you can pick them up and do whatever you want. Find a cabin that's hidden from the main road and stay away from your friends. If you get back together with your friends I'll kill them and you."

She replied, "I won't, and I believe you."

He set a flashlight on the dock, then pushed the boat away from the dock. He gunned the boat leaving her in darkness. She whispered to him, "Please I won't be a bother!" She stood, listening for the boat until it was out of earshot, and then walked to the end of the dock, picked up the bullets and equipment, and dropped it under a maple tree.

Tom drove the boat across the lake to Twenty-five Mile Creek. He pulled the boat up to Garrett's dock, and walked to the house. It was cold, but the wood stove cozied the inside of the big cabin. He lit candles, fed Woody, and sat down in front of the window overlooking the lake. It was dark and the only light was from the stars and moon. In the moonlight it seemed like another wilderness cabin. Come daylight it would not be the same; homes were like tombs, some people had enough time to bury their dead, most did not. Tom and Woody walked out to the end of the dock. His side hurt. Karen's bullets had hit one clip that pushed back on him. He was a lucky man again.

LISA

CHAPTER 23

LISA TURNED THE FLASHLIGHT ON and pulled stuff out of the packs. She found a North Face sleeping bag and a sleeping pad. She was tired, exhausted by a day like no other. She walked away from her campsite to pee, then crawled in her new nylon and goose down sleeping bag. She sat up, loaded the pistol and shotgun, and then laid her head down on the pack. She slept fitfully with bad dreams of loud and destructive gunfire.

She woke to a sound in the nearby bushes. It was early morning. She held the pistol at the bushes. The bushes moved apart and the head of raccoon appeared followed by a body, and four babies. She laughed, watching them move past. As she made a fire and coffee with her new supplies, she was in a good mood. She took stock of the gear Tom had packed for her, a rolled up orange tent, MSR camp stove, Swiss Army knife, first aid kit, small binoculars, headlamp, and a red down jacket. She put it on, and was instantly warm. She found a beanie and slipped it on.

Inside one pack she found ten freeze dried dinners along with packets of granola and trail mix. She pulled out packets of hot chocolate. In the top pouch of her biggest pack she found a nylon bag. Inside was a big bag of marijuana, rolling papers, and a Bic lighter. "This is great!" The weed she would save for another time. She sat, drank hot chocolate, and munched on granola. She finished her meal, picked up the pistol and shotgun, and started up the road. She hiked for an hour, passing cabins and homes. Finally, she crested the plateau. There was a cluster of homes on the downside of the plateau. She looked through four of them taking stock of the supplies. In one of the homes she looked through a dresser, finding women's clothes. In a closet she found camo pants and a jacket. She put them on then looked further. She found a pistol belt with a Browning High power pistol with bullets and two full clips. She put the belt on over her camo jacket and slung the shotgun over her left shoulder. She walked into the bathroom looking in the mirror. Her face was spattered with blood and dirt, and her hair matted together. She laughed, then shuffled in front of the mirror. She pointed at the mirror, and then smiled.

Then Lisa made a more serious face, "You looking at me?" she turned to look behind her. "I don't see anyone else, here … are you looking at me?" She pulled the hi-power pistol out of the holster, and again, and again talked to the mirror. "Are you looking at me?" She cracked up laughing.

Outside in the yard, she walked following a path of stepping-stones past a small greenhouse. The path continued through an old garden. In front of her was a small cottage with cedar shingles, both on the roof and the walls. She looked in the windows. "This is perfect. It's perfect." She put her hands to the sky, "It's perfect."

The entrance was off a cedar deck set up on stilts. The deck was half covered by a mossy roof porch. The door was unlocked. It had a warm, clean feeling to it. In the back corner was a sleeper sofa. Next to that was a Lazy-boy recliner. She sat in it and sighed in comfort. The cottage held a small table and chairs, two end tables, and a coffee table. In front of the window was an old dresser used for games and books. Dead center was a square wood stove. She walked out onto the deck. Big maples and other trees and bushes covered the full 360 degrees around the cottage. It sat, looking over its own gully, deep with leaves. In the garden was a water hydrant. She picked up the handle and pumped it three times. Cool, fresh water poured from the spout. She went through the house looking for keys, and found them in the kitchen. In the barn was an older Toyota-4Runner. She crossed her fingers and turned the key. The motor turned over with ease.

The 4Runner fishtailed back to the boat dock. She retrieved her gear and drove back to the cottage. She spent the remainder of the day scrounging the food, clothes, and gear she would need from the homes around her. When she finally was finished for the day, she walked back to the cottage, crossing the driveway. Her tire tracks were showing in the dried leaves. From the front yard she picked up a fallen branch and swept the driveway until the tracks were gone. Satisfied, she walked back to her new home. She closed and locked the door behind her and set her weapons on the table.

She'd put a three-gallon pot of water on the wood stove. When the water was hot to the touch, she poured it into a five gallon plastic bucket and set a refilled pot on top of the wood stove to heat more water. In front of the small kitchen she stripped off her clothes. The cottage was now warm and cozy. She bent her head over the sink, and poured water over her hair and added shampoo. She lathered and rinsed using a small soup pot.

She tied up her hair in a towel, and opened her eyes. The sink was brown from the dried blood of Steve and Karen. With the soup pot she cleaned the sink pushing dirt and blood into the drain. She looked into the drain strainer. It was full of what looked like pieces of teeth. She picked one up piece, rolling it between her fingers, "That came from my hair?" She reached into the strainer, dumping the contents into her hand. One of the pieces was soft and pliable. She squeezed it. It was like rubber. She held the piece up to the light for a better look, and realized with horror, that it was a piece of skin with grey hair. The harder white pieces were pieces of Steve's and Karen's skulls. She hurried to the door dropping some of the pieces on the ground. When she got the door open, she threw the pieces over the railing.

"Goodbye, Steve and Karen!" she laughed. She stood for a minute, trying to calm down. She was naked. She relocked the door and continued washing. When she finished she changed into sweatpants and a fleece shirt that Tom had given her. When she slipped on a pair of brand new Patagonia socks, she moaned in pleasure. Chicken noodle soup was heated up on the wood stove. She pulled out the sleeper sofa. With real sheets and blankets, the bed was perfect, and no longer would she have to share it with Ted, or allow him to have sex with her so she would feel protected.

Ted was in her thoughts as she fell asleep. She gripped the Browning pistol. She fought off her thoughts of Dorn, his ugly face constantly strained from teeth and bowel pain. Never would she have to deal with his leering stupid looks. For two hours she drifted in and out of sleep; images of Karen's and Steve's ugly heads being shot apart kept entering her mind like a movie. Finally, sleep took over. She dreamt of a journey to paradise, wrought with miles of walking through ugly situations, death and dismemberment.

GEORGE THIELMAN

Morning came, with sunlight seeping through a small hole in the drapes, and warmth covered her face and continued down her body. With a smile, she jumped out of bed. She strolled outside on the cedar deck. The deck steamed as moisture evaporated. She stood at the railing looking through the leafless trees at Lake Chelan. This was a perfect place to be.

The morning was spent making pancakes. She ate until her stomach was ready to burst. The next morning Lisa drove the 4Runner back to the boat dock. Her goal was to catch fish. She tied a shiny new lure to the fishing line, and cast it out into the lake. The work was boring and monotonous. Fishing would become one of the more significant acts in her life. Fresh food would become necessary. Without electricity there would be no refrigerators, without refrigerators there would be no freezers, without freezers there would be no ice, and without ice, fresh meat could not be kept for any length of time.

In the small greenhouse she pulled out old pots and trash. Several holes in the roof let in the cold. She found clear plastic sheeting and layered it over the green house and tucked the trailing edges under the dirt to hold it down and keep the heat in. Seeds were found in the barn: lettuce, tomato, squash, onions, carrots and peppers were set in soil and placed on her windowsill. She would start at the bottom with her own little farm; like her grandma's small backyard in Yakima that seemed to grow an endless supply of food, not only for the family but the neighbors as well. She would do the same.

She was not lonely, at least not for her last roommates. She didn't miss them. Her thoughts turned to the soldier. She had so many questions. Where did he come from? Why was he here? Why didn't he take her with him? Soldiers always indulged themselves in the spoils of war. Why not him? Why not her? His scars had meaning that she could not know. She was willing to lie down for him. His bravery and skill spoke for itself. He wasted her friends with ease and walked away with barley a scratch. The bag of weed perplexed her. What kind of soldier smoked weed? Clearly, a damned good one. He was good-looking too; other than scars to his right side, he looked not only intact, but had the kind of body women would love in a man. She shrugged her shoulders and enjoyed the chair on the deck.

From a pocket she pulled out the bag of weed. On a paper plate she rubbed the bud until it dropped on the plate in small crumb-like pieces. She bent one of the papers, then sprinkled it with just enough pot for one joint. She licked the adhesive strip and rolled it in one of the best joints she had ever made. She lit it and sat back, smoking for a few minutes. The joint had a fruity taste. She held the smoke in and then blew it out slowly, watching the smoke dissipate.

She was stoned out of her mind. Her ears not only rang, but also felt hot. She thought of the soldier again, and about the dog. She liked him. She smiled at the thought of both of them. She felt cramps in her gut and stood up hoping to make the gas pass, but it didn't. Her period was about to start. She sighed in relief. She'd been worried that she was pregnant with Ted's baby, "Ok, maybe a slight possibility." She went into the house, checking the bathroom for tampons, panty shields, anything, but found none. In the neighboring houses she struck out. Finally, she came to realize she would have to go into town. She didn't like the idea, but it was time, and her list of supplies was long.

The 4Runner made tracks to town. She drove within five houses of the condos. She put on the big pack the soldier had given her, now empty. She wanted some of the belongings that she'd been forced to leave behind. Through the same yards Tom had passed through a few days earlier, she stepped carefully, the Browning pistol in her right hand. Her room was empty of Ted's gear. Her things were strewn about. She gathered her clothes and removed a board under the dresser. There she kept everything that was important to her: photos, letters, a jewelry box, and a small Ruger pistol that fit in her hand perfectly. She stuffed the things in her pack and reached behind a folding closet door. She pulled out an AR15 that Ted had given her for emergencies. She dropped the clip, looked at it and replaced it. She racked the first round and left the condo with her stuffed pack. She stayed away from the parking lot, not wanting to see the remains of Steve and Karen. If she had ventured into the lot, she would have noticed that the bodies were gone.

At the shot-up feed store she found more seeds and gardening supplies. Next, she drove straight to Wal-Mart. The front doors were smashed in where the punks had driven inside for a thrill. Clothes and racks were on the floor, and there were black tire and skid marks on the tan tiles. She filled two shopping carts with supplies, food, and tampons. Down a quiet isle she pulled her pants down and slipped a tampon inside of her. She was still stoned from her early morning puff. She found two pair of pants and slipped one on. She stopped in front of a mirror and looked at herself. The red, puffy, down jacket made her look fat. She stopped, looked seriously in a mirror and pulled her pistol. She holstered it after clicking the safety on, and turned the holster around so it was on her left hip. She would have to pull it with her right hand, across her belly, like Sharon Stone in "The Quick and the Dead." She always liked that movie. She practiced pulling the pistol twenty times. From the women's department she picked out a long brown Carhartt jacket. She clipped the pistol belt around the outside and turned the holster around so it was just in front of her left side under her arm. She practiced pulling the pistol some more in front of a mirror.

She pushed and pulled the shopping carts outside to the 4Runner. She unlocked the door and was surprised to hear, "Nice to see yah here, Lisa."

She turned to see Dorn in front of her. He grabbed her hands. She struggled. He was too strong. Helpless, she kicked at him, he was too much for her. He turned her around unbuckled her pistol belt and pulled her pants down. She was bent over the tailgate of the 4Runner. She felt the head of his penis enter her.

In a seductive way, she said, "Wait Dorn, I have a tampon in. It will feel much better with it out."

Dorn stood with his cock in his hand, "Ya , yah get that thing out of there!" He held on to himself with his right hand; the other held on to his pants.

From her jacket pocket Lisa pulled the small Ruger pistol, and pointed it straight in Dorn's face.

"Lisa, come on now. Don't shoot that gun, really." He reached out with his hand, dropping his pants to his ankles. She pulled the trigger, shooting Dorn in the shoulder. He reached for his bleeding shoulder. The bullet had passed on the outside of the muscle, almost a graze. She pushed him in the chest with her foot. He tried to step backward, but tripped on his pants. He lay on his back, trying to pull his pants back up. She fired two shots at his head, but missed each time. He crawled backward to his black pickup. She picked up her Browning Hi-Power, and clicked the safety off. He was now standing up, trying to open the pickup. She aimed carefully, and then fired two rounds, hitting him in the ass with the second round.

He yelled at her, "God damn! Lisa, stop! I've had enough. I'm sorry, I'm sorry!" He laid on the ground his hands over his face cowering. His butt was burning in pain. She walked to him, pistol aimed at him. She couldn't kill him.

She yelled back at him, "Ok, Dorn. You stay there until I'm done loading my car and I'll let you live. If you try anything I'll shoot you in the head." He agreed. She loaded the 4Runner as fast as she could and then walked to Dorn's truck, and pulled out the keys, his Glock pistol and AK47. She looked in the back seat and saw a big rifle, a thirty-pound Barrett .50 caliber sniper rifle. She pulled it from the back seat, and dragged it to the asphalt. She laid it in the parking lot. On her way, Lisa squealed out and drove straight for the .50 caliber. Her left tire ran over the barrel, bending it. She left the parking lot screaming,"Yaaaaa-hooooo!" She felt empowered. She pulled her pistol and fired two rounds in the air. From the end of the parking lot she fired four shots at Dorn. The bullets hit his pickup, and he covered his head cussing at her.

Lisa parked the Toyota in the barn and swept the driveway with the branch. She placed her supplies in the barn and locked it. One wheelbarrow full of supplies was brought to the cottage. Windows were covered with blankets. She made one more trip out to the Toyota to collect Dorn's weapons. She laid them on the table. "Quite an arsenal." She picked up the thick Glock 9mm. It was too big for her hand. She picked up the Yugoslavian AK47. She noticed the difference in bullet size from her own Rock River AR15. She scratched her head as she looked at a .223 caliber and the .308 from the AK. She set the weapon down, and went to work cooking the two fish she caught that morning.

It was another great day, but different from any other. She was truly on her own, on the edge of life. She cooked the fish in flour and Crisco Oil, eating outside on the porch. The wind on the lake was picking up and white caps could be seen in the middle. She smiled in the darkness.

The next day she rode off on a mountain bike she found in the barn. Slung across her back was the AR15. She'd reloaded the Browning, and set the two spare clips the pocket of her new cargo pants. She brought a small pack with a hunting knife. She clipped the gun belt and knife over her jacket and had pocketed a compass, map, headlamp, extra batteries and first aid kit. Her bike rode smoothly over the dirt road. It felt good to exercise. Her heart rate was up; the sky was clear, and the road clear.

She rode past a small farm, and noticed movement. She slowed her bike down and left the bike against a fence. She brought the three spare clips from her small pack. She snuck to the front door and listened, and knocked. She walked around the back of house to a small yard, straining to look through the bushes. She saw movement and put her AR to her shoulder. She was ready. Two skinny chickens stepped out, pecking at the ground. She breathed a sigh of relief, "Bad chickens." She stood up, herding the chickens into the coop, and found a trash can full of chicken feed. She sprinkled a big scoop onto the ground, locked the chicken coop, and left. She hopped back on her bike down a dirt road to the water.

She passed a cedar cabin, and rode straight to the boat dock. She stepped of the bike onto the rickety dock. She stood, stretched, and patted her pistol with her fingertips. She pulled out her fishing gear, snapped the pole together, and looked around for a spot to pee. She ran over to the shore to some green grass. She started to pull her pants down. Unzipping her pants she heard a voice,"Uhhh, 'scuse me, mam."

She pulled her pistol and pointed it at Bill, who was sitting on a lawn chair in the sun. Their eyes locked. Bill continued, "This is my yard please, and I have a outhouse you are more than welcome to use."

She blinked her eyes, then said awkwardly, "Umm, sorry 'bout that. I didn't mean to do that. My name is Lisa."

She smiled at Bill. He stood, "Could you lower the piece, please? Like I said, this is my yard and I'm not armed."

Embarrassed, she holstered the gun leaving the safety off, just in case. Bill handed her a beer. She looked at the handwritten label, "Big Belly Beer."

"Good name. You made it?"

He nodded, "Made it fresh two weeks ago. Name's Bill. Bill Crystal." He sat back in his chair, his hands stretched behind his head, "So Lisa, what brings you to Manson, Washington?"

She paused to think of the right answer, "Well, I was dropped off at the boat dock a couple weeks ago and decided to stay."

Bill was curious. "Dropped off? By who? Didn't know the ferries were running." She took a big pull on the beer bottle. It was the best beer she had ever had.

"It wasn't the ferry. He was a soldier … with a dog, and a kick ass boat."

Bill's eyes lit up. "A soldier in a boat with a dog? Now you have my attention. Was he armed?"

She replied with a big smile on her face, "He was armed all right. Never seen anything like it. I mean, I found myself with these people, didn't know at the time they were a gang. Drugs, booze, guns, and they were violent. They screwed with the soldier, and he … well, he killed five of them. Beat the crap out of a guy seventy pounds heavier than him and six inches taller."

Bill sat on the end of his chair. "Did this happen a week ago?"

Lisa finished her beer. "Yes, it did. He left me at the dock the same evening."

"So he just showed up in Chelan and shot up your friends and left?" He handed her another beer.

"No he showed up to pick up supplies. Some of the punks ran into him in the city and shot at him. He found us that night. Kicked their asses again. The next morning they found him and tried to kill him. Didn't work. He won that day. I helped him load his boat. He was armed with military weapons, and was very good with them."

She pictured the demise of Steve and Karen. "Anyway, he left me at the dock with supplies and a couple of guns, and … he just drove away in the boat. Said he was going uplake."

"Heck of a story, Lisa. Was he a nice guy?" She felt the two beers. She laughed," Ya, I think he's a good guy. Left me with all I needed, and a bag of weed."

"A bag of weed. That's awesome. Have any with you?" She smiled. "Not here, at my cabin. Give me a ride and I'll get yah buzzed."

Bill loaded her bike in his camper. They drove to her cottage, stopping on the way to catch the two chickens, but found a new total of four. They stuffed the chickens in a dog kennel along with the bird feed and drove to Lisa's place.

Bill mended a fence and turned a small storage shed into a chicken coop. They found straw for bedding and moved the ducks into the coupe.

They cooked a duck that Bill had shot the day before, and then sat on the cedar deck, smoking a joint. Bill sat in the chair, blowing smoke into the air. He watched the smoke intently. "I heard the shooting. Sounded like a full-blown battle. Seemed to go on forever." Lisa and Bill talked for two hours. Bill asked, "So how do we get ahold of this soldier?" She told him about the sign, that she'd already made one, and placed a note for him. "You know Lisa, there's some great locations uplake. How 'bout we get a boat and travel uplake, see if we can find him?"

They met up the next day at Bills cabin. He had an Alumaweld boat like Tom's, with a small cabin and a big Honda motor. They filled the boat with food and beer, and placed their weapons upright in the cabin. They started to patrol the big lake. Each day they rode the lake, checking cabins and stopping at small communities along the lake, never finding any life other than the usual wilderness critters. They traveled to Twenty-five Mile Creek, the last spot to launch a boat onto the lake. No sign of life was spotted. They continued north zigzagging from one shore to another, checking cabins and campsites.

Two weeks of bad weather kept them on shore tending to the chickens and garden. On May first they ventured to Lucerne. At the little harbor of Refrigerator Harbor they tied up at the docks and looked through binoculars for signs of life: smoke emitting from chimneys, tire tracks, footprints or barking dogs. Two chimneys were belting smoke; there were tire tracks in the thin gravel, and footprints that were new. Boat ramps looked normal, all clear, with no boats sitting at the docks and no sunken trash or boats. Bill checked nearby vehicles. Two vans sat looking somewhat clean, their white paint smeared from dirty snow. He looked for keys and found none. Two school busses were locked up tight.

Lisa scratched her head, "We could hike to the Lutheran village of Holden, or come back with bikes, 10 miles either way you slice it."

Bill agreed,"Yah, I really don't want to hike that far. A good mountain bike would be the way to go. Nice place, but a trail bike would be better. "

Lisa said, "Seems this would be a good place to survive. Super remote, good water, clean air, probably lots of hunting here."

Bill looked through his binoculars at the chimneys. "All it would take is one person infected, making it to this community. Still, this makes sense. The people that would move here really don't need or want all the trappings in modern society. I went to Holden Village fifteen years ago. It was cool then, and I'm sure it is cool now."

Lisa scanned the town. "Somebody is looking at us right now. I can feel it." Lisa looked around in a half circle, and then watched as two dogs, one small and brown, and the other a fluffy red Irish setter, jogged from a row of cabins. As they picked up speed, a gunshot rang out. A puff of dirt sprayed up by the dogs. Bill yelled at the dogs, and Lisa whistled. They waved their arms. The dogs spotted them, picked up the pace, and ran as fast as they could. Three hundred yards away, a golf cart appeared from the same street as the dogs. Bill and Lisa stopped waving their arms. Men stepped off the golf cart, calmly walked to the back of the cart, and pulled a rifle out. Bill and Lisa started running back to the boat. Lisa slowed and looked back at the dogs. They were catching up to them. She stopped to duck behind a utility cover. The dogs ran straight to her. Panting hard, they seemed to be smiling.

Two shots rang out. Bullets sprayed the dock and wood slivers flew through the air. Bill yelled, "What are they shooting at us with, a cannon?" Lisa looked at the men, pulled the dogs behind her and pulled her pistol, knowing full well that they were out of range of her nine millimeter. She fired six rounds at them. They hit the ground. Both men seemed old. One wore a red and black, checkered wool coat; another wore an Elmer Fudd hat with fuzzy ears. They stopped shooting and ran for cover. Lisa ran down the wooden dock to the boat, and the dogs ran beside her, desperately hoping to go with them. She picked the smaller brown dog and put him into the boat; the Irish Setter jumped in without help. Lisa pulled her assault rifle out of the cabin as Bill fired up the boat. The old men were standing with their rifles pointing at Lisa and Bill. Lisa aimed through the small sight on her rifle, firing ten rounds at them. Again they scattered to cover. As Bill backed the boat out of the small bay, the old men boarded a golf cart and were trying to follow them along the shore. Lisa fired several shots at them. Bill turned the boat around and gunned the engines. He drove full-throttle for a mile before he stopped the boat. As it coasted through the water, he yelled to Lisa,"Wow, that was bullshit. Do you think any of them were your soldier friend?"

"I doubt that."

Bill said, "Oh yah, how can you tell?"

Lisa laughed, "Ha! If that was our soldier friend, we would be dead!"

The two dogs took to Bill and Lisa instantly. They were both skinny and seemed to understand that they were now in safe hands. "I wonder what that was about, "Lisa wondered.

Bill looked back toward the little town, "Probably think we have the plague, don't want to get infected, I guess." He reached down to pet the big setter. "This one's a boy, not more than two; the little one looks older, probably six or seven. Look at the grey muzzle. Must be a terrier mix, little mutt of some sort, looks like a skinny butterball turkey. We need to find them something to eat. Let's troll to Stehekin. We can throw the lines in the water and see about getting some fish for dinner."

Lisa said "What if the folks in Stehekin are like the old men in Refrigerator Harbor?"

Bill threw a fishing line in the water, "I don't think we should assume everyone is like that. If we do we'll be alone forever, and I don't want that."

Bill and Lisa pulled into the dock at Stehekin. They disembarked with the dogs, walked around the small town, checked into the ranger station and found no one. There were signs of bear, broken locks and buildings, and scattered trash. They rode the boat as far as the dock at the Sky Café, but couldn't dock because recent warm weather had increased the flow of the Stehekin River. Huge trees, complete with branches, blocked the docks. If they had made it to the docks they would have met up with Tom and Old Joe Spadafore, who'd shown up at the café only five minutes after Bill and Lisa had turned around and headed back to Manson.

A VISIT

CHAPTER 24

Tom made it back to Stehekin the day Lisa found her cottage. He stayed close to home. With Joe's help, they'd unloaded the boat and stowed the supplies. The cats got a big helping of cat chow. Two had disappeared, probably killed by a coyote. Tom presented Joe with a brand new Remington model 25. It looked like a long-barreled M16 with a scope, but it was made for hunting with a camo covering. Joe received a new version of the .45 made by Kimber. It was OD green military color, and a bit tighter to keep dirt and sticks out. He didn't like the Glock that Tom had given him because of the lack of a safety. While Tom was gone, he'd accidentally fired the gun in the bunkhouse, forgetting that a round was in the chamber. A bullet went through his sleeping bag, embedding itself in the wood floor. He beamed with joy at his new presents.

Both men worked in the garden preparing for planting. Many starts were already planted in the outside garden in the portable plastic greenhouses. Seeds were planted in the dungeon in April. There they nested in the dungeon. As they grew, they moved them to the wood shop, which was without heat. This allowed the plants to adapt to the outside environment slowly. Sky Ranch had many chores that needed work; the compost pile had grown in size, and snow had melted on the ground. Joe prepared the nearby neighbors' 10 acres for the planting of the big crops of corn and wheat. If they had good warm temperatures they hoped to have a crop to sustain them for the following year. The growing season in Stehekin was short. With the help of the heated growing rooms and plastic greenhouses they were sure to make it work.

On May first, a Sunday evening, Tom and Joe rode mountain bikes to the café. They made a roaring fire in the wood stove. Joe cooked up Sally's recipe for elk stew. They went to the bar where Tom had poured Jameson whiskey on the rocks for both of them. On the TV was a movie, "The Stand," about a virus that had escaped by way of military scientists and decimated the population of the world, leaving the survivors to dream of both God and the Devil, both incarnated in human forms that are easily understood. Tom found it to be a happy movie, upbeat, and realistic to a point. In real life the movie had rewritten itself, and never would there be another movie made like it. He laughed at that.

Joe came in the room picked up his glass and sipped it. "That's the nectar of the gods, god damn ill-tell-ya-whu ..." He stopped, with the glass in his mouth. He was in the bar area looking toward the lake. In a calm voice he said, "Tom, we're having company tonight." He pointed behind Tom. Tom turned around to see an Alum weld boat puttering towards them. The boat was bumping logs out of the way and coming toward them.

From behind the bar Tom pulled a pair of binoculars, "Well, I'll be a monkey's uncle. Joe we are indeed having company. Let's greet them." They walked outside to the dock. Tom had his AR-10 strapped over his shoulder. Both men carried drinks full to the brim. They waved their arms. The boat was close and coming their way.

Lisa looked through binoculars at Stehekin. It was quiet with no movement. Bill steered the boat slowly through the shallows, past the town.

He yelled over the motor, "Lisa, there's smoke from a fireplace." She swung her binoculars to the café. Two men were walking down the dock.

With a smile on her face she said, "The soldier! It's him! It's him! "She reached down stroking the two dogs. They jumped with happiness. Bill picked the speed up, driving to the dock. Lisa smiled at the sign over the building, "Sky Café and Trading Post" and in smaller print, "cocktails."

Tom stood waiting for them. Even Woody watched the boat come. His tail wagged slowly back and forth, and when dogs' heads appeared, he barked. The boat stopped in front of Tom and Joe. Tom tied them off. Lisa jumped from the boat.

"You're a hard man to find!" She wrapped her arms around Tom. She said, "This is Bill Crystal. "Turning to Bill, she said, "Bill this is … I'm afraid I don't know your name!"

"I'm Tom Trainer. and this is Joe Spadafore, and my dog Woody. Good to meet you. If you're hungry we have some stew and drinks in the bar."

Bill stepped off the boat. "I like this trip already. Is that whiskey in your hand? "Tom handed Bill the glass, and he took a sip.

"Ice. What a great thing to have," Lisa commented. "Do you have food for the dogs? I think they're starving." Tom watched the two dogs greet Woody, sniffing as they followed their masters. Lisa walked along looking at Tom. He was wearing grey pants with a brown fleece jacket and looked very different from a couple weeks ago. Tom noticed that Lisa looked healthier. Her hair was shorter and lighter in color. She wore green cargo pants with a pistol on her left hip. He liked that.

Joe fed the dogs dry dog chow mixed with stew. They ate in haste, taking huge mouthfuls. When they were done they walked to the other food dishes and checked them out, all the while, their tails were wagging. The two dogs followed Woody to the beach. They stood ankle deep in the fresh water, drinking. The three dogs padded into the bar, laid by the fire, and went to sleep. Bill noticed them sleeping close together, "I guess that's how they made it through the winter." The two dogs slept spiraled together with the smaller brown dog between the legs of the bigger. Both snored happily.

Bill told Tom and Joe his story of being fired from Hanford, and how he came to live at his family's vacation home. He told of hearing a battle and of meeting Lisa on his dock a couple of weeks ago. Lisa told of the old men shooting at them from Lucerne.

Tom spoke up, "They shot at us."

Bill replied, "They shot at you and they're still alive, can't believe that!"

Tom replied looking at the floor,"Gonna have to deal with them sooner or later, before they kill someone."

Lisa said,"Ya … they need to stop."

Tom said, "I'll take care of them. Just don't stop there. Keep a gun on them as you pass, but keep going. I'll find them and deal with it, but I need to do it my way, alone."

Bill and Lisa ate like dogs, with total enthusiasm. Bill supplied his Big Belly Beer; hard drinks were mixed, and drank. The four of them rode bikes to Sky Ranch and the dogs ran beside them. Lisa had never been to the mountains. The wilderness spirit was never in her, but she found the snow-capped mountains which surrounded her breathtaking. The sound of flowing water dominated the area: streams, waterfalls and the river created constant background noise. She noticed the security of Sky Ranch: a six-foot high fence of hard wire, and that the posts were new and so very strong. Bill and Lisa walked amongst the chickens with a hungry look on their faces.

Lisa asked," Do we get eggs and bacon in the morning?"

Tom answered, "Eggs and sausage, apple juice or milk, if you want it."

Her reply was "Nice." Tom walked them through the small ranch. Joe fed the animals and went to Finger Rock to finish the evening fishing. He ignored the new guests, choosing instead to hang out by himself.

The two dogs from Lucerne adopted Old Joe, following him from place to place. He spoke to them in a different tone; cuss words were replaced with a sweet tone. They sat near him as he threw his fishing pole forward and reeled it back. The little brown dog kept his eyes on Joe at all times, not wanting to lose her new friend. Tom led Lisa and Bill down through the wood shop and into the dungeon. Only twenty plants were growing along with new starts. Tom gave each of them an ounce of fresh Juicy Fruit. At Tom's greenhouse he started the fire in the snorkel stove. The cow manure smell was gone, and the inside the greenhouse smelled of mint and tomatoes.

In the cabin, Bill looked at photos of Tom's life. Lisa joined him. The house was filled with weapons and the paraphernalia to take care of them. Bill looked closely at a picture of Tom high on a mountain in Afghanistan, with the massive dry valley below him. Sitting on a flat rock the size of a car, Tom sat smiling, showing the label of Starburst Fruit Chews. His skin was tanned from the high altitude sun. Two long barreled sniper rifles lay on the packs behind him. His face was one of pleasure. Lisa looked closely, her face next to Bill's. They looked at each other and laughed. Lisa whispered, "He's absolutely crazy, you know."

Bill replied with a scrunched up face,"I think he's cool!" They looked at each other again and laughed.

Tom, pointed to the photo and squinted at it. "That was Afghanistan, '02, I believe. Chasin' the Taliban. We were spotters. They came every day and night looking for trouble. We gave it to them. The only defense those assholes had against us was to blow themselves up. They were desperate to martyr themselves; so desperate that they forgot to learn to be soldiers." Tom looked back at the photo, and back at Bill and Lisa. "They learned real fast that they didn't have a chance against us." He walked to the kitchen. "Hey, you want to hot tub?"

Lisa's shoulders drooped at the thought of a relaxing hot soak. "I thought you'd never ask."

Bill carried a cooler full of beer and set it on the bench. They sipped the cold beer, running their hands through the hot water. Bill stripped his shirt off and walked down to the bamboo shower and washed off. He smiled as he ran back up to the hot tub. Lisa went into the house and came back a few minutes later wearing a t-shirt and baggy boxers. There was no initial shock when they sat down letting the hot water surround them. Facial expressions were that of pure pleasure. Both Bill and Lisa's expressions changed when Tom stripped off his shirt. Under the scars and tattoo's was a strong fit bod, clearly the flesh of a military man. They sat in the hot water sharing their stories of survival and travel. The greenhouse windows and skylights steamed up, and drops of water dripped on them from the glass above. Stars lit up the night, and the moon was half full, blurred through the steamy glass. The greenhouse was warm. Bill lightly inhaled a joint, the sweet smell of weed in the air.

Bill squinted at Tom, "So Tom, Do you find it easy to live this life? I mean after all you've been through. Does this life seem normal to you? Can you fight Americans as easy as you fought the Taliban?"

Tom laughed at him, "Bill, I just do what comes naturally, same anybody that's trained in any job. You get up and go to work. In my case, riding in choppers and sneaking around dry lonesome country."

Bill stood up, his gut hanging over his shorts. "Very well put my friend, I'm going to go to bed. Goodnight and happy dreams." He stood, picked up a towel, and left the greenhouse. Tom and Lisa sat in the water sipping at their beer. Lisa floated over to Tom.

Stoned and horny, she spoke quietly, her mouth close to his, "I thought of you every night and day, leaving me on the dock. I didn't understand it then. I do now. I feel I'm different." She brushed her body against his. He reached behind her back. She kneeled over him, her wet t-shirt clinging to her breast.

Suddenly the greenhouse door banged open. "God-dam sumbitch shit heeeehhhhehehee." Old Joe, stumbled in drunk. He bellowed, "Sheeeit ill-tell-ya whut, shit." He looked at Tom and Lisa with big smile on his old craggy face, seeming to be waiting for a reply. He pulled his clothes down to his shorts and hopped in the water with a splash. He told Lisa his tale, how he came to live in Stehekin, as usual yelling the whole time.

"Well ill tell yaw hut my wife died, died of cancer smoked two packs a day, drank cheapest whiskey she could get her hands on, bitched at me every day. 'Why don't you change your underwear? Clean your room!

Stop watching so much football!' On and on she went, dumb bitch. Don't get me wrong I loved her, but after she died something snapped in me. I moved to our cabin here in the valley, take showers, and do everything with ease now that she's dead." He looked up through the clear glass windows, then loudly pronounced, "At her end there, she wasn't in good shape. Hair was white and thin, teeth bad, skinny as a whippet, smoked and drank till the end." He shook his head, "Never could get her to take a bath … her stink could knock a buzzard off a shit wagon, boy ill tell ya whut. After she died, I moved to that old cabin, been there for eighteen years. I have, god dam ill tell ya whut."

He stood up, the water dripping off his grey-haired body. He stood looking at Tom and Lisa. As he stepped over the edge of the cedar tub, he let out a thirty-second fart and walked out laughing.

Lisa followed the old man to Sally's house, found a bed in the upstairs, and fell asleep. She woke to the smell of coffee. Pots and pan clanked together in the downstairs kitchen. Bill and Tom sat at the big table drinking coffee. Joe poured Lisa a strong cup of coffee. She sat down next to Bill. He turned to her, "So Lisa, Joe and Tom have asked us to move in with them, expand the ranch, get some horses, hot showers, good food, and beer. We'll be regulars at the cafe, safe and secure."

Joe yelled out, "All the best weed in the world … ill tell ya whut-shit –fire." He laughed quietly as he cooked.

Lisa sipped her coffee, "Man, that is strong." Tom and Bill laughed. Joe arrived the table with a pot of veggies. Tom said, "This is what we call deluxe: spuds, squash, potatoes, onions, garlic, cilantro, and seasoning, pretty good." He sprinkled salt on the mix as Joe delivered a bowl of scrambled eggs, and set down another plate full of pancakes. Lisa's eyes teared up, "Can't believe this is happening. A month ago I was living with criminals." She shrugged her shoulders, smiled, and then happily tried each dish. With her mouth stuffed with pancakes and eggs she said, "Ok, I'll do it. Just don't twist my arm any more.

Bill and Lisa rode the boat down the lake, quietly thinking. The sun was going down and waves hit the boat hard.

Bill said, "A bit choppy today … so what do you think?"

"About moving in? Think it's a good idea. It feels remote there. Think it will be safe, that's for sure," mused Lisa.

Bill laughed, "I think it's remote anywhere. I think it's too cold, freezing in the winter, but … and this is a big but, what are we isolating ourselves from? We have no choice."

GEORGE THIELMAN

Lisa moved closer to Bill, hanging onto his chair, "Those guys will protect us. I know what kind of people are out there. They are sadistic and ugly. Tom and Joe …" she laughed, and Bill laughed with her. "Never knew a guy that farted so much as that old man." They laughed hard, bouncing with the waves.

Y CREEK

CHAPTER 25

FOUR DAYS LATER TOM CRUISED IN the Sky Boat to Bill's cabin. Bill and Lisa were overdue by two days. It was six in the morning when he pulled up to Bill's rickety dock. Bill's truck was gone, and the cabin was empty. Tom unloaded his mountain bike, locked the Sky Boat, and started peddling to the top of the plateau. With a sixty pounds of gear, food and weapons, he got a good workout. He rode another mile to Lisa's cottage. Her 4Runner was gone and the cottage was empty. He looked down at Woody. "Ok, now what?" Woody looked back at him, then stretched, his front paws straight before him, his shoulders and head dipped to the ground, butt in the air, and yawned loudly. Tom laughed, "You want to run some more don't you? "Tom wasn't worried yet. He inspected the road in front of the house. It was filthy asphalt. He could make out tire tracks on the road; they headed north, away from town.

He rode north, the tracks were clear and easy to follow. After two miles the road came to a stumbling block... The road had been torn up by a bulldozer. The dozer sat next to a utility truck. The road crew must have started the repair and then gotten sick. The road behind the tear-up looked like it dead-ended.

He looked closer at the tracks. Where road turned into gravel, he could still make out tracks. He followed them down a private drive. The trail turned northeast through an apple orchard. It turned east after a half a mile and Tom was looking at the dead end and the construction site with the bulldozer again. Tom had spent thirty minutes going almost in a circle.

This time Tom, continued to ride east along the gravel road. To the left was a good-sized hill, about fifty feet in height. The top of the hill was full of stunted pine trees. The road turned northwest through a small pass. A six-foot high gate had been erected and "No trespassing" signs hung on it. The tire tracks continued past the gate, which was locked with a chain and the biggest Stanley padlock he had ever seen. He set his bike behind a stand of trees and bushes. He had the idea he was onto to something big. Under a tree he put on his combat vest, and checked the six thirty round clips in the vest. Two were for the M4 full of .223 rounds. He replaced them with the bigger .308, then put his Camelback pack on. He sucked up a pint of water, checked the H&K and the four extra clips on his belt. Under his left arm he pulled the small Glock .40 caliber, checking its small clips, and he was ready to go. His vest held two tan smoke grenades, two small tear gas grenades, and two flash bangs. He had four Power Bars in one pouch along with a big baggie of elk jerky. Over the left shoulder strap of the vest was his small dagger and on his belt was the big Gerber dagger. He pulled it out. Small traces of blood stuck in the serrated teeth, no doubt from Ted's thigh. He spit on the blade and wiped it in the dirt. It didn't help. He sheathed the knife, and gave Woody a small bowl of water. He lapped it up.

He took a big breath, pulled out a Gerber multi-tool, and began cutting the barbed-wire fence. He squeezed through and onto the gravel road. He pulled the charging handle chambering the first round. Now he was ready for anything. Weapon ready, he hiked quickly. The pass opened up to the greenest of green. His mouth dropped open in amazement as he walked into a mini valley of a green flourishing cultivated farm. Below him he calculated a thousand meters square. There were a few more passes to the east and one to the north where a irrigation ditch flowed. The ditch dissected the middle of the farm, taking a turn to the east in front of him, probably going underground through the hill. In front of him were a couple of acres of fruit trees. On the sides of the hill that boarded the property grapes were growing. Most of the farm was cultivated for crops that had just been planted. Rows of dirt had recently been turned or moved. The soil looked rich. In the middle of the farm trees and bushes surround all a green and brown farmhouse, with a matching barn and other buildings. Through binoculars Tom saw three dogs walking amongst a group of chickens. To the northeast was a barn. He could see grazing cows and horses beyond the barn. Smoke was puffing from the farmhouse. The area around the house was littered with a vehicles: a big green Dodge pickup with a scoop on the front, a pickup, and a 4Runner sat next to a beat up pickup. Below him in the fruit trees he spotted the roll bar of a tractor. He could see two people, a man and a woman, pruning the fruit trees. No threat could be seen so he continued walking straight down the driveway. He came even with the two pruners. He stood a hundred yards from them. They were working hard and did not notice him. The three dogs noticed him first. They barked as a group. Two of them ran toward Tom. The workers had stopped and hit the ground. The man held a rifle, its barrel in the air.

Tom waved at them, a kind of salute with his left hand. The woman waved back. They cautiously and slowly walked toward Tom. When they were twenty feet in front of him, Tom said, "Hello. I'm Tom and this my dog, Woody." Two German Shepherds caught up to them and circled Tom and Woody. Woody's back fur stood straight up. He watched both dogs closely. He understood the tension. The woman approached Tom. He shouldered his weapon, and they shook hands, they were Anna and Jacob Krause, owners of the farm. Tom thought they looked young to be farmers.

Anna said with a smile, "I have a surprise for you. Some of your friends are in the house. Two got in last night; the other two got in a couple days ago." Tom walked back to the farmhouse with Anna and Jacob. The dogs were now finished sniffing each other and busy irritating Woody by bumping against him and nipping at his back paws. They surrounded Woody. One of Jacob's dogs put his head over Woody's back. Woody swung around, and bit the dog in the chest. The big Shepard jumped backward, stung from by the bite, but continued to test the big red dog. Woody stayed by Tom's side as they walked down the drive. As Anna opened the front door of the farmhouse, Lisa came out of the house and ran to Tom.

"Good to see you!" Bill came out of a building to the right. He was with a Mexican friend, was smiling, and both men held full pints of beer. "

"Tom, this is Jesus Baragon." They shook hands. Lisa led Tom by the hand into the house and to a large wooden table similar to the one in Sally's house. They sat down at the table. Bill handed beer to everyone.

Tom slugged down half of his glass, "Bill that is the best beer I've had." Bill toasted Tom. Inside the farmhouse it smelled of freshly baked bread, sweet and warm.

Tom asked, "What kind of bread are you baking?"

Lisa said,"I've been making bread and pies for you and Joe. We were bringing them to you tomorrow, wanted to surprise you. I have another one in the oven." She raced from the room. Tom hung his vest on a coat rack. Jacob directed him to a gun case along the wall. Tom set the AR10 next to a bunch of other weapons; most were ARS and AK style.

Tom commented, "Got some interesting rifles here."

Jacob spoke, "Found them in Chelan a couple weeks ago next to five dead people."

Tom squirmed in his seat, "Ya, I, ah, know about that. Sorry."

Lisa came downstairs. Behind her was another woman, taller and thicker, her short black hair hung above her shoulders. She looked muscled, and a bit shorter than Tom. Her eyes seemed orange or gold and she was impressive, strikingly pretty. She walked with a cool grace. He noticed blue shorts with big strong legs. His eyes locked on her piercing eyes.

Lisa said, "Tom, this is Becky Smith." They shook hands, and their hands simply stayed together after the shake.

Lisa looked at them both, then snapped her fingers,"Uh, hello. This is earth calling." Tom and Becky both looked at her.

"Would either of you like some bread or pie?"

Tom fumbled for words,"Yah, I wouldn't mind sourdough bread with butter, and apple pie."

Becky finally spoke, keeping her eyes on Tom, "I'll have the same Lisa, thanks." Lisa walked to the kitchen. She felt a bit jealous. From the moment she met Becky she knew she herself was no match for Tom. Becky was a perfect match for Tom. While they looked different, the strong bodies and the way they carried themselves were similar. Lisa was enjoying watching an enchanted moment.

Becky looked at the vest hanging on the coat rack, then at the AR10 and at Tom's two holstered pistols. "Well Tom you are well armed."

Tom slapped the H&K,"What? These old things, just something I slipped on," Tom joked. Lisa set three plates down in front of Tom and Becky,

"Here you go sir, bread with butter and two pieces of pie."

"He looked down astonished, "No way! Man, that looks good." They snacked for an hour before taking a tour of the farm. Tom, Becky, and Jacob each slung their weapons over their shoulders. Jacob carried a well-worn Marlin lever-action rifle. Becky carried a M4 type rifle, a bit smaller than Tom's.

They walked as a group, out the door heading to the building next to the farmhouse. Jacob spoke clear and loud, "This is the bunk house. Actually this was the original farmhouse built in the 1920s by my great grandfather. He built the current house in the late 1960's. The big old barn is over fifty years old." They walked through the barn, "We have ten beef cows, and two milk cows, ten buffalo, six horses, a hoard of chickens, two big German Shepherds and an Australian Shepard." Tom looked out at the pasture. Cows, horses, and a few buffalo grazed in the grass together.

Anna continued the verbal tour, "We need a good bull to breed with our cows, but we can't find any bulls anywhere."

Tom spoke up, "I have a big bull in Stehekin. Don't know what kind it is, but it's big and hairy, real nice though."

Anna pointed at a fenced garden every bit the size of the one at Sky Ranch. The plants were much further along than the plants in Stehekin. "This garden is completely organic, as the entire farm is. It's one and a half acres." She pointed to a greenhouse made of PVC pipe and thick plastic. "We started everything in the greenhouse and then transplant the starts to the garden." They walked to the northwestern corner of the property where a four-foot deep ditch made a y thus the name of the ranch, "Y CREEK Farm." At the crotch of the Y was a small block building. A six-foot water wheel spun on an axle in the water. The axle connected into a block building and to an electric converter, which powered the farm.

Jacob said, "Our little power station is what got us in trouble with the neighbors and the county. They thought the water wheel was impeding the flow of the water, which is bullshit of course. Then the neighbors made a stink because we don't use pesticides. Well, they've got bug problems and blamed us for the stupid bugs, even though we had no problem with them. You found out what kind of friends you have when you go through that kind of crap. Anyway, we became hated outcasts, so we put up a gate and stayed to ourselves."

Anna jumped in, "The hill you see is a glacier moraine. It was pushed up to where it is by the movement of the glacier. From this spot the glacier melted for eons. The Y Creek passed through the area, and the moraine trapped deposits of rich soil and minerals, a perfect place for a farm. We're trying to grow different, hardier, wheat. On other parcels we have corn and potatoes the orchards are apple, cherry, pear and grapes. So far everything we plant grows and grows well."

Tom looked out over the farm, "You have two see Sky Ranch; it is very much a carbon copy of this one."

The upper arms of Y ran downward one along the west side of the farm and the other dead center of the farm. Water flowed into a concrete irrigation tank ten feet round and twelve feet high, and provided the farm with clean water. Pipes ran downhill to the farmhouse and other buildings, providing water to the garden feeding hydrants throughout the farm. A pipe ran to a small rock building. Above the front of the door was a sign that read "Bath House." Inside the north wall large thick metal bucket on hinges was attached to a wall of mortar. Set in river rock under the bucket was a furnace with a fire. The fire heated the water in the bucket. When it was the desired temperature, you dumped the water into the river rock tub below. Tom said, "I gotta find you guys a snorkel tub, its way easier."

At 7:00 pm Tom drove back to Bill's cabin on the water. He radioed Joe that he would be a few days longer. On the way back Tom and Bill laughed about getting a DUI. Tom spent two days at the Y Creek, and for two days Bill, Jesus, Tom and Becky looked for a cedar tub and snorkel stove. They found one in the back yard of a cabin near Bill's cabin. At the ranch they set the tub up in the bathhouse. The cedar tub was six feet around. The stove was attached to the bottom with screws.

Late on the second evening, the seven ate great meal of buffalo stew and bread topped with homemade butter and finished with apple pie. As usual, everyone drank, and then walked to the bathhouse in swimsuits, rifles swung over their shoulders. The tub fit everyone but the dogs who stood patiently outside bugging each other. The two shepherds continued to mess with Woody. The white and black Australian Shepherd didn't care about the other dogs. She wanted one thing, how to screw around with the cows and horses, and she did. This evening she hung with everyone else watching the humans make fools of themselves. Bill was drunk in the tub. He pulled out three joints lit them and passed them around.

"I want to toast Tom!" Everyone raised their glasses as he poured wine into them. "Here's to Tom, a pure badass and we are happy to have him, and here's to Anna and Jacob, what a great place to be, this farm. And here's to Jesus, a great farmer, and here's to Lisa, Becky and Anna who bring beauty to every place they go." His arm splashed down in the tub.

Anna laughed, "What about yourself Bill?"

He raised his glass, "Here's to me."

"What about you?" Jacob asked.

Bill raised his glass, "Here's to me. I'm an engineer. I can fix anything." He sat back down in the hot water. A layer of marijuana smoke hung above the tub.

Tom and Becky sat next to each other in the tub, whispering in each other's ears. They walked back to the farmhouse holding hands. At first Tom and Becky couldn't keep their eyes off each other, but then their self-control, which comes with age set in. However the tub, drinks, and smoking diminished their inhibitions. The need for human sexual contact took over. They slept, in a far corner of the farmhouse, sharing a creaky old bed that kept Anna and Jacob awake for hours.

DECISIONS

CHAPTER 26

BREAKFAST WAS COOKED OVER the barbecue outside in the backyard and served on a picnic table on the porch. Anna stood up, "Ok, everyone, we need to talk about several issues. We need to know who is going to stay where. We also need to know what chores people want to do. There is no doubt that everyone here must work and I want to hear from each of you how you will help or not help in with the work on the Y Creek Farm. I'm also wondering why and if we need all these weapons, and if so, what and who are the threats."

Bill raised his hand, "I want to live here. I'll work on whatever you need, electrical, plumbing, making beer and wine, and whatever needs to be done, and if Tom and Joe need something worked on I'll go up the lake and take care of it." He tapped his cup on the table. "That's what I want to do." He was still buzzed from the night before. He continued, "What about you Jesus?"

Jesus looked up, his big brown eyes sad. "I'm a bit hung over right now, but I think I want to stay here and work with Anna and Jacob on the farm, been doing it for twenty years, the earth is what I like to work with."

He sat down. Anna said, "What about you Lisa?" Lisa said quietly, "I'll go wherever I'm needed. If you and Jake need me here, then I'll be here. If not, I would like to wander to Sky Ranch to snoop around, and explore the big mountains."

Anna looked at Becky, "What about you?" Becky looked at Tom, and then smiled. "Uh, I think I'm going to Sky Ranch, been thinking about it for months, and I have more than one reason to go." She tapped Tom with her leg.

Tom stood up, "I will continue to live at Sky Ranch. I'll do whatever is needed anywhere and any job. Would like to patrol the area, snoop around, and see what's up. I want to add that we should stay close, no further than the town of Chelan, to Stehekin, for safety's sake."

Anna stood up, "Ok. So there we have it. We are staying together for one common good, to survive. We will need to work together for crops, meat, and water. As for security, we were hoping that Tom and Becky would handle security matters."

Tom stood again. He thought of the military, and knew these were not military people. "The most important thing we can do is keep remote, hidden. This farm does that very well with the bunched up dirt making such a fine hill. I found this place by tracing your tracks in the road. But, if I can do it, someone else can."

Anna spoke up, "So should we hide ourselves from other people so we keep the bad from here, or should we open ourselves to the out world so they can use our food and resources to survive?"

Bill said, "If we're here, then others might be about, looking for a way to survive. Maybe we should put up signs, come here and live."

Tom said, "We have to stay the way we are. We cannot advertise our whereabouts. There are those that would take all this from you, without a thought. I've encountered them. They'll do it. Besides, we don't know if the contagion or whatever killed everyone, is still out there. It might still be circulating about the cities and towns. We just don't know."

Lisa spoke up, "I agree with Tom. We should not go checking the cities to see who's about, and we should stay put."

Bill spoke up with a serious tone. "Another thing we have to think about is toxic waste. I worked at Hanford for a decade. Everything that Hanford does produces toxic radioactive waste. I would venture to say that if we were downwind we would be dead or dying of radioactive exposure.

Bill continued, "We have tanks of petrochemicals, all types of man made toxic chemicals sitting in containers that will not last forever. Every home has some type of chemical, whether it is pesticide, or gas; it's dangerous to us. What we should do is empty every home and building upstream and around us of this crap, and dump it downstream of Chelan. If we don't we could allow this place to be contaminated from either a cloud, or mess up our drinking water. What we should do is gather up gas and diesel fuel, store them in tanks, and in barns, out of the weather, so the seals and valves don't rot away so quickly. We'll use as little fuel as possible because sometime in the future there won't be any more, and that goes for batteries too."

Tom said, "Well said, Bill. Let's all stay close to home from now on unless we go as a group. We have some bad guys out there. If they get a toehold in this place, it won't be easy to get them out. I suggest that everyone learn how to shoot and learn some tactics that will help you in an emergency situation."

Anna spoke, "I don't want to get to the point where we are killing people."

Tom interrupted, "Anna, we are already at that point. It happened."

She spoke up with a frightened voice, "I know Tom. I helped bury them that you shot. It was ugly, never seen that before, and I'm struggling with it now, but I respect you for what you did, and I'll do whatever I have to keep this place."

Becky stood up, "We have everything to lose and it's ours to lose. I think we should have radio communication every day from Sky Ranch to Y Creek. It will keep us alive and informed. Weapon training is a must-have for everyone here, and I agree this place must be hidden from whoever is out there. I feel lucky to have Bill and Lisa and the rest of you. Jesus was my companion from Pullman to here. Now I feel like a hitchhiker with only one prospect, and I thank all of you. She sat down, and took big swig from her cup of tea. She was gorgeous and articulate.

Tom was impressed. He stood, "Ok. The first thing is for everyone to do their part, starting today I'll go pick up weapons and bring them back here."

Becky said, "I'll go with you."

Anna stood, "Ok, so we defined everyone's jobs. We are going to stay together, working for the common good of the two farms. We are going to own Lake Chelan and are responsible for it. Tom and Becky are the Sheriff and Marshall. Lisa and Jesus will help with the farm and Bill is the fix-it man.

Jacob and I will continue to own the Y Creek Farm and work it as we have for ten years. I assume that Joe will stay at Sky Ranch. We are dependent on each other, this is our declaration of dependence to each other." She walked to the kitchen and brought back a tray of shot glasses filled with whiskey. "We will have a toast to our Fellowship of the Farms."

UPLAKE

From Twenty-five Mile Sky, Tom and Becky brought six Colt M4s and two of the bigger H&K 417s. Since all the people were inexperienced shooters they brought handguns chambered in 9mm and .40 caliber. The weapons were all Smith and Wesson, brand new in the boxes from Ray's store. The following morning Tom laid all the weapons on the picnic table outside and described each weapon as he would do for a soldier. For two hours he taught his friends how to strip and clean and then put the guns back together. In the fields, weapons were carried. After five days of this practice, the amateurs got to shoot. Each person went through two hundred rounds with their side arms and 100 with the long guns.

With planting to be done, only so much time could be spent on weapons training. Bill, Anna, and Jesus were not enthused by all the work with guns. They understood the need, but were not into it.

Tom went through possible scenarios, "If bad guys come down the driveway in numbers larger then our numbers, turn to your weapons and fire slowly. They will not be military. If they are, they will take cover, which will give you time to get in your vehicles and book through the pasture. Don't stop to open gates, just drive. Make your way to Stehekin and we'll deal with them from there.

COMMUNITIES CONVERGE

CHAPTER 27

Two weeks later, with planting completed, Tom, Becky, Lisa, Jacob, and Anna left in the Sky Boat to help old Joe finish work on the garden at Sky Ranch. Everyone was happy to see Sky Ranch. Joe had worked countless hours in the garden. Joe had given it great care, but he was an old man. They spent three days arranging the garden, mixing compost materials, and spreading it about. Every evening was spent with drinks and good smoke. They toured the valley on mountain bikes every day.

On the fourth day they rode into Stehekin to see the sights. The day was unusually warm, and they all jumped off the dock into the freezing lake naked. Later they pedaled the two miles back home.

When they made the turn to the café, Tom slammed on the brakes of his bike. He stood, looking at piles of horse shit on the asphalt road. He looked ahead. "Come on! Ride fast!" By the time they reached the café, they could see that the horses had clearly passed the cafe, and continued on to Sky Ranch. Tom and Becky were in the best shape and beat everyone to the ranch on their bikes.

In the front of Sally's garage were five horses; one with a saddle, and the other four loaded down with supplies and gear. No rider was present.

Tom stormed into Sally's house, and, ran straight into Philip Sky. He bounced off the big kid. "Philip! You're alive!" They embraced. He seemed bigger and stronger, with crow's feet at the corners at the corners of his eyes. There he was.

Philip was introduced to everyone then sat on the back picnic table and told Tom his story.

"When I left last November, I met up with Uncle Karl on Highway 20. He drove back home with my aunt. I took his rig and my six horses to a place east of Glacier National Park, to do a high hunt for some clients. I gathered the supplies I needed and went on a three-week scout before the hunt, was having the time of my life living in a cabin up high and alone. When the time came for my clients to show over Thanksgiving, they never showed. Since I was paid ahead of time, I didn't care. Just stayed there. Had supplies for five people for two weeks of living high on the hog. I went hunting by myself and shot two deer. Dragged them back to the cabin, each time hoping to find my clients. On the last two days of the trip a nasty storm came from the north, dropped two feet of snow, and then continued to dump for two weeks. At some point the power went out and I was stuck in three feet of snow on a twenty-five mile dirt road. I kept expecting to find a snowplow coming up the road, but it never came.

There was no way I was going to leave my horses. Two of them were older than me, so I stayed. Had a small corral loaded with hay and grain for not only my horses, but the horses that belonged to the clients that never showed. Anyway, I had enough supplies for a couple months, so I stayed after Thanksgiving. Thought I should head into Glacier to call my parents. I couldn't get out, so I stayed after Christmas. Finally, made a try for home with just the horses. It was too cold for them, so I turned back. Next thing I knew, it was February and I was almost out of supplies. Shot some elk and a bear, and then broke into a couple of cabins, stealing all I could. The snow held until March. Finally, a warm front came through, and I booked it out of there with all the horses. Two of the horses went lame and I shot them.

There was a river that had a bridge out and I had to travel for thirty miles along the bank until I found a bridge we could pass over.

I arrived at east Glacier the end of April. Found nothing but dead people! So, I stole a truck and trailer and started for home. Roads were bad so I had to go far south, ended up in Pocatello Idaho. Drove through Boise and then through to I-5, straight up into Seattle, and to Uncle Karl's house, where I found my family, dead. Buried them in the back yard. Was a sad day.

When I was done burying everyone, I loaded up the truck and trailer with two of Karl's horses and all the supplies I could carry. Drove up Highway 20 to about Canyon Creek. The snow was too deep for the truck, so I pulled out the horses and huffed it to here.

He looked at Tom with tears in his eyes. Didn't expect to find dead people everywhere. Man, what a crappy deal! All the time I was gone I wanted to get back here and eat with my family, and sleep in my own bed. Now I get the house to myself."

Next, Philip sat and listened to Tom's story, from the botched drug deal to the battle in Chelan, and then to the meeting with Anna and Jacob. By the time they were done talking it was late in the day. They walked back to the house for supper.

For three days Sky Ranch was a scene of activity. The massive garden was planted, fences were mended and made stronger, buildings were worked, trees were trimmed, and weeds were pulled.

When Tom drove the group back to Y Creek Farm, Lisa stayed with Philip. They had formed a relationship behind the scenes. Quiet and private, Philip wanted to be alone. He had no intentions of leaving the ranch after eight months away, and Lisa was a great distraction for him.

He had matured quickly. Having to bury his family had the most impact on him. He showed a strong face and spent most of his time alone. Lisa stepped her way into his life, cooking and cleaning the house he'd grown up in. Patiently she watched him, and they'd grown close.

With the state of the world as it was, it was only natural they made it together. Both had been through quite a bit in the last six months. Nature had its way with young people.

Philip happily threw himself into life on the ranch. He spent a few days reconnecting with Sky Ranch. Seven months of travel had aged him. His relief at finding the ranch intact and inhabited was huge. Tom, while younger than Philip's father, now became a father figure to Philip. Tom had offered to move from the ranch, since Philip owned it. Philip would not even think about it.

Tom and Joe were now fixtures at the ranch. Joe had moved into Sally's ranch house. He moved his meager belongings into the ground floor room next to the office. The house was kept clean and tidy. Like Anna's kitchen at Y Creek Farm, the kitchen was the meeting place. Joe worked making great meals, usually with a glass of beer or bourbon nearby.

One day, Joe stood in the chicken coop. clucking at the happy and healthy birds. They were high quality chickens, hardy and lean. Old Joe enjoyed the birds. They were simple. Two of the chickens were standing their ground, not letting the two mutts walk by. Three roosters walked over to give added ground support to the chickens. Joe pushed the chickens away. While he didn't smoke marijuana, he did in fact cook it into a special cornbread that he liked and kept from the others. It took the edge off his aches and pains. Known to none of his fellow citizens was that he had broken legs , hands, an arm and most of his fingers in the past. Not all of his bones were set by doctors, and he had pain in all of them.

Meals were somewhat the same: meat, potatoes, and veggies of only what they could grow. Bread and butter were now traded with Anna for fresh meat. Pies and cakes were a treat where before they were merely another choice. Everyone spent time fishing in the river or lake. Food was not a problem.

CRYSTAL CLEAN

CHAPTER 28

JACOB REQUESTED EVERYONE TO A MEETING at the Y Creek Farm. Joe stayed at the ranch as usual. Anna started the meeting, "I want to thank everyone for coming today. This, as you can imagine, is a make or break time for all of us. I've been talking with Bill, our in house environmentalist and engineer about matters that he sees as crucial to our future. These matters will not impact us today, but will in the future. I have asked Bill to talk on these matters and then we'll have a discussion. Without further introduction, and ado, I give you, Bill Crystal."

Bill stood with his beer bottle in his hand. Jesus sat with his signature smile on his face next to Bill.

"Ok. Thank you, Anna, and welcome all of you. Stealing a line from Lord of the Rings, the subject of this meeting is the Fellowship of our Farms, or maybe the future of them. What we need to think is the health of the outlying area around the farm.

As you all know we have corpses rotting in homes and buildings as well as toxic chemicals most of which we'll never be used on this farm or in Stehekin. I think we need to remove anything that could become a hazard to us. This includes cars and trucks, and chemicals of any type: gas tanks, along with their contents, corpses, boats that sit in the lake sinking or polluting their contents into the lake and the human waste we make.

As it stands right now, of course I'm assuming the rest of the world is a dead zone, with pockets of living, similar to here. The good thing is we are no longer polluting the air as we have in the past. No more do we have jet airliners leaving their filth to rain down on us. Cars and trucks are not emitting their filth either, as well as coal and petroleum plants.

That's all good, but in this area where we have all decided that we are going to live. I think we should make an effort to clean this area as best we can. While in that pursuit we should collect anything and everything we can use so we may continue to prosper in the manner we have been. Simply said, we need to get busy collecting the filth from our old world and deposit it downwind and downstream from this place, so this area can become a viable organic growing town of people that live, not to destroy and watch things burn, but a community of people that work together for a common goal. Anna's 'Declaration of Dependence' hit home for me. We should all get it together to get-r–done."

We have a responsibility to help people that want to pass through. Feed them supply them and give them knowledge. We also have a responsibility to protect this area from those that would want to destroy it or take for their own. Another thing that I worry about is nukes, the kind that sit in missile silos on ships, subs, and power plants. We've talked about this before, and there is little we can do about a radiation problem, but we should become aware of all the possibilities."

The group broke up and set about a great meal of barbecued steak, with beer, wine and other drink consumed. The following day, and for two months straight, the people started the cleanup by collecting all they could. Truckloads of supplies were stored in cargo trailers and set inside nearby barns. Two tanker trucks were driven inside a barn for safekeeping. One held gasoline; another diesel fuel. Insecticide, cleaners, solvents, and chemicals that were deemed not useful were driven south along the Columbia River and left in trailers and box trucks on a big empty field. Cars and trucks were moved from their carports, garages and streets and driven to the nearby Wal-Mart parking lot. Siphoning gas from vehicles was started, but stopped when it was obvious it would take too much time.

Lake Chelan was cleaned up as well. Boats that were floating or half submerged were dragged out, placed on trailers, and left in the Wal-Mart parking, next to the cars and trucks. Gas and diesel stored in tanks at the local gas stations were siphoned out and back into tanks for use on the farm and Sky Ranch.

Farmhouses and cabins near the Y Creek Farm were emptied of bodies. All were buried in their in their own yards. The residents dug graves with a small bulldozer. The work was sad and dirty, Only the men could handle this chore. Most corpses were left in their own homes, as clearly there were not enough people to carry through with the cleanup and burial process. Homes were marked, and then the doors and windows were locked. The front doors were marked with spray paint; a simple "R.I.P." was sprayed on the door.

Moving the bodies affected Tom the most. Specifically, after a day of carrying out bodies to be buried, the dreams of Afghanistan began. Digging deep in his mind, they shadowed his every sleeping moment. Dead people, their skin grey and void of any healthy color, the smell reaching deep into the back of the throat and nose, dominated his every dream, and seeped into his waking moments. Finally, he could do no more. Becky insisted the burial process stop so he could see some relief. Jacob and Philip took over for him. Tom went to doctor's offices and the local hospital gathering medical supplies and drugs so that both the Y Creek Farm and Sky Ranch had the most complete mini-hospital with drugs and all the paraphernalia one would need to set broken bones, sew up cuts, and diagnose ailments.

Each ranch was set up with a hospital room. One room on the downstairs floor of each of the farmhouses was set up with exam chair and bed for surgery. Stainless steel medical utensils and sterilized equipment were set the same way in each room. Each room was set up with a medical library.

Anna took the cleanup and detoxification process to a new level when she outlawed plastic bags on the farm. When she outlawed Tupperware she had a rebellion on her hands and she changed her mind. By the end of July, the citizens could spend no more time on the cleanup of Chelan Valley. The crops had grown to record sizes and required constant pruning and weeding, watering was important as well, and the temperatures were well into the 90's. With the cool mountain water and hot temperatures, the crops prospered, and the farm had become a luscious Garden of Eden.

The temperature was lower at Sky Ranch. The smell was of organic life was abuzz. Bees buzzed everywhere, pollinating and working the farms beehives. Snakes, lizards, and frogs covered the cool ground, munching small bugs. Hummingbirds buzzed through, spending their time at the big garden. Deer wandered onto the farm to munch at the crunchy healthy plants. They were either shot and eaten, or chased off by the dogs.

Dogs were important to the farm, they chased off and in some cases, caught and killed varmints before they did damage to the crops. Common enemies of the farm were raccoons, deer, porcupine, skunk, bear, and crows. Most of the animals raided the farm for the fruit, and the dogs always seemed to know where they would appear. The two big male shepherds kept tabs on the white and blue Australian Shepherd named Lady. She was pregnant and waddled along with her male friends, playfully nipping at the big males' heels. They were happy and healthy. Like Woody, they protected their masters. When a rattlesnake was found dead, the Shepherds stood next to the snake looking proudly up at the humans, showing off their catch with wagging tails and smiling faces. Lady, in her final weeks of pregnancy, followed Anna throughout her day in the kitchen and garden.

Once the garden and fields were worked Tom, Becky, Lisa, and Philip drove back to Sky Ranch to tend to the two-acre garden there. With fall near, crops were worked and canned for future use over the fall and winter.

The people had over twenty cords of wood to cut and split. With four cabins on the farm, each one using close to four cords of wood during the winter cold.

General maintenance of the buildings was done: fixing windows, doors, roofs and walls. Philip's house had sat empty for eight months. With Lisa, he worked hard to collect all the supplies needed for the winter. At the suggestion of Bill Crystal, the people collected propane tanks and used them for cooking and heating,. Bill's reasoning was to use propane before the seals went bad and the gas leaked away with no chances of capturing it. Propane stoves and heaters were set up in each cabin. The winter would be much easier. In the areas around both the Y Creek Farm and Sky Ranch big propane tanks were set up in barns and garages to keep the seals from weathering.

While gas, diesel, and propane were now plentiful, Bill set about setting up wind-powered generating units at both ranches. Using smaller windmills set up on telephone poles, when the wind blew they worked great. Set on the roofs of the cabins and houses were solar panels scavenged from other buildings. Power ran through the ranches, unlimited with no power bills. Meter readers didn't come snooping around, jotting numbers in their books, and then driving off. Both ranches were completely unplugged from the old world.

But no matter how independent the people became, signs of the former life existed everywhere. All they could do was ignore the signs and look to the future. The past was slowly moving to the back of their minds.

SEPTEMBER'S PREPARATION

CHAPTER 29

IN THE BEGINNING OF SEPTEMBER crops were being harvested and stowed away, in sacks, then garbage cans, bottled and canned and stored in neighboring basements for use in the future. Everyone worked on the crops and orchards. Joe and Lisa singlehandedly kept the Sky Ranch garden green, picking what they needed and canning all they could. The basements under Sally's and Philip's houses were packed to the gills with stacked jars of every size, full of fruit and veggies, Tupperware and garbage cans full of wheat and flour sat stacked to the ceiling. When the two basements were full, the dungeon under the barn became a warehouse with supplies from both farms. The garden was winding itself down in September. Most veggies had been picked. Squash, pumpkins, and lettuce were still growing. The chickens had the run of the garden now, eating grubs and bugs. Portable greenhouses were back. Clear plastic held up by bent PVC pipe kept the remaining plants warm during the night.

The cows and bull had gained a great deal of weight during the summer. The weight would help them during the long freezing winter. Both calves had been gaining weight as well. They were playful and protected by their mothers and the bull. They, along with the bull, would be moved after the two cows became pregnant again. They would be moved to the Y Creek Farm where the grazing was better and the winter was less severe.

The big bull would be used to stud; impregnating the cows there. Anna and Jacob had yet to find a bull in the Manson area, so the one big Sky bull was it for now.

Philip had found six horses in pastures around Manson and brought them back to the Y Creek. He found two skinny horses in Stehekin grazing in a pasture with four deer. They were brought back to Sky Ranch and sent on to Y Creek to gain weight.

To get the stock from Stehekin to Manson, Bill had been working on a small tugboat that was used for hauling freight throughout the lake. He claimed the tug would be ready for use with a small barge. Two semi-trucks full of hay and feed for the stock at Stehekin waited for the tug to be finished.

MID-SEPTEMBER

Tom and Becky drove the Sky Boat back from Manson loaded with supplies. Jacob and Anna rode along, enjoying a few days off from the farm. They had brought along their pregnant dog, Lady. The boat was full of burlap bags of potatoes and other supplies from Chelan, along with the new rifles for the ranch. Milk crates with fresh bread and butter were stacked in the small boat cabin. Woody and Lady stood, watching the world go by. They passed the Stehekin Landing then to the Sky dock. They unloaded the boat into the Ford pickup and drove to the Sky Ranch.

Philip ran out from the barn, "Your two calves were both born while you were gone. They look like blond-haired Holsteins." This was a big deal; the first birth since the apocalypse had happened. Cats arrived hoping for a bowl of milk. This time they didn't get any.

From Finger Rock Tom and Becky watched the beavers work on the ever-growing dam. They walked to the greenhouse. Tom's crop of Juicy Fruit was over six feet tall, with one-foot buds. The buds were tight and wound together with golden hairs dripping with crystals. Becky threatened Tom with an arrest for growing weed. Anna and Becky followed Tom and Jacob to the dungeon. Part of the room was lit up with only three sodium lights. The rest of the dungeon was a warehouse. There was no longer a need to grow weed except to keep the strains going. The sweet smell of cannabis dominated the room.

Anna and Becky stripped down to bikinis and laid down at the beach to get much needed rest. They loved the beach. It raised the spirits of all. The small tree frogs sat in hiding near the pond, watching the humans.

GEORGE THIELMAN

One ran under the waterfall to a cave they liked to hang out in. Two others followed. They had spent most of the day gorging on flies and mosquitos, and now wanted to sleep and breed.

The frogs watched as Jacob straddled Anna's face then jumped off laughing. The men left the girls alone. They walked to Tom's cabin with a case of Bill's Fat Belly Beer.

Tom and Philip had decided that the two ranches would be upgraded with weapons from Ray's Gun Shop and from the Yakima Proving Grounds. Jacob had agreed to keep the new weapons a secret, knowing that Anna would make a fuss. In Tom's cabin they laid out Remington semi-auto hunting rifles, simply called the 25 and 15s; three of each. The 15s chambered in .223 calibers and the 25s chambered in .308 calibers. All the Remington rifles looked like a military M4 with a camouflage finish. They were semi-auto built more for long-range target shooting and hunting. Four H&K 417 were to be used for defensive purposes along with Four Colt M4s. The 417s were chambered in .308 and the Colt M4s .223 both was fully automatic or semi-auto rifles. Remington rifles received bigger hunting scopes and the M4s and 417s received smaller scopes designed for fast target acquisition for close up shooting and were fairly good for long range shots. Like the military the men decided the long-range hunting rifle would be the Winchester model 70 chambered in the booming .300 magnum.

The .300 was a wicked big bullet with a big charge of powder that could easily send the round a mile and knock out any prey including man. The gun had a good kick and, other than the fact that the kick sent the scope digging into the shooter's eye socket leaving a nasty round cut, the round worked well. These were the weapons that would protect the farms from animals and bad guys alike.

Each ranch would be set up with a thousand rounds for each gun. All would be kept in gun and ammo cases in the ranch houses, and those persons who took a weeklong course would be assigned a weapon. Only Anna and Jesus declined to take the gun course, preferring to work in the fields, or in Anna's case, anything else.

BECKY AGAIN

CHAPTER 30

ANNA SHOWED BECKY, LISA, AND JOE several recipes for bread and pasta dishes, herbs to spice up meat, and easy methods of making bread. Tom knew little of cooking and stayed away from the kitchens. Anna's teachings were taken to heart by all that learned from her; her energy in such matters was endless.

Becky Smith had thought about how happy she was to be living in Stehekin, safe from traveling problems, with great people to learn and live with. She loved the deer, elk, and bears, which strolled by the Sky Ranch looking around, foraging for food, unafraid of the compound. She had always searched out the far away cold places; in her past, Alaska, and Yellowstone. Like everyone else, she was struggling to cope with her new life. Without family members or old acquaintances she felt a bit out of place. She thought of the past year. "Who would have thought such a thing would happen?" She looked out the window toward Tom's cabin. It was not what she had dreamed of, but would do.

On the bed, the two cats snuggled together purring. Big Woody sat, waiting, hoping Becky would come outside for a walk. Downstairs she grabbed two fishing poles, and walked outside with Woody. She loved the late evening fishing sessions. Tom ran out to Finger Rock. They hugged.

Tom asked, "Did you start the tub?"

She looked at him with her new tan from the dungeon heat lamps, "Of course I did. Don't think I would miss out on that, do you?" She thought of the great session they had the night before, and then shook her head, smiling at her man.

They caught four trout, dressed them out and walked back to the cabin. After supper they slipped into the cedar tub, making love on the cedar seats while the two kittens batted at Woody's tail. Afterward, Tom fell asleep. Becky walked around the cabin. She stood for a long time looking at endless tables full of scoped assault rifles, pistols, and equipment meant for the destruction of human beings. She was brought up going to church on Sunday. Her heart was restless. She easily quit religion and turned to individual sports like cross country, swimming, gymnastics and track. Like Tom Trainer, she joined the Air Force after high school, and then joined law enforcement before becoming a forest ranger. She thought of all the trials and tribulations, and how they all led her to being in this place at this time. Training and duty as a M.P. in the Air Force and law enforcement had taught her the art of self-defense and weapons training that had made it possible for her to have survived and made to this place.

She walked outside in one of Tom's fleece shirts, sipping tea as she walked by the horses. She sensed she wasn't alone and looked down. Woody stood not five feet from her, his head cocked to one side. He was ready to do anything she wanted. He was waiting for a signal, "Come on, Big Boy. Let's go to bed." They walked back to the cabin. Woody ran inside the cabin and stood waiting for her. In the loft she looked down at Tom sleeping, she noticed him flinching, and making jerking movements. She had seen it before. With what he had been through and done, she wondered how he ever got any sleep. Then she thought of the couple that had survived the most deadly virus known to man only to die at her hands. She threw the shirt off and picked up the kittens. She set them on a chair. She lay down next to Tom, running her arms between his, and wrapped her feet around his. He jerked back as he woke. He groaned and put his arms around her shoulders. He pulled the covers over her. She thought of all that had happened in the last ten months. With all the death and misery, the heartache and pain, here she was sleeping in a bed with a scarred- up soldier, two kittens, and big, kind-hearted mutt. The word that came to mind was harmony.

INVASION

CHAPTER 31

LISA AND PHILIP SEEMED TO BE THE MOST resilient of the group; they worked at both ranches and at any task that needed a hand. The traveling from one place to the other gave them time to hold onto each other and have sex in strange places. They exuded love, hope and energy, the way only young people could. Lisa was almost three years older than Philip, but felt him to be the more mature one. It was a subject they argued about. They found a small sailboat twenty-five feet long, long enough for four people and a few dogs. The boat cut through the water like a knife. It ran on clean energy, and they enjoyed the sensation of sailing quickly and quietly.

Tom pulled up in the pickup with his gear. Today was his first lesson with a sailboat. He walked to the end of the dock. Anna and Jacob came out of the café. All were in good spirits. The day was still warm. Summer had not yet ended. Tom noticed the boat was named the Lisa Ann.

He teased Philip, "Lisa Ann? Who's that? "Jacob and Anna walked up, chatting loudly. Tom looked off into the distance during the chat. The smaller Sky Boat was coming toward them at a fast clip. Tom said, "Hold on a minute, something's wrong here."

Philip looked through his binoculars, "It's Jesus and he doesn't look good." As Jesus came closer to the dock, Tom put his hands in the air and slowly lowered them, signaling Jesus to slow down. Jesus slammed straight into the dock, denting the front of the boat.

Jacob grabbed the boat, "What's going on dude? "He looked down on the floor of the boat and was startled. Bill was lying on the floor in great pain; the puddle of water in the bottom of the boat was red with blood.

"They shoot him! Shoot in leg, shoulder, arm. Too many of them!" Jacob shut the motor off and tied it up. Anna asked what happened.

"We come back from Chelan and they there at Y Creek Farm with black trucks and many guns. We come through gate and they shoot at us. Bill, he shoot back and they run away, but then shoot more. I drive to Bill's cabin then come here."

Tom yelled to Philip, pointing at him, "Philip, go back to the ranch, bring weapons, your dogs and a radio. I need you to stay at the café and keep watch. Tie the dogs up so they can watch the lake.

Tom and Jacob carried Bill to the back of the pickup and sped to Sky Ranch. They carried Bill to the first aid room they had made in one of the corner bedrooms. Bill screamed in pain as Tom and Becky ripped the clothes from around his wounds.

"Ow man, that hurts!"

"What are ya doing Bill? Trying to catch up to me with the number of bullet holes?"

Bill laughed through the pain, and then burst out in painful screaming.

Tom put his hand to Bill's forehead, "Listen dude, I need you to stop yelling. Just deal with the pain, I'm going to give you something you're going to love, but first I want to know how bad your injuries are, so hang on buddy."

Bill gritted his teeth, "It just hurts like hell, man."

Becky said calmly, "One bullet went through his arm and the other past through his shoulder. There are exit wounds at each wound." She grabbed Bill's hand. Jesus was holding the other.

Tom looked at Jesus, "Jesus I need you to go and do something else. You're in the way here, and tell Anna to come quick." Anna came into the room with warm folded hand towels and two big bowls of hot water. Tom went to the medicine cabinet, fixed a syringe with morphine. "Okay Bill, it's time for La La Land, you're going to dig this. "He slipped the needle into Bill's arm. Bill jumped at the sting and then settled down. His eyes started to wander across the ceiling of the room.

Tom snapped his fingers in front of Bill's face. "How ya doing buddy?"

Bill whispered, "Good, yah … good, Tom," They cleaned the wounds, and applied antiseptic. Tom gave Bill a shot of Demerol and dug around, looking for bone and bullet fragments.

Tom sewed torn muscle and skin and then went to work on the left leg. A bullet had hit bone eight inches below the knee, shattering both the Fibula and Tibia; both leg bones. Another bullet had shattered the ankle joint. Tom got ahold of the bullet. He set it in a metal pan and then went to work looking for bone fragments. Becky used suction to clean the way for Tom's probe and scalpel. After two hours of cleaning and exploring the lower wounds Tom stopped cleaned up and walked into the kitchen.

Anna handed Tom a cup of coffee. "So how is he?"

Tom looked around the table at his friends, took a big breathe, he was nervous. "Well the wounds to his shoulder and arm are ok. Both bullets were small probably .223's from a M16, they went in and out and hit no bone." He looked at Jacob concerned. "Both leg bones the Fibula and Tibia are shattered with splinters everywhere. Below that wound a bigger bullet shattered the complete ankle. He took a big breath then continued. "There's no doubt that the only thing to do is to amputate the lower leg and foot. If we don't take it off he will never be able to walk on the damaged foot, and most likely the severity of the wound well keep him from recovering. Now I've never amputated anything and I'm not a doctor, that's why I know the only way for him to survive and avoid gangrene is to cut it off, I just need to get my head around it."

Becky took his cup from him then set it on the table; she looked up into his eyes. "We have to do this right now, Bills out of it for a while." Anna asked, "Are you sure there's nothing we can do?"

Becky turned to her. "Two years ago trained doctors could fix this with little problem, those days are over." She turned back to Tom and gently led him back to the medical room.

Tom started with cutting the skin around the leg, leaving a small flap on the back side to cover the wound. They pulled the skin down like a sock then cut the muscle to expose bone then cut the bone with special saw. They worked for three hours on Bill's leg.

Anna woke up from the couch and sat next to Tom, "You were right. We had a security problem. They took our house, just like that." Becky held her.

Tom said, "Don't worry, Anna. They won't have it for long. Tom stood up and stretched, his shirt was bloody. He stood shirtless, a body of power, scarred and beaten. Anna noticed the tattoo above his heart. It was a dagger with wings on each side of the blade. On top of the symbol where the words, "That others may live." Below the symbol where the words, "Anywhere, anytime." Tom walked to the office and called Philip. He went back to his cabin after showering.

Jesus came running into the cabin. "Tom, how is he?"

Tom said, "Well, he's alright. Going to be sore. The bullets missed anything vital. His foot is gone. We cleaned him up. He'll be okay and making beer soon. I need you to take care of him; give him what he needs. I have things to do."

Becky came downstairs. "You coming to bed? You worked on Bill for eight hours, must be tired." Tom said he would in a few minutes.

When Becky woke it was 6:30 am. Gun cases and packs were loaded neatly set on the floor. Tom walked into the cabin in full combat gear, camo pants and shirt, with pistol belt and rifle slung over his shoulder. She looked up at him," Well, you're sufficiently dressed. We going to war now?"

He kissed her, "We're in a war now, that's for sure. Jacob and Philip walked into the cabin in their camo clothes; both armed to the teeth. Becky ran upstairs and came down dressed; she had a camo jacket on with grey pants and a new H&K USP pistol in its holster. She gathered up some things as the men talked.

Joe had a huge breakfast cooking; coffee and tea were ready for those that wanted it. He was dressed in his hunting clothes with a Springfield M1A1, and the gun case in the dining room was filled with every type of shotgun and hunting rifle.

Tom checked in on Bill. He was in pain and groggy. Bill winced as Tom probed his wounds and laid clean bandages over the wounds. "Ok, Bill, my man, you're doing good, no infection, no maggots, head lice, or crabs crawling from the wound." They both laughed. Tom gave Bill two Vicadin pills for pain and another shot of antibiotics. "Bill your ankle was destroyed and we had to cut your leg off six inches below the knee."

Bill blinked and said weakly," I was afraid of that, didn't think we had the stuff to put it back together."

Tom said, "We'll find you a peg leg and you'll be making beer soon."

Bill looked up at the ceiling then fell asleep.

Becky said, "Well he took that well."

Tom laughed," Yes he did, he's smart."

Tom and Becky left the medical room.

Jacob said, "We are going to move the bad guys to another location?"

Tom gathered everyone in the dining room. "Ok. Everyone has something to eat and drink? Good. What we know is that the Y Creek is in others' hands; don't know anything other than that. They took it by brute force. No war, no declaration, no request of any type. We need to vote; shall we take it back or let them have it? All in favor of forced eviction raise their hands." Everyone raised their hands.

Anna asked, I hope you all use some restraint and not go in guns blazing, as they did, and please do not destroy my house. Also I want you all to come back here alive."

Tom sipped from his coffee, "Alright, what I think we should do is load the mini Sky Boat, and Jacob and I will go." Tom saw the disappointment in Philip. "I want Jacob to come with me because it's his ground. This ground is Philip's. He can defend it like no one else. We are going to scout only, count how many there are, check out their defenses if they have any. We'll be back in a few days. We'll try to call twice a day, 7:00 AM and 7:00PM. All the boats should be pulled in, windows covered at night so light does not escape, and everyone should be armed and ready to defend this position. Anyone that doesn't have a weapon or has a question should talk to me."

"Now this is not a revenge or a adventuresome shoot-um-up. This is our right to survive. If we allow those people to keep Y Creek. They will come and try to take this place. We have the right to live, and Anna and Jacob have the right to keep the home that's been in the family since 1908. I don't want any of you to think this well be a cakewalk. People will be killed and wounded. Just look at Bill. He was lucky and will live. You must become focused on the task. The people in Anna's home are occupants; like rats they are nothing, and need to be destroyed. Now let's all come together and get this done. I want someone at the café at all times. Dogs are to be outside at all times, they see and hear better than us. Like the Germans defending Normandy we cannot allow anyone to step a foot at the docks. Ok, let's do this. We should say a prayer to God, or ourselves, and again state our Declaration of Dependence to each other!"

They held hands. Anna spoke softly, "Dear God, help us in our struggle, bless them that are about to go to battle, and forgive those that committed crime against us. Amen."

Tom, Jacob and Philip spent the day loading the boat and going through weapons and ammo. Both Tom and Jacob were weighted down with equipment. The list was long. The trip would be recon. Only, but Tom insisted they be heavily armed. Both carried Colt M4s with eight thirty round clips side arms, four flash bang grenades and four smoke grenades, sidearm, dagger, first aid kit, small binoculars, radio, camo paint, pocket knife, headlamp, night vision goggles, one can of mace, several pairs of plastic cuffs, power bars, granola bars and dried fish. In the boat they loaded ten cases of bullets, a box of smoke grenades, a cooler full of food, extra weapons were Toms custom made AWT AR10, two shot guns, and two bolt action rifles and a Remington 25 semi-automatic hunting rifle.

They waited for darkness, said goodbyes, and then drove off in the small Alumweld boat down lake. Clouds came in low, wind picked up, and white caps could be seen.

Jacob looked at Tom. Both were in full camo paint. He asked Tom, "You scared?"

Tom smiled, "No, I'm concerned. Not scared."

Jacob yelled back at him, "I'm not sure … think I'm scared, but I'm so excited. I feel completely focused."

Tom grabbed his shoulder and shook it. "This is not supposed to be fun. This is serious. Stay focused, and do what I say, we'll be alright." Tom's big smile showed through the night. Jacob looked ahead, rolling up and down with the waves. He was concerned and it showed.

After Jacob and Tom left, Joe and Becky loaded the big Sky Boat, coolers of food and drink, camping gear, bullets and more weapons. She checked on Bill, joked with Jesus and then hiked to the café with Lisa and Joe. A passerby would have seen three highly unlikely hunters loaded down with side arms, rifles with packs, and vests brimming with ammo. It was an unusual sight. They checked on Philip, talked, and kept them company. Joe had become more than helpful. He cooked all the meals, and kept water on the stove hot ready for coffee or bandages. Anna took over in Sally's kitchen, cooking foods that would only need to be heated up over a small cook stove. She made everyone favorite buffalo stew, and cried while she prepared the food.

Philip had taken up residence in one of the upstairs bedrooms above the café. Each bedroom had a three by three window. A hallway door led to an outside deck. This is where he stood, looking southeast. He set up a table next to the railing. Three rifles sat on the table: his M1A1, a Colt M4, and a high powered bolt action Winchester model 70 with a big scope. He had it sitting on a folded blanket. With the Winchester he could reach out and touch someone from a mile off. Lisa sat next to him, armed with her trusty Browning high power pistol. Near the table was a Remington 15, the smaller version of the semi- auto hunting rifle. Philip had attached a lightweight Simmonds scope. It fired the smaller .223 bullet, same as a M4. They were determined to repel any attack. Philip was the more experienced shooter, and Lisa was the only who had ever shot at another human.

TOM'S STORY

CHAPTER 32

TOM AND JACOB CUT SOUTHEAST through the lake. Jacob asked Tom, "Tom what's it's like to kill another man?"

Tom looked at Jacob. "Killing another man is ugly. The hard part is that it stays with you forever. We have the fact that we are right in our favor. I can't tell you that it feels any certain way. All that engage in it deal with it differently."

Jacob looked out at the dark lake, "Will you tell me about your last battle?"

Tom rubbed at the scar on his face. "We were coming back from a five day recon of a valley in Afghanistan. I was in charge of a group of twelve Delta and Rangers. We were tired and hungry. We had spent five days and saw no movement of hostile intent. We walked through a rocky area. I mean the rocks were huge, all leaning on each other. A good place for an ambush. There was no way we could have covered every possible ambush point. Sure enough, bombs went off, picking the two soldiers up in front of me and throwing them into me. All three of us rolled down into a bunch of sticker bushes. We were stunned. As usual, I was lucky and not hurt.

The other two guys were injured: one in the eyes; the other had a broken arm and leg. Anyway, I gathered myself up, and stood up to see three Taliban run past us. I fired my weapon, killed them all. Bullets were raining down from every direction. I gathered up all the ammo from my wounded guys and went about defending our position. Two Apaches came in to support our extraction and to soften up the bad guys hunting us. After fifteen minutes Blackhawks arrived to pull us out. I gathered my two guys and pulled them. Directed them to the choppers. When I got there, I was told of another guy who was wounded. Four of us ran to the area. I was covering the medics with a brand new H&K saw. Two Taliban dudes ran past me and I wasted them.

One of Apaches must have thought I was Taliban because big bullets from its gun raked the area around me. Four Taliban ran past me and disappeared through a cave-like hole. Finally, I realized the only gunfire coming at me was from the Apache. I ran for cover in the rocks following the Taliban. As I stuck my head inside the cave door, the blast from a missile lifted me into the cave and knocked a group of bad guys down like bowling pins. I recovered. First picked up the saw and wasted three of them. The others ran out and down through a woody creek bed. I looked around. There was only one way out the cave hole. It blocked by rocks from the bomb blast and the other way was the way the Taliban went. I took four steps to the creek, and gunfire stopped me.

I was stuck in this small cave and had to get out, to extract, with my men, but couldn't. I looked around and saw a hole fifty feet straight up, big enough for a man. The only path upward was by climbing a crack in the granite. I stuck my hands in that perfect hand crack and free soloed my way out of there. I trailed a rope with my pack and weapon. When I got to the top the choppers were gone.

With darkness coming I stayed put on top the rock, had good cover from all around. When full darkness came, I down climbed the crack into the cave and looked through the packs of the Taliban for food. Found American MRE's and Power bars. I filled up my Camelback pack with water and then bent the barrels of every weapon. Left in the cave and then climbed back out.

Sixteen hours later I was still in the same rocky area, but a quarter mile uphill on top another rock. When darkness came I slipped down to a nearby stream, filled up my Camelback pack and hiked back to my bivouac area. Not far from the small creek I walked into straight into a group sleeping Taliban. I think I may have stepped on one of them. Guns went off and I ran out of there. For three days those bastards came after me, night and day. My radio was hit with a big piece of shrapnel, so it was destroyed.

One morning I was sleeping in a shallow cave no more than five feet high. I woke to an arm wrapping around my neck. I saw a knife, grabbed the hand holding it, and then struggled to wake up. I wrestled around with a young man with gold eyes and bad breath. I couldn't get to my weapon because one hand was holding his hand with the knife, and the other was holding his arm from sinking in deeper around my neck. I rolled on my knees and the kid came with me, knife came close to my face. I stood straight up and rammed his head into the roof of the cave several times. Finally, one of the hits dazed him. I took the knife from him and stuck it into his own neck, just below his left ear. The blade must have cut through his brain stem because he went limp, then died. After that I had these cuts on my face. Every time I rammed his head into the roof of the cave his knife cut into my face.

I got the bleeding stopped then down climbed my way out of there. Hardly hit the ground and ran into five Taliban dudes. I shot two guys before they got a round off. After that I ran and shot, trying to get the high ground. I was using a H&K similar to the AWT here, with a smaller scope. I would hide and wait for them to expose themselves, and fire off several well-placed rounds. Then I'd hike off to the next position. I must have shot a dozen of them. It was like playing whack-a-mole. One would die and another would pop up.

Choppers came and I signaled them with smoke and waved at them. They gave great cover. When I finally got to within a hundred feet of a waiting chopper, bullets snapped from everywhere. I ran as fast as I could. Bullets rained down all around me. It was like they had brains of their own, little body-seeking bullets that caught me and entered my body. The first couple just grazed me. Then one hit behind my left knee; that dropped me. Then one entered my back on the left side; wound its way along the inside of my ribcage and out below my left arm. I was put on the chopper and sent home. That was almost two and half years ago. I feel those bullets and dream that nightmare all the time."

Jacob shook his head, "Man that makes me ache. You should write a book; would make a great movie."

Tom turned to Jacob, "I see that uneducated religious fascist kid, his arm strangling me. The messed up part is that I knew when that arm wrapped around my neck that I was going to kill that kid. When I sunk his own dirty knife into his neck he seemed to question me with his eyes. You see, he thought he had the upper hand, and not until the life began to drain from him did he realize that he had no chance. I see that boy's face ragged and full of hate. I see him in my dreams and flashbacks that happen for no reason. Nothing triggers them. It's just that all of a sudden I'm seeing that kid."

CHASING THE BEATDOWN

CHAPTER 33

BOTH MEN LOOKED ON AS THE MANSON DOCKS came into view. There were three speedboats docked. Tom went through each, looking for clues as to how many and who they were. They continued on to Bill's cabin but stopped a half a mile away. Tom jumped off the boat and ran to Bill's cabin. He was checking to see if Bill's cabin was occupied. It wasn't, so they parked the boat; pulled it under an umbrella tree and covered it with a camo net. They went into the cabin and found the keys for Bills brand new Toyota pickup. Tom and Jacob threw muddy slime from a mud hole on every area of the shiny truck and then threw sawdust from Bill's wood shop over the sticky mud.

Tom stood back from the truck. Jacob laughed, "Good job! Looks like we have a future. Camo for trucks, and it only last a day. People well save thousands on camo paint jobs." They laughed as they loaded the pickup with their gear.

Tom asked, "Where do you think we should go?"

"To the woods west of the ranch, there's an old cave I used to use as a fort when I was a kid. It's perfect! "Jacob looked up at the sky. "It's a quarter mile from the ranch I think, camped there many times. It's just seven big rocks that are leaning against each other. My friends and I dug the center out so it would be flat. We camped there all the time, made fires, and mom and dad could never find it, even when we were having a fire. It's like caveman stuff. If you didn't know it was there you could not find the opening."

They loaded the truck with gear, camping supplies, and firewood, and then took off with the lights off. Tom drove slowly with night vision goggles on. They made it to an end of a dirt road, not more than four hundred yards from the cave. They hike in the dark making the cave by two AM.

They dropped the packs and then scooted over some jagged rocks. They crawled under another set of rocks and into the cave. It was as Jacob had said: fifteen feet oval with an old fire pit against one wall. They sat down on the ground; it was soft earth same as the ranch rich and dark full of organic matter.

"I think we should take a rest." Jacob said loudly.

Tom put his finger to his lips," Can't talk loud anymore, and I'm curious, so let's get going. We'll find a good place to hide and observe." They took off quietly, moving to the southwest corner of the property. Tom put his hand up, stopping Jacob.

"What?" he was annoyed.

Tom looked at him and brought Jacob's face close to his with his hand. He shook his head, "First off, don't talk to me like that. And second, close your eyes and count to 120, then open your eyes. You'll be better able to see in the dark. Then stand, your back to me, not moving for fifteen minutes. Its called 'taking in the night,' enhances all your senses."

They stood against each other in the night. Next, they crawled up the rise of the glacier moraine. On top they sat amongst untrimmed cherry trees; grape vines that grew to five feet covered them. They looked out over the Y Creek Ranch. Lights were everywhere.

Jacob looked at Tom, "Never use that much lighting. What a waste."

Tom looked out over the ranch, "Got a guy sitting in a van at the front gate, lots of cigarette butts. Other than that, I can't see anybody guarding anything."

Tom and Jacob sat in the same position for a while, looking out over the ranch. Jacob fell asleep and was awaken by Tom.

"Come on. Let's go to the power house." At the powerhouse they looked through the small block building.

Jacob said, "Why don't we just put a cog in the works and stop their power? They come out to fix it and they get a knife in the back."

Tom shook his head, "Good idea, I can do that ... but I think we should save it for later. What else can we do to get these people out and off the property?"

Jacob thought. "I don't know what we can do." They jogged back to the southwest hide, and continued east above the white van in the front entrance. This area was even better, with big rocks all around bushes, covering the hide perfectly.

"This is a good spot. We can control quite a bit from here, but we'll need to get closer to the buildings." The time was 4:11AM. Tom said, "Let's stay here."

Jacob said, "I need to close my eyes for a while, and I snore so if I fall asleep, kick me."

Tom shook his head no. "You can't sleep here. Have to go back to the cave for that. How 'bout you go back to the cave and get some sleep, and I'll stay here. Maybe haul some loads and then go back to Bill's cabin and make the call to the farm. Remember, they have a radio in the house and might be listening. It seems that we can move around during the day from the pickup to the cave."

Jacob said, "I don't think we should split up. I'm worried, scared. Whatever you want, but I don't think we should split up."

Tom said, "Ok, I hear you, but my job is to recon these losers and I can't do it from Bill's cabin, so you have to go, empty the pickup, and then drive back to the cabin and stay there until nightfall. After you make the call at 7:00PM beat feet back here. Call on the radio headsets before you come." Jacob agreed, shook hands with Tom, and left.

Tom sat watching the ranch. The cows came in to be milked and no one came to milk them. At 7:30AM the door to the house opened. Four men came out with coffee cups in their hands. Five women came out and mixed with the men. From the farmhouse six men and four women came out. Then from the house came three more men, both armed. Two walked with a limp.

Tom laid flat on the ground holding the binoculars with both hands. He was sure that the big guy limping was the guy that was beat up by him and Woody. The other guy limping was the guy he hit in the back of the pickup at the feed store. Finally, the van door opened below him. A scrappy, bearded guy got out of the van and stretched, and walked slowly towards the house. He was wearing a sidearm only. Tom hurried down the opposite slope under the cover of the grape vines. He opened the door to the van. In the van was a pump shotgun. He unloaded it, and set it back the way it had been. He looked around and stole the keys from the ignition. A water bottle sat unopened. He opened it and dropped two oxycontin pills in and shook it. He ran back to the hide above the van. The new guard was now walking to the van, and the other to the bunkhouse.

GEORGE THIELMAN

Tom sat until 9:00AM and then picked up his stuff and went back to the cave. He called Jacob. "Jacob, come in."

"This is Jacob. I'm here. Everything is good."

"This is Tom I'm good and kicking back." Tom made six trips back to the pickup area, hauling loads to the cave area, and then went back to the cave. He was tired and wired. He pulled his pipe from his vest and filled it with good juicy fruit from the ranch. He drank water and laid out a sleeping pad and bag. He fell asleep for two hours and awoke to the radio headset buzzing. He talked to Jacob for a few minutes and then closed down.

He set up his MSR stove then heated up water for tea, and slopped out spaghetti from a Tupperware dish, heated it up, and scarfed it down. The sausage was elk sausage and made by Joe. He found corn bread with butter, and ate like a pig. He found two beers, drank one, and snuck outside.

It was 12:34. He relieved himself and snuck back to the southwest hide spot. While looking through the binoculars he noticed the two German Shepherds; both were tied up and being tease by two men. He tried to take a count, but couldn't. Several people were working in the fields, picking apples and cherries. He watched them pick and snuck back to the cave for lunch.

Rain came while he was eating spaghetti and sipping water. Water rolled down the rock in back of the fire pit. The rest of the cave stayed dry. He laid down, looking up at the grey rock above him. He dozed, dreamed of Woody swimming out to the beaver dam. Standing on the mud and log structure, Woody was digging and sniffing for the beavers. Water dripped off his blond fur. He stopped sniffing and looked back across the shallow bay at Tom.

A loud pop woke him. He rolled to the right with the M4 in his hands. He stood up, rubbing his eyes. Outside he ran up the moraine to the southwest hide. There was commotion by the house. A group of people gathered around at the back of the house. A man with a green vest was pointing a pistol. The people moved back, exposing the two German Shepherds: one lay on the ground bleeding; the other, older one, Barney stood snarling at the man in the green vest. The man fired six rounds into both dogs, walked over and kicked Barney's lifeless head. The man with the green vest then turned to the people gathered around the dogs. The crowd broke up while the man continued to yell, at them.

Tom made note of what people were wearing. A woman with a yellow jacket, and a man with a red beanie, two others wearing brown shirts. All seemed to be ordered about by the man in the green vest. Ted, Dorn, and a big man in a tan ranch coat, all carrying side arms, came outside. The man with the green vest clearly was speaking in a heated tone to the others. He turned and walked down the driveway. He walked past the van, yelled at the guard sitting inside, and walked through the gate. Tom held his riflescope on the man, "Ya, looks like someone had too much coffee. You calm down buddy." The guy turned toward Tom, continuing his fast paced walk. He made it to the woods, talking to himself. He walked right by the cave, looked around, and then turned and walked back to the ranch.

Jacob made the call to Sky Ranch, and then drove back to the parking spot. "Tom, this is Jacob. I'm at the cave waiting for you."

Tom came back to the cave a while later. " Well, the new occupants of your farm had a great day. First, a guy with a green vest yelled at everybody. Then he yelled at some assholes that were doing donuts in the corral. Next, he yelled at some people that were sitting around, and finally, hold onto yourself, he shot both Barney and Bob and kicked them both."

Jacob sat stunned. Anger welled up inside him. His eyes teared with sorrow and rage. He picked up his rifle, "God damn them. I've had enough. They're going down now. I don't care who or what they are doing." He stood and stormed way to leave.

Tom jumped up grabbed Jacob's arm. "No, you absolutely can't go, not now."

Jacob turned and hit Tom in the mouth. "I'm tired of waiting there. They're going to ruin my farm."

Tom jumped across the room, grabbing the bigger, younger man and wrapped around his body with both arms. Jacob dropped his rifle, trying to get away, but Tom held his arms solid at his side. He tried to move backward to slam Tom into the rock, but Tom reached his left foot down wrapping it around Jacob's legs. They tripped together. Tom turned so Jacob took the brunt of the fall. Jacob spun to the right but Tom grabbed his right arm. With his left leg he wrapped it around Jacob's arm and pulled it back toward him.

Jacob screamed in pain. Tom smiled through bloody teeth. He said to Jacob," This is called an arm bar and I can rip your arm up right now. You are not going out there!" He pulled back on the arm just enough to make him feel the pain and then backed off so he felt relief. Jacob was breathing hard, trying to muscle his way past superior training. Tom turned Jacob's wrist backward, and again Jacob moaned in pain.

Tom let Jacob go and rolled to his feet still smiling. Jacob was laying on his side, holding his arm." God damn man, I think you broke my arm."

Tom picked the bigger man up and pushed him against the rock. They looked at each other and then started to laugh.

Tom pulled Jacob by the lapels, closer to him, "Jacob, I need you to mad, angry, and hurt." He shook Jacob, "but stay in control, channel that hurt and anger. Together we will be a much more powerful tool. You're no good to me if this conflict continues. Now calm down."

Jacob said, "Ok Tom, I'm with you. It's just that…"

Tom slapped him across the face, "I don't care! Do what I say!" He pointed his finger in Jacob's face, still smiling. They laughed. Jacob eased up. Tom let him go. Jacob reached into his vest pocket and pulled out a flask, unscrewed the cap, and then handed it to Tom They drank then sat down.

Jacob sat rubbing his arm, "I think you broke my arm."

Tom laughed, "If I broke your arm it would have snapped."

Jacob said, "Ok, I'm your tool. What do we do next?"

Tom handed him a piece of paper. "I want you to go back to Sky Ranch. Pick up the items on the list. Bring Philip, Becky, and Lisa. Leave Joe at the café on guard, and Jesus and Anna to take care of the farm, and Bill of course. I'll meet you back here tomorrow night. You have 24 hours to get everything done and get back here."

Tom went back to his recon of the farm. Finally, he decided to find another hiding spot near the house. He jogged to the east then north for a hundred yards. At the end of the glacial moraine he climbed up to the end the hill. Again there was good cover on top. In the darkness he moved big rocks, stacking them up for cover, with holes between them for shooting. With a small entrenching tool he dug the area out so there was more of a foxhole. He positioned rocks all around it and then threw branches over the rocks. The old, unkempt cherry trees gave good cover. He went back to each hide digging and arranging rocks and sticks for good cover. By morning he had enlarged and dug all three hides so they gave good cover from all sides. Satisfied, he went back to the cave for much needed sleep.

He woke at 9:15 with cramps. He hadn't taken a crap in two days. He reached for his toilet paper and hurried outside, and found a good spot behind a tree. The relief was great. He stood up and looked around satisfied. Smiling, holding his toilet paper, he looked to his right and was startled to see a man and a women looking straight at him. The man carried a rifle over his shoulder; both paused as they looked from one to the other. The man tried to swing his rifle around to shoot, but a tree branch caught the barrel and the gun fell to the grass. The woman was in the middle of pulling her pistol when Tom fired his AR10, shooting her in her in the chest.

She dropped to the ground dead. The man made a spastic move to get his rifle in position but was too late. Finally, he turned his back and ran. Tom aimed and fired, the thump of the suppressed AR10 was the only sound. Tom ran to the man. Blood was pouring from a wound near his heart.

The man looked up at Tom. "Who are you?" His head turned away from Tom and he died. Tom picked the man up and carried him a hundred yards away, and then carried the woman to the same place. He covered them with pine needles and went back to the cave. He tried to calm down. He was breathing hard; not able to catch his breath.

The confrontation had triggered something in him. He sat down, but the world felt like it was closing on him. He closed his eyes. Images of hands and feet slapping against him from bomb blast was what he saw. He felt the charred body parts as they slammed into him. Desperately, he tried to think of something that would make the images go away. He dropped the rifle and cringed as he backed up to the rocks behind him. The smell of dead, rotting bodies, their guts stinking in the air dominated his every sense. He felt dizzy, turned, and vomited in the fire pit.

8:00PM His radio buzzed, "Tom, come in." The call came six times before Tom answered.

"This is Tom. Come on back."

"This is Jacob. We're on our way." Tom had been sitting for hours, trying to get himself together.

Finally, he was able to conjure the image of Woody standing on the beaver dam, smiling at him, as the beavers teased him. He tried to keep that image. It was working. He was coming back to normal. He thought of Sky Ranch, of Sally and Becky, of the two-day old calves, their white lips licking milk from their mom. He thought of making love with Becky in the cedar tub, her short black hair messy and beautiful, and her golden eyes. He saw the kittens batting at Woody's fluffy curled tail.

He took off his clothes and washed himself with a washrag, put on clean t-shirt and pants, and finished dressing. He threw water on his face and walked outside for fresh air. It was now 9:11PM. He took a breath, now feeling a bit normal. It was completely dark; the moon was behind the mountains. The stars were giving off little light; a perfect night for an ambush.

In the cave Tom cut two. He lit them, using them as fire starters. He added pine needles and then bigger sticks until he put the largest pieces wood on the fire. 9:34PM The radio vibrated, "Tom we're parked." Tom ran to the pickup, moving easily through the darkness of the forest to the pickup. Greetings were made with whispers and hugs, Tom helped carry packs and bags to the cave. The fire lit the inside of the cave; shadows on the rocks moved with peoples' movements.

They sat in a semi-circle around the fire pit, eating buffalo stew and drinking beer. Tom stood and began, "Ok everyone. Listen up. It's 10:30 now. We leave here at 4:30AM and take positions surrounding the ranch. I've surveyed three positions, have them dug out, moved rocks and logs, so you'll have good cover. I think we should do a quick practice run to each position. That way you can each think about what you have to do in the morning. So let's do a quick practice run. I'll explain what each person should do. They moved out of the cave. They wore camo, and were armed and weighed down. Tom had them stand in the dark for fifteen minutes and close their eyes to, "take in the night."

Tom hiked to each position with each person, explaining their fields of fire and pointing out where the rest of the team would be and where their fields of fire were. They left water bottles and three hundred rounds at each hide site.

Back at the cave everyone was ready and tired. Tom lay down with Becky in his arms, sleeping until 3:30 when his Casio watch alarm went off. Anna made coffee for each person, and put a stainless steel thermos in each pack along with chicken sandwiches. Jacob passed a flask of whiskey around until it was gone. Tom picked up each weapon and pistol, checking the first round and showing each person the safety, then dropping the clip and putting it back in.

Tom took the lead again, "Ok, this is it . Everyone seems to be ready. Make no mistake. We are making history tonight. What we are about to do is the most important thing we will ever do. If we don't succeed, this could affect our future. You will be shot at. Maybe you will shoot someone. I don't know. We have to win this. Make this your morning, your day. This is your farm. Take control of the farm. They are thieves. They stole from us with force, now we will take them in force. People will die. Maybe some of us. This will be necessary to complete our mission. This day will be their last day. Never again will they be allowed to do this. They must be made to understand that if they steal they could be on the receiving end of pain. I want all of you to do what I say. Watch out for each other. Most of all, remember that we are making a statement: brute force.

Anna led another prayer. Tom was jacked, ready to go, and he felt in control. He walked Becky and Anna to the southwest hide, and Philip to the southeast hides above the front gate. He walked Jacob and Lisa to the east hide nearest the bunkhouse. Jacob and Becky used the Remington 25 shooting the .308 caliber. Lisa and Anna each used the Remington 15 chambered in the smaller .223 caliber, and they had the same Leopold scopes and camo colors. Philip covered the front of the farm. He had clear vision of the complete front of the farm, fields, and orchards as well as the front driveway. His weapon was a Winchester model 70. He moved dirt and rocks around so he could sit cross-legged with the rifle barrel resting on a branch. Butterflies were playing in his guts. He felt happy to in the hide, excited for the upcoming task.

Tom carried his customized AWT AR10, and his Colt M4. He was weighed down with fifty pounds of ammo and gear. Everyone carried small Motorola radio headsets. To talk they had to press a button that led from the headset to the radio in the front pocket of the jacket.

Tom and Philip walked to the little block powerhouse at the northwestern end of the ranch. They stood in front of the gears that turned the generator. They placed a small chunk of soft aluminum in the cog so when the gears came around, the generator slammed to a stop, ending all power down the line to the house and all the other buildings.

It was now 5:45. Daylight was filtering from the mountains to the east. They waited until 6:35 for someone to come to take care of the problem at the powerhouse. No one came. Philip laughed, "Guess they're sleeping in today," They ran back to the front gate, and then to the hide above the front gate. Tom slapped Philip across the face. Tom said, "Think of Sally and Lisa. We cannot fail, be strong.

Philip watched as Tom slipped out of the hide, down the small moraine, and quietly ran off in the darkness.

"This is Tom, I'm approaching Becky and Anna. Don't shoot me." Becky hardly had time to reply when Tom appeared between her and Anna.

Anna jumped annoyed, "Man you're like a cat!"

Tom laughed. He pointed out their area of fire, the west end of the farm and the beginning of the forest to the west. They had good sight of the area around the bathhouse and powerhouse. He checked each rifle, suggesting how far to lead ahead of the intended target. Satisfied he had told them all he could, he picked up his rifle. As he did, Becky grabbed him by the pack straps kissing him deeply. They looked at each other. Tom laughed, and then was grabbed by Anna. She kissed him deeply too. Becky looked at her and quietly whispered, "Hey!" They sat in silence.

Tom ran to the front of the gate, and crawled under the van to the driver's side. Philip smiled in amazement as Tom stood straight up by the window. He reached through the open window with his dagger, The guard watched a hand with big knife enter the window, stop under his chin for a split second, and he felt a razor sharp pain to his neck. He tried to speak. His hands wrapped around the retreating dagger and then let go and held onto his wounded neck. Tom pulled the dying guard from the van. He dragged him through the front gate where Philip pulled the dying and helpless man to a ditch near the road. He laid the man face up in the grass. The man jerked as his body used the last of its oxygen.

Tom scratched the blood into the dirt and climbed into the van to wait for the new guard. Philip, now back in his hiding spot, came on the radio," Tom he's on his way now." Becky kept a bead on the new guard as he walked to the van. Tom watched in the side view mirror as the guard walked up to the now closed window. Becky jumped when the guard opened the door to the van. Through her riflescope she saw the black silencer of Tom's pistol move straight to the man's head. The head then blew apart in a mess of blood and gore. She looked away. The only sound was that of the body hitting the ground. Tom and Philip pulled the body and set next to the other one.

Tom smiled at Philip, his face and jacket spattered with blood, "Ok, Philip, now it's time for the business." He slapped Philip on the back and ran to Becky and Anna. He called them, "Becky, I'm coming up to you." Before she could reply, he rolled between them. They gasped at the blood spattered on his face.

He announced over the radio, "Everyone ready to go. Now's the time we take this farm back. Remember that you have a safety on your rifle. Don't run up behind one of our people without calling them. Remember there will be shooting so hearing will be affected."

Tom kissed Becky and Anna leaving them bloody. They watched as Tom calmly rolled down the moraine and into the apple orchard. He stopped midway through and looked at his watch, 7:25AM. He kneeled down in the grass under the bushiest tree. A porcupine calmly crawled down the tree and out of the orchard. Tom called, "Ok, I'm waiting for the morning meeting. At my signal sight your scopes on the people that are armed the best, but keep the crosshairs away from me. They will scatter when the shooting starts. Oh ya, Becky and Anna, there's a porcupine coming your way."

At 7:30 AM the door to the bunkhouse opened. People walked to the picnic tables in the front yard of the ranch house, just as Jacob and Anna used to have morning breakfast. There was some discussion. One guy took off around the house. Becky called, "I think they're dealing with the power. A guy is walking past the house to the bathhouse and he's armed with a rifle." Philip watched through his riflescope as the guy with the green vest started talking. The guy with the tan ranch coat walked around unarmed, eating an apple.

Philip called Tom, "What's next Tom?"

Tom called back, "I'm going to walk straight up the driveway. Make sure you call your victim out so we don't have four people shoot the same guy. I'm going now, and Lord help us to shoot straight." There was a collective, "Amen" on the radio. Tom turned left and then straight to the farmhouse. He was one hundred fifty feet from the house, his AR 10 pointing straight ahead at the group of people.

"Tom, your secret is blown. They see you. This is Philip. Have the guy with the Levi jacket." Tom kept walking straight ahead to the farmhouse. The people at the picnic table stood up. Dorn and Ted stood up.

Vaschilli stood up, his hand on his pistol, "Hey you, boyz, you vorst nitemere is back to kiek your fucking asses." His mouth showed a crooked smile.

A big guy wearing a Levi jacket walked in front of everyone, his assault rifle ready. He raised it to fire. Philip fired a round into the heart of the Levi jacket. Blood spattered the people behind the Levi man. One report from Philip's rifle followed. The group of people froze.

Tom yelled at them. He had his rifle aimed at the group and on full auto. "All of you, stay where you are. Don't move. As you saw, there are rifles aimed at all of you. Any of you that want to live beyond today, move to your right, drop your weapons, raise your hands and turn your back to me."

Four people put their hands straight up, and had started to move to their right when Dorn pulled his pistol. Dorn fired two shots at Tom. Both missed. Tom fired, on full-auto, hitting two people. He aimed away from the people with their hands raised.

All at once bullets rained down from everyone. Tom ran to cover behind the wall of the bunkhouse. Shotgun blast ripped through the bunkhouse wall, missing Tom by inches. He dropped to the ground, firing at the cedar walls of the bunkhouse. The shooting stopped.

Ted, Dorn and three other people used assault rifles to fire at Tom from the kitchen. All missed. From the bunkhouse bullets fired through the walls, but Tom was already gone, running through the pear orchard and around the hill and up to Jacob and Lisa. He rolled between the two of them. "There are three people down. Don't know how many are hit."

"This is Philip. I'm seeing a big dude at the stable. He just rode off to the north with a big pack."

Tom said, "Ten four Philip. Guess he wants to live. Let him go. Be aware. We have people in the apple orchard that want to surrender."

Tom yelled through the radio, "We have people walking down the road. Give cover." The back of the house and bunkhouse erupted as bullets hit from all points.

Philip radioed, "I'm going to pick the people up. Wouldn't mind some help."

"This is Tom. I'm on my way to Philip." Tom pointed to the bunkhouse. Jacob and Lisa looked out onto the farm as Tom ordered, "Keep fire on the bunkhouse. Look for good targets." He rolled over the rocks and to the front gate. Gunfire was sporadic. A shot here and there, and a loud long response from the people in the farm, and then a selected shot or two from Tom's group.

The people came through the gate. Tom was waiting for them. He yelled at them, "Lay on the ground, hands behind you." The three women and a man laid down. As Tom flex-cuffed the people around a nearby telephone pole, he spoke to the them, "All of you, be good, and you'll be released unharmed. Just be patient, and don't panic."

Becky came on the line," This is Beck. I'm getting shot at by the guy that went to work on the generator." Sustained fire could be heard. Jacob and Lisa kept up a steady fire on the house and bunkhouse, but they couldn't see targets. They continued to shoot to keep the heads down.

Again Tom came to the rescue. As the attacker on Becky and Anna got closer to them, the attacker ran into the woods trying to get a clear shot on the women. Tom ran straight behind Becky into the woods. He moved easily, the AR 10 ready. The attacker ducked behind rocks, out of sight. Tom had a good idea where he was and hit the deck, using bushes and logs to cover his advance. The attacker thought Tom was the shooter from the southwest hide. He crawled back toward the farm, and then stood up to run back to the farmhouse. Tom fired. Bullets sprayed all around him. He ran quickly past the bathhouse. He stopped in midstride when Becky delivered a double tap to his chest. He hit the ground with a dusty thud.

Tom watched from fifty feet away as the man was cut down by Becky. He crawled through the irrigation ditch near the farmhouse. Crawling on his stomach, he looked up at the house. Two assault rifles fired at him. One bullet cut through his jacket and skimmed along the back of his left shoulder. The pain came on like a burn. He threw a tear gas grenade into the house and fired ten rounds into the window. He ran through the ditch and tripped. Bullets raked the ground around him. While Tom ducked in the ditch, Anna and Becky ran the thousand yards to the bathhouse.

From the farmhouse garage one of the pickups burst through the doors, and continued straight through the horse corral. It jumped the ditch and came down with a dirt explosion that covered their escape.

Tom made his way to the bathhouse. The women were already inside. Becky stood, weapon pointing toward the house, but was out of her element, frightened near to panic.

"You should take Anna back to your position, and wait there." The women jogged back. Tom keyed his radio, "Listen up, we need to flush the bad guys from the house. We need constant fire to the front of the house. I'll run through the bunkhouse and clear it,. I'll give them a chance to live and then I'm going in. If anyone escapes out the back of the house, let them. We'll pick up their trail later." Crawling back through the ditch, he heard the shooting start. It was accurate, meant to draw the bad guys out the back of the house. Tom crawled out of the ditch and ran through the orchard to the bunkhouse. He stopped along the wall, careful to stay below the bullet holes in the wall. He burst through the back door. A blond haired woman looked up. Her hands together she yelled to Tom, "Don't shoot anymore! Please, please!" Snot was running from her nose. She wiped it away.

Tom ordered, "Put your hands up and turn around." She turned around, put her hands behind her, and sat down. Tom flex-cuffed her to a chair and turned it over so she would be out of the way of gunfire. Tom walked through each room of the bunkhouse. It was empty. "This is Tom. I'm going to go between the two buildings. Don't shoot me. Everybody acknowledge." Everyone called in to acknowledge. "Ok, I'm going in." He rolled through the door, low, and to the outside below the farmhouse kitchen. He yelled into the house, "I'm burning the house down now! Get out or you'll burn." He pulled the pin on three tear gas grenades, one after the other, and then two grey smoke grenades. He waited as the gas did its job.

"This is Becky. Three guys just ran from the back of the house. They're running through the garden."

"This is Tom. Let them go. We'll get them later." The three men ran past the bathhouse. Becky watched them through her riflescope. She took a bead on the last one. As he jumped the ditch, he looked back. She pulled the trigger, hitting the man in the shoulder. She fired several more shots but they had disappeared into the woods.

Tom ran through the house. In an upstairs bedroom two men fired at him. They ran into a closet. Tom fired a full clip into the closet. Everyone inside died instantly.

"This is Becky. Three guys in the woods, one wounded."

"This is Tom. Everyone be careful. Keep a lookout. Becky and Anna, stay low and go to Philip. Jacob, you and Lisa run to Philip, and Philip, when everyone is in place, run through the apple orchard to me and we'll go through the house."

Tom ran through the bunkhouse. When he came out Philip was running past him to the stables." Come, on Tom," Tom followed the big kid. In the stables three big American Studs stood saddled. Philip yelled to Tom, "Those shitheads have kept these horses saddled for days. Now they're gonna be sorry." Tom and Philip jumped on the horses, kicking them into a fast trot, following the tire tracks through the fences, past the pasture and out into the neighboring pastures. The horses were wound up and ready to run. The truck tracks continued west.

Tom called, "This is Tom. We'll be back in a few." He turned and waved to the group above the entrance as they rode west.

Ted and Dorn's black 4x4 drove through several fences, smashed through a grape orchard, picked up the main road, and took the road to the Manson dock. Philip and Tom rode the horses hard for ten minutes, stopping the horses on the ridge that overlooked Lake Chelan; they patted the big black horses as they scanned the lake through binoculars. A speedboat was headed northwest on the lake.

Philip yelled, "Fuck! God damn it!"

Tom smiled at the kid, "Down the hill to Bill's cabin. Come on kid, let's catch them." Philip looked at the speedboat disappearing in the distance. He pulled his horse around, dug into the horse's side, and rode hard to Bill's cabin. It took them just fifteen minutes to make it to the cabin. Tom jumped in the boat, and started the two big motors as Philip untied the boat and shoved off. Tom pushed the boat's engine as fast as it could go. The bow stood up as the boat skimmed over the waves.

Philip had to yell over the screaming engine, "We can't catch them, Tom. Slow down."

Tom laughed, "Don't be so sure, my man." He smiled and looked ahead. Philip, assured, looked ahead. Tom asked, "How many rounds do you have left?"

Philip panicked, "I'm almost out. I have four rounds left." He looked dejected, Tom handed him a full 30 round, and Philip laughed, "Oh yah!" He transferred the bullets from one clip to several Remington clips like a happy child at Christmas.

Tom yelled, "Get on the roof and stay alert. Don't miss nothing," He handed Philip his binoculars.

Dorn sat at the steering wheel trying to turn the motor over. Ted yelled at him, "We're out of gas you asshole. You finally killed us, shit." Dorn cowered behind the wheel. They looked desperate. All three were feeling panic set in, when Dorn's forehead blew apart. He hit the windshield. Dorn thought how weird he must look. He looked to the right at the inside windshield. It was splattered by bloody skin and bone pieces. He tried to stand up but couldn't. He had a terrible headache. He looked off to the distance. Several puffs of smoke and then the reports. Three bullets spun his brother and then turned his neck into a bloody mess.

Jessie, the guy with the green vest, was horrified. He thought of jumping overboard. Another set of bullets rained on them. He felt two hard punches to his back, slumped over, and then gagged on his own blood. Ted slumped in the passenger seat , watching his brother's upper torso disappear. He seemed to move like he was being electrocuted. He stopped moving and started to die, falling toward the driver's seat.

Tom and Philip pulled alongside the speedboat. Tom tied the boats together. He jumped onto the speedboat with his H&K pistol and stood over Ted. Ted looked up at him. Blood was pumping from a hole to the right of his heart.

He pointed a bloody finger at Tom, "You're a tough fucker." Tom pushed his finger away. Ted asked weakly, "Bury us somewhere nice, please." He turned his head, and looked up at the mountains and the lake. "What a cool place."

Dorn's boat was tied to the old dock at Bill's. Tom and Philip jumped back on the horses and rode at good trot back to the farm. It was 12:13 noon. They rode back to the farm to shouts of joy. At the entrance they were hugged. Tom turned to the three people cuffed around the telephone pole. He pulled his knife and cut them loose. The man, a balding, fiftyish, thin guy said, "Thank you." He stood looking at Tom . He looked stoic, angry, and stressed. The three just looked at him.

Finally, he said, "You're gonna help them, starting now." He pointed his finger at them. They all agreed and shook their heads yes.

Anna said, "Come with me." She walked them to the barn. "All right, I need you all to feed the animals, gather them up, water them, and be kind to them. They're distressed."

One of the women said, "Listen, we didn't want to fight. They said they had a farm, and we came here and started working."

Anna put her hand up. "Please, just go to work. Help us out and we'll give you a meal and you can go on your way." Tom, Philip, and Becky were checking bodies in the house. Becky came out of the house with the woman that Tom had flex-cuffed to the chair. She pushed the woman with the barrel of her rifle. The woman turned around rubbing her wrists. Her face was dirty, and her hair bloody. She rubbed her nose smearing blood. She looked back at the dead bodies.

"I was a nurse." She broke down sobbing. Becky directed her out of the building to the picnic tables. Spent bullet casings littered the area, and the walls were pockmarked with bullet holes.

Anna walked into her house with a wet rag over her mouth. The tear gas and smoke was lingering, and she felt the sting of the gas. At first she was horrified and sad, and then she became hopeful. New sheetrock and wood siding would cover over the destruction wrought by the five-hour gunfight.

Tom directed, "The weapons should be gathered first. Secure them, and then get the bodies in the ground. Get the power going, keep the floodlights on all night. The three bad guys that survived might be the three best,. Get some cover up around the yard here so no one can get bead on you. Stay as a group, with your weapons ready. Don't let the captured people mingle amongst you … yet. Get to know them first. They need to earn our trust. Someone should be in the birds' nest keeping an eye out.

Becky asked, "And just what do you think you're going to do?"

Tom shrugged his shoulders, and smiled at her, "I'm going after the three." He grabbed her face, kissing her hard. "I've got to go." Jacob and Philip demanded to come along. Tom answered, "No. Stay here, need you guys to get this farm up and running. It's yours." He turned and jogged to the cave.

Inside he set the AR10 against a rock. They were out of .308 bullets. He replaced the empty clips with clips for the M4, and then loaded up 100 rounds of .300 magnums. He slung his Winchester hunting rifle over his back, picked up the Colt M4 and crawled out of the cave. Jacob and Becky stood, weapons hanging low. Tom said, "Don't try to stop me. This is my thing. I'm made for this job." Becky stuffed three apples in his small pack along with along with eight of Anna's granola bars.

She kissed him, "Come back to us!" He took off to follow the trail. He looked back. Becky and Jacob were already jogging back to the ranch. He jogged on, energized, emboldened, and motivated as only a person could be that was doing the right thing. Under any law their actions were legal and moral. He was pushed forward by those laws to ensure that the criminals that did the crimes would not bother them again. Without a jail or a prison system, Tom knew that the end game could only mean death sentences for the men he was hunting.

Greg and Chris Boller hurried through the woods; their wounded buddy Barry Neville slowed their progress. The bullet that Becky shot had entered at the shoulder and traveled under the skin, exiting his back and stopping at his pack. He was flung to the ground by the impact of the burning bullet hitting the pack. He was lucky, but very sore. Barry struggled to keep up with them; his back was screaming with pain. The Boller brothers had been good suppliers of food and security for three months now. Fresh meat was plentiful with the brothers around. They were always shooting something, then reliving the story all night long. They were colorful braggarts that entertained their mates by eating weird animal parts, cooking them with different methods that made the taste buds party. They had raided a Cabalas store a month before, so they were clothed in Cabalas newest camo rags. They had the latest Weatherly hunting rifles and Bushmaster assault rifles. For pistols they carried Smith and Wesson .45's on their hips, with light packs.

Greg and Chris stopped, waiting for Barry again. Barry asked, "How long do we have to keep this up?" Greg pulled Barry's pack off, then divided the contents between him and his brother. They checked Barry's wounded back. There was a red welt six inches long with an exit and entrance hole, and bleeding was minimal. Greg squirted antiseptic across the wound and applied two bandages over area.

"You'll be alright. Just try to keep up. No telling if we're being followed." He looked back at the ground they had covered. They were traveling through the lower valleys of the foothills. The idea was to cover as much ground as possible, to turn east away from the wilderness, find a farmhouse and start over. The brothers were not worried. Chris started hiking again. Barry grumbled, then started his legs moving. Chris thought they should cover ground faster. His military history was as a supply sergeant in the Army. It wouldn't take a general to tell him that they had been sufficiently hammered. He was worried about the ferocity of the attack. The soldier guy that stood before them had the confidence of a real live rubber soldier.

Tom followed footprints, broken twigs, moved sticks and rocks, and Starburst candy wrappers. He jogged and then squatted down to check signs. He moved one way, then came back to the track, looked around, found tracks, and then moved forward. It was clear which way they were going, northwest staying within a quarter mile from the inside of the forest cover. It was clear they would make a break at some point. Tom was covering more ground than they were, zigzagging from their tracks to the end of the forest cover, trying to anticipate their moves and keep an eye on the open ground. It was time consuming. He walked with the lightweight M4 in his hands, and was concerned with an ambush. Nothing helped to counter an ambush better than aggressive automatic fire.

Chris and Greg continued through the day through the woods. Soft pine needles and rolling hills allowed them to cover ground quickly. 6:00PM They finally made the break into the open when they spotted an old bathtub used for watering animals. A windmill pumped water into the ancient bathtub, the area was perfect. A road led east to a nice-looking farm a couple miles away. They moved out of the cover of the pine forest to the pasture, cutting a barbed wire fence, and hiked two hundred yards to the windmill. Barry slammed his rifle down on the ground, and dropped to his knees, his lips in the old bathtub. The water had algae growing in it , but it tasted good and was clean and cold. They washed their faces and hands, and filled their pack bladders with water.

Barry stood up, and drank from a small plastic bottle of 5-hour energy drink. "Man, I think we're going to make it!" Chris gave his brother a skeptical look. Barry stood up straddling the sides of the tub. He stretched his arms out, and thumped his chest.

Chris snapped at him, "Would you please get down from …" The right side of Barry's face blew off. Chris counted five, then heard the report from Tom's model 70. "Five seconds, about five hundred yards," he yelled. Chris and Greg jumped down, behind the tub and the cover of the bushes. Greg pulled Barry down from the tub. The right side of his jaw was gone. He groaned. The broken jawbone was out of place and showing. The brothers cringed from the sight. Barry looked at them with pain in his eyes. He mumbled something and then started to scream and cry at the same time. The movement of the screaming caused his jaw to move and worsened the pain, but he continued. Barry had no control over his predicament. He knew he was not mortally wounded, and the wound was not going to be fixed without a hospital. He thought of eating, never would he be able to eat a steak again. He was frightened like never before.

Greg and Chris laid low against the bathtub, watching Barry and his spastic bloody movements. Barry stood straight up with rifle. He screamed in pain and anger, aimed his rifle at the tree line, and fired his rifle one bullet after another.

Tom watched Barry standing up. He knew he was wounded but didn't know how bad. He ducked as Barry started to shoot. His aim was way off, but Tom moved to cover anyway. He moved to a fat pine tree and used a low hanging branch for a gun rest. He could have hit him anywhere, but chose the right shoulder. The bullet slammed into Barry's shoulder joint and exited, taking bone and flesh with it. Barry spun to the ground screaming louder. Tom wanted him to be wounded so the brothers would have to carry him.

Greg and Chris picked up their weapons dropped down into a ravine and ran, leaving their mortally wounded friend writhing in pain. Staying low through the bush, they hacked at the bush with their rifles. Not caring about noise, they continued running through the damp ground, splashing through mud puddles. After fifteen minutes of jogging they stopped in the cover of three-foot high sagebrush.

From the cover of the woods Tom appeared running the high ground. He stopped, and took aim at the bathtub, now a ravine away. He shouldered the model 70 and ran straight down the ravine, to the bathtub, firing the M4. He hit Barry four times in the arm and shoulder. Once he arrived, he looked down at Barry. The wounds were horrific. The pain that Tom imagined Barry to be experiencing almost made him sick. "No wonder your buds ran."

TOM'S BATTLE

CHAPTER 34

TOM WAS CROUCHED LOW NEXT TO BARRY. Tracks to the little stream below showed the way. Tom was about to take off after the Boller brothers when Barry's hand grabbed Tom's arm. Tom looked down, and saw a pistol. Barry fired a bullet into his own head. His brains scattered out the left side of his head. Warm blood and gore spattered Tom's body. Tom wiped the blood from his mouth. Barry's face now, without a great deal of bone, seemed to have deflated like an ugly rubber mask.

Tom stood up to run, but stumbled head over heal. He kept the M4 in his hands, stood to run, and tripped again. He focused on the tracking of Chris and Greg. He had a hard time running. His body was not sending the correct signals. He wondered if he had been shot. He stopped and felt his body. No wounds but the one on his back. He stumbled to the ground again, stood up, and ran faster. He crashed through the ravine as the brothers had. He felt the darkness starting to envelop his vision. He saw the burned hands and feet, Barry's deflated, bloody, boney face, the blood almost hot to his face, he ran faster to escape the sickening sight.

The brothers sat under a tree, low in the bushes, crouching in a mud puddle. They heard Barry shoot himself. They sat listening and heard breaking branches, a splash, and then running. They called to Barry, "Barry, over here."

Tom could only see straight ahead now. He was sweating profusely, almost in a panic. He heard the brothers call. He tried to stop but tripped again. This time twenty feet from the brothers. Tom locked eyes with them as he crashed to the ground. They fired, point blank, at him but missed. Their aim was high and low.

Tom hit the ground and rolled twice, almost perfect somersaults. Spotting the brothers, he stopped against a tree with a thud. His finger pressed the trigger. He fired full auto at them and missed.

The brothers ran fast down the ravine, east, in a full sprint. Tom emptied the M4 and sat with his finger depressing the trigger. He heard them running away. He sat up against the tree breathing hard. His spent clip dropped to the ground; another was loaded in. He snapped the safety on and sat down on the grass.

Fresh cow pies. How simple they were. Grass stuck together, good fuel for the fire. He put his head on his knees and laughed. Tears rolled down his face, yet he was laughing. He thought, "How does that work?" The thought of the brothers firing at him sobered him. The darkness left his mind. He felt clearheaded. He stood and walked to the spot where the brothers had been crouching. There was a half a pack of Starburst candies. He picked it up, unwrapped a cherry flavored chew, and popped it in his mouth. "Mm ... cherry." He looked at the next flavor, yellow, lemon. He looked at the tracks heading east, and then looked south. "If I start hiking now, I could make it home for supper." He turned toward the farm and jogged. He stopped when he crested one of the ravines, looked around, and continued.

Greg and Chris ran in the opposite direction for two hours, finally making it to a small farm where they found an old Ford pickup. They put it in gear, and push started it. When it started, they high-tailed it down a dirt road. By 2 AM they were fifty miles away. They pulled into a farmhouse for much needed sleep. The next day they were up and driving north.

Tom walked for three hour. He had hit the wall. He stopped, ate an apple, and then pulled out the granola block. A bullet was stuck in it. He tore off a chunk and sat down eating, looking at the deformed bullet. "Must have been a .223." He put the remaining bits into the pack and continued his hike. He made it to the Y Creek powerhouse at 12:00 midnight. The water wheel was turning, and the house area was lit up with halide lights. He cautiously walked through the garden. He heard barking. It came closer. Around the house came Woody with Beau and Buck. They looked at Tom, then Woodies tail started to wag furiously. Tom called to the others as the dogs surrounded him, jumping.

He heard Jacob's voice, "Is that Tom?"

Tom yelled back, "This is Tom. I'm coming in." He walked between the buildings and around to the kitchen. Becky opened the back door. She looked at him, "You coming in or what?" She was wearing a t-shirt and sweatpants; her nipples were poking through the t-shirt. "You always walk around like that?" From inside he heard "God-dam-sumbitch you two gonna blab all night?" The lights were low, but he could see Joe walking from the kitchen with a piece of pie. "Shit boy ill tell yaw whut." His cussing faded out as he walked upstairs.

ARMISTICE FOR THE COWBOY

CHAPTER 35

BECKY LED TOM TO THE BATHROOM, undressed him then dressed his shoulder wound. They took a hot shower together and made love. Tom fell asleep, waking four hours later in a panic. He looked around the room. Becky slept curled up with Woody in her arms. Her short hair hung over her face, and strands of hair moved with her breathe. Downstairs he found Jacob and Anna drinking coffee in the kitchen with Joe and the four women and man that surrendered the day before.

The man and one of the women were a married couple from Seattle. Walt and Jeannie Trumble had been on a hunting vacation, outside of Coulee City, celebrating becoming empty nesters. They had rented a nice cabin and hung out. Bad weather socked them in. When the virus took over, they were well stocked with supplies and stayed put. Eleven months later they had lost thirty pounds each and had struggled to survive on canned food. They'd met Dorn and Ted, and had nothing to do with the hijacking of the Y Creek farm.

The young women were caught up at Spokane Airport while the virus made its way through the Spokane Valley. How they'd avoided the killer virus, they didn't know. They all stayed at the farm for a week, and then found a good SUV, and headed back to find their families on the West side. Two weeks later they all came back, having found each one of the three major passes through the Cascade Mountain Range to be blocked by avalanches.

Walt and Jeannie moved to a small farm to the northeast of the Y Creek. They found a herd of straggly goats and took up goat farming, a dream come true. They ran their house with no electricity or running water. They made candles and wood furniture, walked their property nude, and made a wood fired steam room and a wood fired greenhouse on the south side of their house.

The two blond women moved to a small cabin next to Walt and Jeannie's small goat farm. They worked whenever they were needed, and were hard workers.

Tom, Becky, Lisa, Philip and Joe moved back to Sky Ranch, and sent Jesus and Bill back to the Y Creek Ranch. Bill's leg stayed in an open bandage. An infection set in around the bullet wound, but not gangrene. Tom opened the wound up and found small pieces of foreign matter, removed them, and the leg healed. However, Bill needed crutches the rest of his life. He made beer throughout the winter. Jesus worked every day, taking care of the animals. He cared for and rode the horses to herd the cows and buffalo from one pasture to another. Greenhouses were built to further the growing year, and in the winter. start the crops early.

Tom and Becky went for runs and mountain bike runs every day. When the first snow fell they switched to cross country skiing. One evening they found horse tracks in the snow coming from Stehekin. They followed the tracks to a small cabin about two mile from the café'. They snapped out of their ski boots and hiked high around the cabin. From about 100 yards away they watched a big man chop wood in the back yard. Four horses were in a small barn. While he chopped wood, Tom and Becky snuck up on him. The guy was wearing winter Carhartt pants, with the whole cowboy getup, pistol, rifle, saddles and cowboy hat. The cowboy was chopping when he happened to look up, seeing Tom and Becky. He set the big axe into his chopping block turned to face them with his hand on his pistol.

"Vot may I do for you on this day?" he asked in a Russian accent.

Tom aimed his AR10 straight at the Russian. "Get your hand off that pistol mister." The Russian moved his hand away. Tom moved to within five feet of the big Russian, "You're Vaschilli. Lisa told us about you."

Vaschilli said, "Yes. This is true. I am that man."

Tom asked, "What are you doing here?"

Vaschilli made a sweeping hand gesture. "I move here after you and friends kill Ted and Dorn. I leave there to be cowboy. Always I want to be cowboy and now I be cowboy. I get gun, put on hip like gunfighter. I find cowboy rifle like John Wayne. Bring food and supply to here, and now here I am to be cowboy, here at this place."

Tom looked at the horses, "One of those horses belongs to my friend."

Vaschilli shrugged his shoulders, "I take dis horse from ranch in Manson. Did not know to see you, in dis place. I mean no harm, just vant to be cowboy live in dis place. Is it not free country to live?"

"It is a free country if we still have one. But this is our home and you have attacked us! Maybe I should put a bullet between your eyes and be done with it," Tom said. Becky stood with her rifle aimed at the big Russian. She wasn't sure what to say, and she kept quiet.

Vaschilli asked, "I give you my gun?" He reached into his holster, pulling the pistol out. He handed it to Tom by the barrel.

Tom took the pistol and rolled it over, "A Colt .45, long, good gun. That's a badass gun. The question is, what you are going to do with it?"

Vaschilli replied quickly, "I veil do nothing to you people with my gun. I vont to live here. I shoot, catch vaht I vant in forest and stream. I shoot elk for you and cook, very well on fire. You eat much, I find, I shoot, you eat. Like very much to do this."

Tom stepped back, "Ok, you bring us an elk tomorrow, come and cook it, we'll talk then." He gave the pistol back. Vaschili holstered the pistol. Tom turned his back to him. Vaschilli looked up at Becky. Her AR10 was still pointing at him. He smiled at her, "It is good to see you. I make you meat you vell love." He waved to them. Tom walked backward watching the Russian. Vaschilli stood watching as they walked around the cabin to their mountain bikes. While they were mounting the bikes, they heard the axe chopping into firewood.

The next evening Tom and Becky were walking through the garden. The dogs started barking. Clearly something was at the gate. Tom and Becky made it to the gate first, weapons ready. Vaschilli was leading three horses to the gate. One was Vaschilli's own ride. The second horse held a shot elk, and the third horse carried a big black fellow, in his late teens or maybe, early twenties. Vaschilli waved at Tom and walked over to him smiling. Vaschilli pointed back at the big kid. "I find these kid wit just pack and knife. No want to talk to me." Tom turned to the kid. The kid looked back. A dog ran up to the kid's horse and sat down by Woody.

As the kid stepped off the horse Tom noticed a Bear Grylls knife strapped to the kid's thigh. His pockets were bulging with far too much stuff. The kid walked over and Tom stepped in front of him. The kid stuck out his hand, and said, "I'm Simon." He then walked straight past them stopping at the chicken coup. He raised his hands chest high and gripped the thick chicken wire. Looking down in a wooden box were over twenty chicks warming under a heat lamp. His brow furrowed, eyes opened wide, he stared hard at the little chicks. He could feel the warmth from the heat lamp on his skin.

His eyes traced out the image of one big chicken dancing in the dirt. He smiled, blinked his eyes and the image disappeared. He looked through the chicken coup at the cows, "This is a good place."

About the Author

GEORGE THIELMAN is a stone mason and tilesetter in the Seattle area, and spends his spare time in the mountains hiking and climbing.